ולא יראה פְּנַי ריקם
אישׁ כמתנת ידו כברכת וכו'

אחד המרבה ואחד הממעיט ובלבד וכו'

עי' מנח' מד. עס גפ"ת

חולין קטו: ותוד"ה זויקו

מהרש"א ח"א על יומא סז:

כתובות יג: ופנ"י שם נד"ה אמר להס

ע"ע ידיס ג:ה ושהש"ר א:א.יא

וק"ל וד"ל ואכמ"ל

ALSO BY DANIEL ROSS GOODMAN

Somewhere Over the Rainbow:
Wonder and Religion in American Cinema

A Single Life

A Single Life

Daniel Ross Goodman

KTAV PUBLISHING HOUSE

BROOKLYN, NEW YORK

A SINGLE LIFE

KTAV PUBLISHING HOUSE

527 Empire Blvd

Brooklyn, NY 11225

www.ktav.com

orders@ktav.com

Ph: (718) 972-5449 / Fax: (718) 972-6307

Cover and frontispiece illustrations © 2020 by Devorah Lapidoth

Typeset in Arno Pro by Raphaël Freeman MISTD, Renana Typesetting

ISBN 978-1-60280-404-3

Printed and bound in the United States of America

For

DAVID G. ROSKIES AND COLM TÓIBÍN

and for

P.M.

❧

זכרתי לך חסד נעוריך
אהבת כלולתיך

"Let America be the dream the dreamers dreamed."

– Langston Hughes, "Let America Be America Again"

שאלה מטרונה את רבי יוסי בר חלפתא אמרה לו לכמה ימים ברא
הקדוש ברוך הוא את עולמו, אמר לה לששת ימים, כדכתיב כי ששת
ימים עשה ה' את השמים ואת הארץ. אמרה לו מה הוא עושה מאותה
שעה ועד עכשיו, אמר לה, הקדוש ברוך הוא יושב ומזוג זוזגים, בתו
של פלוני לפלוני, אשתו של פלוני לפלוני.

– בר"ר סח:ד

A matron asked R. Jacob son of Halafta: "In how many days
did the Holy One Blessed Be He create the world?" He said
unto her: "In six days, as it is written (Exodus 31) 'For in six
days the Lord made heaven and earth.'" She said unto him:
"What has He been doing from that hour to this day?" He
said unto her: "The Holy One Blessed Be He sits and makes
matches: 'this man's daughter with that man. That man's wife
with this man.'"

– *Bereishit Rabbah* 68:4

PART I

ONE

Eli opened the door to his musty apartment, dropped down on to the hard plastic chair in front of his metal desk, and let out a moan like a maimed animal.

"What's a matter, Eli?" asked Yoni Braun, Eli's roommate – a tall, angular, smooth-faced, tawny-skinned, sharp-elbowed boy with big blueberry-blue eyes, tufted dirty blond hair the color of ocean floor sand, and a wide smile that seemed to be permanently painted onto his colorless face. He was snacking on bite-sized Butterfinger bars and sipping a diet Peach Snapple.

"I don't know," Eli sighed, casting a deadened glance at the ceiling as if expecting a flock of quails to fall in through the roof. "It's the same story every time. Here's the text I just got from Tamar." Eli handed Yoni his phone so that Yoni could read the text:

Dear Eli, thank you for the date. I think you are a great guy and I enjoyed our conversations, but I'm just not sure I see it working out with us. Take care and all the best.

"I really thought this time it was gonna work out," said Eli despondently, almost as if in mourning, shaking his head and dabbing his moist eyes. "I really thought Tamar would be different than all the others...honestly, I don't even know why I still bother going out on dates at all...you know, I've been thinking a lot about Ben Azzai lately..."

"*What*?" Yoni, who was sitting at his desk, straightened his back, picked his head up from his hardcover copy of *Nisuin Kehilchosuh*,[1] and eyed Eli quizzically. "Why Ben Azzai? Because he was one of the *arba'ah shenichn'su laPardes*?[2] Are you thinking of studying Kabbalah?"[3]

"No, no, no, don't be ridiculous!"

"Then why have you been thinking about Ben Azzai lately?"

"Because of how whenever they presented him with *shidduchim*[4] he kept turning them down, saying, 'I don't need a woman! '*Nafshi chashkah baTorah*'!'[5] I'm liking that idea more and more these days... of just, you know, being married to learning..."

"Oh, come on, Eli, that's the most ridiculous thing I've ever heard."

"It's a *mefurash*[6] Gemara![7]"

"I know it is, but – "

"And the Rambam[8] says that if you're crazy about learning like Ben Azzai and want to devote your life to learning without being *mekayem*[9] *p'ru urvu*,[10] '*ein b'yado avon*.'"[11]

"Okay, Eli," said Yoni dismissively, rolling up his long sleeves and exposing his hairless, shapeless forearms and a black digital watch wrapped tightly around his pudgy left wrist. "But you know we don't hold like that. Ben Azzai was an exception. Everybody else is *chayav*[12] to get married and have children. Ben Azzai didn't have to because he was such an exceptional *masmid*."[13]

---

1. *Marriage According to the Law.*
2. Four Talmudic sages who engaged in mystical speculation.
3. Jewish mysticism.
4. Marriage offers.
5. "I'm in love with Torah."
6. An explicit passage.
7. In the Talmud.
8. Moses Maimonides, the great medieval Jewish philosopher and legal scholar.
9. Fulfilling.
10. The commandment to have children.
11. It's not considered a sin.
12. Obligated.
13. Diligent learner.

"I know... but why should he be the only one ever to be allowed to not marry? Why can't you have, I don't know... at least a few *masmidim*[14] every generation who are allowed to not marry? Does *every*one really need to get married and reproduce in order for the species to be perpetuated? We can't have even a couple people, a couple real *masmidim* sitting in yeshiva[15] devoting their lives to Torah, who are allowed to not get married? The Christians let their elite holy people be celibate and they've survived just fine, so why not us? Why should they get to be the only religion that allows its clergy to practice celibacy? If the Catholics get to have all those bishops and cardinals I don't see why we can't have at least a few Ben Azzais in every generation. Besides, the Rav[16] says *b'shem*[17] the *Chofetz Chaim*[18] that if you teach others Torah, '*ma'aleh hakasuv k'ilu yelado*,'[19] and you can be *mekayem*[20] *p'ru urvu*[21] that way, at least partially. So, *ka mashma lan*,"[22] said Eli in a sing-song voice, "even if you don't get married and have biological children – even if you don't do the **mayseh** mitzvah of *p'ru urvu* – not having children is not *me'akev*[23] in the **kiyum** *mitzvah*[24] of *p'ru urvu* because you can still be *mekayem* it through teaching Torah! And that's *taka*[25] what I plan to do. I'll take a teaching job somewhere and teach others Torah. That'll be my *p'ru urvu*. Okay, so maybe I won't be *mekayem* the *mitzvah bishleimusah*[26] but at least I'll be able to have

---

14. Diligent students.
15. Jewish seminary.
16. Rabbi Joseph B. Soloveitchik.
17. In the name of.
18. Rabbi Yisrael Meir Kagan.
19. You're considered as if you've given birth to them.
20. Fulfill.
21. The commandment to have children.
22. We see from here.
23. Absolutely necessary.
24. Fulfillment of the commandment.
25. Actually.
26. The commandment in its optimal way.

something I can point to after *me'ah ve'esrim*[27] when the *beis din shel ma'alah*[28] asks me '*asakta bifiryah verivyah?*'"[29]

"Come on, Eli. Enough with this crazy *lomdus*.[30] This is absolutely ridiculous."

"It's not crazy. I heard it from Rav Millner, who was saying over this exact idea from the Rav when he came here last year and gave that *shiur*[31] – don't you remember that? Weren't you here for that *shiur*? Or were you out on a date that night with Chani? Yeah," he added sarcastically. "*Mistama...*"[32]

"Eli... I don't know where this is coming from, but I think you probably just had a bad date, that's all. Don't give up. You'll find somebody eventually. Everybody does. *Tav Lemeitav*.[33] Get some sleep, forget about the date and you'll be fine by morning *seder*[34] tomorrow."

"Thank you for the *chizuk*,[35] Yoni... but no," said Eli with a strident tone. He bit his lip and momentarily closed his eyes, exhausted from the enervating evening he had spent in the Marriot hotel lobby talking to the twenty-two-year-old seminary girl he had been fixed up with. He leaned back in his chair and spread his legs straight out in front of him, with his left foot draped languidly over his right foot. "No," he continued, his voice cracking. "I don't think so... I don't think you understand, Yoni. I don't think you understand how humiliating these dates are for me. Date after date after date after date... it's the same *shakla v'tarya*[36] every time. They play nice, they string me along, I make some good conversation – at least I think it's okay – because they're into it too – at least they seem to be... until the end of the

27. I die.
28. The Heavenly Court.
29. 'Did you engage in procreation?'
30. Fancy learning.
31. Lecture.
32. Probably.
33. "People would rather dwell as two than dwell alone."
34. Learning.
35. Encouragement.
36. Back-and-forth.

night, after an hour, an hour and a half, after all that nice talking and schmoozing and *v'chulei v'chulei*,[37] when I ask if I can see her again, it's always, 'well...you're a very nice guy...but I just don't see it...it just doesn't seem right. Thank you for the drink, though.' I can't...I can't go through with this anymore, Yoni. *Ad kan v'su lo*.[38] There's only so much of this a person can take...I don't think you understand..."

"Hmm..." Yoni mumbled, smacking his lips and inserting his fists into his armpits. "You know, there *is* something I've been thinking about..."

"Oh yeah?" Eli reopened his unenlivened eyes and looked at Yoni warily. "What's that? You're gonna magically fix all my problems? You're gonna miraculously make me fit in here, magically make it so that girls I go out with suddenly start paying less attention to how I look on the outside and start caring about what I'm actually like on the inside? Let me guess – you hired a *tzadik*[39] to *daven*[40] for me for *shidduchim*[41] at the Kosel.[42] No – *five tzadikim*![43] No – *ten*! You have a whole *minyan*[44] of *tzadikim davening*[45] for me for forty days and forty nights!...No?...So then what? What do you have for me? You have some *segulah*[46] that I can use for *shidduchim*? A dollar from the Rebbe?[47] A hand-written copy of Tikkun Klali[48] from Rebbe Nachman?[49] A love-potion from the Baba Sali[50] that I can drink that'll

---

37. Yada yada yada.
38. This is the last straw.
39. Righteous person.
40. Pray.
41. Marriage.
42. The Western Wall.
43. Righteous people.
44. Quorum.
45. Praying.
46. Mystical good-luck charm, prayer or behavior.
47. Rabbi Menachem Mendel Schneerson.
48. A set of ten Psalms whose recital is said to effectuate atonement for certain sins.
49. Rabbi Nachman of Breslov.
50. Twentieth-century Moroccan kabbalist.

finally get me past a second date with a girl? Nu?!^{51} So what is it?
What do you have for me, Yoni? What have you been thinking about
for me?" He gave a dry, tortured laugh and shook his head hard, his
face flinching with jaded cynicism. "Look at me, Yoni – look at me. I
think it's pretty obvious why none of these girls here will go for me. I
just . . . I just think that, after all these years of dating, after eight years
of going through this charade, the *pashtus*^{52} is that for whatever reason
I'm just unacceptable to these girls . . . I hate to say that the reason is
based on how I look, but I can't think of any other reason. It can't be
based on money; I mean, there are plenty of guys in this yeshiva who
have no family money and who've gotten married without a problem.
It can't be based on learning. There are guys in this Beis Medresh^{53}
who can barely even make a laining^{54} and they've somehow gotten
married . . . I hate to say it, Yoni, but it's *poshut*^{55} – I really do think it's
based on looks. After all these years, all these dates, it just seems like
these girls just can't imagine being with a guy who looks like me . . .
and don't want to have *children* who'd look like me . . . Yeah, sure, a
guy can be the *shtarkest*^{56} guy in the Beis Medresh and he can have all
the *mai'luhs*,^{57} he can be a great *lamdon*^{58} who's *amel baTorah yomam
valailah*^{59} with great *middos*^{60} and great references and great *rebbeim*^{61}
and *chaveirim*^{62} and *yiras shamayim*^{63} and *ahavas Torah*^{64} and he can

51. Well?
52. Simple fact.
53. Study hall.
54. Learn a page of Talmud without the assistance of a translation.
55. Simple.
56. Most dedicated.
57. Most excellent qualities.
58. Torah scholar
59. Studies Torah diligently day and night.
60. Character traits.
61. Teachers.
62. Friends.
63. Fear of Heaven.
64. Love of Torah.

be *makpid al kala k'chamura*[65] and maybe he's even already published *chidushei Torah*[66] and has five-hundred *blatt*[67] under his belt and said over[68] a Shaagas Aryeh[69] at his Bar Mitzvah – no no – he said over a Reb Boruch *Ber*[70] at his Bar Mitzvah – and maybe he's even finished *Shas*[71] three times with Rashi and Tosfos[72] and the Maharam and Maharsha[73] and answered every bomb *kashya*[74] of Rebbe Akiva Eiger[75] on every *amud*[76] and he could be *baki b'chol haTorah kulah*[77] but if he doesn't have the kind of appearance these girls are looking for they won't want him. *Ha b'lo ha lo sagi.*[78] And whatever look it is they're looking for I clearly don't have it. Let's face it, Yoni. I just don't have it…I'm convinced that this is why it hasn't happened for me…call me crazy – and I wish it weren't true – but I really believe that this is the case. That's why I feel it's useless to even try anymore. That's why I – "

"No no no – Eli, Eli…I know you've had a rough time dating, but – "

"'Rough'?!" he burst out, his dark, rich eyebrows rising in angry incredulity. "Eight years and not even once do I get past a second date?! – not even *once*?! – That's not 'rough'. It's…I don't even know what the word for it is…it's a *kilayon*[79]…a complete *kilayon*…"

65. Stringent in his observance of Jewish law.
66. Torah scholarship.
67. Folio pages of Talmud.
68. Gave a talk on.
69. An insight from R. Aryeh Leib ben Asher Ginzburg, eighteenth-century Lithuanian Talmudist.
70. An insight from R. Boruch Ber Leibowitz, 19th–20th c. Lithuanian Talmudist.
71. The Talmud.
72. Medieval commentaries on the Talmud.
73. Commentaries on Rashi and Tosfos.
74. Extremely difficult question.
75. Nineteenth-century Talmudic scholar.
76. Page of Talmud.
77. Knowledgeable in the entirety of traditional Jewish learning.
78. One without the other doesn't work; you need both.
79. Disaster.

"Well..." mumbled Yoni, nodding his head; tufts of blond hair poked out underneath his black velvet skullcap. "Okay...I'm *modeh*[80] that maybe that wasn't the best choice of words. I hope you can be *mochel*[81] me for saying that. But the point is," he continued, in a calm, cajoling voice, *"ein hochi nami*[82] – you've had a real lousy time dating. But you just haven't found the right one yet, that's all. You're a great guy, Eli, and you will find somebody who wants to be with you – you *will*. And I really do believe that your appearance has nothing whatsoever to do with it. I just think you haven't found your *bashert*[83] yet. But you will, Eli, you *will*. It just takes some people longer than others."

"Yoni," said Eli in an agitated tone, shaking his head and drumming his fingers on his thigh, "you say this every time. After every date that leads nowhere, this is your response. And I've had enough of it. I've had enough with dating. With this whole thing. It's all a crock. It's – "

"So, what, then – you'll get married without dating? You'll find some woman off the street like the way the Rambam talks about how they used to do and you'll just bring her back to your apartment and be *mekadesh*[84] her?"

"No. I mean I won't date, and I won't get married either. No more of this charade. It's not *kedai*.[85] You're engaged, Yoni. You can't understand....you can't understand what it's like to...to never feel wanted. To never feel accepted...you can't understand what it's like to keep being set up and keep showing up for date after date and to keep having your soul spit back in your face at the end of the night."

"Look, Eli...I feel for you, I really do...But this whole 'I'm gonna be the next Ben Azzai' thing, 'I'm gonna be a Jewish celibate'?! No you're *not*! Of course you will date. And of *course* you will get married – at some point. Maybe not now, maybe not next year, but you will. I really believe it...and the next time will be different."

80. I admit.
81. Forgive.
82. This is true.
83. Predestined spouse.
84. Marry.
85. Worth it.

"Why?!" Eli smirked; a sarcastic laugh escaped his mouth. "What in the world makes you think *that*?! My appearance will magically change by the time I have my next date? Hashem[86] will make a *nes*[87] for me like He made for Rebbe Elazar ben Azaryah[88] and one morning I'll wake up completely metamorphosed? 'When Eli Newman woke up one morning from unsettling dreams he found himself changed in his bed into a white man...'"

"No, no...none of that...forget about Rebbe Elazar ben Azaryah. Forget about Ben Azzai. Forget about your looks altogether...I know a girl who will like you regardless of your looks – she'll probably even like you *because* of how you look, for all I know...I mean, I never asked her what her type of guy is, I have no idea if she even *has* a type, but I'm almost positive that she'll like you."

"Who is this, some miracle-girl you created through the *Sefer Yetzirah*?"[89]

"Ha! Yeah right. I don't know the nearest thing about Kabbalah... She is a real person – a real person I happen to know very well..."

"Oh yeah?" said Eli disbelievingly, looking at him in mock-amazement. "And what makes you think she'd have even the slightest interest in me after every single girl I've ever gone out with has never expressed even the slightest iota of interest in going out on a third date, let alone wanting to marry me? After the past eight years I have a very hard time imagining that such a person even exists."

"Well, you don't have to imagine her, because she actually exists... and I think she would like you because, well, all these books you're always reading that you're not supposed to be reading, these books you keep here in the apartment hidden behind your *sforim*[90] – all these books that should've gotten you kicked out of yeshiva years ago – these books that I've never tattled on you about even after that time when you stole my Snapple caps – "

---

86. God.
87. Miracle.
88. First-century Jewish sage.
89. An ancient Jewish book of mysticism.
90. Holy books.

"I never stole your Snapple caps, Yoni. You *lost* them."

"Sixty-eight Snapple caps in a desk drawer don't just one day magically *disappear*, Eli."

"Well, I never touched them.... besides, that was like, fifteen years ago! That was the first year I got here, my first year in this yeshiva! You still remember that?!"

"Of course I still remember that. I was really into those."

"Who in the world collects *Snapple* caps?!"

"*I* did."

"That's the stupidest thing ever to collect!"

"Well, *I* collected them, and you were my only roommate, and no one else had access to this room or to that drawer, and one day they just, hmm, mysteriously disappeared..."

"Why in the world would you think I'd ever want anything to do with your stupid Snapple caps?! I mean, what would I even *do* with *Snapple* caps?!"

"Whatever...forget about it...the point is, I could've told on you right then and there. I could've gone to the Rosh Yeshiva,[91] told him about all these things you read, all these books that they don't allow in yeshiva, and you would've been kicked out on the spot, right then and there...but I didn't."

"Well...that's very nice of you...I really appreciate that...I don't appreciate you harboring a grudge against me after all these years for some stupid Snapple caps that I never even laid a finger on, but – "

"I'm just *saying* – "

"I know," said Eli, looking at him with half-closed eyes. "Well...I really appreciate it...but I don't see why somebody should be kicked out of yeshiva for reading Mann or Márquez after he's put in twelve hours in the Beis Medresh,[92] but – "

"Who?"

"You know...some of the writers I read..."

"I have no idea who or what they are."

91. Head of the yeshiva.
92. Study hall.

"Of course you don't. You've never taken even the slightest interest in what I like to read."

"That may be true…But at least I've never told on you. I mean, c'mon, Eli – the policy of the yeshiva has always been very clear: no secular literature of any kind, except math and accounting textbooks – and that's only if you're studying for your CPA. I respect the yeshiva's policy. But I also respect you…I would never read any of those things myself, but I respect your choice. I always have."

"Thanks, Yoni. I appreciate that…I certainly don't think anyone else here would respect it."

"No, not here. Not in this yeshiva, that's for sure. You're pretty lucky you've had me as a roommate all these years. Anyone else would've told on you a long time ago the minute you accidentally woke them up at 6am while you were doing your morning pushups or whatever it is you do before *davening*."[93]

"I'm sorry for the *gezel shayna*."[94]

"I'm *mochel*[95] you…but the bigger issue is these *sforim chitzonim*[96] you keep bringing in here. I don't think anyone else here would much appreciate what you've been doing with these books all these years… But I do know someone who would."

"Oh yeah?" Eli said impatiently. *He's joking around*, Eli thought. *He's playing me for a fool, just like all these girls on my dates do. He's stringing me along…what is this all about?*

"You remember my sister?"

"Umm…Rena?"

Yoni had hardly ever spoken about her to Eli. Eli recalled meeting her only once, when he had first arrived at Yeshivas Chelkas Yaakov. Yoni, his assigned roommate, had invited Eli to his family's suburban Baltimore home for the fall holiday of Sukkot after Yoni had found out that Eli, who had just arrived from Houston and who didn't know

93. Prayers.
94. Theft of your sleep.
95. Forgive.
96. Secular books.

another soul in Baltimore, needed a place to stay for the holiday. During the first two days of the holiday, he had met Rena, Yoni's older sister, and Tzvi, Yoni's younger brother. A few years later, Tzvi followed Yoni and Eli to the yeshiva, but Eli had never seen Rena since that second day of Sukkot. She wouldn't leave her room at all, Eli recalled, even to go to synagogue; she only left her room to eat, and as soon as the Braun's holiday meals concluded – and often even before they concluded – she would leave the table and retreat to her room, where she would remain for the rest of the day and night. He couldn't remember exactly what she looked like, but he remembered her being very pale and very thin, almost wraith-like; he couldn't remember the sound of her voice at all, but she had been so quiet over the course of those two days that he wasn't sure whether he had ever actually heard it.

"Yeah," said Yoni, eyeing Eli with an unusually upbeat look. "Did you know she became a librarian?"

"No," replied Eli. *How in the world am I supposed to know that when you haven't said a word about her to me in fifteen years?* "I had no idea... wow."

"Yeah. In one of the branches of the Baltimore public library. She loves it. We barely ever speak, but I know she loves it...it took her a while, but she finally found the right thing for her."

"Umm..." *I don't khap*[97] ... *Where is he going with this? Mai kulei hai?*[98] "So...?"

"Oh, right – the point is, I know she'd really be *machshiv*[99] what you've been doing all these years, with all this outside reading you do. Because she's been doing the same thing. Actually I think that's why she left seminary."

"She was in seminary?"

"Yeah, of course. That *yontiff*[100] when you were with us for Suk-

<hr>

97. Understand.
98. What is this all about?
99. Appreciate.
100. Holiday.

kos,[101] that first-ever *yontiff* of yours in Baltimore, that time you met her – that was her last year of seminary. Right after that Sukkos she dropped out. Told my parents she was leaving. Told them she couldn't take it anymore."

"I'm sure they couldn't have been too pleased with that."

"No...not at all. But that wasn't the worst of it. She finished up high school in some public school in Rockville, then when she was at the University of Maryland some friends of ours told us that they saw her shopping on Shabbos[102] in the school bookstore and eating in the non-kosher cafeteria."

"Huh...what did your parents do when they found out she went off the *derech*?"[103] asked Eli, playing nervously with his tzitzit.[104]

"Nothing, really, if you can believe it. Probably because they were so shocked by it, I think. They never really said anything to her about it. Or to me. They were never good with these things, you know them. But I think they assumed it was just a phase that she was going through in college – experimenting, you know?...and that she would get over it soon enough."

"Is she still off the *derech*?"

"Yeah...but as far as I know, she was never really on it. She never really seemed to take much to Torah and *mitzvos*[105] even when she was younger. I think she just went through with it up until high school because that's what her family – our family – was doing, because that was what was expected of her, and as soon as she had a chance she dropped it."

"Oh...well," Eli began, his eyes ranging around the room, unsure of what he was supposed to say. "...I'm sorry to hear that."

"You don't have to be sorry. That's just the way she is."

"Oh...okay..."

---

101. Sukkot.
102. Saturday.
103. Became irreligious (lit., "went off the path").
104. Knotted ritual fringes hanging out of his shirt.
105. Religion.

They sat without speaking for a few seconds in the snug, low-ceilinged room, the silence broken only by the whirring of an engine somewhere off in the distance. Yoni edged his chair closer to Eli's and leaned toward him.

"I think it might work," said Yoni, propping up his dimpled chin with his right fist.

"*What* might work?"

"You and her."

"Umm…what?" Eli asked sharply, unsure whether he had heard him correctly.

"Yeah. You and her. I've been thinking about it. Especially seeing the way your last couple of dates have gone…I think you two could really get along…I see it now, I really do."

"Huh…" Yoni's words seemed to Eli to be floating in the air, like colorless autumn leaves caught in the wind; he waited for them to land on the ground of his comprehension before reacting to them. "Well…she's still off the *derech,* you said?"

"Yes."

"So – "

"I think you could be *mekarev* her,"[106] said Yoni, nodding his head as if he'd just hit on the solution to an insoluble mathematical quandary.

"Yoni, I don't do *kiruv.*[107] That's not my – "

"You won't have to do any *kiruv.* If you go out on a few dates with her and it goes well I think she'll get back on the *derech* just for you… she'll see your example – she'll see that you can read all the kinds of books that she does and still be *frum*[108]…it'll be like a mini-*Kiddush HaShem*[109] – a *Kiddush HaShem* that affects just one person – the kind of *Kiddush HaShem* that could convince her to get back on the *derech*…and I think that she could really go for you – she's always been looking for a kind of guy like you."

---

106. Make her religious again.
107. Jewish outreach.
108. Religious.
109. A sanctification of God's name.

"But I'm *frum*, Yoni."

"Yes... and all the better. She's always been looking for a good, solid guy who could appreciate a quiet, smart, bookish type like her, a guy who'd appreciate all the books she's into. I've never been able to have a conversation about those kinds of books with her. I don't know the first thing about them. But you'd certainly be able to... I think you might really hit it off with her. Waddayou say, Eli?"

"Well..." Eli inhaled so deeply he nearly hurt his lungs. *What in the world... Can this be serious? Is he really doing this?...* "I mean... after eight years of nothing but failure with dating, I guess it might be worth a shot... sure... why not."

"Great!" Yoni wrapped his left arm around Eli's shoulder and hugged him; his eyes were gleaming as if he'd just discovered a pile of gold underneath his volume of Talmud. "I'll give you her email. You guys can be in touch."

"Umm... okay..."

"Then I'll step out of the way. You two can take it from there. The ball's in your court... *b'hatzlacha!*"[110]

---

110. Good luck.

TWO

For his first date with Rena, instead meeting her in the Marriot hotel lobby like he did every other time he had a first date, he met her at a Starbucks a few blocks from where she worked at the Baltimore public library. She had told him that she would absolutely refuse to meet him in a hotel lobby, which he assumed was because an off-the-*derech*[1] girl like her didn't want to date the way normal *frum*[2] girls dated.

Eli stood outside waiting for her, casting furtive glances about him and anxiously watching the shadows of passersby dance along the sidewalk. When fifteen minutes had passed with no sight of her, he checked his phone to see if she had texted or emailed him to say that she was running late, but there were no messages from her. After waiting another five minutes, he was about to leave and head back to the yeshiva when he saw a tall, thin, fair-haired woman wearing a plain white dress approach the entrance of the store.

"Rena?" he asked, half-hoping it wasn't her.

"Hello Eli!" she said cheerily, nodding her head. "It's great to finally meet up with you in person after our emailing."

"Likewise," he responded, straining to hear her soft voice,

1. Irreligious.
2. Religious.

16

which was nearly swallowed whole by the growl of the cars passing through the street.

"Well? Shall we?"

"Yes," he replied uneasily. The timbre of her voice excited him, which made him even more uneasy; it was an uplifting, rhythmic voice that made him think she would burst into song at any moment.

As they walked into the coffee shop, Eli felt his frozen flesh sprouting goosebumps, and his heart began beating furiously, hammering against his chest as if it had an urgent message that he needed to read immediately before it was too late. He didn't feel comfortable being in a restaurant in which less than one-hundred-percent of the food and drink products were certifiably kosher. He felt even more uncomfortable going on a date with a girl who wasn't one-hundred-percent religiously observant. *What are the chances she'd actually become* frum *again for my sake?*, he asked himself, his eyes darting nervously around the coffee shop, worried that someone from his yeshiva might just happen to be there. *No woman has ever bought me a cup of coffee, let alone gone out with me on a third date. And all the sudden this one's gonna change her whole life for me?* But what made him most uncomfortable was that he had felt himself becoming attracted to her before they had even exchanged two words.

Her black boots and knee-length white dress oddly matched his standard yeshiva-issued outfit: a white button-down shirt, black slacks, black shoes, and a black velvet *kippah*[3] that covered two-thirds of his close-cropped jet-black hair. Her frizzy, unkempt blonde hair, slightly reddened by rose-tinted streaks, was the color of golden beets, and her girlish, untweezed eyebrows made her look younger than her thirty-one years. She wore no earrings, necklaces, bracelets, or rings of any kind; her only adornments were her silvery grayish-green eyes fringed with dark lashes, the black bow in her hair, and her thick, black-rimmed glasses, which perfectly complemented her high cheekbones, narrow chin and oval face. She ordered an almond-milk macchiato;

---

3. Skullcap.

he ordered a plain decaf coffee. She laced her drink with extra cream and sugar; he drank his black.

"So I heard you love books, too," she said excitedly, as they sat down across from each other around a small circular table in the back of the shop. Eli had strategically chosen this table rather than a table near a window because he was afraid of someone from his yeshiva chancing by and spotting him. *If they find out I've been talking with a girl who's not frum*, he said to himself, *that's the end of me… if I get kicked out of yeshiva, where would I go? What would I do? I have no other real skills. Never got a real education. All I can do is sit and learn. This is it… man o man is Yoni putting me in a bind. I can't believe I agreed to this date…* "Yoni told me all about you," she continued, smiling demurely; goosebumps formed upon his goosebumps. "He told me all about your reading, about all these books you smuggle in and hide in your drawers and behind your *sforim*[4] and under your bed. It's wonderful that you've been able to maintain this passion for reading even in yeshiva. Me, I couldn't. I couldn't do it… it was either seminary or literature, and I felt like I had to make a choice, and so I did… But you – that's inspiring…"

"Well," he said, taken aback by how excited her simple compliment had made him feel, "umm… I guess I never felt like I should have to give up reading just because I was in yeshiva. Books are essential to me."

"Books are like water to me, too," she said, picking at one of her fingernails, "but *frumkeit*[5] was, well – *frumkeit* was like this macchiato. Except much worse-tasting… I guess you could say it wasn't *geshmack*[6] for me…"

Eli was so nervous that he could barely think of a single question to ask her. Because he was naturally quiet, he was pleased that she was doing most of the talking. He thought it was slightly odd that whenever she was speaking she would gesture animatedly with her left hand, but with her left hand only, and upon finishing a sentence she

4. Religious books.
5. Religion.
6. Tasty.

DANIEL ROSS GOODMAN · 19

would raise it behind her head and leave it there for a minute, as if it needed to rest from all the exertion, before lowering it back down to her lap; but he preferred to concentrate on what she was saying and not how she was saying it. She talked about her love of Emily Brontë and Hermann Hesse, and her impish, olive-shaped eyes widened when he mentioned that some of his favorite writers were David Foster Wallace and Richard Wright.

"Well, I should get going," Eli said after they had been talking for nearly two hours, content that the date had gone as well as it had. "What are your plans for the rest of the day?"

"Not too much," she said, shrugging her shoulders and looking to her left. "I have to do some errands. I was planning on going to Target to get a few things. And then if I have time I'd like to get some shooting in."

"You play basketball?" he asked, his eyes widening.

"No," she chuckled, her eyes sparkling with amusement. "I mean I'd like to go to a shooting range."

"Uhh..." He scratched his head. "You mean...like...with guns?"

"Well, what else?" she laughed, her reddish hair dancing on her shoulders.

"You're...you're into guns?"

Eli held back a yelp of astonishment and feigned a curious expression.

"Yeah."

"Really?" he pressed, eying her alarmedly.

"Yeah, why not?" she said with a charming shrug.

"Well...umm...I just never really knew a Jewish person who was into guns...and especially a woman..."

"So if you're a Jew or a woman you're not allowed to be into guns?"

"Umm...no!...I mean...I don't know...it's just not something I've ever heard of, or, ever expected, I guess..."

"I thought Yoni told you that I'm not exactly the most conventional kind of Jewish girl..."

"Well, yes, he did, but I wasn't sure exactly what that meant...he didn't tell me about this part of you..."

"I guess he didn't want to scare you away from me..."

"I guess so..."

"Well I am just full of surprises, amn't I?!"

"You sure are," he laughed nervously, gripping his sagging collar. "Especially the way the you say 'amn't I.'"

"There's a lot more to me than meets the eye, Eli."

"That's for sure," he nodded, his face rounding into bewilderment. *Who is this girl?*, he wondered, scratching his head. *Guns!? Be'emes?!*[7]

"So," he continued, scratching his neck, "umm, how, umm...how did you get into guns?"

"Honestly," she said, her lilting voice rising ever so slightly, "it started with my former boyfriend. He was interested in shotgun shooting and he asked me if I wanted to go shooting. He was like, 'it'll be a fun date, trust me,' and I was like, 'hmm, I don't know...' I was a little skeptical at first, and very nervous. I'd never shot before. I'd never even held a gun before. But I really liked him, so I figured, 'okay, why not try it? Worst that could happen is we go to the shooting range and I hate it and never go back again.' So we went, and he brought his shotguns with him, and we put on these big black electronic earmuffs to protect our ears, and he showed me how to load the bullets and how to aim and fire... and I was actually pretty intrigued...especially by the mechanism of it – I had never seen a gun up close like that before – they're just really interesting machines. Especially the first one I shot, the pump-action shotgun. It's a more complicated machine than I could ever invent but yet it was still simple enough where I could see how it worked. I was interested in just how it worked, I guess, and then it went from there. It took me a few rounds to get used to the recoil, but once I did and once I was able to shoot more smoothly it was great. I really liked it, so I wanted to buy one. And I liked the idea of becoming proficient with them. To have a skill, like fishing or carpentry or something like that. I thought that being able to handle a gun was a good skill to have. And I also starting getting curious to learn about how different kinds of guns worked. So I started out with just two pistols – "

7. Seriously?

"*Just* two?" Eli's head recoiled. He looked at her dumbstruck.

"Yeah, why not?"

"Umm...ok..."

"Yeah. So the first one I got was a Sig Sauer P320. A year or two ago it was selected to be the US Army's standard pistol. And then I got a Glock 19, nothing fancy. They're both nine-millimeter handguns, nothing too crazy. And two shotguns. Both 12-gage, pump-action shotguns.

"*Also* two?" Eli exclaimed, his jaw becoming slack and his mouth opening.

"Yeah. One's a Remington 870, and the other's a knockoff of the same thing. I bought the second one stupidly and now it just sort of sits there and I don't use it, but I don't like the idea of selling it, because even if I sell it to a reputable place, they might sell it to whomever... and I know that as long as it's in my possession it won't be used for anything nefarious...So yeah...two shotguns, two pistols...and an AR and an AK."

"A *what*?"

"An AR-15 and an AK-47."

Eli scratched the back of his head uncomfortably; he stared at her as if she had just said that she had discovered life on Neptune. His mouth hung agape as he looked at the light-haired woman in front of him.

"I have my eye on a couple of new ones," she continued nonchalantly, acting as if she were telling him about a new kind of cantaloupe she wanted to try. "There's a shorter version of the AR rifle I'm interested in buying – a new one that just came out with a shorter barrel – and a completely different one that folds in half that's convenient for storage. There are some hoops to jump through because it's a restricted item as delineated by the National Firearms Act. But once I jump through those hoops it'll be fun."

"And, umm," Eli started, shifting back and forth in his chair and opening and closing his mouth several times before continuing, "you don't ever, uh, carry these guns with you, right?"

"Not unless I'm going to the shooting range. And even then I never have them loaded until I'm at the range and in the firing lane. Until then they're in the backseat of my car. But no, I almost never carry them with me. It's very hard to get a license to carry in Maryland. Owning one is different from carrying. I'm looking into it but it's hard. It's crazy – right next-door in Virginia you can get guns so much more easily. They're so much more permissive down there … The gun laws in this country are all so different from state to state. Which is one of the stupid things, it's such a patchwork – so a lot illegal guns come into Maryland from Virginia. And because there's no federal framework for these laws it's pretty hard to stop it … it's just really too bad, and it probably won't change for a long time … well, anyway, would you like to go shooting with me sometime?"

"Umm …" Eli had to stop himself from bursting out laughing. "Me? Shooting? Uhh … I don't think so …"

"C'mon, Eli, it'll be fun! I promise! Besides, it's a really important skill to have. Everyone should know how to handle a gun. Whether you're a man or woman, Jew or non-Jew. It doesn't matter. It's a skill everyone should have."

"Uh … yeah … I guess so … but maybe another time … I don't know if I'm up to it just right now …"

"Well …" She started to smile but only one side of her mouth arched upward; she looked at him with a mixture of disappointment and hope. "I know that when you do come shooting with me you're really going to like it. Especially once it gets nicer out and we can go shooting outside. It can be unpleasant when it's cold and too boring sometimes to just go to an indoor range, but in the spring and summer, when the weather's nicer, and we can go shooting outside – that's the best!"

"That could be," he responded perfunctorily, his legs shaking and feet twitching. "Maybe another time … but, um, for now, I should be getting back to the yeshiva …"

"And I should be getting back too …" She looked at him expectantly, her eyebrows raised and her back arched.

"I really enjoyed talking to you."

"I enjoyed talking to you, too," she said, playing with her hair and crossing her legs in his direction.

"So...umm," he said, his voice trembling, "would you, uh, like to go out again sometime soon?"

"Yes, definitely!" she beamed, her lips curving upwards into a wide, radiant smile.

"Great!" he blurted out, immediately regretting expressing himself with such enthusiasm. "So...umm...I'll be in touch..."

"Sounds good, Eli!" she said, raising her head ever so slightly and exposing a few more millimeters of her neck to him.

"Alright, Rena...see you soon."

"You too, Eli!"

THREE

'I can't believe she agreed to a second date,' he said to himself after they parted; he felt light-headed and giddy, as if someone had spiked his coffee with whiskey. 'In eight years of dating I've never met a single girl like this – a girl from a *frum*[1] family who actually reads, who appreciates what I appreciate – at least aside from the guns thing... I wish I knew how to describe what I'm feeling, but one thing I know for sure – she'd know how to describe it. A girl who reads like that, who knows as much as she knows – she'd know how to use words in ways that I don't... this one – I can't believe I'm already thinking this, but I think she could really be the one... I would be married to my best friend's sister – this has to be *bashert*[2]... I know I shouldn't get ahead of myself – I wouldn't want to be *k'bo'el arusaso b'beis chamav*[3] – but I have such a good feeling about this... Yoni would think I'm crazy if I told him that after just one date I met my *Bashert*,[4] but I really do have that feeling... it just – it just feels right... it feels more than right – it feels...'

It feels "perfect" was what he wanted to say in his head; he knew that only one obstacle stood in the way of Rena being a

1. Religious.
2. Meant to be.
3. Putting the cart before the horse.
4. Predestined spouse.

perfect match for him, but he preferred not to think about it. The question of whether she would actually take up observant Judaism again was such a troubling question to him that he simply chose not to think about it. Why bother himself with such concerns when he had met a girl who suited him so ideally? Why disturb himself with such worries when he had finally met a girl who evidently was not only not bothered by the fact that he looked like few other Orthodox Jews in the world but even seemed to like his appearance, if the consistency with which she had made eye contact with him and the frequency with which she gazed at him with a playful glint in her eyes and by the way she leaned toward him when talking to him was any indication. She had been raised in an observant family, he reasoned, so it wouldn't be that much of a stretch for her to take up observance again; it wasn't as if she was a non-Jewish woman to whom observant Judaism was as foreign as the moons of Saturn. When the time would come for him to ask her to marry him – the date had gone so well that he couldn't help but think about that eventuality – surely, he reasoned, she would pick up her observant religious life where she had left it some fifteen years ago, wouldn't she? Wouldn't she do it for him? Or if not for him, then for herself? For the chance to be married to her brother's best friend – a friend who would love her and fully appreciate the bookishness that unnecessarily drove her away from observance – and for the chance to be reintegrated into her community, for the chance to be fully accepted and fully loved again by her family... wouldn't she? Of course she would, he assured himself; it was the reasonable, even romantic thing to do. Wouldn't she change her life for love if she believed that she had finally found it?

'But what is it that I like about her?' he asked himself as he neared his apartment, excited that he'd finally get to tell Yoni about a date that had actually gone *well*. 'I mean, beyond the fact that she also likes books, what do I like about her? She's certainly not your average Jewish girl... She taught herself Russian in high school and then went off to St. Petersburg and taught high school English there for a year... I've never heard of a Jewish girl *or* guy doing that before, to want to go *back* to Russia... What else?... She's working at the library now but studying for the GRE's so that she can get a masters in international relations and eventually – what was it she said she wants to do? Work in the Pentagon? Or in Homeland Security? That's pretty cool...It's scary how much she knows about Russia...scary but also pretty cool...She's really into Star Wars – I wasn't expecting that. She didn't seem like that type...Then there was the thing with her being so paranoid about D.C. being the first U.S. metro area that'll be targeted in a nuclear exchange that she has a bug-out bag ready to go and a bed in a cabin in her college friend's parents' place in Vermont that she knows she can hide out in while Washington and New York are being taken out during the nuclear Armageddon...I'd never even heard of a "bug-out bag," let alone anyone actually having one, but she actually has one! And what did she say she has inside it? Water purification tablets? I've never even heard of such a thing....And there there's the thing with her and guns...that was the weirdest part...She has *six* guns?...*SIX*?!...*Ribbono shel olam!*[5] Does Yoni know about this?!...I better not bring it up...I've never known a single American Jew who owns one gun, and she owns *six*!?! *Ribbono shel olam*...I can't believe she actually asked me if I wanted to go shooting with her...*me* shooting?!' He laughed and shook his head, smiling amusedly. 'I wouldn't last a second in a shooting range! I'd be like, "you guys have fun firing at those targets, I'll be off here in the corner with my *Chumash* and Rashi[6] doing *shnayim mikra!*[7] Let me know when you're done!"... Yeah right...me with a gun...the thought of it...' he laughed again. 'If I'm ever sad and depressed in the future I'll just picture myself with a gun and that'll be enough to crack me up...Okay, so maybe she's a little weird. No – not weird...*Different*. She's different. And I like that...yeah...different...that's what I like about her...'

5. Good God.
6. Torah with the commentary of R. Shlomo Yitzchaki (1040–1105, France).
7. Studying the weekly Torah portion.

FOUR

'This is no time for a fun, cute, pottery-making or walk-in-the park date,' Eli said to himself during yeshiva night *seder*[1] as the day of his second date with Rena drew near. 'I have to really go for it here. I have to show her how serious I am about her. Like Rav[2] Kramer always tells me, "Eli, when you find the woman whom you are sure will be your wife, you have to act very quickly – you have to ask her to marry you right away. *Nisuin*[3] is a great mitzvah,[4] the greatest mitzvah there is, because it is only through *nisuin* that you can fulfill the mitzvah of *p'ru ur'vu*,[5] which is the first and most important mitzvah given to mankind. *Chazal*[6] say that '*mitzvah haba'ah al yad'cha al tach-mitzenah*' – when an opportunity to perform a mitzvah comes to you, don't wait even one instant! And when it comes to *nisuin*, the *Gemara*[7] says that you're allowed to become engaged during *Chol haMo'ed*[8] because '*shema yekadmenu acher.*'[9] *Chazal* knew

1. Learning.
2. Rabbi.
3. Marriage.
4. Commandment.
5. Having children.
6. The rabbis of the Talmud.
7. Talmud.
8. The intermediate days of the festivals of Passover and Sukkot.
9. Someone else might beat you to the punch.

that once you find your eventual wife you have to close the deal quickly. When the opportunity comes to you, Eli, don't wait – do it right away!" Rav Kramer's right: there's no time for fooling around here,' he said to himself. 'Not when I know I've finally found her...'

Eli borrowed Yoni's car, a navy blue 2007 Toyota Corolla, to pick up Rena at the library. He was driving at a normal speed and humming the tune of "Od Yishama,"[10] unable to stop smiling, when he was five miles from the library and spotted a cop cruiser in his rearview mirror.

"*Oh no...*" he moaned, his heart beating like a bass drum as he noticed that the cruiser was tailing him. 'Just stay calm,' he told himself, throwing nervous glances at his rearview and side mirrors. 'Drive normally...and stay calm...' He drove for several more miles with the police car following behind him the entire way; when he was two blocks away from the library, he heard a siren flare up behind him.

"Oh *no*..." he muttered, flinging a helpless glance upwards at the pale blue sky. "Please...not this...not now..."

Grimacing and beginning to feel nauseous, he pulled the car over to the side of the road, reluctantly obeying the siren's shrill command. He rolled down the driver's side window, braced himself, and waited restlessly for the police officer to approach the car.

"License and registration, please," declared the officer, a dough-faced, pot-bellied, puffy-eyed man with an arching nose and a jutting, pointed chin.

"Yessir," Eli hastened to respond, trying to breathe deeply and speak placidly as he handed him the requested documents.

"This your car?" asked the officer, eying Eli leerily and shining his flashlight into every nook and crevice of the car.

"No, sir. It's my friend's."

"Your friend's, you say?"

"Yes, sir. Just borrowing it for the night."

"Uh-humm..."

"Officer, may I ask what the problem is?"

"You were driving suspiciously, Mr. Newman."

10. A Jewish wedding song.

"How else was I supposed to drive? You were following me for five miles."

Eli! he shouted at himself in his head, pressing his lips together and slapping his palms on his knees. *You shouldn't have said that! You KNOW you should NOT have said that! You idiot!*

"Mr. Newman, I'm gonna have to ask you to step out of the car."

What?, Eli shouted in his head while obeying the officer's command. *Why?! What did I do?!*

"Mr. Newman, I'm gonna have to ask you to face forward, put your hands on the front of the car, and hold them there until I tell you you can remove your hands."

Oh, you have got to be KIDDING me, Eli said in his head, standing stock-still as the officer patted him down from his wrists to his feet. *This is – this is the biggest ball of – I cannot believe this…*

"You may remove your hands from the car and turn around. Please open the trunk, Mr. Newman."

Ribbono shel olam,[11] Eli bellowed in his head as he popped open the trunk, rolling his eyes. *What is this?! He thinks I have drugs or something?! He cannot be serious…. THIS cannot be serious…*

The police officer, apparently satisfied after rummaging through a few empty duffel bags and a couple of Yoni's tennis racquets, turned to Eli and narrowed his eyes, nearly squinting at him.

"This is not your car, Mr. Newman, is it?"

"Yes, sir – uh – I mean, no sir – it's … as I said … it's my friend's car. He gave it to me to borrow for the night."

"Uh-humm…" mumbled the officer, scrutinizing Eli's license and the car's registration for a second time. "And can your … *friend* … confirm this?"

"Yes, sir. You can call him. Here's his number," said Eli, shaking, and handing the officer his cellphone. "His number's the first one listed in my recent calls."

The officer dialed the number and put the phone to his ear.

---

11. Oh God…

I cannot believe this, said Eli in his head. *I cannot believe he's actually calling him...*

"Yes, Mr. Braun, this is Officer Charles Wallace, Baltimore Police, Central District. I have found your car. It was being driven by an Eli Newman. The suspect is –.... oh.... oh.... uh-huh... I see... yes.... I understand.... well, then. Thank you for your time, Mr. Braun. I'm sorry to disturb you. Have a pleasant evening."

"Well," said the officer, handing Yoni's registration and Eli's license back to him. "I apologize for the misunderstanding. Thank you for your cooperation. Have a pleasant evening... and stay safe out there, young man."

"Yes, sir," Eli rasped out, still shaking. "Thank you, sir."

Eli, clenching his jaw and crinkling his nose, got back in the car and drove one more mile to the library, gripping the steering wheel as if he were trying to strangle it. Fury gnawed at him, but he refused to let it devour him. He tried to push the incident out of his mind as quickly as possible by humming "Od Yishama" again and forcing himself to smile, but his mind was replaying the conversation with the police officer over and over as if it wanted to force him to fully come to terms with what he had just experienced. 'I can't be thinking about that stuff now,' he told himself, shaking his head vigorously. 'I have to focus – *shema yekadmenu acher*.[12] The time is now...'

The scant autumn light had begun to wane, and dusk was steadily deepening. As he approached the library, he could barely see Rena, who, in her full-length black dress and black leather shoes, looked more like a shadow than a full-bodied person underneath the library's white-painted portico.

"I'm so sorry, Rena," he said with sunken shoulders, looking away from her as she got into the car. "I'm usually very punctual, but I was stopped... by the police..."

"Why?" she asked, peering at him over the top of her glasses.

"I wish I knew," he said, laughing sarcastically, as he started driving toward Rockville.

---

12. If I don't marry her someone else will.

"Has this ever happened to you before?"

"Only once...but then again, I don't own a car, and I almost never drive. Yoni lets me borrow his car when I go on dates, but even then I don't always use it..."

"So..." she asked, biting her right ring finger's unpainted nail, "you're saying you think this would happen more often to you if you drove more often?"

"Well...that's hard to say, but...I mean, I've gotten stopped at grocery stores and CVss, so...I don't know...maybe..."

"Wow...that's terrible...I feel so badly about this."

"Thanks," he said, wishing he could come up with something better than that but not knowing what else to say. He took a sip of water from the plastic Yeshivas Chelkas Yaakov water bottle that he always carried with him, waiting for her to ask a follow-up question about the incident – or about similar prior incidents in his life – or about what it was like to be him – but she merely pursed her lips, folded her arms and looked out the passenger side window, as expressionless as the clouds drifting miles above them.

Why isn't she asking me about what's it's like to be me? he asked himself as a prickly silence sprouted between them, making them both complicit in each other's discomfort. *Why doesn't she want to go there? She's a cool girl...educated, worldly, different...I thought she was different from all these other white Jewish girls...I thought she would actually care a little bit about me, about my background, about what makes me who I am and what it's like to move through the world as me – I thought she would at least be a little curious about it...Really?...Nothing?...She's not gonna ask me about it at all?...No?...Not even one question?...Is it really too uncomfortable of a subject for her to bring up? She can have all these intelligent conversations about Russia and nuclear proliferation and the latest DOD appropriations bill but she can't have one real honest conversation about race?...Wow...I didn't expect this from her...but then again maybe I should've...for all of her intelligence and worldliness and weirdness and distinctiveness, at the end of the day she's still white...*

"So," he began uneasily, "you were telling me last time that you were into movies, too?"

"Yeah, definitely," she said, a wide smile forming across her vanilla-hued face. "I could actually talk about movies for hours."

Though he thought it was slightly odd that she intermittently bit her fingernails – and as soon as she became conscious that she was doing so, she quickly pulled her fingers out of her mouth and hid them under her chin as if to pretend that she hadn't been doing what she had just been doing – he chose to pay attention to what was coming out of her mouth and not to what she was putting into it.

He had decided to take Rena to an upscale restaurant in an affluent Washington, D.C. suburb. The meal, he figured, would cost him nearly a quarter of his monthly yeshiva stipend – but for Rena, he told himself, it was worth it. 'Ishto k'gufo,'[13] he told himself, 'and you have to treat her like you'd treat yourself if you were celebrating a great occasion – and isn't this a great occasion? You need to take her to the nicest restaurant you can find. Maybe it doesn't have to be ki'seudas Shlomo b'shayto,[14] but it has to be the best you can find... And don't care about how much it'll cost – your grandchildren won't care about how much money you had to spend on this date... these are the kinds of sacrifices you have to make for mitzvos,[15] and there's no greater mitzvah than kiddushin.[16] You need to do this mehadrin min hamehadrin[17]...'

"Yeah," he said midway through the meal, confessing that in addition to sneaking secular books into his yeshiva dormitory room in high school and college, he would also sneak out of yeshiva to go to movies. "Whenever I go to movies," he said, emptying his glass of water, "I put on a blue shirt and my blue 'Stros hat so that no one'll recognize me."

"'Stros?" she asked, leisurely chewing her honey-glazed chicken.

"Oh... the Astros... I'm a Houston Astros fan... well, used to

---

13. "Your wife is like yourself."
14. Like the feasts of King Solomon.
15. Commandments.
16. Securing a spouse.
17. The best possible way.

be – I'm not so into baseball anymore, but I still have the hat…I'm from Houston, originally."

"Oh…right," she said, slowly nodding her head. "Yoni told me that…so, what are some of your favorite movies?"

"Well," he said, holding her gaze and leaning back in the leather-paneled seat. "The Coen brothers are probably my favorites…I think I've seen every one of their movies."

"Really? I probably have too."

"Neat…" He took a sip of his kosher Italian Chianti; he never drank wine except on the Sabbath and holidays, but he figured it was a special occasion – a 'seudas mitzvah,'[18] he told himself, because it was the first meal he was having with his future wife – and what greater mitzvah was there than marriage? "I'm also a big Wes Andersen fan. 'Grand Budapest Hotel' was probably the best thing I've seen all year."

"I totally agree!" she exclaimed, twirling a strand of her hair between her forefingers and moving the golden lock in front of her lips as if it to kiss it. "I *loved* that movie!"

"Wow," he said, his face suddenly as pink as the cedar-plank salmon he was eating; he practically had to restrain himself from springing out of his seat.

"Yeah…I love Wes Andersen, too," she said, raising her glass and taking a sip of her Merlot, her eyes riveted on Eli the entire time. "Even though all of his movies are basically awkward stories about dainty people wearing bow ties while sitting in chairs that are a tad too small…but yeah, I still love his films…have you seen 'Magic in the Moonlight' yet?"

"No, I haven't, but I'd really like to."

"We should go see it."

"Yes, we should…I would love that."

"I would love that, too," she said, leaning toward him and grinning widely. He noticed that her voice had become even more buoyant, like a bubbling brook overflowing after an overnight rain-shower.

'This is amazing,' he thought, sighing dreamily and trying to

18. Festive meal celebrating the performance of a ritual commandment.

moisten his dried lips and parched throat with a few more sips of wine. 'No date has ever gone this well in my life... and if I'm reading her body language correctly, this could go very far indeed...'

And yet, on his way back to his apartment, he asked himself again why it was that Rena had still not asked him a single question about his background. He had so badly been wanting to share his experience with another sympathetic soul – his painful, discomfiting experience of feeling as if he never fit in, no matter how Jewishly he dressed and acted; his disillusioning experience of feeling that, no matter how many tractates of Talmud he mastered and no matter how many ancient texts he deciphered, he would never be regarded as fully "Jewish" as his white Jewish friends. He so badly wanted for Rena to be the one that he could share his disheartening experiences with – his experience of being insultingly asked in synagogue, "So, what made you want to become Jewish?"; his experience of being watched whenever he would go into the synagogue kitchen to wash his hands; his experience of congregants in synagogues simply not greeting him at all – that he was almost more disappointed that she had been so silent and uncurious about the incident with the policeman than he was overjoyed that for the first time in his life he had found a woman who actually wanted to go out with him on a third date.

'Should I bring it up with her on the next date?' he asked himself as he approached his apartment, excited to report back to Yoni about how well the second date had gone. 'Should I just come right out and say something about it?... Or should I just – what's that expression? – let sleeping dogs lie?... Yeah... maybe best not to bring it up now... why rock the boat... she's clearly uncomfortable talking about it, so why make her uncomfortable? Yeah... best not to bring it up now... best to treat this as a *davar sh'yesh lo matirin*[19] and wait till after we're engaged to bring it up...'

---

19. Something that should be avoided now but which will be permitted later.

FIVE

During the week leading up to his third date with Rena, whenever he tried to fulfill his obligations to the yeshiva and earn his stipend by studying Talmud in the study hall, Rena's waifish image wafted before his eyes like the single flame of a freshly lit candle. And even when he concentrated very intently and tried to push her image away, it still lurked in the back of his mind, ready to reignite itself as soon as he had a lull in his study. Whenever he went to the water fountain for a drink of water, she was there; when he went to brush his teeth, she was with him; at night, in bed, when he moved his head onto the cooler side of the pillow and shifted his body from one side to the other in accordance with the procedure mandated by Jewish law, she was by his side, glued to his consciousness like melted wax on a candlestick holder. 'Will she like the name Menashe for our first-born boy?' he wondered, as he tossed and turned in bed the night before his third date. 'If our first-born is a girl, I'll let her choose the name. But I get to choose the boy's name. Everything else, I'll let her choose. I'll let her choose the dishes and the cutlery and the drapery and the bath-towels and the bed-sheets – whatever she wants, I'll let her choose. Everything except the first-born boy's name...but she's a nice enough person, I'm sure she'd agree to that without much of a fuss...but otherwise, I'd give up anything for her, anything. I'll eat what she eats, drink what she drinks, live where she lives – anything for Rena. Anything for my *Mekudeshes*,[1] my *meyuchedes* – my *mezumenes*…'[2]

At the movie theater, Eli, wearing a button-down blue dress-shirt, saved a seat in the back of the theater for Rena. As he sat through the previews and waited for her to arrive, he clamped his hands upon his shaking kneecaps and squirmed in his seat. 'This is the time,' he said to himself as he finally saw her She was wearing a frayed pink sweater, a jean skirt and black shoes, and holding a small bag of popcorn in her right hand. '"*Shema yekadmenu acher*" – I have to act now – I have to tell her now…or at least after the movie…Knowing my luck, if I don't say something to her at the end of this date somebody'll stop by the library tomorrow, somebody smarter, richer, cooler, better looking and more confident than I am and she'll fall for him and completely forget about me…the time is now – *im lo ach'shav eimasai*[3]…'

"Hey there!" she greeted him, smiling good-naturedly as she sat down to his left. He was pleased to notice that this time she was even wearing jewelry – a simple silver bracelet on her right wrist and two jade studs in her seashell-shaped ears. "I'm so happy to be seeing this with you."

"Me too."

"And so happy to be with you in general," she continued, toying with the strap on her purse and eying him expectantly. "It's really a delight to spend time with you. This is only our third date, but I really feel – I don't want to be presumptuous, but I really feel a real bond…"

"I…I feel the same way," he said, his heart racing. 'Could this really be happening? Really? Right here? To *me*? To have what I dreamed of for so long about to finally come true?…'

"I brought this for you," she said, reaching into her silver suede handbag and handing him a bottle of water.

1. Bride.
2. My One.
3. If not now when?

"Thanks," he said, smiling and giving her a grateful, knowing glance. "That's so thoughtful of you."

"I also brought you some popcorn." She moved the bag to her right and set it upon the armrest. "I already had like half the bag on the way into the theater, so the rest is for you."

"Oh, thanks. That's so nice of you!"

When the opening credits began to roll, Eli reached into the bag with his left hand and intoned the Hebrew words *"Blessed are You, Lord, our God, King of the Universe, who creates the fruit of the ground"* under his breath.

"Oh...wait a sec," he said, just before he placed the fistful of popcorn into his mouth.

"What?" she asked, raising her eyebrows slightly.

"Did you buy this at the concession stand outside here?"

"Yeah...what's the problem?"

"You know that the popcorn here is not kosher."

She fell silent and averted her gaze from him. Her face clouded, and her eyes became lifeless.

"Oh," she finally said after a second that felt like an hour. "Oh right... I'm so sorry...it's been so long since I worried about that stuff...I'm really sorry..."

"That's ok," he said, looking straight ahead at the screen as the movie began. "Don't worry about it...let's just enjoy the movie."

'Don't worry,' he told himself, sitting back uncomfortably in his seat and biting his tongue. 'Once we're married she'll start keeping kosher again. It'll be no big deal. She did it once before. She did it all the way through high school...or at least for most of the time she was in high school...it'll be just like riding a bike for her...she'll get right back into it without a problem – nothing to worry about here...just forget about it and enjoy the movie...But how exactly should I ask her to marry me?' he asked himself, continuously sipping water in a futile attempt to wet his parched throat and moisten his dry lips. 'And when?...I can't do it *now*! Not after only the third date!...And there's that small aspect of not having a ring yet...where do I go to get the ring?...And how am I supposed to find out what her ring size is? Am I supposed to measure her finger?...Is there even such a thing as a 'ring size'? *Ribbono shel olam,*[4] I can't believe how ignorant I am of these things!...Yoni would know...I'll have to ask Yoni...But what would he think about me wanting to marry her after only three dates? He'd probably be happy about it...but wouldn't he think I'd be acting too soon?...But how can it be too soon if it's a mitzvah?[5] *Zrizim makdimim lemitzvos...*[6] If I have an opportunity to do a mitzvah I have to do it now, I can't wait! *Hayom la'asosam – ha'yom v'lo l'machar!*[7] ...So how should I leave things with her at the end of this date? I suppose we can talk about the movie, but shouldn't there be some way for me to say something that'll plant the seeds for what I intend to ask her the next time? *Ribbono shel olam,* I wish I knew how to go about this and wasn't so in the dark about these things!...Maybe there's something about this in *Nisuin Kehilchosuh*[8]...I should ask Yoni if I can borrow his *sefer*...'[9]

Two-thirds of the way through the movie, as the main characters were conversing in an astronomic observatory, Eli looked to his left and smiled. Rena ran her hand through her hair and smiled back. Even in the darkened theater, amidst the spare silky light being emitted from the wide flat screen, he was able to notice that on this night, unlike during their previous two dates, she was wearing lip-gloss and makeup. Her hair was also straighter, less frizzier, and even somewhat wet; she looked as if she had just showered prior to meeting him at the theater. He looked back at the screen but couldn't resist trying to steal one more glimpse of her. The next time he turned back toward her, she caught him looking at her. Her prominent pale lips puckered; she leaned toward him, wrapped her bony right arm around his shoulder and placed her mouth on his.

4. God.
5. Commandment.
6. The diligent ones perform the commandments at the first possible opportunity.
7. "'And you shall do them today': 'today' and not 'tomorrow.'"
8. The book *Marriage According to the Law.*
9. Book.

Eli flinched as he felt her wet lips on his dry mouth and her cool jasmine-scented breath on his warm neck; his knees buckled, and his heart began to race like a car with broken brakes. 'Ribbono shel olam,'[10] he said in his head, 'what do I do?' His heartbeat resounded in his ears like a jackhammer, and his thoughts became a mound of mush; he didn't move his lips, and his now-moist mouth was as irresponsive as a dead fly. After four seconds of her lips maneuvering upon his inert mouth, she pulled herself away from him and faced forward, locking her eyes on the screen as if trying to pretend that what had just happened had not in fact happened.

As soon as the closing credits began to roll and the ceiling lights gradually came back on, Rena, staring blankly at the screen, exhaled audibly.

"I'm so sorry," she said, ashen-faced, her jaunty, high-spirited voice finally beginning to flag. "Please forgive me."

"It's ok, Rena," he said, straining to hear her sunken voice, which was muffled by the murmuring of perplexed moviegoers collecting their belongings and exiting the theater. "Don't worry ab – "

"I know I shouldn't have done that … you're shomer,[11] aren't you?"

Eli nodded his head; hers drooped. A shadow passed across her freckle-flecked face.

"I knew you were, I just … I … I shouldn't have done that … I'm so sorry."

"Rena, please … really … there's no need to ap – "

Before he could finish his sentence, she had already sprung out of her seat and was hastening toward the exit. Eli watched her leave without saying a word. 'Just let her go,' he said to himself, rubbing his temples with his knuckles. 'You're not supposed to try to calm someone down when they're upset. You're just supposed to let them be, let the emotions play out … don't go running after her … don't even call her later tonight. Or tomorrow. Give it some time … then

10. Oh my God …
11. Refrain from touching non-family members of the opposite sex (other than one's spouse).

call her in a few days. She'll have forgotten about the whole thing by then and it'll be back to normal between us...'

When he called her back five days later, he got her voicemail and left a message. "Hi Rena," he said in a quivering voice. "It's Eli. I just wanted to say I had a great time with you at the movie the other day and hope you did too. I hope you're having a good day, and, uh, I hope to see you again soon." After waiting three days without hearing back from her, he sent her a text message: "Hey Rena, hope you're having a good week, just wanted to say I've really enjoyed spending time with you, looking forward to doing so again soon." After another three days had passed without him having heard back from her, he debated with himself about whether he should bring up the incident at the movie theater the next time he messaged her. 'Maybe that's why she's not writing or calling back,' he thought. 'Maybe she's still upset about what happened. Maybe she feels guilty about what happened. But I don't understand... why would she want to do that to me in the movie theater but then completely go silent on me and not respond to any of my messages? It's a *tartei d'sasrei*;[12] it's a *stirah minei ubei*[13] ... it makes no sense... Maybe she's waiting for me to say, "hey, forget about it, it was no big deal."... But maybe it would be even worse to bring it up. It would be like reopening a scab... or like reminding a *ger*[14] who's repented and converted and is now a new person, *"emesh hayisa oved avoda zara... peh she'achal neveilos utreifos shkotzim urmasim..."*[15] ... She probably just wants to forget about it, and I'd only be making it worse by reminding her of it. Yeah... probably best not to bring it up at all...' And so, convinced that what had happened between them in the movie theater was no more than a little dirty puddle in the middle of a long clean street that would quickly evaporate after a few days of sunshine, when he sent her an email the following week, he simply wrote: "Hi Rena, how have you been? You're probably real

12. Contradiction.
13. Complete contradiction.
14. Convert.
15. "Just yesterday you were worshipping idols and eating non-kosher food..."

busy with work, but I just wanted to say hi. Haven't heard from you in a bit, hope all's well. Best, Eli."

After another week passed without having heard from her, Eli briefly contemplated texting her one more time but decided against it. 'If you ask a person for forgiveness three times and each time he doesn't forgive you,' he thought, reminding himself of a teaching from Maimonides' Laws of Repentance, 'you're not *chayav*[16] to ask a fourth time...three times with no response means no, and I'll just have to accept that, as hard as it is...'

As he sat in the back of the yeshiva study hall and reconciled himself to the prospect of a future without Rena, his bottom lip was quivering, and his eyes were moistening. He knew that he wasn't supposed to feel sorry for himself – the holy texts of his tradition instructed him to simply and humbly accept the decree of God in all matters – but his emotions overwhelmed his intellect. Everything he had so ardently been hoping for evaporated before his eyes like a beautiful night's dream dissolving in the daylight. He buried his head in the open volume of Talmud in front of him and let the overflowing fountain of his inexpressible feelings pour themselves forth.

16. Obligated.

PART II

ONE

The New England Hebrew High School building, set on the slope of a scenic meadow, was like a stylish silk suit that was two sizes too large for the wearer but which the man still wore because, after all, he was the one who had commissioned it. The building, constructed at the turn of the twenty-first century, was designed to accommodate two hundred students, but by the time Eli arrived to teach there, only forty-five were enrolled.

After the fifteen years Eli had spent at the yeshiva in Baltimore, the New England high school was like an astounding alien landscape filled with bewildering sights he had never before seen. Every room number outside every door was also written in braille, and next to the six steps of stairs that led to the school's main entrance was a wheelchair-accessible ramp. There were Purell dispensers on every floor, and signs posted outside of bathrooms that perplexed Eli to no end: "Please use the restroom that is most consistent with your gender identity. A gender-neutral restroom is available on the first floor." The building had an actual working P.A. system, school-wide Wi-Fi, and smart-boards in every classroom that he was too scared of ever learning how to use. 'Baruch Hashem[1] they kept the old green chalkboards even after they installed these new smart-boards,' Eli would think every time

---

1. Thank God.

he looked at them. '*Mistama*[2] they kept them for the over sixty-five-year-old teachers – they probably never would've imagined that the thirty-and-under teachers might need them just as much...'

Eli marveled at the school's clean cafeteria that served quinoa and kale; its in-house IT department that responded immediately to every kind of technological request conceivable; its on-site secular library; vending machines stocked with vitamin water and vegetable chips; clearly marked exit signs, functioning fire alarms, and professional security guards; separate garbage bins for recycling – and separate bins for paper, plastic, and metal recycling at that; potted plants – filled with real plants and real flowers – inside every classroom, watered regularly by the school's expert custodial staff; hallways decorated with paintings by contemporary Jewish artists; a computer lab with twenty-first century computers – which actually worked, and which even had internet access and Microsoft Office; a state-of-the-art gym with an indoor basketball court, three indoor tennis courts, and a weight-room and aerobics center; a spacious auditorium with a globular-shaped theater in which weekly performances of music and plays were held as well as monthly guest-lectures from elite Judaic and secular scholars from Maryland to Massachusetts. The entire environment of the high school surrounded him like a pool of fresh spring water, and he eagerly immersed himself in it every day, bathing in all the manifold, revitalizing ways it differed from Yeshivas Chelkas Yaakov – an institution whose disdain for the *"goyisher velt"*[3] surrounded it like the ozone layer encircling the earth, shielding it from almost all foreign intrusions which could potentially damage the yeshiva's fragile biosphere.

But to Eli, star-struck anew everyday by the new world he was now living in, the biggest difference of all was that there were women around him. Not since his days as a callow middle-schooler at Houston Hebrew Academy had members of the opposite sex been a part of his everyday world. For fifteen years at the all-boys' Baltimore yeshiva he

2. Probably.
3. Secular world.

had lived without girls and had not even missed them – at least this is what he would say to himself; the fact that his natural urges never subsided spoke otherwise. He was proud of having made it through his entire adolescence – from twelve to twenty-nine – without a woman in his life to speak of and had, despite his dating disappointments, maintained his equilibrium. He had plunged into the height of his hormonal phase without women and had made it out alive, and now that his body was no longer as insistent as it had been during his teens and mid-twenties on having its way, he felt himself at ease, almost serene, finally able to fully devote himself to his Torah studies and to his reading without needing to worry about women. But now, chafing at having to be in the same building as Emma Yates – the brilliant, blue-eyed English teacher – every day, he wondered, 'Why? Why, Hashem,[4] did you put me in this situation? How come when we're having lunch in the teacher's lounge and she's eating her prepackaged pineapples and apple slices she won't even look at me – as if she's embarrassed to do so, as if she wouldn't want anyone else to find out that she had been looking at me? But then why does she smile at me whenever she passes by me in the hallway? *Vas meinst*[5] that smile of hers?' He wished he could take her smile with him and give it to a forensics lab to analyze it; he wished he could show it to a psychologist, or a 'smile-ologist,' if such a thing existed, to probe what was going on beneath it and determine its true intent.

Every day, as he taught portions from the Talmud to a group of wide-eyed ninth graders, he did his best to avoid Ms. Yates; the mere thought of her was enough to make him jittery, and he did all he could to spare his strained nerves any further stress. He studied her class schedule, and only left his classroom when he knew she was in the middle of a class of hers. He started eating his lunch at his desk in his classroom, and he kept his socializing with the other teachers in the school to the most minimal degree possible lest they somehow entangle him with her. When he needed to go to the restroom or to

4. God.
5. What does it mean.

the Judaics library to retrieve a book, he kept his head down when he walked through the hallway, fearful of catching even a glimpse of her and what that one glimpse would do to his mind for the rest of the day – or for the rest of the week. The mere sight of her was enough to make him instantly drop his carefully conceived plan to become the next Ben Azzai – his plan to revive the long-lost tradition of Jewish celibacy, his plan to show the world that principled bachelorhood could indeed exist once again in the Jewish tradition. His dating disasters had convinced him that this was God's plan for him. 'HaKadosh Baruch Hu,'[6] he would tell himself, 'is preventing me from marrying because he wants to use me to show the world that it's not only Catholics who can do it – Jews can do it, too. We can use our willpower to conquer our natural desires in order to devote ourselves completely to a life of Torah and *kedushah*.[7] If the priests can do it, why not us? If Ben Azzai can do it, why not me? Sure, I was disappointed by all the rejections from all those girls in my twenties, but I really shouldn't have been. It was *hashgacha pratis*.[8] Not since Ben Azzai some fifteen-hundred years ago have we had a genuine, celibate, life-long bachelor-scholar. Just think of how much I'll be able to accomplish without a woman. Newton, Democritus, Kant, Thoreau, Locke, Brahms – they lived alone, without anyone to *batel*[9] them, and look what they gave the world: science, literature, philosophy, music...imagine what I'll be able to accomplish without anyone *batelling*[10] me,' he would tell himself, constantly reassuring himself and strengthening his resolve whenever his thoughts turned to women. 'The reason you've been so unsuccessful in your dating life is because HaKadosh Baruch Hu is saying to you, "Eli, my son – you are not cut out for a *stam*[11] *balabatish*[12] life. That

6. God.
7. Holiness.
8. Meant to be.
9. Distract.
10. Distracting.
11. Regular.
12. Domestic.

kind of life is for other, weaker souls, not for elite *lamdonim*[13] like you. *Ha lan v'ha l'hu.*[14] Yes, it may be difficult, at first, to live without love, but in the end, you shall accomplish so much more; the reward for doing without a partner will be much greater – and I am reliable to compensate you faithfully for the reward of your efforts. Newton and Kant, Jane Austen and John Paul – ask yourself, Eli: do you want to be like every other Yosef Yitzchak, or do you want to accomplish what Newton and Brahms and Benedict and Francis accomplished? If so, leave your silly dreams of a married life behind you and embrace who you truly are: a Ben Azzai for the twenty-first century – a celibate, bachelor Talmudic scholar. It is your destiny, Eli. Don't fight it. Accept it – and all will be good with you, in this life and in the life of the world to come." It's as easy as that...forget about dating, forget about marriage, forget about women. All you really need is right in front of you: your Torah, your Talmud, and your books.'

But this Emma Yates...the mere sight of her would cause him to forget all this, and he needed to remind himself every day that he was 'cut out for other, "higher" things,' as he told himself. 'What Ben Azzai accomplished in Talmud, what the popes accomplished in theology,' he would tell himself, 'it doesn't just happen by accident. It's because they made sacrifices for it. Living without an intimate relationship is a difficult sacrifice – maybe the most difficult one of all – it's a kind of death, *epes*.[15] But *"ein divrei torah mis'kai'min ela b'mi sh'meimis atzmo aleiha"*[16] – it's ultimately an infinitely rewarding sacrifice, the most rewarding sacrifice there is...and that's the *hishtadlus*[17] that I have to make. But this woman – why, Hashem? Why do you have to make it so hard for me? One look from her and she sets me on fire...'

Whenever their eyes would meet in the school hallway, his mind – his strong-willed, highly disciplined, Talmud-trained mind over which

13. Scholars.
14. "That (marriage) is for them, not for you."
15. Somewhat.
16. "Torah is only preserved by one who kills himself for it."
17. Effort.

he usually exercised such tight control – would, like a mighty ocean wave that for all its power could still not prevent itself from crashing upon the rocky shore, always wander back to that sultry August day when he had first seen her...

She had been wearing a pansy-colored short-sleeve dress and had been looking at him throughout the introductory faculty lunch. It was one thing, he had thought, for her to be looking at him as he was being introduced as the school's new, highly recommended Talmud teacher, having been hired out of the elite Baltimore yeshiva of Chelkas Yaakov to fill an opening in the Judaic studies department of New England Hebrew High School, a small co-ed modern Orthodox high school in West Hartford, Connecticut; it was another thing for her to still be darting glances at him while the rest of the twelve faculty members and administrators were being introduced to one another. Her gaze was making him fidget, and he never fidgeted; he had made a career – albeit hardly a lucrative one – out of an unmatched ability to sit still for hours on end. His *"hasmada,"* as they called it in yeshiva – his remarkable ability to literally keep his bony behind glued to his chair as he toiled away night and day for sixteen years in the rear of his seminary's spacious study hall, mastering the Talmud, Bible, and the Jewish law codes and commentaries – had given him everything he had. His friends would always come to him whenever they had a question about a difficult passage in Talmud or the Jewish law codes, because, as they would say, *"haKol tz'rikhin l'marei chitai'ya".*[18] Granted, all he had to show for his efforts were eight years of subsistence-level seminary stipends and now this, his first actual full-time job, but at least it was something. At least he had survived. At least he now had his first shot at a legitimate, decently paid, yeshiva-free existence – and his first chance to act upon his long-cherished wish of living an independent, unattached life. 'And now this,' he thought, as her consistent, on-and-off glances that so agitated him continued to fall upon him – glances that seemed so inappropriate to him that were her

---

18. "Everyone needs the owner of the wheat" (i.e., the one who knows the most).

parents present he was sure they would have told her, "that's enough, sweetie, it's not polite to stare."

It was the gaze of a woman the likes of which he had never felt before: charmingly non-resistant yet magnetically insistent, and above all, *interested*. He didn't need her to raise her hand and say, "hey you, over there – new guy, whatever your name is – you really pull off that white-shirt black-slacks black-shoes black-skullcap look rather well" to know that she was interested; he could tell from the way she was strategically trying to look away from him. Every time he shot a look in her direction, she quickly looked away from him, her rosy cheeks reddening ever so slightly as if she had relapsed back into her schoolgirl phase, unconsciously ogling an attractive adolescent boy as the reigns of self-control – which she surely must have been grasping as tightly as if her life depended on it every second of every minute of her illustrious professional life in order to attain the position she had, Chair of the English Department and Director of the NEHH English and French honors programs – had, for the first time in her adult life, momentarily slipped from her deathly tight grip.

And now, as they sat around a large rectangular table in a small square room and listened to the principal prattle on about the importance of "proactive pedagogy" – evidently the latest educational fad *du jour* which she had picked up at some private school administrators' conference over the summer and was now preaching as if it were the *sola scriptura* of schooling, the only possible path to scholastic salvation – he was sweating. He ran his right hand across his damp, clean-shaven face; even though his cheap electric razor never gave him that close of a shave, he had always abstained from using a real razor because *halakhah* – the system of Jewish law that he observed as carefully as a chemist supervising a spacecraft's gas thrusters – prohibited it.

'I can't believe this,' he said in his head, hoping the English teacher's intermittent glances cast in his direction would soon cease. 'No woman has ever made me sweat before ... well, maybe Rena – but only once. And not like this ...'

He – the cool, calm, collected Eli Newman, the imperturbable

Eli who barely broke a sweat while running a mile and certainly never perspired under pressure – was as sticky as if he hadn't put on deodorant in a decade. The new building's central air-conditioning was undoubtedly working, counteracting the early August heat with a steady stream of strong arctic air, but despite the polar temperature which prevailed throughout the principal's protracted scholastic sermon, the sticky droplets of sweat leaking out of his armpits were slowly seeping through his four-cornered string-fringed undershirt and were staining the sides of his starched white dress shirt.

'*Beis Din*[19] would be *mechayev* her[20] to pay *nezek tzaar ripui sheves* and *boshes*[21] for all this,' he quipped to himself, swallowing hard and tapping his foot briskly. 'Or at the very least she should have to pay for my dry cleaning bill...'

'Well, what should I do about it?' he asked himself, as two long-tenured teachers motioned for him to pass the large platter of sesame noodles perched in front of him. 'Should I reciprocate this – whatever this look is she keeps giving me?... Should *I* look at *her*?... Should I?'

'Of course I *want* to,' he said to himself, as the math teacher to his right refilled his plate with a pear-sized portion of noodles. 'But that's not the question... am I *allowed* to look – that's the question... *Chazal*[22] would say I can't... my *rebbeim*[23] would say I can't...' He rummaged through every recess of his Jewish-law-filled mind for a source that would justify his desire to look, hunting through his book-cluttered brain like a starving beggar scavenging through a mound of trash, desperately hoping for just one piece of discarded food that could provide him with sustenance, but he could not find even a single scrap that would allow him to satisfy the painful cravings of his hungry eyes.

It wasn't a question of whether she was beautiful – that, she certainly

19. A Jewish court.
20. Would obligate her.
21. Damages for embarrassment and emotional distress.
22. The rabbis of the Talmud.
23. Rabbis.

was, with her long, slim limbs, svelte figure, smooth, cream-colored skin and silky, sun-streaked strawberry-blonde hair cascading down her slender neck and nestling softly upon her wiry shoulders. Not, it wasn't a question of whether she was alluring enough to attract his gaze – that, she certainly was, with her sparkling sea-green eyes fringed with long, dark lashes, her well-tended eyebrows, her symmetrical, narrow-nosed face, and her plush, paradise-pink lips. It wasn't a question of whether she was elegant – that, she certainly was, with her perfect posture, her unprepossessing demeanor, her stylishly cut dress, and her well-placed, tastefully worn bracelets, earrings, and pencil-thin necklace. And it certainly wasn't a question of whether she was intelligent; when Principal Penske, a short, plump, well-dressed woman with graying blonde hair, wide-set gray eyes, green horn-rimmed glasses and a pre-ternaturally pleasant disposition, had introduced her at the beginning of the lunch, Eli had been astonished at her credentials: after graduating summa cum laude from Amherst College with a B.A. in English and a minor in Philosophy, she had earned a dual M.A. in French and Comparative Literature from Yale and stayed in Connecticut to take the post of Chair of the NEHH English department, where she had taught English and French for the past nine years, earning all sorts of teaching distinctions the names of which Eli had long since forgotten as he fidgeted and sweated and bit his lips and twitched his toes for the greater part of the hour, consciously bridling – yet unconsciously ebullient – because of the unremitting attention of this brilliant woman that he had somehow managed to attract. Her master's thesis – written on Joseph Conrad's *Victory*, a novel Eli had never heard of – had been published by a small but prestigious academic press. And, to top it all off, she had published prize-winning poetry in highly regarded journals, said Principal Penske – in literary reviews with names like "Ploughshares" and "Threepenny Review," none of which Eli had ever heard of either – and was now working on her first volume of collected poems, soon to be published by an elite academic press whose name Eli had also forgotten, preoccupied as he was with other, more-pressing mental demands and more insistent visual and sensual stimulations.

All he could remember, blinded as his brow-beaten brain had been by the aquamarine brilliance of her deep-set eyes, was her name: Emma Yates...As soon as those three simple syllables emerged out of the slow-moving mouth of Principal Penske, Eli had been involuntarily repeating them in his mind as if they were the three-digit combination that would unlock the hidden treasure chamber of his most secretly cherished desires. As soon as he caught himself repeating her name to himself in his head, he stopped, but not before irrevocably imprinting those three smooth syllables in his memory, from where he could now recall them as quickly as he could recollect the three letters of his own name.

'It's not right that I should look at her,' he said to himself, as the head of the school's Judaic studies program, a short, stocky, black-bearded rabbi with large wire-framed glasses and a knitted blue-and-white yarmulke sitting atop a full head of steel-gray hair, began to give an overview – mostly for the benefit of the new faculty members – of how the school's excellent secular studies program synthesized with its rigorous religious studies program. 'The Torah[24] says *b'feirush*[25] *"lo sasuru,"*[26] Eli reminded himself, 'and *Shulkhan Arukh*[27] *asir's*[28] even looking at a woman's *etzbah ketanah*.[29] There's no *heter*[30] to look at her. Not even at her hair. *"Sei'ar b'isha erva."*[31] And you definitely can't ever talk to her... it would be one thing if she were Jewish... but Emma *"Yates"*? That doesn't sound very Jewish..."Yates"...hmm... I don't know...I don't think so...No...There's no way she can be Jewish with a name like that...And even if she were Jewish, it wouldn't matter – it'd still be *asur*[32] for me to look at her – unless...unless it

24. The Five Books of Moses – the first of the Hebrew Bible's three sections.
25. Explicitly.
26. "Do not wander after your heart and after your eyes."
27. The Code of Jewish Law.
28. Prohibits.
29. Pinky.
30. Halakhic (Jewish legal) Permission.
31. "A woman's hair is in the category of 'nakedness.'"
32. Prohibited.

was for *shidduchim*[33] ... unless there was a possibility that we could get married and I needed to find out whether I was attracted to her ... but "Emma *Yates*"? No ... there's no way ... it's *asur* ...'

Besides which, becoming attached to another person was a highly dangerous prospect, he reminded himself. He knew from personal experience – bitter, luckless, disenchanting personal experience – how dangerous it was to get one's hopes up about the prospect of finding a woman who actually wanted to marry him, and he had vowed that he would never again let himself fall prey to the human heart-eating Venus fly trap that was the flower of love.

'Why should I change my entire way of life just because of one stupid, meaningless look of hers?' he thought defiantly, as the school's Judaic studies director discussed, in needlessly extensive depth, the school's endlessly complex, hopelessly ambitious educational philosophy. 'Besides, how presumptuous of me to assume that she's actually interested in me from just a few looks! The *yuhara*![34] *Mistama*[35] she's staring at me for the same reason that everyone else, at least in Jewish settings, has stared at me all my life. She's probably sitting there and wondering, "who are you and what are you doing in a Jewish school?" She's probably wondering the same thing that all those other Jewish girls I've gone out with on dates were wondering: "How are you even Jewish?" they'd all ask me without saying it – asking it with their incredulous eyes, asking it with their furrowed brows and their pursed lips the first time they set eyes on me, those doubting eyes that said so much more than their mouths could ever say, those suspicious, disbelieving eyes that said, "I've never seen anyone Jewish who looks like that ... the *shadchan*[36] who set me up with you told me you were a *masmid*,[37] a *ben Torah* ...[38] But this ... this can't be right ... there

33. Dating for marriage.
34. Chutzpah.
35. Probably.
36. Matchmaker.
37. Diligent learner.
38. Learned, devoted, genuinely religious Jewish man.

must be some mistake. The *shadchan* must've set me up with the wrong person, because no way can the person she was describing to me be you." This Ms. Yates may not be phrasing it in her head that way, but I'm sure she's asking herself something along those lines, some kind of question like, "I have nothing against people who look like you, nothing at all – it's just that I can't actually believe you're Jewish…I mean, not that there'd be anything wrong with that if you were, it's just that I wasn't expecting the school to hire someone who, how should I put this, looks like you for a Judaic studies teaching position." But still, that look of hers…her on-and-off and on again three-second-stares…it's *not* the same kind of look I used to get on those dates. There's something else about it – something more… some, I don't know, look of *interest*…She's not just eyeing me as if I'm a circus oddity, the answer to the question "which of these doesn't belong"? – but eyeing me as if I'm actually a *person*, not just a thing, as if I'm a person worthy not only of her passing curiosity but of her sustained, genuine interest…I don't know how I know this – I don't even know *that* I know this – but I do feel it…I sense something different here. Something different both about the way she's looking at me, and something different about her – her way of looking is not like the others' way of looking…and *she* is not like the others…but what is it? What's the difference? I don't know what exactly it is, I just know that her looks are different…'

That she should be someone of interest to *him* – someone sufficiently attractive, in every sense of the term, to draw his gaze and command his attention – was not surprising to him. That he could possibly be of interest to *her* – not merely as a "how did someone who looks like him wind up in a place like this?" curiosity, but as a person of real, genuine interest – was astounding to him.

As Principal Penske concluded the opening faculty luncheon with a few remarks which sounded to him like the same lines she must have been repeating at the conclusion of every opening school session since 1982 – something along the lines of how no group of people on earth loves the first September chill as much as teachers do because it signals the beginning of a new school year, the moment teachers wait for all summer long, the moment they get to resume doing what they most love doing, "what God put us here on earth to do" – Eli vowed to avoid ever speaking to this Ms. Yates lest the slightest possibility arise that something occur between them that wouldn't be sanctioned by Jewish law. 'I know it's the height of absurdity to think that just because of a few looks from her that there could ever be a possibility of anything like that ever happening between us,' he thought, unnerved as much by the flickering fluorescent light above as by the intermittent glances being directed at him by the English teacher below, 'but *Chazal*[39] say you can never be too careful – an inviting look here, a suggestive word there, and the next thing you know you're alone in a room together and the next thing you know you're... *halakhah*[40] knows that one thing leads to another, so it says to cut it off right at the outset, to not even touch a woman – to not even look at her or speak to her – to nip it in the bud before it even gets a chance to go anywhere... and *kal va'chomer*[41] with a woman who's completely not *shayikh*[42] for you on any level... Even though Rashi[43] says in Beitzah[44] "*asu mishmeres lemishmarti v'lo mishmeres l'mishmeres,*"[45] sometimes like in Chullin[46] with the *g'zierah ha'ala'a atu achila*[47] by *b'sar oaf v'chalav*[48] we do make a *lig'zeirah lig'zeirah,*[49] not necessarily because it's *kula chada g'zeirah*

39. The rabbis of the Talmud.
40. Jewish law.
41. All the more so.
42. Appropriate.
43. Medieval Talmudic commentator.
44. A tractate of Talmud.
45. "Make a safeguard for my decrees, but not a safeguard for a safeguard."
46. Another tractate of Talmud.
47. The prohibition of putting meat and milk on the same table lest you come to eat them together.
48. Fowl and milk, which according to Maimonides and most Rishonim (medieval rabbinic authorities) one is rabbinically (but not biblically) prohibited to mix and to eat together.
49. Decree on a decree.

he^{50} like the $g'zeiros^{51}$ in Beitzah but because *"ee lo ha lo kaymi ha."*[52] Sometimes you really do need a second *mishmeres*[53] around the first one because without the second one everything will collapse. And this is one of those cases, because it's an *inyan*[54] of *arayos*[55] – *v'harai'yuh,*[56] the Torah itself makes a *mishmeres l'mishmeres*[57] in these *inyanim,*[58] according to those *achronim*[59] who hold that the *lav*[60] of *"lo sik'revu"*[61] is a *s'yag de'oraisa*[62] ...I need to make a *mishmeres l'mishmeres* here that I shouldn't even talk to her...

But as the pale fluorescent light inside and the gray, overcast weather outside conspired to dull his spirit, he was secretly hoping – though he would never in eighteen thousand years admit it to himself or anyone else – that precisely what *halakhah* had been designed to prevent was exactly what he wished would come to pass between him and Emma Yates. All he had to go off of was a few long looks, a few three-second stares – but it was more than enough for his perfervid mind to concoct the most creative concupiscent fantasies imaginable. Forbidden thoughts began to seep into the center of his mind like water from a leaking faucet that he couldn't turn off. A feeling of foreboding came over him; he felt as if his mind was trying to tell him an incontrovertible truth about himself that he had been refusing to acknowledge. It was a terrifying, feverish feeling that threatened to tear him apart at his roots; he felt as if he was standing at the gates of

50. Decree.
51. Decrees.
52. Without the second safeguard not even the first will be preserved.
53. Safeguard.
54. Matter.
55. Forbidden relationships.
56. The proof is that...
57. A safeguard for a safeguard.
58. Matters.
59. Post-renaissance Talmudic commentators.
60. Prohibition.
61. "Though shalt not come close to uncovering nakedness."
62. Biblical safeguard.

hell and all that stood between him and permanent perdition was one more look – a single suggestion from her sea-green eyes, and a single split-second reciprocation from his.

After Principal Penske formally concluded the luncheon and dismissed the faculty, ending by emphasizing how important it was for a school of such small size that its faculty members get along with one another and "act as a team, not as individuals," Eli's heart began racing uncontrollably. Eli could not conceive of how Emma Yates, an evidently brilliant, unattached young woman who wore no rings of any kind on her long, finely formed, well-manicured fingers would ever want anything to do with an unaccomplished first-year Talmud teacher from a school that no one outside of a few rabbis and teachers in Judaic studies departments had ever heard of. His navel knots at last loosened and his furiously fidgeting toes finally stopped twitching when he noticed that Ms. Yates was no longer looking anywhere near his vicinity.

Confident that her gaze had been completely innocuous but still uneasy about what the sight of her glances directed at him – and the fleshy, full-bodied fantasies that his mind had so speedily brought to life from the few measly bones of those intermittent stares – portended for him, Eli hastily collected his books and left the faculty lunchroom without exchanging pleasantries with any teacher, determined to carry out his new professional duties as he had vowed to live out his personal life: free from attachments, free from absurd, irrational romantic dreams, and free from the devastating disappointments that always accompanied the inevitable crushing of his reckless hoping.

TWO

Eli began to feel the famed New England cold he had heard so much about on the night after the fall harvest festival of Sukkot. As he walked home from synagogue that mid-October night, snowflakes flittered through the frosty air, and a wintry wind whipped at his weather-beaten body. 'It's probably seventy and sunny right now in Houston,' he thought, admiring the pumpkin, magenta, and cranberry-colored leaves glimmering in the benign autumnal light while cursing the cruel northeastern climate and realizing that he'd have to take his winter jacket out of his still-unpacked boxes months earlier than he'd thought he would have to. 'But at least now I can be *mekayem*[1] that first Mishnah Berurah[2] in *Hilchos Sukkah*[3] for the first time in my life, that one where he brings down from[4] the Tur[5] that we go outside to eat in *sukkas*[6] during *yemos hag'shamim*[7] and not *bimos hakayitz*[8]

---

1. Fulfill.
2. Authoritative nineteenth-century halakhic work.
3. The Laws of Sukkah.
4. Cites.
5. Fifteenth-century halakhic code.
6. Temporary outdoor huts.
7. The rainy season.
8. The summer.

because if we were sitting outside during the summer it wouldn't be *niker*[9] that we were doing it *l'sheim mitzvah...*'[10]

As soon as he arrived back in his apartment – a small, under-furnished, ill-lit one-bedroom residence with curtain-less windows that felt to Eli like a halfway house but which was nonetheless an Eden compared to the cramped hovel that was his Yeshivas Chelkas Yaakov apartment in Baltimore – he made himself a glass of tea, took a long, hot shower, and turned on his computer.

In his Baltimore yeshiva community, living on the same block as the study hall, he would always hear his fellow yeshiva companions coming and going from the study hall, talking excitedly about various Talmudic points with one another as they arrived back at their dormitories or apartments at 12 a.m., 1 a.m., and often even later. But now, in sleepy West Hartford, without even a radio or a roommate, his laptop was all he had to pierce through the thick silence of suburban New England, where everyone seemed to be in bed by 10 p.m. and where even the dogs would stop barking by 10:30. He still studied by himself, but it wasn't the same without a study partner; *"ein divrei torah nik'neis ela b'chabura,"*[11] he knew – his silent studying could not come close to the quality of learning that he used to enjoy while studying with a *chevrusa*[12] in yeshiva, and this realization made the eerie Connecticut quiet even more disquieting to him. The silence of West Harford after nightfall was a silence unlike any other he had ever experienced. It was a disturbing, unnerving, monstrous silence that seized him every night and wouldn't let him go until the first golden rays of dawn broke through the ink-black night and mercifully surged through his window. It was a terrifying, inescapable, all-encompassing silence, enveloping him and everyone around it in its ghostly embrace.

When he logged on to Facebook and saw a friend request from Emma Yates, his entire body began to pulsate as if he were an astronaut

---

9. Recognizable.
10. For the purpose of fulfilling the commandment.
11. "Torah is acquired only in group study."
12. Study partner.

being launched into space. He marked the date of the request in his mental calendar as if it were a court summons crossed with an invitation to an exclusive masked ball – Wednesday night, October 15. His unruly imagination had already irresponsibly created a thousand and one different fantasy scenarios involving the two of them, but none of them included an internet interaction with her. He had thought that his imagination was boundless, but it had strictly confined itself to physical, not virtual, possibilities; a Facebook friend request from Emma Yates was something he had never even considered conceivable.

'Is it *mutar*[13] to accept her friend request?' he ruminated, his knees shaking and his hands quivering. 'Being Facebook friends doesn't mean we'll actually ever have a real conversation…I can't just ignore the request. She's the head of the New England Hebrew High School English Department and in charge of the Honors program… it wouldn't be professionally responsible to ignore it…or polite…the polite thing to do is to at least respond to it…it's *derech eretz*,[14] and *derech eretz kad'ma laTorah*…'[15]

When he clicked the "confirm" button and accepted her friend request, he could hear the words of his Baltimore yeshiva rabbi reverberating in his mind: "Remember, *bochurim*,[16]" Rav Simcha Kramer used to say whenever he warned his students about the dangers of computers, "nowadays, the gates of *Gehenom*[17] no longer open with a clamor – they open with a click…"

'This is purely for professional reasons,' he said to himself, pretending that the primal, non-rational reasons for doing what he had just done did not exist. 'I'm sure she only sent the request because she knows it's important for her to be connected with the other teachers in the school…Besides, why should I delude myself for even one minute that a woman like her would want anything to do with someone like

13. Permissible.
14. Good manners.
15. "Good manners precede Torah."
16. Boys.
17. Purgatory.

me? She knows I'm *frum*,[18] she knows – well, I guess that's all she does know about me. Maybe she wants to find out more...no, not a chance – there's no way she could possibly be interested in me. And anyway, even if she were,' he told himself gruffly, 'she's completely not *shayikh*[19] for you. Forget whether or not she's *frum*. She's not even Jewish. And she's a fellow teacher. Don't they always say it's a bad idea to date someone from your workplace?...and there are probably rules against these things too...But you're overthinking it...It's just a simple, harmless friend request. Best not to think too much of it. You have work to do – lesson-planning, home-work grading, and your own *k'vias itim*[20] to keep up. Stay focused and do what you need to do. Don't let this distract you...'

18. Religious.
19. Appropriate.
20. Daily study regimen.

THREE

Three nights later, immediately after the Jewish Sabbath had concluded, Eli returned from synagogue and turned on his bedroom lamp, which cast a dull yellow glow over the bare-walled bedroom. After turning on his computer and answering two work-related emails, Eli mindlessly opened up his Facebook page. When he saw a message waiting for him from Emma Yates, he instantly began to feel as if a herd of wild boars were stampeding inside his chest. 'Are these palpitations?' he nervously asked himself. 'Are they? How young can you be to experience palpitations? What is this all about? Why would she message me? Probably just a school-related matter. Nothing to get excited about.'

"Hi Eli," he read, flush with excitement,

I hope you had an enjoyable holiday. I just wanted to say that I think it's great that you have come to us from Baltimore. Everything I've been hearing about you leads me to believe that you are a terrific addition to the faculty and that you've already really improved NEHHS's Judaic Studies department. I know that you are a Talmud specialist, so I was wondering why I always see you carrying around some kind of novel. I would be interested in getting to know you and would love to hear about how you've developed these literary interests and where and how they fit into your Talmud studies. Hope to hear from you soon. All the best, Emma

He stared at the screen with the bewildered gaze of a lost pedestrian. Without having the slightest clue as to how he should answer her – or whether he should even reply to her at all – he rose slowly and ambled to the kitchen to make himself a cup of chamomile tea. When he returned to his desk, he read the message again, probing it for any clues about her intentions. When he couldn't find any hints, he read it a third time. Then a fourth time. He read it a fifth time, this time pairing it with the memory of the way she had looked at him on that day he first saw her at the introductory faculty lunch and with the more recent memories of the way she would look at him when they would pass each other in the school hallway. Was it possible that there was a hint – even the slightest, most miniscule hint – of desire in those looks? Was it possible? No – he dismissed the thought from his mind as soon as it arose. He was ashamed at himself for even thinking she was capable of such a thing. She was a professional, an experienced teacher – she wouldn't let herself be susceptible to those kinds of urges, even if she were to have them. And how could he be so preposterously presumptuous to even think for a single second that she would have such desires for *him* when no woman in his life had ever looked at him in that way?

'All you're doing is torturing yourself,' he said to himself, as he heard the hissing of the teakettle and walked back to the kitchen to pour the white-hot water into his raisin-black Yeshivas Chelkas Yaakov coffee mug. 'You're just working yourself up over nothing. Remember all the *issurim*[1] that you could be *over*[2] if you get anywhere near her ... I don't know if we say *issur chal al issur*[3] by[4] *arayos*[5] but you could probably be *over* two or three, easy, if you ever get anywhere near her ... And remember your life-goals ... remember Ben Azzai – and Newton and Kant, and Gaudí and da Vinci, and Jane Austen and Henry James ...

1. Prohibitions.
2. In violation of.
3. A prohibition being added upon a preexisting prohibition.
4. Regarding.
5. Forbidden relations.

Don't worry about her. You have a different destiny. Focus on your learning and on your work and on your reading and you'll be happy – they're all you really need. If those things were good enough for Ben Azzai and Thoreau – they didn't need a woman in their lives, did they? – then they should be good enough for you. *Nafshi chash'ka baTorah...*'[6] He shut down his computer and put off responding to her until the next day.

6. "My soul is in love with Torah..."

FOUR

"Hi Emma," Eli wrote to her on Facebook the following day, as the sparse light of the fall morning peeked through his bedroom window,

> Thank you for your message. I spent more than enough time in Baltimore, so I was happy to come here. Connecticut is nice. And the school is great. The short answer to your question is that I had a friend back in Houston, in middle school, who used to read a lot of novels. This friend got me into it. I kept on reading in yeshiva even though I wasn't supposed to. And I still read, obviously. I don't know how it fits into the rest of my life or even if it does 'fit in' at all, it's just something that I like doing. And yes, I would be interested in getting to know you as well. I hope you have a good day and an enjoyable weekend. Best, Eli

'*Ribbono shel olam*...'[1] he thought immediately after sending the message, running his hands over his head. 'What am I getting myself into? I should not have done that...I should take it back. I should write to her and say, "look, this is very nice that you've taken an interest in me for some odd reason, but I don't think it's appropriate that we communicate further." That's what I should

---

1. Oh God.

write. Is it too late? No it's not – it's still *tokh k'dei dibur*² – I can still write that...'

Before he could finish typing those words into the chat box, he received another message from her:

> That is fascinating! I would love to hear more about this. Would you like to go for a cup of coffee after work sometime?

'What?!' he said in his head. A shudder passed through his shaking body. 'What did she just write? Is she...is she asking me out? Impossible...she could never –...but why? She finds my reading to be "fascinating"? She must be exaggerating. I don't see what the big deal about sneaking novels into yeshiva is. So what? People do stuff they're not supposed to do all the time. It wasn't like I was sneaking in drugs, or...but why would she say that? *Ribbono shel olam*...she really wants to go out with me? With *me*? There must be some mistake... and anyway the school probably has some policy against it...but why? No – I can't do it,' he told himself, pretending to himself that he did not want to have a cup of coffee, and much more, with Emma Yates. 'It's completely *asur*.³ Not even Rav Ovadia⁴ could find a *heter*⁵ for this...'

'It wouldn't be right,' he thought, clasping his hands behind his neck and raising his head to the ceiling as if looking for a sign from heaven for guidance. 'I have to refuse this. I should just be honest with her. "Emma," I should write: "Look, this is awkward to confess, but I made a vow last year that I wouldn't ever date again. I don't want to get married. I want to devote the rest of my life to Torah study and to reading. And even if I were to change my mind, I am a religious Jew, and you are not Jewish. I wouldn't be able to marry you even if I wanted to." That's all I need to say. That would end it right this instant – nip it in

2. Not that long of a time-lapse.
3. Prohibited.
4. R. Ovadia Yosef, an Iraqi-born twentieth-century halakhic posek (decisor of Jewish law).
5. Halakhic source of permission.

the bud before anything has a chance to develop. That's what Rabbi Kramer always used to say: we say in *davening*,[6] "don't lead us into *lidei nisayon*[7]" – it's not just temptation, but the *hands* of temptation that we don't want on us, because once it so much as lays its hands on you, you're done for...No,' he said to himself, springing up from his chair and beginning to pace back and forth, 'I can't say that to her, that would be too weird – why should I imagine that she wants something more with me than just coffee? How ridiculously presumptuous of me! I can't write that...I'll just write, "Emma, thank you for your offer, but I don't drink coffee." Yeah, I think that should do the trick...I think I can write that...'

"Emma," he wrote with trembling fingers,

I would love to learn more about you as well. I'm just a little worried about being seen with you in public. I could lose my job. And if the news of our meeting spreads beyond Connecticut – which I'm sure it would, knowing the way these things tend to get around in my world (the Jewish world is VERY small) – I'd never be able to get another Judaic studies job again. It wouldn't be your fault, though. Quite the contrary. You are great. But in my circles, unfortunately, for me to be seen with you would be disastrous for me. I know this sounds terrible but that's how it is in my *"velt"* (that's Yiddish for "world"), as we say. But I would still love to talk to you. Maybe we can continue this conversation some other way and see where it goes?

'What are you doing?!' he yelled at himself after hitting the 'enter' button and sending the message. 'Why would you write that? Are you crazy?! All you have to do is say "no!" It's so simple! Just say "no"! Instead you have to write her a whole long *arichus*[8] about how the Jewish community would ostracize you if they heard you had been out with a non-Jewish woman?! What's that thing people sometimes

6. Prayer.
7. The hands of temptation.
8. Lengthy discursus.

say these days? "TMI"? That's exactly what that is! She doesn't need to know all that! And what is this "maybe we can continue the conversation and *see where it goes*"? "*See where it goes*"?! Where, exactly, do you want it to go?!'

"Sure, Eli," she wrote back,

> that sounds like a good idea. I look forward to speaking with you again. Have a good night, and I hope you have an enjoyable weekend as well!

'Oh God,' he said to himself, pacing back and forth across his bedroom. 'You know *exactly* where you want this to go. You better stop this right now. *Asu mishmeres lemish'marti*[9] – stop this before it's too late…'

---

9. "Make a safeguard around me decrees."

FIVE

On the night before classes resumed following the school's fall holiday break, as Eli was preparing a lesson-plan and source-sheets for a series of classes on the "rebellious son" passage from the Talmud, the disquieting silence of the New England night was broken by a chiming electronic "bing" which alerted him that a new message was awaiting him on Facebook.

'Oh, God,' he thought, shaking his head and biting his lower lip. 'Not now...I shouldn't have left Facebook open...I should've closed that tab hours ago...'

"Hello Eli!" Emma had written,

I hope you've had a good weekend. Would you like to talk now? Is this a good time?

'Just tell her no,' he said to himself, inhaling deeply. 'It would be so easy – N-O. Be cold with her and end it now before it goes too far... You know very well what *chazal*[1] say about *kol hamarbeh sicha im isha*...*[2] "I really shouldn't be communicating with you at all" is what you should write to her,' he thought, while in the polar regions of his consciousness he could feel the ice of his

---

1. The rabbis of the Talmud.
2. A man who speaks to much with women.

inhibitions slowly melting away. 'But is a Facebook messaging chat really "*sicha*"[3]'?

"Sure," he typed,

"now's a good time. So...forgive me, I'm terrible at this – I'm terrible at asking people questions about themselves, which is probably why I never had much success at dating – but I wanted to ask you where you're from, what your background is, the kind of things you like doing, and all those sorts of questions."

"That's funny," she responded. "I was never very good at those questions either."

"Really?"

"Just because I'm an English teacher doesn't mean I'm an expert at using the language in all its facets. If I was good at asking people questions about themselves I would've been a journalist, not a teacher."

"Good point."

'What are you doing?!' he shouted at himself in his head, running his right hand over his face. 'You need to just be cruel with her and cut this off right now! You know very well what chazal say on[4] Shaul and Agag Melekh Amalek[5] – what's the *lashon*?[6] "*Kol mi shena'asa rach'man bim'kom ach'zari, sof na'aseh ach'zari bimkom rach'man*"?[7] Now's the time when you need to be cruel with her and just cut it off!' But he was already enjoying himself too much to want to cut off the conversation. 'This is so much better than the way my in-person dates used to go,' he thought, his body beginning to relax like a shoe whose laces have just been untied. '...And this format is probably better for me too – no talking, just typing. If she asks me a tricky question, I

3. Conversation.
4. About.
5. Saul and the King of Amalek.
6. Precise phrasing of the saying.
7. "One who is merciful when he should be cruel will eventually become cruel when he needs to be merciful."

have time to think about it before responding. I just wish I could write better…she's probably judging my writing already…oh God, how embarrassing this'll be for me. I should drop out of this conversation right now before I make a complete fool of myself…'

"In that case," she typed, "I'll go first. I'll get the 'tell me about yourself' details out of the way and then we can move on to the better stuff."

"'*Better stuff*'?' Eli asked himself, his body temperature beginning to rise. He let out a nervous chuckle. "'*Better stuff*'?' he repeated. 'That doesn't exactly sound like great English. Maybe she's not trying to write on such a high level herself…relax…it's just an internet chat. She's not trying to write poetry with me. She's knows she doesn't need her Facebook messages to be publishable, and neither do you. If she can write casually on it, then so should you…'

"So," she began. "I grew up in a small town in Pennsylvania called Scranton, not sure if you've heard of it."

'Scranton?' Eli asked himself, casting an oblique glance at the screen. 'Scranton…sounds familiar…where have I heard of it?…'

"Yes," he wrote back. "I have heard of it."
"I grew up there as an only child in a very strict Catholic family."
"I'm also an only child. Raised in a strictly Orthodox Jewish family. I should say 'raised by a strictly Orthodox father' – I never knew my mother."
"Why is that?"
"She died shortly after giving birth to me."
"I'm sorry to hear that. I lost my mother only a few years ago."
"I'm sorry to hear that as well. Does your father still live in Scranton?"
"No. Last year he moved to Chicago because of a woman he was dating. They didn't end up together, but he ended up staying there. Did your father ever remarry?"

"No."

"Why not?"

"Good question. I always wondered why myself. I always thought it was hypocritical of my father to never remarry."

"You sound like you were – and maybe still are – angry at your father."

"That's a fair assumption. I haven't spoken to him since he put me in an all-boys' yeshiva in Baltimore in 9th grade."

"I'm not on good terms with my father either. We barely speak. He's been angry with me ever since I changed my name."

"What did you change it from?"

"Emily. When I turned 18 I changed it to Emma."

"Why?"

"I never liked the name 'Emily.' It just seemed too ordinary to me. There were three Emilys in my elementary school class alone – three out of sixteen girls."

"What's wrong with being ordinary?"

"Nothing. I just never wanted to be ordinary. I never thought of myself as a Nullachtfünfzehn."

"A what?"

"Oh. That's a German term for something or someone that's common, ordinary."

"That, you are certainly not."

"So what about you with your father? Were you mad at him because the school he put you in was a yeshiva, or because it was an all-boys' school?"

"A bit of both. This yeshiva had almost no secular studies to speak of. A little bit of math, and some chemistry, but that was it. In middle school I had fallen in love with literature but this yeshiva offered no English classes, so I had to do all my reading on my own. I felt, years later, like I had it in me to be an English teacher if only I'd had the proper education and training. But I had nothing."

"Do you not like being a Talmud teacher?"

"It's not that I don't like it. It's that I think I would've made a better English teacher than Talmud teacher. The only thing my father ever prepared me for was to be a Talmud teacher. He saw that I had a good aptitude for it from an early age. 'Good aptitude' – does that make sense? Can I say that?"

"Don't worry about it. It's only a Facebook chat. No one else is ever gonna see this."

"Ok. Well, he started me off when I was four years old – from the moment I was able to read Hebrew – on Bible. When I was six he started me on some basic Talmud. By the time I was eight he was drilling me on Talmud every day. Constantly. Lobbing questions at me round-the-clock. 'Eli, why does Tosafot (a medieval Talmudic commentary) call carrying on the Sabbath a *"melacha geru'ah"* (inferior labor)?' 'Eli, what is the disagreement between the Rosh and the Rambam (two other medieval scholars) about the nature of the blessings recited under the *chuppah* (Jewish bridal canopy)?' 'Eli, what does *"ein on'shin min hadin"* mean?' 'Eli, what is the exception to the din (law) of *"v'heishiv es hag'zeilah"* ("You shall return a stolen object")?' 'Eli, who does stam Mishnah (unattributed legal rulings) in Zevachim follow, Rebbe Meir or Rebbe Elazar ben Azaryah?' He would drill me at all hours of the day. Literally. When I was six he started waking me up at 5 in the morning to study Talmud with him – and not even the 'relevant' parts. He wanted me to study even the parts that talk about the sacrificial service in the Temple and the laws of purity and impurity – things that people haven't been practicing for 2,000 years. And at night after dinner I couldn't have dessert unless I could repeat to him what I had learned hours earlier that morning."

"And could you?"

"Yes. Always. I knew that the exception to the rule of returning stolen objects is when there's a change in the object. (The Talmud refers to this as *"ganav koneh b'shinui,"* a thief can acquire an object if the object has changed.) I knew what *"ein on'shin min hadin"* meant but it would take me too long to explain it to you and I don't want to bore you. I knew that even though in the rest of Shas – in the rest of the Talmud – 'stam mishnah' is according to Rebbe Meir, in Tractate Zevachim 'stam Mishnah' is like Rebbe

Elazar ben Azaryah. I'm sorry if none of this makes any sense to you but this was my life and my life probably makes no sense to anyone anyway, so...Yeah...If there were such a thing as Talmud tournaments or Talmud pageants I'm sure he would've entered me into them. Instead he just put on his own Talmud tournaments at our house – me against his expectations of me. And every day without fail there was a match."

"I thought my parents making me go to early Mass once a week and not getting to sleep in on Sundays was rough, but what you had – geez...that's a whole 'nother level."

'A whole 'nother level? Lich'ora[8] she really is serious about not taking her writing on Facebook too seriously,' Eli thought, reflexively darting his eyes around the room as if he were in a coffee shop with her and afraid that someone from the high school might spot them together. 'I guess that's a good sign. I wonder what the expression is on her face now...I wonder whether she's in her pajamas now. Or maybe in a t-shirt and sweatpants. I wonder what color t-shirt...I wonder what she looks like at nighttime. I wonder if her hair looks redder after dark... I hope I'm not scaring her away with all my talk about my strange childhood...then again, maybe it would be a good thing if I scared her away right now before this goes any further. Talking to her at all is completely pastnisht.[9] You should not be doing this. You should never have even started this...'

"And then when he sent me to this Talmudical academy in Baltimore, this yeshiva," Eli typed, "that was the end of it."

"What do you mean?"

"It was the end of me having a chance to do anything else other than be a Talmud teacher. It's the only thing I'm trained for. I never really had a choice. I have to do what I'm doing. I have no other way of making a living."

"You mentioned that you were also mad at him for not remar-

8. I guess.
9. Inappropriate.

rying. What did you mean when you said this was 'hypocritical' on his part?"

"Because my father was a rabbi, and he knew very well how much the Jewish tradition emphasizes marriage and how much it insists that 'it is not good for man to be alone.' He was also well aware that according to Jewish law you haven't fulfilled the commandment to 'be fruitful and multiply' until you've had at least two children, so I can't understand why he just stopped at one without ever even trying to have another. And this was a man who was so punctilious about fulfilling every detail of every aspect of Jewish law that every day after morning prayers he would put on a second pair of tefillin just in case the first pair hadn't been good enough."

"What's 'tefillin'"?

"It doesn't matter... the point is, he was so careful about fulfilling every single jot and tittle (that was an old-fashioned expression he used to like but that I hated) of Jewish law, so I always wondered why he never remarried, considering how much importance Jewish law places on marriage..."

"Did you lose your father?"

"What? No."

"Then why are you speaking about him in the past tense?"

"Oh. Sorry. He's not dead. But – I know this is a terrible thing to say but it's the truth – sometimes it feels that way to me."

"What do you mean?"

"Because I haven't seen him or spoken to him in fifteen years."

"That was your own choice?"

"Yes."

"Did you ever ask him about his decision to not remarry?"

'My father is the last thing I want to talk about!' Eli exclaimed inside his head. 'Do I really have to keep talking about this?!...Does she even care at all about this? Or is she just asking all these questions to be polite, feigning interest in my background as a way to...a way to *what*?'

"No," Eli responded. "I never asked him."

"Why not?"

"I never felt comfortable asking him those kinds of questions. Personal questions, I mean. I know those were things he just never talked about, so I never brought them up. He thought those kinds of discussions were frivolous, that they wasted time that could be spent studying Torah." 'Can we please stop talking about my father?!' he yelled in his head. 'I have to get out of this conversation...' "So what about you?" he typed. "What were your parents like? What was your upbringing like?"

"My parents were fairly strict, but nothing like your father, it sounds like. My mother was a nurse, and my father, until just recently, was a policeman."

A cold shiver shot up Eli's spine. 'What if I have to meet him?' he wondered, his dry eyes drifting uneasily to the window. 'Don't you eventually have to meet the parents? Maybe there'd be a way I could get out of it. I'd have to find some excuse – "I don't feel well," I'll tell her on the day I'd be supposed to be meeting her father. "I'm sick...just came down with something."... *Ribbono shel Olam!*,[10] how presumptuous can you be?! Just because she's shown a single sliver of interest in you, *mimeila*[11] you think it'll automatically get to that point?!...But what if it does?...what *if*?...'

"So yeah," she continued, "they took me to Mass every week, made me go to Sunday school, made me say prayers every night and before every meal. But I got out of all of that nonsense pretty quickly."

"What do you mean?"

"When I was nine or ten I started questioning the things they were teaching us in Sunday school, and I wasn't getting any good answers. I would ask them something like 'how do you know that these miracle stories in the Bible really happened?' And they'd respond by saying something like 'because the Bible says so.' Which

10. Good Lord.
11. Consequently.

is just circular and ridiculous ... or I'd ask them something like 'how do you know that heaven and hell exist,' and they'd say something like, 'because so-and-so died on the operating table and went to heaven and when he came back to life he described his vision,' but everyone knows these kinds of accounts are not very reliable, and they certainly aren't scientific proofs of the existence of heaven. By the time I was in my teens I came to the conclusion that they were supporting this whole restrictive lifestyle with a few flimsy threads, and it just didn't hold up. I started realizing that everything they wanted me to believe in was based on miracles, and no real proof existed as to whether any of that stuff actually happened. Everything they had been teaching me was based on fantastic stories that had no basis in reality. For somebody who likes to use her brain, to be told to shut it off and 'just believe' was not something I could live with. I guess you could say I chose my brain over my beliefs – not that I ever had any beliefs to begin with ... but that's besides the point."

"That's an interesting way of putting it ..."

'Now how do I finesse this without being *merachek*[12] her? Not that I actually "want" her,' he told himself, even though, without admitting it to himself, he really did desire her more intensely – almost painfully so – than he had ever desired anything in his life. 'But I still have to be careful here ...'

"But isn't that what literature is?" he wrote.
"What do you mean?"

'I should stop this,' he said to himself, turning his glance away from the screen and playing nervously with a pen. "*Ad kan v'su lo.*[13] I'm getting into dangerous territory here ...'

"I mean," he wrote, "fantastic stories that have no basis in reality."
"Yes, but literature actually has a basis in reality. The stories have

12. Alienating.
13. This is enough.

to be grounded in real life – or at least in settings and situations that resemble real life. Miracles, prophecy, supernatural revelation – all the things that the Church required me to believe in have no basis in real life."

Eli squirmed. The last thing he wanted to do with Emma was to get into a debate with her about religion.

"So you have no interest at all anymore in religion?" he asked her, hoping like he never hoped for anything before that she would write back something along the lines of, 'not entirely – you never know,' or 'I could be open to changing my mind if someone made a persuasive case to me,' or – as he already found himself fantasizing – 'Catholicism, no; but Judaism, since I'm so attracted to you… I would do anything for you, Eli – convert to Judaism? If that's what it would take to be with you? Sure. Why not.… '

"Not in the slightest," she wrote back. His shoulders slumped. "Not in a thousand years could I ever go for any of that religious nonsense again. I've been done with it since I was fifteen and I've never once felt even the slightest desire to go back. My life has been great without it – whereas when I had it in my life, all it ever did was make me feel terrible about myself and terrified that I would go to hell for missing Mass or for eating meat during lent. Why would I want any of that in my life ever again? No thank you."

Eli's cheeks contorted painfully; he bit his upper lip and pressed his fingers uncomfortably into the keyboard. "But don't you know I wouldn't be able to be with you unless you converted to Judaism?" he was tempted to write. Instead, he typed:

"So is that a definite NO to *all* religion, or just to the one you were brought up with?"

"Yes. It's a definite NO to all religion. I'm interested in people, not gods; in fictional stories that actually know they are fiction, not in fictional stories that are pretending to be factual. I have no patience for religion of any kind. Never have, never will."

Eli felt a pang in his chest. "But what about for me, Emma?" he was tempted to write, "wouldn't you do it for me? I thought you liked me. It wouldn't be a genuine theological commitment, just a demonstration of your love, that'd be all. You wouldn't even have to confess to any doctrines. All you'd have to do is to just have a quick dunk in the ritual bath, commit to doing a few rituals every now and then, and that's it! Is that really so much to ask? You wouldn't do it for me, Emma? Because I would do anything for you, Emma, I would. *Anything*. Well, except if it would be against my religion. But otherwise, I'd do anything for you. Anything…" Instead, he wrote:

"So what else do you like besides books and reading and having no religion lol?"

"Lol indeed… sometimes I think that there really is nothing more comical than religion. At least when it comes to other superstitions, people haven't built temples and cathedrals and created communities and constructed entire canons of scripture all based upon the proposition that it's bad luck to walk under ladders or to have a black cat walk by you."

"Lol," Eli wrote back, even though he was cringing instead of laughing.

When am I supposed to bring up my Judaism with her – and how?, he asked himself, wrapping his left hand around his drooping head. *She knows I'm an observant Jew… right?… Doesn't she care about how all these comments are making me feel?… And what about my race? Doesn't she know that – doesn't she see that? Doesn't she see who I am?… Wouldn't she want to ask me about that at some point?… Or is she no different from Rena… Maybe she's really no different from all the other white women I've dated, all those other girls who are so eager to talk about books and literature and even about guns and nuclear weapons but the minute race comes up they snap back into their safe white shells like scared little turtles… Is Emma really no different? No… I can't make any assessments like that about her just yet… it's too soon… way too soon…'*

"What else are you into?" Eli typed into the chat-box, his eyes beginning to grow heavy.

"Oh, many things! I like gardening and taking care of plants... embroidery and sewing... I like to draw and paint – nothing too complicated, just simple sketches with crayons and occasionally some paintings with watercolors. I probably like to sketch more than draw. And I really love animals. After college I became licensed as an animal rehab specialist in Connecticut and I'd take in all kinds of animals into my apartment – cats, dogs, squirrels, turtles... all kinds of birds... ducks, geese, loons... once I even had a deer... but I gave it up."

"The deer?"

"Well, yes. Obviously. But I meant animal rehab. I stopped doing it."

"Oh. Do you ever miss it?"

"Yeah, of course."

"So why don't you go back to it?"

"Teaching is a very demanding profession, as I'm sure you're discovering, Eli, and I just wouldn't have time to care for that many animals, unfortunately. My writing takes up a good amount of time as well. I felt like I needed to make a choice... You can't do everything in life that you want to do – and if you tried to you'd end up shortchanging something. And as much as I love animals I don't want to shortchange my students... Besides, the animals really got on my roommate's nerves. That whole experience, of working in animal rehabilitation, was wonderful, but it made me think about things – like if I could ever find a partner who'd want to live that kind of lifestyle, with all kinds of animals around all the time, and I figured I'd never find anyone who'd really want that kind of life, so it made the choice between teaching and animal rehabilitation easy for me... well, not 'easy' – easier."

"You seem like a woman of many talents and many interests," he typed, groaning silently. *Is this woman for real?* he thought, his fingers slipping off the keyboard momentarily. *Talk about having no basis in reality... She is too perfect... she must have at least one mole somewhere or something. Some kind of flaw, some kind of shortcoming, some kind of ugly scar...* "And someone who cares about animals as much as you do must have a kind heart and a compassionate soul.... So what else?"

"What do you mean?"

"I guess what I'm asking is, what makes Emma Yates tick?"

"'What makes me tick?' What kind of question is that? What do you think I am, a clock!? MDR!!!"

"I guess that is a funny expression," he typed, shrugging his shoulders and laughing silently. "I never really thought about it... by the way, what is 'MDR'?"

"Oh, that... it's French texting slang for LMAO."

"What is 'LMAO'?"

"That's an inappropriate expression for you. You're a good yeshiva boy, Eli. You shouldn't know what something like that means."

"Ok... Then can you at least tell me what MDR means?"

"Sure. *Mort de rire.*"

"Ok thanks... and now maybe you can tell me a bit about what makes you tick? (And if you really don't like that expression maybe you can teach me a better one in French?)"

"MDR! Yes, absolutely! Alright... I guess I'd say this: for as much as I love books, I love being in nature even more. Sometimes I feel like I use books to make up for other things, like not being out in nature as much as I should, or not being with animals as much as I used to be. Some people might feel spiritual when they're in church or in synagogue but for me it's when I'm in nature. Some of my best memories growing up are of going hiking in the Poconos..."

"That's lovely," he typed, even though nature and the outdoors didn't interest him in the least.

"So there's that... and, if you must know... even though this might seem paradoxical to you, for as much as a realist that I am, I also have a romantic soul. A *very* romantic soul. Not just in terms of watching rom-coms all the time – I WILL cry during movies, I have no shame! – so you've been warned!"

Why is she 'warning' me?, Eli thought, his heart beginning to beat faster. *Is she implying that she wants this to go further?...That she believes this WILL go further?...But she hardly even knows me...*

"So," she continued, "I've always been so frustrated about why I haven't found the right person yet. I try to do everything right – and I think I do – but I keep getting let down. It's the story of my life... Two years ago my boyfriend of five years broke up with me. He had kept on telling me for years about how much he loved me and how much he adored me and how much he was looking forward to a life with me and to having children with me, but whenever I asked him when he actually wanted to get married or whenever I tried to bring up wedding-planning with him he'd change the subject. Maybe I should've taken that as a sign. But I loved him too much. I guess I was blind. In retrospect I should've seen it coming, but how could I? When you're in love to that extent you don't think straight, you don't see things that you should be seeing... So when he broke up with me I was completely shocked, and very confused – just the week before he had been telling me how much he loved me and was saying things to me like 'guess what your groom just bought today at Target?' And he was still cooking for me all that week and doing the dishes and getting blood oranges for me at the grocery store (my favorite fruit) and picking up my dry cleaning... I just didn't – and still can't – understand the behavior of someone like that. Can you, Eli? How can someone keep telling you how much he loves you and keep doing all these things for you and then the next minute want nothing to do with you ever again?... I was absolutely devastated... Luckily it was during the beginning of the summer, so I didn't have any classes to prepare for three months – otherwise I don't know how I could've gone through with teaching after that. I bawled my eyes out for three weeks and then woke up sick to my stomach every day for the next three weeks and then I was numb and zombie-like for another three weeks... I hope you never have to endure heartbreak, Eli. It's the worst thing in the world. It really is. It's unimaginable pain, Eli, just unimaginable..."

Yes it is, Emma, he said to her in his head, as if she could hear him. *It really is…oh, Emma, I wish I could reach through the screen right now and hug you…and if you're crying, I wish I could be there to wipe away your tears…I will never do anything like that to you, Emma – NEVER. No 'bli neder.'*[14] *NEVER. You have my word…I will never let you down in that way. You have nothing to worry about with me. I'll never treat you the way that terrible boyfriend treated you. Never. You can trust me…*

"At the end of the summer," she continued, "one of my friends invited me to her place in New York to hang out for two weeks, and that was really good. Being with my friend really helped. As did the change of scenery. There was one day where we were coming back from some museum exhibit and we got on the subway and sat down across from this couple, they looked like they were in their 50s, and we were overhearing them talking and laughing with each other and planning their day together and my friend Samantha – who's much more talkative and outgoing than I am, I'm actually kind of shy, more on the introverted end – she blurted out to them, 'You guys seem like you work really well together. How long have you been together?' 'Seventeen years,' they said. She asked them how they met. The man said that they were both working in a nursing home in Yonkers. He was a physical therapist there and she was a receptionist. They'd pass each other in the halls every so often without saying anything to each other. 'But I was attracted to him,' she told us; 'he might've not been the best-looking guy in the world, but he was pretty close to my type, and every day I kept wondering *is he gonna ask me out? Is he gonna talk to me? Is today gonna be the day?*, but it never came. I was brought up with this idea that only men should ever ask women out and that it's not a "womanly" thing for a woman to approach a man, but heck, I was 37 years old, what importance did being "womanly" have to me anymore when all it had done for me that far in life was to keep me

14. "Without a vow" (a statement uttered to take away the binding force of a vow in case one is unable to follow through with the commitment).

single and lonely and childless? So I approached him and asked him out.' 'You asked *him* out?' I asked her. 'Oh yes. And it was the best thing I ever did in my life. Two days later he took me on our first date, to the Bronx zoo. And he proposed to me. Right in front of the zebras.' 'How did you know?' I asked her. 'Sometimes you just know,' she said, smiling at him. 'Well, first of all, he took me to the zoo – and I love animals – so that went a long way to winning me over. But I also just had a really good feeling about it . . . I think that so often in life we're taught to be "rational," to "think with your head," to be "sensible," to not get married to someone unless you've known them for X amount of time and vetted them and screened them and this and that and this and that . . . but sometimes I think you just need to go with your feelings, to trust your heart . . . and that's exactly what I did. And it was the best decision I've ever made in my life.' I asked them what they thought the key to a good marriage was. 'The key?' they said. 'Well, I'll say this,' said the man. 'I married my best friend. There was this one time when we were on a double-date with some friends and she was driving and her friend wanted to sit next to her up front, and at first I said "okay" but then I sensed myself getting unhappy about it, so then I told her, "no, I want to sit up front – I want to be close to my friend." I realized that I would've missed being near my friend.' 'And whenever we go to parties,' she said, 'we always tend to just stay close to each other. We'd rather spend time with each other than with anyone else.' 'It's not like we don't have fights,' he said. 'Everyone has fights.' 'But we do work well together,' she said. 'We're a good team.' I asked them if it was important to have a lot of things in common. 'Things in common?' she said. 'No, I don't think it's that important. We actually don't have a lot of things in common. We have some things, but he kind of has his own things and I have mine. He's really into old records and movies and old comic books – he has this huge comic book collection. Over 20,000 comic books. I'm not into comics at all. I do like some of his records. And occasionally I'll go to movies with him. I think the last movie we saw together in theaters was Lord of the Rings. I'm much more into animals and he's not. But we work well together, we make each other laugh, and we're each other's best friend.' I told them how wonderful that was, and how wonderful their marriage seemed – secretly growing envious inside, wondering whether I'd ever get to experience that – and then told them my story, about my 'wonderful' boyfriend breaking up with me and breaking my heart. 'Oh, we're so sorry,' they said. 'But you are a lovely young woman,' she said, 'and I am sure you'll find the love that you deserve. Sure of it. It will happen. It just takes time, sometimes. It took me till I was 37, almost 38.' 'And it'll probably happen when you're least looking for it,' he said. 'I met her,' he said, turning to his wife – I wish I'd gotten their names, they were the most adorable couple I've ever seen – 'I met her,' he said, 'when I wasn't even looking for anybody. I was 41. By that point I figured I'd never be married and had basically made my peace with it. I had just gotten into this new career as a physical therapist after working for almost 20 years with DC comics. DC had just laid me off. This was in the nineties, when comic sales really started slumping,' and then he started telling us all this stuff about comics and the comic book industry, like about how a new Superman comic would sell something like 300–400,000 copies in the seventies but by the nineties it would only sell about 6,000 copies. He had been an editor for DC – it was a dream job for him, he said, and it was devastating, heartbreaking to get laid off. He had grown up collecting everything, he said: Archie, Casper, Dennis the Menace, Weird Science – I had never heard of half of these comics. I had thought that the only comic books that existed were superhero comics. And then he told us about how he had had to build himself up from scratch and get into a new career and a new field and how difficult that was but how rewarding his new career eventually turned out to be. 'I was finding physical therapy very fulfilling,' he said, 'and I was content with my life, at peace with everything, not looking for anybody or anything, and all the sudden she comes along…' And then he turned to her and smiled at her and she smiled back, and I just wanted to kiss them both, they were so adorable – they were both blond-haired and slightly overweight, he was balding and slightly gray but he had a hand-somely chiseled face, and she was a little stoop-shouldered but she had these beautiful blue eyes and sun-gold skin...and she had a crutch with her. Just a single crutch...You could tell they absolutely adored each other. And then it was our stop, and Sam and I got off and we never saw them again...But hearing their story really made an impression on me. It changed my outlook on everything. I had been so depressed and hopeless that entire summer and meeting that couple so randomly like that changed my perspective 180 degrees. I starting thinking, 'yes, I WILL meet someone. These kinds of romantic stories really DO happen. This couple, they weren't from the movies, nothing was scripted about it – they were a real-life couple. And their story is a real story. If these kinds of things can really happen, then why not for me?' And so I kept that hope alive. And I kept thinking, 'I WILL meet someone – and it'll happen when I'm least expecting it, when I'm not even looking for it...' And then, Eli, when you arrived at the high school, and I saw you and I was – okay, I'm going to admit this, but I was immediately attracted to you – I kept replaying that couple's story in my head, about how attracted she was to her husband-to-be, about how they were working together in the same space, seeing each other every day...and about how she kept waiting for him to say something to her but when he wasn't, she took the initiative and SHE was the one to ask HIM out...and how well it worked out for her, and for them, for both of them...and how they became engaged after only one date...I know that that might not be 'typical,' but I kept asking myself, 'is there such a thing as "typical" when it comes to love?' And I kept thinking about that couple and about how they met, and whenever I'd pass by you here in the hallway I kept thinking, 'why not? If you're attracted to him, and he's not taking the initiative, maybe *you* need to take the initiative...maybe you need to be a little forward sometimes in life, even if you're a woman – or some-times *especially* if you're a woman. So...yes...that's why I messaged you...I had no idea I'd be getting into this tonight and never would have imagined I'd be revealing all of this to you so soon...but then again, after hearing that couple's story, I'd never have imagined that I would be doing a lot of the things that I've done in the past couple of weeks…"

"Wow," was all he managed to type back in reply, too over-whelmed and too tired to come up with anything else. "Well, I think I should be going to bed. I have to get up early tomorrow. I look forward to talking to you again soon, Emma."

"As do I, Eli," she wrote back. "A+."

"Is that my grade for this conversation?"

"MDR no! (though you did do very well :)) It's French texting slang for "'see you later'."

"Oh. Neat. Well, then…A+ to you too."

"A+, Eli. And sweet dreams."

His eyes widened; he stared at the screen in disbelief. 'Did she really just type all that?' he asked himself, sitting up a little straighter and drawing his hands away from the keyboard. 'Or have I been dreaming? I'm not *mekabel*[15]…' He rubbed his eyes and looked at the screen again. He saw that she had signed off from Facebook, but those two mysterious, monosyllabic words – "sweet dreams" – still stared back at him from the screen like two smiling sentinels.

During that sleepless night, and throughout his terribly distracted next day at New England Hebrew High School, a single unforgettable phrase that she had written – "I was immediately attracted to you" – remained blazing in his mind like six torch-lit lamps, pointing the way to a road of heart-pounding possibilities. 'Why would she write that?' he asked himself in between his Talmud classes. 'She could've just been trying to be nice … maybe this is just her way of being charming, or sweet,' he thought, cycling through all the possible permutations of what she could have meant by those six words, 'but "attracted to you"? Isn't that a little much for a first conversation? Why would she be saying that so soon? Or maybe this is her idea of a joke. Maybe she was bored and she just wanted to have a little fun so she decided to

15. I don't believe it.

play this elaborate joke on the new teacher in school...Or maybe I shouldn't think about it too much. All it'll do is drive me crazy. Besides, there's no way this can ever actually lead anywhere. She told me very clearly how anti-religion she is. There's no way she'd ever convert. I'd never be able to marry her.... Yeah...This has been fun but I need to cut this off. There's no way I should be talking to her...'

'But what if she *would* convert?' he asked himself. 'What if she would do it for me? Maybe she would...if she really likes me that much, maybe she would do it for me...maybe that's what I'll do – I'll use that as my test for her – as her way to prove her love for me...I'll say to her, "Emma, you can be with me, but only on one condition: you have to convert to Judaism," and then – '

'No, Eli!' another voice inside his head shouted in reply. 'No! You have to cut this off *right this instant*! Why are you bothering with *any* woman?! Remember your vow! Remember Ben Azzai! And Emily Dickinson, Hans Christian Andersen, Leonardo da Vinci – they didn't need marriage. They didn't need a partner. They got on just fine without anyone else. So can you! You're not cut out for that sort of *balabatish*[16] life anyway. Don't cave in to conventionality!'

During school hours, Emma faithfully observed Eli's request that there be no interaction between them lest people become suspicious; if they were to continue talking, Eli told her, they would need to confine their conversations to their emails and online chats. But this did not prevent Emma from smiling at him whenever they occasionally passed each other in the hallway – smiles that pleased and tortured him to no end. 'Why *me*?' he would anguishedly ask himself upon the grateful receipt of each smile. 'I'm sure she's crossed paths with hundreds of men who are far more "eligible" and much better "fits" for her than I am. Who am I that she could be even remotely interested in me? I'm religious. I don't like animals. Or nature. I don't even have a college education. And of all those others, the one she's interested in is the one who's trying to *avoid* all possible contact with women, the one man whose personal prime directive is to avoid intertwining

---

16. Bourgeois.

himself with another at all costs – *this* is the one she sets her eyes on? I don't get it…Why are you doing this to me, Hashem?[17] Why??'

Though he kept telling himself to stay as far away from her as possible, he took her small book on Conrad's *Victory* out of the school library – 'for no other reason than simple curiosity,' he told himself – and began reading it. Titled "A Postcard from the Volcano: The Quest for the Autonomous Self in Joseph Conrad's *Victory*," it began with an epigraph from a writer he had never heard of, Karol Wojtyła: "Man longs for love more than for freedom." He began reading *Victory* as well, and the more of the novel he read, the more he began to admire what she had written about it, even though he needed someone to translate the vast majority of what she had written into English for him. "What happens to the character who travels in the novel," she wrote in the first chapter,

> is that, though we may not even see her original place, that place has an uncanny effect on her – it has greater substance than the place in which she exists in 'real time.' Lena leaves behind London yet still feels more at home there. Conrad's characters – Heyst and Lena in particular – are living at a remove from themselves. The self in movement dissolves; when the self is in movement, the self becomes protean, less real, jumping from island to island, and the soul has been left elsewhere, in a place somehow more solid, more real.

This, like so many other passages in her book, was too philosophical for him to understand. Still, he found himself growing more attracted by the page to the remarkable intellect who had penned such an impressive study of one of the greatest writers in the English language.

The more he told himself that he wanted nothing to do with her, and the more he insisted to himself that his decision to live alone was set in stone, the more he crumbled into thousands of little pieces whenever she gave him so much as a quarter of a smile. Even the sight

17. God.

of her shadow was enough to drive him mad with desire. He wanted to hold her shadow, to touch it, caress it; he wanted to cradle it in his arms and carry it home with him; he wanted to eat dinner with it and take it with him to bed. And on those infrequent instances when he actually saw her, his heart starting pounding as furiously as it had done during that time in Baltimore when the policeman had pulled him over on his way to his date with Rena, and he would need to hold his hand to his chest and remind himself to breathe. On one occasion in January, when he saw her wearing a low-cut top that revealed a few square inches of her upper chest, with her collarbones protruding beneath her skin like tree roots underneath the soil, he was so seized with desire that in that moment he would have given anything for five-to-nine minutes with her – his books, his learning, his bank account, his yearly salary, his share in the world to come – anything for just five-to-nine minutes with Emma Yates . . . He quickly regained his composure, reminding himself, as he so often needed to do, that it was the height of impropriety to consider being with a non-Jewish woman for even one moment, but not before the unquashable craving had crept into his head – the unquashable craving that made him question every religious avowal he had ever made and every spiritual principle he had ever believed he stood for . . .

SIX

'Scranton...?' Eli asked himself the following week, still thinking about the conversation he had had with Emma about their
childhoods when she had mentioned her hometown. 'So that's
where Emma grew up? Hmm...Scranton...I know I've heard
about it before, but from where?...Is that one of those small rural
Pennsylvanian towns that Updike used to write about? Scranton? Scranton...where have I heard of Scranton before...'

He had never been to Pennsylvania, and the only two other
Pennsylvanian cities he had ever heard of were Philadelphia
and Pittsburgh. He searched through is mind for "Scranton" as
if his brain were a room in which he was sure he had placed his
car-keys but just couldn't remember exactly where, and now that
he actually needed them he couldn't find them anywhere. After
a few minutes of staring open-mouthed at the computer screen,
it came to him: 'Yes, of course...Yaakov of Scranton – that story
that Rabbi Kramer always used to tell us about the famous yeshiva
bochur[1] of Scranton...'

The story of Yaakov of Scranton was a true story that Rabbi
Kramer, the *Mashgiach Ruchani*[2] of Yeshivas Chelkas Yaakov
in Baltimore, used to tell his students every year at the end of

1. Student.
2. Spiritual Advisor.

93

the post-Passover semester: not too long ago, there was a boy named Yaakov who was the top student in the Yeshiva of Scranton. His intelligence was unparalleled, and his diligence in study knew no bounds. Every rabbi in the yeshiva believed – *knew* – that Yaakov would eventually become one of the greatest Talmudists in the world; he was a near-genius, and had already developed a reputation as one of the greatest *lamdonim*[3] in North America. Throughout the Torah *velt*,[4] Yaakov of Scranton was already known as an outstanding "*Sinai*," a scholar who possessed encyclopedic knowledge, and a preeminent "*oker harim*," an unparalleled Talmudic analyst. One day, his rabbi came to him with some unsettling news.

"Yaakov," his rabbi said to him that day, "a very successful businessman who lives in Rockland County – Norman Stone, perhaps you've heard of him – came to the yeshiva last week asking me who the top *lamdon*[5] is in the yeshiva. He wants to be *meshadech*[6] his daughter to a great *talmid chochom*.[7] So of course, Yaakov, I told him that you were the *bochur* he was looking for. He assured me that you will be provided with all the funds you need so that you can continue learning in comfort for the rest of your life – and your children and your children's children will be able to learn in comfort for their entire lives as well. He very much wants a son-in-law who will make great contributions to Torah. The only thing he requested from me is that he wanted to know a bit about your family – your father, your mother, your father's parents, your mother's parents – you know, standard stuff. So I had the staff here do some simple research into your *yichus*,[8] and, well...we found something that's a *shtikel*[9] *shver*[10] ..."

"What did you find?"

3. Torah scholars.
4. World.
5. Scholar.
6. Marry off.
7. Torah scholar.
8. Ancestry.
9. Little.
10. Difficult.

"Well, Yaakov...how should I put this...you remember the story that your mother told you about how her father met her mother? Your grandfather claimed that he met her at a DP camp, which is true. But, you see, Yaakov, in these DP camps, there weren't only Jews...there were many Poles in these camps too, and, well...we double-checked – triple-checked this, and... *bekitzur* [11] ...the truth is that you mother's mother was a Pole. She was Catholic. She and your grandfather raised your mother Jewish, and your mother raised you Jewish, of course, but, Yaakov...you know very well what this means..."

"I'm not Jewish..."

"Correct, Yaakov. But this should be no cause for concern. As you know, we'll be able to fix this very easily and very quickly. So okay – *halakhically*, [12] you are not 'Jewish,' but, let's be honest, Yaakov – you know more about Judaism than anyone else in this yeshiva. You know more Torah and Talmud than anyone else in America. Your *giyur* [13] will be such a formality that we'll barely need to do anything to make it happen – it's completely assured. You'll walk right through with no questions asked...Yaakov, I know this must all be coming as a great shock to you, and this is very understandable. You're probably angry at your mother for never telling you the truth, but don't be – she didn't know, either. You grandparents hid this from her. Perhaps you're angry at your grandparents, but don't be – what they did by raising your mother as they did enabled you to be brought *tachas kanfei haShechinah*. [14] So do not be angry at them...but yes, I certainly understand the shock you must be feeling at this time. So, Yaakov, here is what I will suggest to you: you're probably thinking, 'I'm just going to continue with my regular *sedarim* [15] as usual, why should I do anything different?' This would be an understandable approach. But I would advise you not to do this. Instead, Yaakov, I would suggest you do the following: take a break from the yeshiva for a few days. Have a few days to yourself. We

11. In brief.
12. Based on the letter of Jewish law.
13. Conversion.
14. Into the Jewish faith.
15. Learning schedule.

have a lot of *tayvuhs*,[16] Yaakov – forbidden foods we've always wanted to eat, things we've wanted to do on Shabbos[17] and Yontiff[18] that the Torah prohibits us from doing. Other *tayvuhs, ich veis*[19]...And perhaps you may now want to *khap a rein*[20] to, *ich veis*,[21] act on some of these *tayvuhs*, to do some of the things that you've never had a chance to do and will never – once you officially come back and go through the pro-forma *giyur*[22] – be able to do again. Now's your chance to do all these things completely free, *'sine pecunia*,' as they say – I had to study Latin in high school, *rachmana litz'lan*,[23] that's one of the few phrases I remember...Now's your chance to do all these things with absolutely no *din v'cheshbon*.[24] And now that you've heard this news, you're probably wanting to do exactly this. So, Yaakov, I would suggest that you take a few days off from yeshiva – three, four days, maybe a week – and do these things, whatever it is they may be. Get it out of your system. And when you come back next week, we won't ask you any questions about what you've done. When you come back, it'll be as if you've never left. You'll have a quick dunk in the *mikvah*,[25] a quick and easy *hatafas dam b'ris*,[26] and that'll be that. You'll be back to learning your *sedarim* and learning beyond the regular *sedarim* as you always do."

"Thank you, rebbe...but I don't want to leave the yeshiva. Not even for a day. Not even for an hour."

"Yaakov...as your *Mashgiach Ruchani*,[27] I'm telling you that I think

---

16. Desires.
17. The Sabbath.
18. Holidays.
19. Perhaps.
20. Take advantage of this opportunity.
21. I don't know.
22. Conversion.
23. Unfortunately.
24. Repercussions.
25. Ritual bath.
26. Drawing a drop of blood from the area of circumcision.
27. Spiritual Advisor.

you should. Just at least for one day. Process this information that you're receiving. Clear your head. Do whatever it is that you've always wanted to do but have never done, whatever it is that that may be. It's a once-in-a-lifetime opportunity, Yaakov. Have a Big Mac. Go out to a movie on Friday night. Go to a Phillies game on a Saturday and have a ballpark frank with a side of nachos. But you know your own *tayvuhs*, Yaakov. Maybe it's a Philly cheesesteak. Maybe it's, *ichveis*, lobster... or shrimp... or those waffle fries from that *treifadig*[28] chicken place that that *baltshuva bochur*[29] was telling me about last week... I can't imagine them for you – they're your *tayvuhs*, not mine. And this is your one chance to act on them with no *din v'cheshbon* whatsoever. Do it this week. Then come back. Think of it as a *bein hazmanim*[30] – but, you know... with a few more *heteirim*[31] than usual... And once you're back in yeshiva, and once you've gone through the pro-forma *giyur*, it'll be as if you've never left."

"Well... okay, Rebbe... if Rebbe says so... I'll do it."

"Good, Yaakov. I'm happy to hear that. As soon as you come back, and as soon as you *tovel*[32] and have your *hatafas dam bris*,[33] you'll marry Mr. Stone's daughter, and you and your children and your children's children will be *mamesh*[34] set for life. And it will be a wonderful life, Yaakov – filled with Torah and *mitzvos*[35] and *seforim*[36] with all the *chidushei Torah*[37] that you'll compose... I'm very excited for you, Yaakov. Very excited. Have a good break. And see you soon."

Yaakov did as the *Mashgiach Ruchani* said – he never once disobeyed his rabbis – and took a break from the yeshiva. When three days had

28. Non-kosher.
29. Formerly irreligious student.
30. Mid-semester break.
31. Permissions.
32. Immerse in the ritual bath.
33. Drawing a drop of blood.
34. Really.
35. Commandments.
36. Books.
37. Talmud scholarship.

passed and Yaakov had not returned to the yeshiva, his rabbi was happy. "I'm glad that Yaakov did not just take a one or two-day break," the *Mashgiach Ruchani* told the other rabbis of the yeshiva. "That would have been insufficient. This way, when he comes back, he will truly be able to say that he has tasted everything the *goyisher velt*[38] has to offer and has found that none of it compares to the taste of Torah. When he comes back, he'll be an infinitely greater *Kiddush HaShem*[39] than he ever could have been had he only been a brilliant *bochur*: now, he won't just be the greatest *lamdon*[40] of his generation – he won't just be a *gadol haDor*[41] – he'll be a *tzadik haDor*,[42] someone who has known the *tayvuhs*[43] of the non-Torah life and utterly rejected them in favor of Torah. He will be our Onkelos,[44] our Koheles,[45] our Reish Lakish[46] – Yaakov will be even greater than them all."

When eight days had passed and Yaakov had still not returned to the yeshiva, his rabbi was even happier. "Yaakov has wisely chosen to take the full one-week absence that I suggested he take," the *Mashgiach* told the other rabbis of the yeshiva. "This shows that he not only has *emunas chochomim*,[47] but that he knows that it will only be possible for him to fully affirm Yiddishkeit[48] if he has fully known all of the *tayvuhs* of the world and rejected them. Now, he'll be able to be *mekabel ol malchus shamayim b'lev shalem*,[49] without any *sfeikos*[50] and without any *dayguhs*[51] that he's 'missing out' on something else. I have never

38. Secular world.
39. Testimonial to the merit of Judaism.
40. Scholar.
41. The most outstanding Torah scholar of his generation.
42. The most outstanding righteous person of his generation.
43. Temptations.
44. Ancient Torah translator.
45. Ecclesiastes.
46. Talmudic rabbi.
47. Faith in the sages.
48. Judaism.
49. Accept Judaism wholeheartedly.
50. Doubts.
51. Worries.

once doubted Yaakov's *chochmah*[52] and *tzidkus*,[53] and this is only a greater proof of it."

When another week had passed and Yaakov had still not returned to the yeshiva, the rabbinic staff of the Yeshiva of Scranton began to worry, but the *Mashgiach* calmly reassured them. "There is no cause for concern," said the rabbi. "*Aderaba*.[54] Yaakov is merely discovering that there are many more *tayvuhs* in the world that he had no idea of when he was sitting and learning here in yeshiva all day, and in order to fully embrace Yiddishkeit, he knows that he has to discover them all so that he can fully reject them."

When a month had passed and Yaakov had still not returned to the yeshiva, the rabbinic staff of the Yeshiva of Scranton began to grow alarmed, but the *Mashgiach* once again calmly reassured them. "There is no cause for concern," the rabbi said to them. "The fact that Yaakov is taking this long is merely a *gilu'i milsa*[55] that he is discovering that there are far, far many more *tayvuhs* in the world than he had ever imagined, and that he knows he has to experience them all so that once he returns to yeshiva, he'll be able to fully and knowingly reject them all – and once he does, he'll be able to fully and knowingly embrace Yiddishkeit out of his own *bechirah chofshis*."[56]

When three months had passed and Yaakov had still not returned to the yeshiva, the rabbinic staff of the Yeshiva of Scranton began to become distressed. They asked the *Mashgiach* to go find Yaakov and tell him that it was time for him to return to the yeshiva. "Absolutely not," said the rabbi. "Yaakov must come back out of his own *bechirah chofshis*, and he must embrace Yiddishkeit out of his own *bechirah chofshis*. And he *will*, he absolutely will – how can you have any doubts that Yaakov, the greatest *bochur* in the yeshiva, the greatest *bochur* in all the Torah *velt*,[57] will do otherwise? Right now, Yaakov is merely

---

52. Wisdom.
53. Righteousness.
54. On the contrary.
55. Sign.
56. Free will.
57. World.

discovering that there so many more *tayvuhs* in this world – not only in the *treifah medina*,[58] but all across the world, and he needs to know and experience all of them in their totality in order to fully embrace Yiddishkeit in all its totality."

When six months had passed and Yaakov had still not returned to the yeshiva, the *Mashgiach* took out a pen and paper and composed a letter to Yaakov, asking him how his experience in the *goyisher velt*[59] was going and whether he was thinking about returning to the yeshiva in the next few months. When the *Mashgiach* went to put the letter in the outgoing mail, he saw a letter addressed to him from Yaakov in that day's incoming mail, and instantly became elated. "A report from Yaakov's experience in the *goyisher velt*!" the *Mashgiach* excitedly exclaimed to the rabbinic staff of the Yeshiva of Scranton. "The complete and utter rejection of the *goyisher velt* that we've been waiting for!" The *Mashgiach* eagerly removed the letter from the envelope and read it aloud to the yeshiva's rabbinic staff:

> Dear Rabbi Glickman,
>
> You're probably wondering where I am and why I have taken so long to return to the yeshiva. I have gone to many places and have done many things I never imagined doing. I don't feel comfortable telling you about the things I have done, and in any case I don't think you would want to know. I have returned to Scranton. But I will not be returning to yeshiva. I have decided that I would like to go to college. This fall I will be enrolling in the University of Pennsylvania. Thank you for all your encouragement and support over the years. I wish you, my *rebbeim*,[60] *chaveirim*,[61] and everyone at the yeshiva the best.
>
> Sincerely,
> – Jack
>
> P.S. I will not be returning to Judaism either

58. The United States.
59. Secular World.
60. Rabbis.
61. Friends.

"*Rabosai*!!!"[62] Rabbi Kramer would thunder each year upon finishing the story. "*Rabosai*, what a *busha*!!*[63]* What a *shanda*!!*[64]* The greatest *bochur* in the yeshiva *velt – farfallen*!!*[65] Farfallen in ganzen*!!*[66]* And *why* was he lost, *rabosai*, *why*? Because during all his years in yeshiva, no one once ever asked him – nor did he ever ask himself – '*mai taymuh.*'[67] He never asked himself *why* he was observing Yiddishkeit.[68] He didn't understand the *ta'amei haMitzvos*[69] – he didn't understand the reason why he *should* choose Yiddishkeit. All those hours in the *beis medresh*,[70] all those *blatt Gemara*[71] that he learned, all those *chidushei Torah*[72] that he wrote, and he never once asked himself *why* he was doing it. His Yiddishkeit had no *ta'am*[73] – he didn't understand the *reason why* he was doing everything he was doing. The learning he was doing was *gevaldig*,[74] of course it was – but it was lacking in something essential: it lacked *ta'am*.[75] It lacked a reason, and it lacked taste. Torah wasn't *geshmack*[76] for him. And his *shmiras haTorah*[77] lacked *simcha*.[78] And when he finally experienced some *simcha* and some *ta'am*, when he finally experienced a *geshmack*, it was out there, and not in here – it was in the *goyisher velt*,[79] not in the Torah *velt*..."

62. Gentlemen!
63. Embarrassment.
64. Disgrace.
65. Lost.
66. Completely.
67. Why.
68. Judaism.
69. The meaning of the Commandments.
70. Study hall.
71. Pages of Talmud.
72. Talmud scholarship.
73. Reason.
74. Tremendous.
75. Taste.
76. Tasty.
77. Observance of Judaism.
78. Joy.
79. Secular world.

Here, Rabbi Kramer would lower his voice and pause for dramatic effect, letting the melancholy of the *schoomze's*[80] adagio sink in to the student's souls, before winding up again for the *schoomze's* final movement, a rapturous, rousing, rollicking allegro that left no heart unmelted and no soul unstirred:

"*Rabosai!* We ask Hakadosh Baruch Hu[81] every day in *davening,*[82] "*v'ha'arev na,*"[83] to make our learning *sweet*!! 'Please, Hashem,[84] make it *sweet*! Make it *geshmack*!!' Because our Talmud Torah[85] *has* to be sweet, Rabbosai!! It *has* to be! Aye,[86] "*mitzvos lav lehenos nitnu*"?!![87] Yes!, *ein hochi nami*!,[88] we say "*mitzvos lav lehenos nitnu*" *b'chol haTorah kulah,*[89] *except* for ***Talmud Torah!!**, zugs*[90] the Eglei Tal!![91] You're *mechuyev*[92] to get *hana'a*[93] from Talmud Torah! It's a *chiyuv*![94] It's the *ikar mitzvah*[95] of Talmud Torah! So we ask Hakadosh Baruch Hu every day 'make it sweet! Make it *geshmack*! *V'ha'arev na*! Please, Hashem, make it sweet!!' Because if it's not sweet, if it's not *geshmack* – if it doesn't have *ta'am*, if it doesn't have *simcha*! – our learning won't be *mispashet*[96] into our *neshamos*![97], it will only remain on the surface!, it

80. Talk.
81. God.
82. Prayer.
83. "Please make it pleasant."
84. God.
85. Torah study.
86. Okay, so what about…
87. "The commandments were not given for pleasure."
88. True.
89. Everywhere else in the tradition.
90. Says.
91. Nineteenth-century book on the laws of the Sabbath.
92. Obligated.
93. Pleasure.
94. Obligation.
95. The essence of the commandment.
96. Spread.
97. Souls.

won't *transform* us, it won't get into the *chadrei chadarim*[98] of our very beings! *Rabosai*... you must always remember to inject *ta'am* into your learning, into your *davening*,[99] into your *mitzvos*.[100] Do everything *b'simcha*[101] – because the essence of *Avodas Hashem*[102] is joy: '*ivdu es HaShem besimcha*'!'[103] And never forget to ask yourselves every day *why* it is that you do what you do: you do it because it adds *ta'am* to your life fills your *neshama*[104] with *simcha. Rabosai!* We often make the mistake to think that learning and obeying is the *ikar*[105] and *ta'am*[106] is the *tafel*[107] – no!! *Ta'am k'ikar*,[108] *rabbosai*!! *Ta'am* is the *ikar*!! Because without a preservative – without *ta'am*, without *simcha* – everything you have been working for in your *avodas Hashem*[109] can be lost in an instant! This is the *Bris Melach*,[110] *Rabosai!* The *Bris*[111] can only be preserved through *ta'am*, through *simcha!*.....*Rabosai!!* You must always remember this *yesodis'diger*[112] point: you are *ov'dei Hashem*[113] because it is *good* for you!, because *Hashem*[114] wants to reward you!, in this world and the next! *Ratzah Hakadosh Barukh Hu Lezakos es Yisroel!*[115] Hashem gave us so many commandments and prohibitions not because He wanted to burden us but because He wants to reward

---

98. Innermost regions.
99. Prayer.
100. Ritual observance.
101. With joy.
102. Judaism.
103. "Serve God with joy."
104. Soul.
105. Main thing.
106. Taste.
107. Ancillary.
108. Taste is the essence.
109. Judaism.
110. Covenant of salt.
111. Covenant.
112. Fundamental.
113. Jews.
114. God.
115. "God desired to reward the Jewish people."

us! Every single *mitzvah*[116] is for our own good! *All* of Yiddishkeit, *all* of Torah, is for our own good! Every single mitzvah gives us a world of *simcha*! Even if none of you are ever presented with the choice of Yaakov of Scranton, you must still make a choice every day of your lives: you must ask yourselves what you *would* do if you were presented with his choice. And, *im yirtzeh Hashem*,[117] if we do so every day, and if we learn, *daven*,[118] and perform *mitzvos* with *simcha*[119] every day – if we always remind ourselves *why* it is that we choose Torah! – then we will continue to freely choose Torah *b'simcha*,[120] *b'tuv levav*,[121] *ub'rov kol*,[122] and we will be *zocheh*[123] to the supreme *simcha* – the *simcha* of *kirvas Hashem*[124] – each and every day of our lives."

Rabbi Kramer's annual end-of-year *schmooze*[125] never failed to electrify the spirits of every student in Yeshivas Chelkas Yaakov. Immediately following the conclusion of the *schmooze* the entire yeshiva would erupt into spontaneous song and dance, singing the words "*ivdu es Hashem b'simcha*"[126] and with all their might, followed by an evening prayer that was always the most inspiring *tefillah*[127] of Eli's year. The story always served to stir Eli to pray, learn, and perform his *mitzvos*[128] with greater diligence and heightened intensity for a few days until he settled back into the normal, even-keeled, scrupulous yet unzealous way he prayed, learned, and performed *mitzvos* throughout most of the year. He never once had given a thought to the concrete

116. Commandment.
117. God-willingly.
118. Pray.
119. Joy.
120. With happiness.
121. Wholeheartedly.
122. And out of everything.
123. Merit.
124. Closeness to God.
125. Talk.
126. "Serve God with joy."
127. Prayer service.
128. Religious rituals.

reality of the story of Yaakov of Scranton. He knew that it was a true story, but for him it was still just a story, not a factual event; it was a legend, not something that had actually happened in the real world. For Eli, Scranton might as well have been Sleepy Hollow, and Yaakov Ichabod Crane. And now, as he thought about linking his life to Emma's and perhaps some day going with her to the actual place where the legend had happened, he was filled with an excitement infinitely greater than the excitement that would briefly lift his spirits after Rabbi Kramer's annual end-of-year *schmooze*. 'This will be amazing,' Eli said to himself, licking his lips and raising his head to the ceiling. 'Being with Emma – *marrying* Emma...and doing it in Scranton, of all places...and then going with her to Paris for our honeymoon, or to Barcelona, or Rome...and when we return to the U.S., we'll have the whole wide open country all to ourselves. We'll be able to go wherever we want to go, do anything we want to do...but it will all start in Scranton. Of *course* it will start in Scranton. It couldn't be any other way...'

As Eli let such enticing possibilities run like an unleashed greyhound through his mind, he watched the silvery shadows of the silent moonlit night crawl across his bedroom and soon sunk into a restless, dream-ridden sleep.

SEVEN

"So...what was it like growing up black in the South?" Emma asked him the next time they chatted on Facebook.

Eli cast a sidelong glance at the wintry landscape outside his bedroom window as he pondered how he should answer her. A bright glare of sunlight reflecting off of the sun-splashed snow razored in from the window and shone directly into his eyes, making him wish he had bought blinds or curtains for the apartment's windows. He put on his Astros hat and lowered the brim, protecting his tired eyes from the assaults of the white mid-morning light. From somewhere within his distracted consciousness, the idea arose in his mind that he was being punished by Heaven measure-for-measure for having used his eyes to look at things he shouldn't have been looking at, but he ignored the thought; he had more pressing matters to think about, he told himself – like Emma Yates, for instance, whom he knew was sitting by her computer and eagerly awaiting his response.

"Well, I should correct two misunderstandings you seem to have," Eli typed, less surprised that she had brought up the subject of his race than that she had waited this long to do so.

"First of all, Houston is not really the South. It's a bigger and an even more cosmopolitan city than Nashville, New Orleans, or even Atlanta. It's a very diverse city. Second, I'm actually half-black."

"Oh. Ok."

"Can I ask you something?"

"Of course, Eli. Anything."

"It doesn't bother you that I'm black?"

"Why would that bother me?"

"I don't know...it's just that it seemed to bother all the other girls I've ever dated. They never said it did, but I could always sense it."

"How could you?"

"I just could. It's hard to explain...It had to do with the way they would look at me. I could tell from their eyes. It was that strained, trying-to-be-polite look that really said 'I don't think this one will fit in so well with the rest of my family and friends.' And because you just know when you're not someone's type. And I was never their type."

"Well, you're my type."

Eli's heart skipped a beat. 'Just breathe,' he told himself. 'Breathe...'

"Really?" he typed, his fingers shaking. "Why?"

"Because you just are. *Le coeur a ses raisons,* as they say... This surprises you?"

"Yes."

"Why?"

"Because I've never been anyone's type."

"Eli...I have a hard time believing that you've never met a woman who's been attracted to you. You're a handsome guy. Tall, lean, athletic-looking...has anyone ever told you that you look like Trevor Noah?"

"Who is that?"

"He's the new host of the Daily Show."

"What's that?"

"It's a TV show."

"I don't watch TV."

"Oh...right. So which side is your white side, and which side is your black side, if I'm putting that correctly?"

"You probably are. You'd know better than me."

"Just because I'm an English teacher doesn't mean I know how to phrase these kinds of questions correctly."

"Right…"

Eli sensed that she was being overly concerned with not wanting to seem racially insensitive, but he stopped short of telling her not to worry; the worst experiences of his life had occurred when he had interacted with people who were under-sensitive, not over-sensitive, about his racial identity, so why should he tell her not to be concerned? If she were to err at all, better for her to err on the side of caution, he reasoned, than on the side of recklessness. He was ready to charge her with an error for comparing him to another black man – at least to a man he assumed must have been black, as he could not imagine her comparing him to a white man – because no matter how accurate her comparison may have been, he was always dubious of comparisons between black people made by white people; such comparisons always rubbed him the wrong way, regardless of how innocent or well-intentioned they were. He didn't know whether it was because he sensed that such comparisons seemed to reveal a smidgeon of subconscious racism or whether it was because he sensed that white people who made these kinds of comparisons demonstrated a certain lack of sensitivity for the feelings of black people; he just knew that he didn't like it.

"Anyway," Eli continued, content with letting Emma's error slide; he felt it would be unfair to apply *kansu shogeg atu meizid*[1] to her. He wanted Emma to associate him with good feelings, and critiquing her for her slight insensitivity would not have helped him get closer to his goal – a goal which he knew was completely inappropriate for him to have, but which he nonetheless could not help but harbor in his otherwise sternly disciplined mind.

---

1. To punish her for unintentionally insensitive comments on account of intentionally insensitive comments [of others].

"My father is white. My mom was black... She died when I was eleven months old."

"I'm so sorry."

"Me too. I wish I would have at least gotten a chance to know her."

"At least your father must have been able to give you a good sense of her, I assume?"

"No. Unfortunately not."

"What do you mean?"

"Believe it or not my father never talked about my mother. My grandmother – my father's mother – told me a few things about her, but she hardly knew her either."

"What about your mother's family?"

"Never knew them."

"Why didn't your father ever talk about your mother?"

"I don't know. He just didn't."

"But you could've asked him about her, couldn't you?"

"No. Not really. You know how in some homes, you just know you can't talk about certain things with your parents? Like money? Or, 'other things'?"

"Sounds like the home I grew up in. Lol."

"Well, in my house, my mother was the taboo subject. I learned early on that this was just not something that could be discussed in the Newman household. From the little that I gleaned from my grandmother my sense was that my father was made to feel ashamed for marrying a black woman."

"Why should that be?"

"I know it's hard to understand now, but back then things were different."

"Obviously."

"My father grew up in a very conservative, insular Orthodox Jewish community in Dallas – conservative both politically and religiously. In the community he grew up in there were no black Jews – the term was an oxymoron back then in his community. Even after he moved to Houston, met my mother and fathered me, I still think he felt embarrassed at having brought a black child into what for him was an exclusively white Jewish world. It was as if he felt guilty for ruining his closed community's carefully guarded homogeneity. My grandmother told me he never brought my mother back with him to Dallas to visit, not even to meet his parents. The only time my grandmother ever saw her was at the wedding – and even there, she said there were only ten people at the wedding. He wanted to keep it as quiet as possible, most likely because he was ashamed about it – wrongly so, obviously, but he was brought up with these old-fashioned notions that races shouldn't mix (he wasn't a baby boomer – he was a bit older than that), and I guess it's hard to change the ideas in people's heads that they're brought up with, even if they're terrible or nonsensical ideas."

Eli wished with all his heart that he wouldn't have to talk about his father any further, but he felt compelled to go on; it was Emma, after all, who was the one asking him, and 'for Emma,' he told himself, 'I'll do anything…anything for you, Emma,' he said to her in his head. 'I'll do *anything* for you. Even if it's painful. Even talking about the thing I least want to talk about. I'll do it for you, Emma, I will. Anything – *mah she'eilasech umah bakashasech?*[2] – just ask, and I'll do it. I'll even talk about the person I hate most in the world…yes, I will – I'll talk about my father, if that's what you want. I'll talk about anything you want to talk about, do anything you want me to do – *ad chatzi hamalchus v'yinasen lach…*'[3]

"And so," he continued, starting to tremble because he suddenly felt cold – but also, he realized, because talking with Emma, even if it wasn't a real face-to-face conversation but a Facebook-messaging conversation, made him nervous in the way that only talking with Rena had ever made him nervous,

"I understood that my mother was simply a subject not to be

2. What is it that you want?
3. I'll do anything – *almost* anything – for you…

talked about. And I never learned anything about her aside from the fact that she was African American – not an Ethiopian Jew, but a black American woman, from Houston...But that's all I ever found out. The only thing I ever learned about her was her Hebrew name: Leah. My father never took me to meet her family – and I never learned anything about her family besides for the fact that they had been in this country for at least several generations. And my father, it goes without saying, never took me to any black kids' playgrounds or black neighborhoods. He never arranged any play-dates with other black kids for me. During my entire childhood I only ever knew one other black kid – she was a classmate of mine at the Houston Jewish day school – and the moment it seemed like I was starting to know her a little 'too well' for my father's tastes, he pulled me out of the school and put me in an all-boys' yeshiva in Baltimore."

"This is why you never spoke to him again after you turned eighteen?"

"Yes. Mostly because of this.... and also because of all those other things: for waking me up at 5 a.m. every morning to study Talmud with him; for ensuring that I never got a proper secular education; for ensuring that I wouldn't be fit for anything else in life other than being a Talmud teacher; for ensuring that I'd never learn how to talk to girls; for raising me as a white kid when I wasn't; for pretending that I wasn't black when I was; for trying to hide my blackness not only from my friends and my teachers but even from me...yeah...because of all these things..."

"Oh...ok. I guess that explains it...I'm getting a feeling that this is not the most pleasant subject for you. I hope you don't mind my asking. I was just curious."

"No, not at all," he lied. "Anything you want to ask me is fine. Anything..."

It was after midnight, and even though he felt himself becoming tired, he pushed on, partly out of the sheer thrill of chatting with Emma and partly because of a visceral, inexplicable fear that this

would be his last chance to do so; it was as if he was terrified that the
moment the Facebook-messaging conversation would end he'd turn
into a pumpkin and would never be able to talk to her again.

"And what about you?" he typed, tapping his toes and stretching his
neck in an effort to keep himself awake. "What was your childhood
like?"

"Not anywhere near as interesting as yours sounds," she wrote.
"Certainly nowhere near as tumultuous. My father was pretty strict,
but nowhere near as strict as yours."

He wondered if she was aware that she had just written "nowhere
near" in three consecutive sentences. 'Maybe because she feels she
can be looser with me because I'm not an English teacher grading her
writing or a literary journal editor judging her submission,' he thought,
a subtle smile forming around the edges of his tickled mouth. 'Maybe
she feels she can let down with me...maybe I like that...yeah...
maybe I do like that...'

"My father wouldn't allow us to watch TV on Sundays," she continued. "And he wouldn't allow me to have any friends over on
Sundays either. When I would complain, he'd yell: 'what, your
own family's not good enough for you?!' That time he'd *really* yell;
most other times when he spoke, it only sounded like he was yelling
because he had one of those really loud voices that made him sound
like he was yelling at you when he was just speaking in his normal
voice. But if I ever asked if I could go to a friend's house on Sunday
or if I could go to the movies on Sunday, then he'd *really* yell. That
was not very fun. But he did teach me the importance of hard work,
so I was always working ever since I was thirteen – all kinds of
afterschool jobs, summer jobs...I tried to find time for reading in
between schoolwork and working at Walgreens but it wasn't easy. It
wasn't until college that I started reading for pleasure. Before that I
simply didn't have the time for it. But even in Amherst I didn't have
as much time as I would've liked; I had to work my way through
school. The scholarship helped but it didn't cover everything."

"Well," he wrote, the thought of not being fully alert for his next day's classes beginning to overweigh the exhilaration he was experiencing on account of merely chatting with her on Facebook, "you certainly didn't have an *un*interesting childhood... but I should be getting to bed."

"I should too... I hope you have a good night, Eli."

"You too, Emma. A+"

"A+, Eli."

'Is this what it's like when people fall in love?' he wondered, his heart throbbing and his mind racing. 'Can you fall in love this quickly? Are you *allowed* to fall in love this quickly? What are the rules for falling in love? Are they written somewhere? Can I look them up in a book? Has any *posek*[4] written a *sefer*[5] like *"His'a'havus K'hilchasah"*[6] that I can take out of the *Beis Medresh*?[7] I wonder what it would say about whether you're allowed to fall in love after just three Facebook conversations. *Mistama*[8] most *poskim*[9] would say that falling "in love" only through social media alone doesn't have the *din*[10] of "love," that it's impossible to fall in love through social media alone because of some reason like *"his'ahavus b'Facebook lo mik'rei ahava,"*[11] that all a Facebook conversation can be is a *"mayseh sicha b'alma"*[12] and not *ahava mamesh*[13]... Yeah... they'd probably say it's *asur*[14] to fall in love until you've had an actual face-to-face conversation.... But what if it's a

---

4. Jewish legal authority.
5. Book.
6. "Falling in Love According to the Law."
7. Study hall.
8. Probably.
9. Jewish legal authorities.
10. Halakhic (legal) force.
11. Falling in love on Facebook cannot be called "love".
12. A mere act of conversation.
13. Real love.
14. Prohibited.

she'as had'chak?[15] Like when you can't meet in person for some reason and *l'may'seh*[16] this is the only way you can meet? Maybe it could be *mutar*[17] to fall in love this way?...Maybe?...Maybe *b'di'eved?*[18]... *Ribbono shel Olam*[19]...where is that fifth *cheilek*[20] of *Shulkhan Arukh*[21] when I need it...'

15. Special circumstance.
16. Practically.
17. Allowed.
18. If this is the best you can do.
19. Gosh...
20. Section.
21. The Code of Jewish Law.

PART III

ONE

Seeing Emma every day in school had an almost trance-like effect on Eli. It made him do things he would never otherwise do, like forget to wash his hands before eating bread. It made him say things he would never otherwise say, like when he told Principal Penske that her new pair of red horn-rimmed reading glasses looked nice on her – in flagrant violation of the religious law he had been observing scrupulously his entire life which strictly prohibited men from complimenting a woman on any aspect of her appearance. And it made him remember things he had been trying for nearly two decades to forget – tender, melancholic memories that lay tucked away in the back of his mind like dusty albums in an attic which he could not resist replaying whenever he rediscovered them, no matter how painfully nostalgic listening to those sweet sounds yet again would always make him...

As much as he had tried to forget it, he could no more forget September 9, 1997 than he could forget his own birthday. It was the kind of hot, humid Houston day Eli loved, the kind of day when the air was so thick that to breathe in was not much different than inhaling a milkshake, the kind of day that was so hot that one could hardly believe that such a thing as winter actually existed on planet Earth. Because his Houston Hebrew Academy classmates had chosen to play soccer at recess instead of basketball, he had shuffled away from the sports field and had wandered up the short hill overlooking the school. When he reached the top of the hill, he saw Jessica David – the honey-voiced girl who never went anywhere without a book in her hands – reclining on the grassy knoll, her raven-black hair swinging silently in the soft midday breeze, seemingly unconcerned about getting grass stains on her short-sleeve blue shirt and knee-length white skirt. She smiled sweetly at him and he smiled bashfully back at her.

When he was nine years old, he recalled realizing that she was the only other kid in the entire school who looked like him, but he never believed that that was the reason he was attracted to her – though it did give him a strange, inexplicable feeling of comfort whenever he was around her, feelings which evolved from comfort to nervous excitement after he turned twelve. He didn't know if he felt nervous and excited around her because of the cute way she wore her hair – perpetually plaited into a single shoulder-length ponytail – or because of the charming way she would laugh when another girl would make fun of her or "accidentally" spill something on her at lunch; he just knew that he liked her. He wished he could remember what they had said to each other that day up on that sun-warmed hill, but all he could remember was how her clear blue opal-sized eyes sparkled under the crystalline sky when she rested her book on her lap and took his hand in hers, filling him with an indescribable sensation that made him feel as if anything was truly possible.

Throughout those next few weeks and months, whenever the boys in his class would play soccer instead of basketball at recess, he would walk up the HHA hill and sit next to Jessica. She would usually blush whenever she saw him coming over toward her, which he instinctively interpreted as a good sign, though he wasn't sure why. He tried to repay her displays of affection by talking to her about whatever it was that she wanted to talk about at the time. He had never given much thought to asking her about the books she was reading because he knew they were novels, and he had never cared for reading much of anything except for books about basketball and history.

In October, she asked him if he was interested in auditioning for a part in the play that the HHA middle school had chosen to present that year, *Romeo Juliet*. "Why would I want to audition for a part in a stupid play?" he responded.

"Because I'm going to try out for a part. Maybe we'd be able to act in it together. Wouldn't that be fun?"

"Why would we need to act in a play together when we can be together with each other in real life? Plays are just made-up things, no different from all those made-up things they make us read in English class. Those stories are all fake. They're not real; history, science, math, Torah – that's all real... I don't understand why we even have English class. We might as well have a class about dreams.... besides, if I want to do something fun, I have basketball for that – I don't need plays. What a huge waste of time. I'm surprised the rabbis at this school even allow them. In the time that students are practicing their parts for the play they could be studying Torah. Or even studying science or history. A play? What a useless, time-wasting thing for a school like ours to let students spend their time on."

"I understand, Eli," she said, sighing and shrugging her narrow, sloping shoulders, adding gently: "I guess we just like different things. But that's okay."

On a warm Friday in the middle of March, he trudged to the school auditorium, compelled, like every other middle school student in the Houston Hebrew Academy, to attend the annual school play. Sitting on one of the hundreds of hard, uncomfortable metal folding chairs that bedecked the basketball-gym-sized auditorium, Eli couldn't wait for the play to end so that he could get home and finish studying the weekly Torah portion; his father would never let him play basketball on Friday afternoons until Eli had finished studying that week's Torah portion – and when Eli would tell him that he had finished it, his father would quiz him about it to make sure he had actually studied it, asking him questions such as: "On behalf of which individuals can a Kohen[1] make himself impure?"; "what was the name of the Simeonite prince

---

1. Priest.

who was caught coupling with the Midianite princess?"; "what is the one activity that the Torah explicitly prohibits on the Sabbath?"

When the lights in the auditorium dimmed and the stage curtain was raised, Eli began to grow antsy. 'We're gonna be let out of here much later than usual,' he thought, tapping his toes and continuously shifting his legs in search of a comfortable sitting position which he could never quite attain. 'I'm never gonna be able to finish being *ma'avir sedra*[2] by three o'clock. What a *bitul zman*[3] this all is!' But when Jessica – playing Juliet, wearing a simple white dress and with her straight espresso-black hair loose and unpleated – appeared onstage, he immediately became transfixed.

When Romeo – played by Avi Rosenberg, a short, freckled, boney-nosed, pasty-faced boy with oily, slicked-back hair who also played point guard for the school basketball team and whom Eli considered one of his few friends in the school – began making sweet faces to Jessica, Eli's face flushed angrily; he gazed at Avi imperiously, as if to say to him, 'what do you think you are doing?!', and tried to give him the evil eye. When Avi put his arm around Jessica and pretended to kiss her – Eli was sure it was all pretend, because HHA was a religious school and it strictly prohibited any physical contact between boys and girls – he was ready to leap out of his seat and hurl a javelin toward the stage – if he had had one at his disposal – that would have impaled this Romeo on the spot. 'Shaigetz!!!'[4] he shouted at "Romeo" Rosenberg in his head, his nostrils flaring and his eyes flashing red. 'This isn't right! You can't do that! This is a *frum*[5] school! You're not allowed to do that! This is *asur*![6] *Asur asur asur asur*!'

He had never felt so helpless in his life. 'It's just a play,' he told himself, trying in vain to calm his frazzled nerves. 'It's all make-believe, all of it. All the words, all the actions, even the smiles they're exchanging

2. Reading the weekly Torah portion.
3. Waste of time.
4. Scoundrel!
5. Religious.
6. Prohibited.

with each other are make-believe. There's nothing to worry about. This is the stupidest thing in the world. You're making yourself crazy for no reason.' But nothing he told himself cooled his boiling blood or loosened his tensed torso. He involuntarily balled his hands up into fists and kept them locked in that position for the remainder of the play. When Romeo Rosenberg drank the poison and died, Eli finally felt his limbs relaxing and his body temperature returning to normal. 'Ribbono shel olam,'[7] he thought, as he calmly rested his hands on his knees. 'What's happening to me? Am I... *jealous*? All I've done is just hold hands with her a few times... wow... well, I guess if she really likes this stuff, these plays, those books she's always reading, then maybe I should take an interest in them, too, if that's what it takes to get closer to her, to be able to have those kinds of nice moments with her... maybe if I start reading what she reads, I'll be able to have moments like that with her, too...'

During the following weeks and months, whenever Eli would take a walk up the hill during recess to sit next to Jessica, he would ask her about what she was reading. And as soon as he found out what she was reading, he would take out a copy of that book from the school library and would carry it with him wherever he went. She liked reading a lot of Isabel Allende and Sandra Cisneros, so throughout the rest of the school year, instead of reading biographies of basketball players, he started walking around the school with copies of *The House of the Spirits* and *The House on Mango Street*. 'Maybe if she just sees me holding them that'll be enough,' he thought. 'Maybe if I just carry them around with me – *mid'agbei nafak bei*[8] – that'll be enough...' Soon enough, however, he opened up the books and started reading them himself. He couldn't recall ever having a conversation with her about those books; in fact, he couldn't remember having many extended conversations with her at all. The only conversation he could ever clearly remember having with her was in mid-May of that year. A warm, lilac-scented breeze was fanning the pages of her book and the braids

7. Oh my God.
8. "Once you have picked it up you have fulfilled the obligation."

of her hair. They were both reading quietly, sitting side by side like an old married couple; she reached into her lunch-box, rummaging for some sort of snack or drink, and when she couldn't find it, she put down her book and turned her face toward his.

"You're the chocolate thief, *that's* who you are," she said, winking at him and swinging her ponytail around her neck. "You stole my chocolate!"

"What are you talking about? *What* chocolate?"

"I had a piece of chocolate in my lunch-box, and now it's gone! It was right here, and now it's not! You took it!"

"I have no idea what you're talking about!"

"You *must* have taken it," she said, grabbing his wrists and prying his closed hands open. "Who else could have!? You're the only other one up here!"

"I didn't touch your chocolate! I swear! I didn't even see it!"

"Fine," she said, as sunlight stroked her soft, moon-shaped face. "I believe you." Her lips spread into a toothy smile; she bent her head toward his and kissed him on the cheek. "You're a good kid," she said, laughing playfully. "I believe you."

His mouth was open but no words came out; not a single thought coursed through his head. He held her hand for the rest of that recess, wishing that the bell would never toll, wishing that he could hold on and never let go of the passing shadow of that momentary bliss, wishing that he could stay with her up on that sun-drenched hill forever, to loaf with her on the grass – without music, or rhyme, or meter, or customs or lectures, without even words, only with her and the lull that he loved, the hum of her honeyed voice...

At the end of that school year, Eli's father told him they would be moving to Baltimore that summer.

"But why?" Eli protested. "I like it here. All my friends are here."

"Because I got a new job in a very big *shul*[9] in Baltimore," said his father, a tall, austere, black-bearded man whom Eli never saw without a tie on and whose voice always bore the gravid, deathly serious tone

9. Synagogue.

of a Yom Kippur sermon. "The *shul* is expanding and looking to bring in a second rabbi."

"But *abba*,[10] I don't understand," Eli persisted, looking listlessly at his expressionless father. "The *shul* in Houston didn't fire you?"

"No," said his father in a deadened voice. "I have no problem with the *shul* here. But in actual fact, the *shul* in Baltimore is a better opportunity for me. And it'll be better there for you, too. The Jewish community in Baltimore is bigger and better than the one here."

"But the community here is good, *abba*."

"Yes it is...but Baltimore is closer to New Jersey and New York. And in actual fact, that's where the center of American Jewish life is, Eli – on the east coast. Especially *frum*[11] Jewish life."

Eli hated the phrase "in actual fact"; he wasn't sure whether he hated it because his father overused it or because it sounded strange to him, he just knew he hated it, and vowed that he would never use that phrase himself.

"But *abba*, Houston is a great community. And the communities in Dallas and San Antonio are great too. Who cares about New York. We have Houston. Our life here is good."

"Eli," said his father in a sharp, commanding voice, "I know this is difficult for you, but one day you'll understand. The other reason we're moving to Baltimore is because there is a great yeshiva[12] there – one of the best in all of North America. And you will be going to this yeshiva. I've already spoken to the Rosh Yeshiva[13] and he's assured me of your place in it. I have told him all about your *bekius*[14] and *omkus*[15] and he is very much looking forward to having you in the yeshiva. This may be a difficult move for you now, but one day you will thank me, Eli."

"I...but...but I really like it here, *abba*...all of my friends are

---

10. Father.
11. Religious.
12. Talmudical academy.
13. Headmaster.
14. Extensive knowledge.
15. Advanced abilities in Torah and Talmud study.

here…" A lump formed in his throat; he wiped a few tears off of his reddened cheeks. "…I don't want to move, *abba*…Please, *abba*…"

"No, Eli," said his father with crushing coldness, his stony tone of implacable finality sealing the conversation shut. "It's settled. I've already accepted the position in Baltimore and resigned from my position here at the *shul* in Houston. We're moving in two weeks. So start packing your *seforim*[16] and saying goodbye to your friends."

Eli wanted to continuing protesting, but he knew that no amount of objecting could avert his father's decree; he felt as powerless as a crippled leaf caught in a gust of autumn wind. He cursed at his father in his head, and continued cursing at him in secret every day for the next three years; he would have cursed at him to his face had the Bible not prohibited it. His father had given him a reasonable-sounding story about getting a better job in Baltimore and about wanting him to go to some great yeshiva, but Eli was sure he knew the real reason why his father was moving him across the country: to keep him away from Jessica. He was sure that one of his classmates must have spotted him holding hands with her one day and – out of jealousy, or out of a desire to play a cruel joke on him, or out of sheer spite – must have told his father. His father, Gerald Newman, a prominent communal leader and rabbi of the largest Orthodox synagogue in metropolitan Houston, would not have been able to tolerate any rumors of his only son engaging in inappropriate behavior with a girl, and so, to punish his son for his sins, and to prevent the possibility of Eli establishing any further connection with this girl, Rabbi Gerald Newman exiled his son – and himself – to the Eastern Seaboard. Eli could not know with absolute certainty whether this was the real reason he had been banished to Baltimore, but he was sure that it must have been the reason. But he was also even more sure that his father had wanted to get him out of Houston because it wasn't just any girl that Eli had been caught holding hands with – it was because he had been caught holding hands with a girl who looked like Eli. 'It's bad enough,' Eli imagined his father thinking, 'that my son looks the way he does. And

16. Books.

I have only myself to blame for that. But of all the Jews of Houston, the one Jewish girl my son finds is the only other one who looks like *him*? There is no way in *Gehenom*[17] that I am allowing this – I will *not* have grandchildren who look like that. I have to get him away from that girl. In Baltimore, once he reaches the *perek*,[18] I'll have a *shadchan*[19] find him a real *eishis chayil*.[20] He'll have real Jewish-looking children. *Seder*[21] in the family will be restored. I can't allow him to make the same mistake I made. I have to get him away from that girl...'

'That girl' was suddenly on his mind more than ever during Eli's early days at New England Hebrew High School. For whatever reason, the daily sight of Emma was making Eli think of that girl – and whenever he thought of her, he cursed his father in his head yet again for taking him away from her. He would never forgive his father for what he had done to him. 'But at least I have Emma now,' Eli would say to himself. 'At least I have Emma. That makes up for everything. It'll all turn out alright. Everything I've gone through will have been worth it in the end as long as I end up with Emma...'

17. Hell.
18. Marriageable age.
19. Matchmaker.
20. Jewish girl.
21. Order.

TWO

Though it was the middle of winter, the Sunday sun was strong enough to knock a few mounds of snow off of several nearby tree-boughs, giving the illusion to those like Eli sitting indoors that it was warmer outside than it really was. Eli wished that he could simply sit inside his warm apartment and peacefully contemplate the fanciful snow-laden New England landscape shimmering under the rose-tinted sky, but the charming scenery wasn't potent enough to overpower the irrepressible human image that kept creeping up in his mind every time he let down his guard.

All day long he tried as best as he could to occupy himself with other things so that he wouldn't come to think about Emma. In the morning he read a strange story that Emma had recommended to him – "The Secret Sharer," by Joseph Conrad – which diverted his attention for three quarters of an hour before the image of Emma's strawberry-blonde head resurfaced from the cloudy waters of his consciousness and prompted him to log on to Facebook to see if she had left him any new messages. There was nothing. Of course there was nothing – it was only 10 a.m. on a Sunday morning and he had only just messaged her at 10 p.m. the night before. Why should she reply so soon? 'Give her some time,' thought Eli, trying to speak rationally to himself; 'there's no reason to think that the first thing on her mind on a lazy Sunday morning is also the same thing as the first thing on *your* mind. *Mistama*[1] she's sleeping in, fixing herself a late breakfast of toast and jam, thinking about the lesson-plans she needs to prepare today for the coming week... you're probably the *last* thing on her mind! How ridiculous of you to assume that you've become her center of attention just because she's become yours!'

Still, he thought, as he put on his waterproof parka, fleece-lined snow-pants, thermal mittens, winter hat and woolen scarf, preparing himself to go out into the New England winter as if he were preparing to trek through the North Pole, *it would be so great if – if...* As he mechanically moved his legs and quickened his pace, he inhaled the brisk, snow-scented air, and involuntarily began to picture himself sitting at the breakfast table with Emma...

The lazy Sunday morning sun was sauntering through the half-opened blinds, painting stripes of bright white light on Emma's peppermint-colored pajama top. They were sipping coffee, sharing an omelette, and looking at the Sunday Arts section together – she wanted the classical music portion of the section, and he wanted the movies portion, but because the last page of the classical music article she was looking at was the first page of the movies article he wanted to read, he let her read what she wanted and pulled out the Book Review instead. She put her hand on the back of his head and began stroking his hair, signaling her satisfaction for whatever it was that he had done for her the previous night, and he smiled, taking another sip of coffee and flipping through the first few pages of the Book Review to see if there was an interview with one of the authors that he'd been hoping the Book Review would interview...

His nose began to drip from the cold; he took off his gloves and warmed his fingers by breathing hot air into his cupped hands. 'You're doing it again!' he reprimanded himself, his arctic eyes squinting in the scintillating morning sun. 'This is the same thing you did with Rena! Don't you remember?! After only one conversation – *one* conversation! – you were picturing yourself standing under the

---

1. Probably.

chuppah[2] with her! Don't you remember? Don't you remember how disastrously that turned out?!' His mind quickly transported him back to his brief relationship with Rena, forcing him to remember how speedily his hopes for a life with her had come crashing down upon him like an asteroid falling to earth, creating a crater in his heart that he feared would always remain unfilled. 'You were convinced, absolutely *convinced* that she loved you and wanted to spend the rest of her life with you based on – based on *what*? Based on one shred of flimsy evidence that wouldn't hold up in the most lenient court of the imagination anywhere, based on *svaras*[3] that could be shlugged up[4] by any six-year-old who hasn't even learned *Elu Metzios*[5] yet – and all because she *smiled* at you. And because she asked you if you had ever read Updike – because *she* asked *you*! That was *it*! *That's* what you were *somech*[6] on! Based on that *one* reckless *diuk*[7] you were rushing off in your mind to the *sheva brachos*[8] and then to the delivery room and the three-bedroom-house with the two-car-garage and living happily ever after with her and with your children and grandchildren and *mechutanim*[9] and *rayim ahuvim*[10] *v'chulei*,[11] all off of that one meaningless smile – don't do this again, Eli! You think hope is this wonderful life-giving thing – no it's *not*! It's lethal! It can kill you! Hope is a balloon of nitrogen dioxide that inflates itself inside your heart and you stupidly keep blowing into it and making it bigger and bigger and bigger until she eventually pokes it with the tip of her pink-painted pinky and it pops and releases all those toxic gases into your system and leaves you with a poisonous depression for weeks, months, maybe

2. Marriage canopy.
3. Reasoning.
4. Refuted.
5. The second chapter of Tractate Bava Metzia (in the Babylonian Talmud).
6. Relying
7. Inference.
8. Wedding hall.
9. In-laws.
10. Well-wishers.
11. Etc.

years, maybe for the rest of your life – and those poisons from that Rena balloon are only *just* getting out of your system *now*, after over a year! And you want to go through this all over again!? This hope thing, this is *dinei nefashos*[12] stuff you're messing around with here! It could *kill* your! It could – '

He tried to snuff out those thoughts by focusing on the soft, strangely comforting crunching sound his boots were making whenever he stepped on ice-crusted patches of snow, but on his way home his mind still couldn't help itself from thinking about Emma and imagining what it would be like to meet her father…

"Hello there young man," said her father, a stout, well-built man with a white mustache, a sharp, chiseled chin, wire-framed glasses and close-cropped salt-and-pepper hair. "I'm George Yates."

"Pleased to meet you, sir. I'm Othello Shylock."

"Well I'll be damned – that is one mighty strange name…" He looked Eli up and down, knitted his thick, bushy eyebrows and squinted. "I ne'er heard so much as either one of them names in my life, but I guess folks these days have all kinds a strange names…well, then, young man – Otto, was it?"

"Othello."

"My daughter speaks very highly of you, Otto. She says you also read them books like she does. Now, I ain't read so much as one of them things in my life, but if you both like them wordy things and you believe you'll be happy together, then God bless ya."

"Yes, sir. We are to be married."

"Well, then – congratulations, young man," said Mr. Yates, clapping him forcefully on his right shoulder. Eli staggered momentarily but remained upright. "I wish you both much happiness."

"Thank you very much, sir. Now would you please hand over your white Christian daughter so that I may go unto her."

"Whoa whoa whoa…hold your horses there, young man. Now, listen here, Otto: I appreciate directness as much as anybody – I ne'er was

12. Life-endangering.

one for sneaky kikey lawyer-talk and what-not – but don't you think you are being a bit too direct with me, boy?"

"Not at all, sir. I'm being no more direct with you than my forefather Jacob was being with his father-in-law Laban when he asked him for Rachel's hand using those very same words."

"Ahum…I see…well, gosh darnit you do know your Old Testament, young man – that is commendable…I'll tell ya what, Mr. Sherlock – "

"That's Shylock."

"Whatever you say, Otto."

"That's Othell – never mind…"

"As I was saying, Otto: I'll hand my daughter over to you – so long as you agree not to convert her to Judaism or Blackism."

"Um…okay…fine…Agreed…"

"Listen, Otto – I didn't bust my behind in the force for six days a week for forty-two years and I as sure as hell didn't miss not one single Sunday Mass my entire life so that I could have goddamned kike-n@#$%* grandkids. Do I make myself understood, Mr. Sherlock?"

"Yes sir. I understand, sir. Very clearly, sir."

"So then, Mr. Sherlock…I takes it we have ourselves a gentleman's agreement: you will raise my grandkids as good proud white Americans, and you will raise my grandkids as good godfearin' Christ-lovin' Christians."

"We're not raising them as anything," Emma interjected. "We don't even know whether we'll have kids."

"Oh, for Chrissakes, Emily! Stop that nonsense talk! Of course you'll have kids! So, when you do have kids – "

"If, dad."

"Good Lord…fine…if you have kids, when you come visit, you will let me take them to Mass. Understood?"

"No, dad. Our kids will walk with you, talk with you, play Scrabble with you, watch football with you, maybe even eat with you – but they'll never pray with you."

"But what about Christmas?" asked her father. "You'll at least have a tree, right?"

"No, dad, remember? I don't believe in any of that stuff anymore. I never believed in any of it."

"But a tree isn't even 'Christian,' honey. It's just a decoration…It's not even that religious of a thing…It's really more of an American thing, really. It's not like having a baptism or taking communion or somethin' like that. What's wrong with a tree? All Americans have – well…I mean, all real Americans – have trees."

"Sorry, dad. No tree."

"How about a poinsettia? You can at least have a poinsettia."

"No, dad. Nothing."

"But – "

"Dad, I already explained this to you. I don't want any vestiges of that stuff in my house, even things that remind me of it. I know you still haven't come to terms with this but at some point you're just gonna have to accept that I'm no longer a Christian – just like Eli has come to terms with the fact that I'll never convert to Judaism."

Emma glanced over at Eli for a supportive "yes"; for an encouraging nod; for at least a sympathetic look.

"Umm…" Eli began, fidgeting noticeably on the couch, his stiff legs beginning to shake. "Sure…yeah…exactly what she said…"

The scene was still playing out in his mind – Emma's father was asking whether Emma, Eli and the kids would at least *visit* for Christmas, prompting Emma to repeat that they weren't certain if they'd even *have* kids, and even if they did they would only come as long as her father agreed to hide the tree and not mention anything about "Christmas" or "Santa Claus" so that the kids wouldn't get confused and only on condition that if her father gave the kids gifts they were to be called "winter holiday presents" and not "Christmas presents" – when Eli arrived back at his apartment, quickly tore off his winter coat and gloves, stripped himself of his snow-soaked boots, and opened up his laptop computer, giddy with anticipation for a new Facebook message from Emma. But there was nothing. Absolutely nothing. Not even a "hey, thanks for that long message, I'll get back to you later" message.

And suddenly, as quickly as he had torn off his graying black boots, the scene in his mind had changed – Eli was no longer meeting Emma's father but was in his fifties in some other far-off corner of the country, living in an under-furnished studio apartment and silently lamenting his loveless life.

Even he, who had become so skilled at registering the rapid revolutions of his temperament, was astonished at how swiftly his spirits had changed. He was even more dumbfounded to find his eyes somewhat moist. The strained conversation between Emma and her father, though almost as uncomfortable for him to imagine as getting stopped by the police officer in Baltimore had been for him in real life, was in other ways so heartwarming and so illustrative of everything he'd ever truly desired out of life that he was absolutely distraught over its instantaneous disappearance.

'There's no way her father could actually be that racist,' he told himself as he poked around inside his near-empty refrigerator and fumbled through the Tupperware in his cluttered kitchen cupboard. 'Or that antisemitic...that's just a ridiculous fantasy...white Americans are much more sensible these days...the KKK is a shell of its former self... white supremacy is a thing of the past...people in this country don't really hate blacks and Jews the way they used to...it's not like all these white people are running around today killing blacks and Jews like they used to do...and just because he used to be a policeman doesn't mean – no, I can't let myself jump to conclusions, that's not right...I need to be *dan es kol ha'adam lechaf z'chus*...[13]...Maybe once he'd get to know me he'd actually like me...maybe I shouldn't be so sensitive about this stuff all the time, so on guard and so – and anyway, Emma still hasn't messaged me back...so maybe this is it...maybe it's over... maybe she's lost interest and I'll never have to worry about this whole meeting-her-white-Christian-father thing anyway...'

He washed his hands and made himself a tunafish sandwich, but when he sat down at his small kitchen table and stared at the toasted rye bread, he found himself unable to eat. His stomach seemed to

13. Give people the benefit of the doubt.

be full of some sort of noxious, unwholesome vapor mixed with the butterfly sensations he used to get before his middle school basketball games. The thought of food started to make him feel sick. He quickly wrapped the sandwich up in tin foil, placed it in a paper bag and stuck the bag in the refrigerator.

'Look at you,' he said to himself scornfully, walking back to his desk and refreshing his Facebook page. 'You've done what you know you were not supposed to do... How many times did I tell you to not get your hopes up?! How many times did I tell you!? *Chochom einav b'rosho!*[14] You *know* what happens when you let yourself go for a girl like this, and now look at you! Absolutely miserable. Practically *crying*! Unbe-freaking-*lie*vable! You shed a *tear*! A *TEAR*! You're *crying*, for godssakes! *Shoiteh!*[15] Crying as if you've broken up with her after a five-year relationship when you haven't even been out with her on a *single date*! Crying more than you did that time in Rav Kramer's *shiur*[16] when you got points off the *bechina*[17] because you couldn't remember the *shita*[18] of the Rashba[19] by[20] *chad bit'rei batil!*[21] *Ribbono shel Olam!*[22] Get it together, man! *Yisgaber ka'ari!*[23] ... You'd be much better off if you'd never responded to her friend request in the first place!...'

The rest of the day wore on for him like every Sunday since he had started teaching at New England Hebrew High School. He prepared his lesson-plans for the upcoming week, did his cooking for the next few nights, and mindlessly recited the words of the afternoon prayer

---

14. "A wise man's eyes are in his head."
15. Fool!
16. Class.
17. Test.
18. Opinion.
19. R. Shlomo ibn Aderet, thirteenth-century Catalan Talmudist.
20. In the case of.
21. When three pieces of food are mixed together and two are kosher and one is not.
22. Good Lord!
23. Get over this!

service – focusing for four seconds on the words "God is close to all who call upon Him, to all who call upon Him in truth" was about as much concentration as he could muster – before settling back into his books for the rest of the evening, trying as best as he could to let the analytical brilliance of the Dagul Mervavah[24] and the brazen buffoonery of Don Quijote distract him from the demoralizing setback of Emma having dropped him. The more of *Don Quijote* he read, however, the more concerned he continued to become with Emma's statement to him in one of their email exchanges that she was "devoted to finding my Quijote." '*Lichora*,'[25] he would think, as the more of the incorrigible knight-errant's antics he read of, 'Quijote would be the *worst* possible *shidduch*[26] a woman could want! He's irresponsible, irrational, unreliable…recklessly romantic…overly guided by books…unless it's *mashma*[27] that for whatever reason that *is* the kind of *shidduch* she's been looking for?…and maybe she sees a bit of Quijote in me?… And that's why she came on so strong at first?…All the *frum*[28] girls I dated were looking for a steady Sancho Panza but Emma Yates has been looking for a Man of La Mancha?… Well, whatever the case was with her, it doesn't matter any more now that she's out of the picture. At this point it's *b'toras*[29] *d'rosh v'kabel s'char*…'[30]

It hadn't even been twenty-four hours since he had messaged her, but he was sure she had dropped him. Girls had always done this with him, he reminded himself. He'd go on a date, he would think it had gone well, he would call her or email her the next day, and then he wouldn't hear from her for days. Eventually he'd get some "you're a nice guy, but…" message, and that would be it. He knew from experience that if a girl didn't write back within two days, it meant that

24. A commentary on the Shulkhan Arukh (Code of Jewish Law).
25. Maybe it's just me, but…
26. Marriage partner.
27. Possible that.
28. Religious.
29. In the category of.
30. "You shall receive reward for the learning alone."

it was over. With Emma, he was certain that it was over before it had even begun. He knew that it was the height of foolishness to entertain for even one *minute* the possibility of him and her ever ending up together. And then, as if he had magically cured himself without even trying, his anger overtook his sadness, and he began to feel angry at himself for having let his guard down. He thanked God for the sudden providential transfusion of anger into his emotionally drained system; it was much more pleasant to feel angry than to feel sad.

THREE

On Thursday night, mindlessly scrolling through his Facebook page and looking forlornly at pictures of his friends with their wives and children, he saw an orange light in the upper-right-hand corner of the page that signaled a new message. He looked away from the screen and inclined his head toward the window, gazing at the attractive glow of the street's Christmas lights glimmering like earth-bound stars against the milky, snow-laden lawns. He looked back at the screen; the orange light glared at him like a warning light, as if it were cautioning him against doing what he was about to do. He clicked on it and saw that it was a message from Emma; with his legs shaking and his heart racing, he read:

Hi Eli! I hope you're having a good day. To get back to you about what you asked me the other day about how I like being a teacher, I'll say that, first of all, it's a privilege to teach literature, and I wouldn't give it up for anything in the world. It has its challenges, sure, but it can also be fun and even rewarding...I always wanted to be a teacher, and growing up I got different sorts of part-time teaching jobs. In my teens, during the summers I would teach for a non-profit, and during school-years I would run a lot of the youth programs at church. (Fortunately they didn't test me to see whether I was really a believer – otherwise I would've been out of a job faster than you can say Jesus Joseph & Mary lol. They just liked how I was with kids.)

I always thought I'd be a public school teacher, so it's been interesting having been a private school teacher for nine years now. I've heard from some of my friends who've become public school teachers that it's gotten more difficult recently due to things like states' cuts to their education budgets, lower teachers' pay and larger classroom sizes combined with national movements toward testing, in addition to other factors (but my friends who are public school teachers in Massachusetts and Connecticut seem to be happier – probably because of the resources they devote here to education and because of other benefits teachers in these states receive)... but at private schools, like here at NEHH, even though we have our own pressures from the dual Judaic/secular curriculum, we don't have the same sense of pressure you feel in public schools to teach toward tests, and it actually makes for a more relaxing and creative teaching environment.

Well, I think that's enough from me for now, I could go on for hours about teaching, schools etc. but I don't want to bore you... how have you been? What have you been reading lately? How did you like "The Secret Sharer"?

I hope you have a good evening and look forward to chatting again soon.

– Emma

The aftereffects of her message percolated through his body like a slow-release caffeine pill. In the depths of his mind, without consciously realizing it, he had already decided that if she were to ask him to marry her, he would say yes. He couldn't imagine what his yeshiva friends would think if they were to find out that he would marry her without her having converted to Judaism – so he didn't think about it. He told himself, as if to appease himself, that of course he would only marry her if she converted – marrying her if she didn't convert was out of the question, he said to himself – even though he knew that there was about as much of a possibility of Emma Yates adopting any religion as Eli Newman walking on Mars. So he simply chose not to think about it; even though he refused to admit it to himself in a conscious manner, he knew in his heart that he would still marry her even if she did not convert...

And even if she *did* convert – even if the impossible miraculously came to pass – even if she were to fully embrace observant Judaism, what would his yeshiva friends say? 'Who *cares* what they'd say,' he would tell himself when the question arose in his mind. 'Outside of Yoni, they never really cared about me anyway, so why should I care about what they would think?'

But even though he wouldn't admit it to himself, he *did* care about what they would think; in his heart, he really did care about what Aharon and Avrum would think, he really *did* care about what Shmuel and Yosef and Yitzchok and Doniyel would think. Because, while his mind rejected them, his heart told him that he wanted them at his *chasunah*;[1] he wanted them sitting by his side during the chosson's tish;[2] he wanted Avrum and Shmuel to sing *im eshkacheich*[3] while he was under the *chuppah*;[4] he wanted them to dance him into the *yichud* room;[5] he wanted them to sing with him and dance with him and be happy for him, because in his heart he knew that he wouldn't be completely happy unless they were happy for him – but in his head he knew that they wouldn't be happy for him unless they'd approved of his choice of bride. But what would they think when they'd hear that he had finally found a bride – and that it was Emma? He preferred not to think about it, because he knew that the prospect of his friends' disapproval was too hurtful a thing for him to think about. Still, he couldn't help but think about it; in his mind he could already hear what they were saying:

1. Wedding.
2. The groom's reception: a pre-wedding meal for men during which the *ketubah* (the traditional Jewish marriage contract) is affirmed and signed.
3. "If I forget thee, O Jerusalem."
4. Bridal canopy.
5. A private room where the bride and groom retreat to for several minutes immediately following the formal bridal canopy ceremony.

'*Nu?*[6] So Eli's finally getting married? Mazel Tov. When's the LeChayim?[7] It's all the way up in Connecticut? *Ribbono shel Olam.*[8] Why doesn't he just come back to Baltimore for it? It would be so much easier. He can stay by[9] the Brauns and his kallah[10] can stay by the Herstics. Instead he has to be *mat'riach*[11] everyone to come up to Connecticut? Why not at least make a *p'shara*[12] and have it in New York? It's halfway, no? Whatever he does he'll have to at least make[13] *sheva brachos*[14] in Baltimore if he wants any chance of *panim chadashos*[15] ... So *nu*, who's his kallah? What type of girl is she? A Bais Yaakov[16] girl, *mistama?*[17] What? No? Then from what seminary? ... She didn't go to seminary? Nu, so what, she's a Stern girl? She's modern? He's marrying a modern girl? ... What? No? So she's a Touro girl? ... No? Not even a Touro girl? ... She went to *college?* ... To a *secular* college? And no seminary? *This* is the type of girl Eli is marrying? Eli *Newman?* I'm not *mekabel*[18] ... Nu, so what else? She's older than him? He's crazy. But that makes sense. He was always looking for a mother ...'

The mere thought of what Eli knew they'd surely say made him want to throw a chair against the wall and smash his hand through a window. How could they be so reductive?! To reduce everything to some simplistic psychological impulse – an impulse they were one-hundred-percent wrong about anyway, he was sure – when nothing could be further from the truth?! How dare they demean

6. Well?
7. Engagement party.
8. Good lord.
9. At.
10. Fiancée.
11. Bother.
12. Compromise.
13. Have.
14. Post-wedding meals.
15. New people showing up.
16. Religious Jewish girls' school.
17. Most likely.
18. I don't believe it.

him and degrade him by saying that his whole life was guided by some blind psychological compulsion! Didn't he have a will of his own?! And how dare they debase *Emma*! Couldn't they understand that he hadn't fallen in love with a "type" of girl?! Couldn't they understand that he had fallen in love with a living, breathing, three-dimensional girl – a *woman*, not a "girl" – who is the incarnate contradiction of the flat, fake "type" of girl they seem to believe a yeshiva *bochur* is supposed to marry!? *K'tanei amana!*[19] *She is a real person, not a dating resume!* And couldn't they understand that he would have fallen in love with Emma whether she was five years older than him or five years younger than him? What did age matter when he had found a woman with whom he could share Brontë in bed and Beckett at breakfast? What did age matter when he had finally found a woman who didn't just merely tolerate him but who actually loved him – physically, emotionally, and intellectually loved him – precisely for who he was, not in spite of who he was? Were their imaginations so limited that they couldn't conceive of him marrying unless he had found a "type" of girl who crossed off all the boxes of their dating checklists (cooks; bakes; only wears skirts; went to seminary for at least one year; has two references from two rabbis; will fully cover her hair upon marriage; father is a doctor, lawyer, businessman or banker; no older than 25)? Couldn't they understand that Emma was not – and never would be – a "type" of anything?! Couldn't they understand that she was an individual, not an idea – a genius, not a genus – a woman, not a wife – an *Emma*, not an *eema*?![20] Couldn't they?

---

19. They of little faith!
20. Mother.

FOUR

Two days later, while walking to class amidst an early March snow-shower that mercilessly pelted the leafless, defenseless black birches and brown oaks with an unrelenting stream of little white pellets and transformed his forest-green parka into the color of his off-white prayer shawl, Eli pictured the birthday message that he envisioned Emma posting on his Facebook wall in fourteen months' time, after they would have been married for three months: "Happy birthday to the man of my dreams!", she would write, accompanied by a picture of them standing side-by-side, smiling the satisfied smiles of first-year marital bliss, so that all his friends could finally see that Eli Newman was no unmarried failure-of-a-human-being after all. He didn't actually think she would write something as commonplace as that – after all, she was Emma Yates, summa cum laude in English and Comparative Literature from Amherst College – she was Emma Yates, prize-winning poet published in The Threepenny Review – she would surely write him a birthday message that was a bit more sophisticated than the average "happy birthday to the love of my life!" message he seemed to see scrawled on the Facebook wall of every one of his married friends on their birthdays. She would probably write him a line from Rilke or Keats, or maybe one of those lines from a Thomas Mann novel that looked innocuous to others but that they both found secretly suggestive.

"To Eli Newman on his birthday," she would write: "Whose eyes are ripening fruits, whose torso sparkles…whose mind gleams like a lamp, whose chest dazzles, whose shoulders glisten, whose arms burst like stars, whose smile runs through my placid lips…oh Eli Newman, I verily did change my life for you!" No…even that would be too unoriginal for her, he thought; it would be too clichéd – what poet hasn't riffed on the Torso of Apollo? Maybe she would simply settle for posting a poem by Emily Dickinson on his wall that they could try to parse later in bed…"Happy birthday to the man of my dreams"?! She would never post something as hackneyed as that! Not Emma Yates, Chair of the New England Hebrew High School English Department and Director of the Alfred J. Soffer English and French Literature Honors Program, thrice-published poet in The Kenyon Review! No, she would never write anything as banal as that! That his mind even pictured such a senseless thing was the greatest proof yet of the pathetic paucity of his juvenile imagination.

And yet…and yet, as he struggled on through the whirling snow, his befogged eyes occasionally glimpsing a pine-tree or spruce thoroughly frost-covered from the foot of its trunk to its outermost bough, he sensed that somewhere in the shadowy, unexplored polar regions of his wintry mind, he secretly – though without actually realizing it – really did desire that she *would* post something as hackneyed as that on his wall. He really did want her to call him "the man of my dreams." Forget the Rilke, forget the Shakespearean sonnet, forget the fancy Flaubertian flourish – all he really wanted her to say was that he was "the man of my dreams" – not her Torso of Apollo, not her "dream of clouds which methought would open and show riches ready to drop upon me that when I waked, I cried to dream again" – no… just her "dream" would be enough. Just the "man of my dreams." His desires were truly – though he would never admit it to himself – as simple and as conventional as that…

Because, for the past eighteen years, he had doubted whether he could really ever be *any* woman's "man of my dreams." Who would ever want *me*, he would think, a scrawny, painfully shy, under-educated yeshiva *bochur*[1] with no money and no prospects whose only knowledge of anything outside of Talmud came from the books that he'd smuggle in from the local library? What NJG,[2] as the *shadchanim*[3] called them, would ever want to become involved with an NJB who would never amount to anything more than a high school Talmud teacher – and it wasn't even clear if *that* would materialize, in which case he'd be stuck sitting in yeshiva and making a pittance for the rest of his life as an aging, past-his-prime *kollel*[4] fellow? He was the opposite of a "catch," he used to think – he was a disease that no woman in her right-thinking mind would ever want to catch unless she herself had some sadomasochistic death-wish to live in poverty for the rest of her life, sacrificing herself for the sake of spirituality while her husband would slowly reveal himself to her as man who cared more about his own scholarship than her precious spiritual ideals. Catching Eli Newman, he used to think, would be as disastrous as catching the bubonic plague.

And yet...and yet, as he trod steadily on through the miserable March wind, occasionally espying a few distant junipers glittering with ice, he secretly did believe – though he would never expressly admit it to himself – that he really *could* be the man of some woman's dreams. Why else had he been exercising and keeping himself in shape for the past twelve years? It was as if he were the backup quarterback to Tom Brady – working out every day, practicing every day, memorizing the playbook, attending all the film study sessions, keeping himself in tip-top shape – knowing all along that the chances of him actually seeing the field were about as good as the chances of him becoming the Crown Prince of Denmark. He knew that his career would probably be over before he ever saw any real action...but maybe, *maybe*, he thought, someday, he just might get a chance to play. It was a mad,

1. Student.
2. Nice Jewish Girl.
3. Matchmakers.
4. An institute for advanced Talmud study, often housed in a yeshiva.

almost unimaginable notion to him, but without that burning desire for action combined with that wild, inexpressible belief that he *would* get a chance to play, he never would have continued with his ridiculous exercise regimen for as long as he had. Because in the unexamined recesses of his mind lurked the wild belief that there just might come a day when all of his skills and all of those hours he had put in on the practice field and in the film room and in the study sessions *would* come in handy and it would all pay off in one great burst of spectacular, real-life action. He had harbored that hope without realizing it, but it was there, hovering in the background of all the reading he'd been doing and all the push-ups and sit-ups he had been doing and all the running and walking and mental fitness exercises he had been doing for eighteen lonely years. Because "why not me?", he secretly, inexpressibly thought, his unutterable thoughts swirling in his mind like the ambiguous undulations of casual pigeons. "Why not me? Why can't *I* be the man of some woman's dreams? I'm not asking for a boatload of women, or even a bucket-full or a binder-full; I'm just asking for *one*. Just *one*. **Achas** *sha'alti.*[5] Why can't I be *one* woman's 'man of her dreams'? Am I really *that* repulsive that I can't be *one* woman's 'man of her dreams'? Surely there must be *some* woman out there crazy enough to want to catch Eli Newman. It's just a matter of finding her – or her finding me. That's all..." And until then, he would keep himself ready for that off-chance that some day, somewhere, the unthinkable might actually happen; he would keep himself ready for the day when the nothing that had been his life would somehow, someway, at last amount to something more than the sound of the wind and the wafting of the leaves.

He heard back from Emma again later that evening. "Sure, I'd love to have a Skype date," she wrote back to him on Facebook. "Does Tuesday evening work for you?" Her message immediately set off a flurry of feverish feelings within him, suffusing his body with warmth and fueling his mind with more fantastical visions of the marital bliss

---

5. "One, is all I ask for..."

that he unconsciously – though he would never expressly acknowledge it – believed would soon be theirs...

"*Your rabbi told me the most unbelievable things about you,*" Emma said to Eli as their wedding was winding down. *All the guests had left, even their family members, leaving them alone at last in the spacious social hall.*

"*Which one?*"

"*Rabbi Bleich, I think...yeah, that was him.*"

"*Oh God...I can only imagine what he'd have to say about me.*"

"*It was all good.*"

"*Really?*"

"*Yeah...I couldn't get over it...he was practically saying you're a saint... he loves you...*"

"*What did he say?*"

"*He said, 'Emma, you should know, you're a really lucky woman. Eli – let me tell you something about Eli. Eli is a "tzadik," which means a "righteous person." He's extremely smart – one of the smartest students I've ever had – and very hard-working. Kind, compassionate, considerate. You know, Emma, when I was younger, I used to be really impressed by people who had great minds. But now that I'm older, you know what impresses me most? People with big hearts. And Eli – let me tell you about Eli...Not only does he have a great mind, but more importantly, he has a great big heart...Eli is a very, very special boy...which makes you a very, very lucky woman.' Then he gave me a big hug...I didn't think Orthodox rabbis were allowed to touch women.*"

"*They're not...but that's just Rabbi Bleich. That's his thing. He's a hugger. He hugs everybody, indiscriminately, all the time.*"

"*I still can't get over what he was saying about you...and that wasn't it. He just kept going and going and going...I've never heard such nice things in my life about anybody.*"

"*Well,*" said Eli, grinning playfully, "*I guess paying him off really worked...*"

"*What? You paid him to say those things?*"

"*No, no,*" said Eli, chuckling and shaking his head. "*He's just...for whatever reason, he's always thought very highly of me. I'm not really sure why, but he always has. He's the one who's a saint. Me? I'd be lucky if I was a beinoni.*"

"A what?"

"That means 'an average person.' … I know he loves me, but he has no business calling me a 'tzadik' when he's the real tzadik… Well…" he said, as a sly smile crossed his reddened face, "shall we make our way to the hotel?"

"Yes!" he immediately starting typing in response to her Facebook message before deleting the exclamation point and simply writing "Yes"; he didn't want to come across as overeager, even though over-eager was precisely what he was. "Tuesday night definitely works for me," he wrote, his legs trembling. "What's the best time for you that night?"

After sending the message, he closed his computer and opened his volume of Talmud in order to finish preparing the passage that he was planning on teaching his tenth grade class that week. The faint, liquid light from the thin sickle of the moon trickled in through the window and dripped like clear honey onto the word-cluttered page. 'Could it possibly be my turn?' he thought, scanning the words with glassy eyes while his mind took him elsewhere – to the wedding hall, to the bridal canopy, to the marital home, to the delivery room… 'Could it be? Why not? Why not *me*? Thousands, millions, maybe *billions* of people do it – can it really be such a hard thing to accomplish? It's not like you need some special advanced training in order to do it. It's not like you're an astronaut preparing to be launched into space, training to be one of the mere handful of people per decade who get to do it… maybe I can do it too… yeah… why not me?… maybe it's my turn…'

FIVE

Over twenty-four hours had passed since he had last heard from Emma and she still had yet to message him back to confirm the time for their Skype-date. After every hour that passed without him having heard from her, another petal from the flower of his wilting soul fell to the earth, unwatered by the fructifying fountain of that heavenly New England poet who had already become his only corporeal desire, his sole source of spiritual sustenance. As he was taking out the garbage following his dinner of tofu and broccoli, the old worries began to overtake him once again.

'She's no longer interested,' he thought, throwing the small plastic bag of refuse down the hallway's incinerator shoot. 'I know it…She's decided I'm not good enough for her – she knows she can do better…she met someone else – some real literary type, not an amateur like me…but who else could she have met in such a short time? *Here*? In *Hartford*? Who could she have met in *Hartford* in the past twenty-four hours on a snowy Monday in the middle of March? It's not like Mark Twain or Wallace Stevens are still living here…Oh, come on, Eli, you're being absurd – just thirty hours go by without hearing from her and already you think it's over?! Where's your *emunah*?![1] Is that really all it takes for you to give up all hope?!'

1. Faith.

Over the next few hours, while reviewing his lesson-plans for the upcoming school week, he tried to use rational arguments to calm himself down – 'the *pashtus*[2] is she's busy preparing for her classes'; 'she meant to message you but she got caught up talking to an old college friend'; 'it's almost April, she's probably doing her taxes…' – and at the ground level of his mind, he was appeased. As the night deepened, and as the sinister shadow of the midnight moon lengthened, he had gradually convinced himself that there was nothing to worry about, and that it was completely reasonable that she should wait over twenty-four hours before responding. Even though it was already 12 a.m. on Monday night and their Tuesday night Skype-date had still not yet been confirmed, he had persuaded himself that it was entirely irrational and utterly absurd for him to believe that she had already lost interest or had met someone else. And yet, below the placid surface of his mind, in the turbulent region where his darker, unexamined thoughts lay, he *did* believe she had already dropped him, and he did fear, as absurd as it sounded to him, that she had met someone else. He did not dare air out those beliefs and let them speak for themselves, but they were nonetheless there – unassessed, unheard, yet imperceptibly coloring his every clear thought and shading his lucidly argued views one shade darker. He did not want to believe that Emma had left him before she had already even arrived – the pain of her premature departure was simply too great to contemplate; but he couldn't help but feel that that was precisely what she had done. And in that same turbid, unexplored region of his mind, dark clouds began to swirl, forming themselves into a toxic cocktail of thoughts that mercilessly poured down their poison upon every corner of his consciousness: 'You will need to get back on one of those dating websites now – J-Date, J-Wed, J-Swipe, J-Lo…. You'll need a new screen-name. Yaal Kegam didn't work out so well last time. Maybe you'll have better luck with Yad Shachatdam … or Nat Barnat. Hmm … no … too American … Yak Nehaz … no … too Persian … Shatnez Getz … too German … Kim Lei Bidrabaminei … no, too Korean … Uchla de Efras … no, too French …

2. Simple explanation.

Tashrat Tashat Tarat...Boutros Boutros Ghali...no...it's hopeless...
You should just stick to your plan and forget about this whole dating
shtus[3] altogether. It's just *bitul zman*.[4] Not something fit for a serious
talmid chacham[5] like Ben Azzai. Just think of all the advantages there
are to staying single. You'll be able to keep reading all night without
ever having to stop to make conversation...you won't have anyone
around to *batel*[6] your learning...you'll be able to continue listening
to all the sports podcasts you want to whenever you want to without
anyone ever telling you to turn them off...you can keep spreading
your bath towel over the length of the entire towel bar without having
to worry about making space for another towel...you won't have to
worry about anyone seeing the strange way you eat, which would
truly drive any sane person mad...you won't have to worry about
waking anyone up with your early-morning exercise regimen...you
won't have to worry about someone yelling at you for leaving your
socks at the foot of the bed...you won't have to worry about sharing
a bed with someone who might snore and cause you to never be able
to get a good night sleep ever again...Don't worry so much about
it. Being married can be worse than being single. Didn't Reb Yaakov
Emden[7] write that he was married to three different women and didn't
love any of them? I wonder why...And what about your whole "I'm
gonna forget about marriage and devote my life to learning" plan?!
The second a woman finally comes along who's interested in you, you
drop your whole "I'm gonna be the next Ben Azzai – the-next-Jewish-
celibate-monk" life-mission as quickly as Rena dropped *you*?! Have
you no resoluteness?! You weak, worthless, pathetic – '

He cut himself off from thinking such thoughts and reimmersed
himself in his work, fortifying himself – as he had grown expert at
doing over the past dozen years – with the ancient armor of Torah and

---

3. Ridiculousness.
4. A waste of time.
5. Torah scholar.
6. Interrupt.
7. Rabbi Yaakov Emden, eighteenth century German Talmudic scholar.

the medieval chain mail of the Talmud and its commentaries against the relentless assaults of dating disappointments that threatened to rend his brittle heart in two.

When she finally did message him back Tuesday afternoon at 1 p.m. to confirm their video-chat date for 9 p.m. that night, he felt as if he had been boosted out of the stratosphere – as if he had left his earthly existence and had suddenly been propelled into a gravity-free state where none of his former fears and anxieties weighed him down any longer. All it had taken was that one message of confirmation, and he was once again mentally planning his future with Emma without even realizing that he was doing so...

"How about Santa Fe?" Emma said to him one morning at the breakfast table, having coffee and oranges in a sunny chair; spring robins warbled softly, and dust motes danced lazily in the warm morning breeze. "I've always wanted to go there. Maybe that should be our next trip."

"I don't know," said Eli, taking one more sip of coffee before getting up to clear the dishes. "What exactly is there to see there?"

"Well...there are lots of cute little art galleries...the Georgia O'Keeffe museum is there...Los Alamos is not too far away..."

"That doesn't sound like too much to me. You don't just wanna save up and go back to Paris the next time we can?"

"Eli, we've already been there twice. Where's your sense of adventure? Besides, if all you care about now is French culture, then we should definitely go to Santa Fe. Simone de Beauvoir said that of all the places in the US, if she'd have to live in one, it'd be Santa Fe. I think that's reason enough to check it out at least once in our lives. It's supposed to be beautiful out there."

"What about San Francisco? We haven't been there yet. We haven't even been to Chicago."

"True," said Emma, sprinkling another teaspoon of cinnamon into her oatmeal. "Well, we can always go visit my dad in Chicago anytime...and I'm sure we'll get to San Francisco at some point. Why not Santa Fe?"

"Well...if you insist..."

"I don't insist, Eli, I just thought it would be nice..."

He taught his final Talmud class of the day with a light, almost carefree attitude. He hoped the material still somehow came across clearly to his students, and was grateful that none of them asked any follow-up questions after class about that section's finer points; all he could think about was getting home as quickly as possible to prepare for his video-chat date with Emma.

At eight o'clock, as the hidden moon rose from above the tips of the towering oaks and evergreens into the cloud-covered Connecticut sky, he changed into a cobalt-blue dress shirt – it was one of the few non-white button-down shirts he owned – thoroughly checked his face for any trace of pimple or imperfection, and rinsed his mouth with mouthwash. Even though he knew he wouldn't actually be sitting across from her, he still wanted to get himself 'in the mood,' as he said to himself; he wanted to pretend that it was as close to a real, in-person date as possible. 'It's like Rav Kramer's *schmooze*[8] about the importance of wearing a jacket during *davening*,'[9] he reminded himself as he fixed his collar and buckled his belt. 'When he would talk about the way people watching football on TV dress up in the jerseys of their favorite teams and shout and cheer even though they're not even at the game, because they want to get into the spirit...I need to do the same here...'

At ten minutes to nine, he poured himself a glass of water, turned on his computer, and made sure the lighting in the room was adequate. He sat in his seat like a defendant in a courtroom waiting for his verdict, waiting to see whether Emma would actually show up or whether – as he expected would happen – she would send him an email or Facebook message at two minutes to nine saying, "Hi Eli, after thinking things over, I decided it just wouldn't be right for us to do this. Even though it's not a real 'date,' I still don't think it's right. We teach in the same school – we need to maintain appropriate boundaries. Besides, I've met someone else...I'm sorry, Eli..." To calm himself down, he practiced the deep-breathing exercises he had learned from a yeshiva

8. Talk.
9. Prayer.

classmate who had studied kabbalistic meditation techniques and hummed the song *"Toras Hashem temimah"*[10] under his breath.

At 8:58 p.m., he opened up his internet browser and logged into his Gmail account. Never before in his life had he been this concerned about being punctual – not even for his NEHH interview, when he had showed up three minutes late. 'There will always be more Talmud-teacher jobs,' he said to himself, breathing rapidly as he checked himself in the mirror one final time. 'But there will never be another Emma Yates…'

He waited with breathless anticipation for the clock to strike 9, but the minute-hand on his wristwatch had seemed to slow down; it was as if the universe itself was conspiring against him, he felt – as if the very atoms and molecules that constitute the entirety of material existence were trying to prevent the consummation of this forbidden conversation. When nine o'clock at long last arrived, he entered Emma's email address into his Gmail browser, brought up her contact details, and moved his mouse over the video-camera icon underneath her blue-lettered name, bringing up a one-line text box that read: "Start a video call with Emma Yates." With his right finger trembling, and with his highest hopes and worst fears gnawing at his insides like two ravenous Rottweilers, he clicked on the video-camera icon, bringing up a small black screen, and waited. After two minutes of waiting without seeing anything materialize on the small black screen, he ended the video-call.

'Exactly what I thought,' he said to himself, his shoulders slumping. 'She finally decided she's not really interested – and why *would* she be? What do I have to offer her, really? Why would she possibly want anything to do with me? I'm not even – '

His thoughts were interrupted by a pop-up message on his computer screen: "incoming video-call." He clicked "accept" and took a deep, kabbalistically-trained breath.

"I'm so sorry, Eli," said Emma, her face appearing on his screen in

10. "God's Torah is pure."

a slightly blurred form, like a faded photograph from the pre-digital age.

'I know,' he thought to himself. 'You're sorry for needing to end this. I knew this moment was coming from the moment I started talking to you. That's fine. We don't really have much in common anyway. And we – '

"I'm so sorry for being late, Eli. All night long I was reminding myself, 'gotta get ready for Eli, got be ready at nine o'clock for Eli,' and then I get this call from my dad at ten minutes to nine. I was like, 'dad, I really can't talk right now,' but then he started telling me how he wasn't feeling well and how he's had this cough for weeks now that hasn't gone away and how he's been experiencing *this* symptom and *that* symptom, and I was trying to tell him, 'dad, I'm not a doctor – there's really nothing I can do to help. Get yourself to a doctor, dad. And that cough sounds terrible – for the love of God, dad, how many times do I have to tell you to quit smoking?! Get yourself to a doctor and get yourself some nicotine patches!' When I finally got off the phone with him it was two minutes past nine and I'm like, 'oh my God, my date with Eli!' So sorry about that!…but here I am!"

"Yes you are," he said, smiling widely and nodding cheerfully, presenting a relaxed face while trying in vain to calm his somersaulting heart. Her picture was starting to come in more clearly now; her hair, somewhat frizzier than normal and looking to him like it was uncombed, was hanging nonchalantly across her shoulders, like a lazy cat, and she was wearing a white t-shirt with a purple-and-red pattern whose full image he couldn't quite make out – 'perhaps a butterfly?' he thought – because the screen cut off her image at her chest. In her clear, carefree look was the composure born of cravings that had already been satisfied countless times – a look Eli never recognized whenever he looked at himself in a mirror. "Yes you are indeed."

"Here I am! Albeit in pixelated form! – but hey, it's still me!…at least I *think* it's still me – not sure if the philosophers would agree with that, but…"

"Why not?"

"Well, you know…maybe my 'screen-self' is not my 'real-self' –

maybe this digital, computer-transmitted version you're seeing of me isn't the 'real me.' Maybe what you're seeing is only a faux-version of myself, whereas the true me – the one and only 'real me' – is sitting here in my apartment, looking at you ... and telling you how nice you look in blue ..."

"Oh ... thank you ..." He blushed, and when he realized that he was blushing, he blushed again. He was warmed almost as much by what she had said as by how she had said it, with a soft, lulling voice – a voice like the lapping of a lake in midsummer, gently inviting him to dip his toes in to see how the water feels. "You ... um ... look very nice, too ... but that's right, you took philosophy in college, didn't you?"

"Yeah. I minored in it. I'm not sure how much I really got out of it, but I did take several courses in it ... how about you?"

"I didn't go to a secular college."

"Oh, right ... sorry ... forgot about that for a second ... Did you ever read any?"

"What?"

"Philosophy?"

"Oh ... well ..." Eli bit his lower lip, unsure of whether he should make up something about how many philosophy books he had read in order to impress her or whether he should just tell her the truth.

"Honestly," he began, "I hate philosophy. When I first started sneaking 'extraneous books,' as they called them, into yeshiva, I tried reading a little philosophy but found it impossible. I abandoned it almost as quickly as I started it. I couldn't understand their abstractions and couldn't wrap my head around these impossible phrases they'd use like 'epistemic holism.'"

What an awful, bone-chilling phrase, Eli remembered thinking when he had tried to read philosophy; that phrase alone – and there were hundreds more such beauties he had encountered in those philosophy books – was enough to scare anyone away from philosophy. It made the entire discipline seem like a haunted house at the end of a dead-end street; why go anyone near it when there were terrifying apparitions like "epistemic holism," "ontological relativity," "discursive regularity," and "enunciative modality" lurking inside? And even if he had tried to approach it, it would have taken him two lifetimes just to understand what it meant – one lifetime for "epistemic" and another for "holism." All he could understand from philosophy books was the phrase they always seemed to use whenever they wanted to test out a logical proposition: "all bachelors are unmarried men." For Eli, that was no mere philosophical abstraction; it wasn't a logical proposition to be tested out – it was his concrete, all-too-real everyday reality. It felt like a personal attack; it was almost as if the philosophers were taunting him. Couldn't they have come up with something else – *anything* else – to test out a logical proposition than that gut-wrenching phrase? And besides, what was their fixation with unmarried men? Did they all arrive at that statement because they were drawing upon something they were all confessing – either proudly, or embarrassingly – about themselves? Was it that "all *bachelors* are unmarried men," or was it really that "all *philosophers* are unmarried men"? Was *that* what they wanted to say, but couldn't, out of personal embarrassment? Were there so few women philosophers because women knew that to be a philosopher you needed to be an "unmarried *man*"? And was that why they condescended to Hannah Arendt by calling her a "journalist" rather than a real "philosopher"? Or maybe it was the case that female philosophers usually ended up getting married but male philosophers didn't because their penchant for abstractions and absent-mindedness made women flee from them as if they were lepers? Wasn't that why Nietzsche had said that Western culture was so pathological – because its philosophy was all written by unmarried men? Eli decided to stick with fiction for his extracurricular reading; "leave philosophy for the unmarried men," he would say to himself. Next to collecting comic books and spraying himself with skunk-scented deodorant, philosophy seemed to be the surest path toward lifelong bachelorhood, and though the world had thus far conspired to make Eli Newman a bachelor, he subconsciously had no intention of remaining one – even if he had consciously vowed he would always remain one. 'The only part of Descartes that I can understand,' he remembered thinking at the time he had made his impetuous vow of bachelorhood, 'is why he never got married. Just squirt a few sprigs of philosophy on yourself and you'll be able to repel all women for the rest of your life. If any priests out there are struggling to stay celibate, all they have to do is start spouting Kant – they'll be guaranteed to never come close to being led into temptation ever again.'

"Well, I found it pretty interesting in college," she continued, licking her lips and running her fingers through her hair. "Maybe you were just reading the wrong books."

"That's always possible...hold on a sec, Emma."

"What's the problem?"

"Nothing...it's just that I'm hearing an echo."

"What echo?" Her eyes darted around her room as if she were looking for the sound instead of listening for it. "I don't hear anything."

"Maybe it's only on my end."

"Hmm..." She tapped her right index finger on her lower lip several times and raised her eyes to the ceiling before looking back at Eli. "We could try FaceTime. Or Facebook – they have their own video-chat service."

"That could be a good idea."

"Alright. I'll hang up now and call you back on Facebook."

"Ok. See you in a – wait..."

"Yeah?"

"The echo...I think it stopped."

"It did?"

"Yeah...it stopped. The echo's gone."

"Ah, I see..." she said, winking playfully. "The good people at Google have obviously been spying on us and once they heard that we were about to drop them for Facebook or Apple they were like, 'it's ok, it's ok, we'll fix it! Stay here, stay with us! We'll fix it! See?! It's alright now!' Thank you Google!"

"Thank you Google indeed," he deadpanned.

"With the way the world's going," said Emma, a broad smile spreading across her moon-shaped face, "fifty years from now more people will be saying 'Thank Google' than "Thank God.' I mean, even now we already should be saying that. We're getting far more help these days from Google than from God, so isn't that where we should be directing our gratitude? Not to some imaginary, nonexistent old man in the sky but to the omniscient, omnipotent presence in the cloud that we *really* can't live without? I mean, seriously – who's *really* the master of the universe at this point?"

He laughed, but – worried that his laugh might reveal a smidgeon of religious doubt that Emma would pounce on – soon stifled it as quickly as he could and tried to steer the conversation away from theology.

"Well…" said Eli, unsure of what to pivot to and how to do so. "That's very clever…um…" He took a sip of water and swirled his tongue around his mouth. "How did you become so smart?"

"Oh, you are too nice," she said, her unpainted lips widening into a genial smile. "Well, I guess I was always a curious person. So it might come from that. You know, always wanting to know more about things I didn't know, always wanting to read…"

They talked for another forty-five minutes without any further technological interruptions, and without any further theological speculations, even though Emma did talk to him about the possible connections between Dante's *purgatorio* and the Catholic conception of purgatory.

"It's been great talking with you," Eli said around the one-hour mark of their date. "I'm glad we got past the technological glitches… Even though we can't really go out here, because of, you know… because of this thing about how I can't afford to be seen with you in public… but at least we have the technology that lets us do this, so – "

"Yeah, it's great what technology allows us to do these days, isn't it? At least for now… though maybe we won't be saying the same nice things about technology seventy years from now when we're all enslaved by the robots."

"True… or we *will* be saying the same exact nice things, because they'll be whipping us if we don't."

"Right…" She broke into a laugh; by his count it was the eighth time he had made her laugh over the course of the conversation. He had been keeping track of the number of times he made her laugh the same way he had used to keep track of the number of points he had in his middle school basketball games. Not since his first date with Rena, by his count, had he made a girl laugh this many times on a date. "Well, this was really nice," she continued, wearing an amused smile on her pale, pink-hued face. "You wanna do this again?"

"Oh... Yeah – yes," he stammered, his voice squeaking like an out-of-tune trumpet. '*She* is asking *me* whether I want another date?!' he exclaimed in his head. 'I'm not *mekabel*[11] ... can this really be happening? What is her aim here? Is she trying to set me up for some big humiliation in the end, some grand finale where she says she was merely leading me on the whole time just to get a rise out of me? Is she doing this just to entertain herself after nine ho-hum years as a high school English teacher? Messing around with the new guy – is this her way of having fun?' "Yes I do, absolutely... of course."

"Great!" she beamed, flashing him a full-toothed grin; her smile was like a cosmic ray that annihilated any sliver of doubt from his distrustful mind. "Let's be in touch," she said, tossing her hair to the side, tilting her head and gazing at him with soft, dreamy eyes. "See you soon and have a great night, Eli!"

He clicked on the large red button inside the small black screen, ended the call, and exhaled for what felt like the first time in months. He had loved so many aspects about his experience of speaking to Emma for the first time, but what he had loved most of all was the Americanized way she had been pronouncing his name – pronouncing the "E" like the "E" of "east" and the "I" like the "I" in the word "high," instead of the way his father and everyone else had always pronounced his name, with the "E" like the "E" of "west" and the "I" like the "I" of "spaghetti." He had always hated that pronunciation of his name; it sounded soft, weak, effeminate. But the way that Emma had pronounced his name – making it sound like "Eli Manning" rather than like "Elie Wiesel" – sounded strong, hard, even heroic; it sounded like a real American name. An "*Eh*-lee" Manning could never have led a Super Bowl-winning drive against the greatest coach and quarterback of all time – but an "*Ee*-lie" Manning? He could not only do it once

11. I don't believe it.

but *twice*. If an *Ee*-lie Manning could pull off that unheralded feat, who knew what an Eli – rechristened as *Ee*-lie – Newman could do? 'Let her keep calling me that,' he decided. 'If my father ever found out that I was changing my name he'd have a heart attack – he always talked so much about the importance of Jewish names, about how the Jews merited to be redeemed from slavery in Egypt because *"shelo shinu es sh'mam"*[12]...but if I found out he had a heart attack what could I do about it anyway? I'm not a doctor...I love the sound of my new name too much to care what he'd think of it – and I especially love the way it sounds coming out of her mouth..."Hi, *Ee*-lie" – it even rhymes...'

He tried as hard as he could to not think about Emma for the rest of the night lest he come to do something with himself that was prohibited by Jewish law. *"Barasi yetzer hara barasi Torah tavlin lo,'*[13] he reminded himself, sauntering to his bookshelf in search of a *sefer*[14] that he could be sure would be powerful enough to eradicate the *kedusha*[15]-killing poisons of his inappropriate thoughts. He pulled out his *Ketzos*,[16] read for a few minutes about the subject of *kinyanei meshikha v'hagba'ah kal'sah kin'yana*,[17] and as the clear, liquid light of the cream-colored moon trickled into his room, the hefty brick-red book fell from his arms and he fell asleep. He dreamt that the sportswriter Bill Simmons had stopped by his apartment and asked if he could use Eli's microwave to heat up his beef jerky.

"No. I'm sorry, Bill. You can't," Eli told him after taking a look at the ingredients. "This jerky is not kosher. It contains dairy in it, and the Torah prohibits eating meat and milk together."

"But it's not for you, it's for *me*, and I don't keep kosher. I'd be eating it, not you. So why not let me use your microwave?"

---

12. They didn't change their names.
13. "The antidote to temptation is Torah."
14. Book.
15. Holiness.
16. A book about complex matters in Jewish business and financial law.
17. Acquisitions effectuated through pulling and raising can only be accomplished in the moment during which the action is taking place.

"Because not only am I forbidden to eat a mixture of milk and meat, but I can't even cook it."

"You think warming up something in the microwave is 'cooking'?"

"Yes. When I was growing up my father used to make yams in the microwave all the time. People use microwaves to cook nowadays, and *derech bishul asrah Torah.*"

"What?"

"It'll take me too long to explain that. How about we just stick to sports?"

"Sure. But I'm hungry... How about you just let me use your micro-wave for a minute so I can eat this jerky? I'll press the buttons and you won't have to do anything."

"Sorry, Bill, I can't. Not only am I not allowed to eat meat and milk together and not only am I not allowed to cook meat and milk together but I'm also not even allowed to derive any benefit from a meat-and-milk mixture, and if I let you use my microwave for your jerky, that would be a benefit for me."

"Why would that be a benefit for you?"

"Because I like you. I listen to your podcast all the time. So if I helped you microwave your jerky, I'd be doing you a favor, and I'd feel good that I'd done you a favor."

"You like the podcast?"

"Yeah. And especially your columns. But you never seem to write anymore, so maybe I should just call you a podcaster now instead of a writer."

"Hey! I resent that. Haven't you been reading my weekly NFL Column?"

"True, you still do write that column...sometimes...so who do you like in this week's games? Ravens vs. Patriots? Bears vs. Texans?"

"I made all my picks this week in my Friday column – you'll have to read it to find out."

"I look forward to doing so."

"Well, I gotta get going...got another podcast to record with Malcolm Gladwell...are you sure you don't want any of this jerky? It's good stuff."

"No thanks, Bill. Remember? I can't have anything that has meat and milk mixed together."

"Oh. Right. So why aren't you guys allowed to mix meat and milk?"

"It's a good question. There are a lot of answers given but the truth is that we really don't know why. All we know is that God told us not to, so we don't do it."

"Oh. Ok... Well, I gotta go. Nice seein' ya."

"See ya, Bill."

At seven in the morning, the glimmering daylight glided into his dark, dank bedroom like a reliable coworker coming to relieve him from his grim nightshift. As he sauntered to the bathroom to wash his weary face and rinse his sun-flecked eyes, the lingering peculiarity of the dream began to make him feel uneasy. 'Why would I dream about beef jerky?' he wondered, slipping his arms into an unironed white shirt and putting the blue shirt he had worn the previous night back into his closet. 'I've never had jerky in my life – I never even *think* about jerky... I don't even know anything about it... Does jerky have dairy in it?... And *microwaving* it? Do people microwave jerky? I don't know the slightest thing about jerky but it doesn't seem like microwaving it would be a good idea... And did I even answer him correctly? If I let a *nochri*[18] use my microwave for *basar b'chalav*,[19] beyond the fact that he'll *treif* up[20] my microwave, maybe I'm *taka*[21] not *over*[22] the *issur hana'as basar b'chalav*?[23] After all, I didn't own the *basar b'chalav* – it was his jerky. All I'm doing is letting him use my *keilim*[24] to cook with. On the other hand I'm still getting *hana'a*[25] from letting him cook with my *keilim*... maybe it depends on whether the *issur hana'as basar b'chalav*

18. Non-Jew.
19. Meat and milk.
20. Render non-kosher.
21. Actually.
22. In violation of.
23. The prohibition of deriving benefit from meat and milk.
24. Pots and pans.
25. Benefit.

is an *issur cheftza*[26] or an *issur gavra*?[27] ... Ugh. Look at you. Claring[28] a *chakira*[29] on a dream. You've really hit rock-bottom. It's not even a *mayseh shehaya,*[30] it's just a dream, Eli! Get your head on straight and focus on the real-life *shaylas*[31] that are facing you right now!...'

26. Prohibition relating to the object.
27. Prohibition relating to the person.
28. Doing.
29. Advanced Talmudic and Halakhic analysis.
30. An event that actually happened.
31. Problems.

SIX

He sent Emma a short email at 9 p.m. that night, figuring it would
be best to wait about twenty-four hours before contacting her
again. He had to hold himself back from emailing her any sooner
so as not to seem overeager. "It was great video-chatting with you
last night," he wrote. "Glad we got past the technical glitches!
I hope you had a good day. How did your classes go? Thank
you for sharing more about your experience in that previous
relationship with me. I'm glad you feel you can be so open with
me. I was really sorry to hear more about that boyfriend and
how awful that breakup was for you. It does sound like maybe
the fact that he had had a kid from a prior relationship and that
he didn't seem too eager to have any more kids may have made
him less willing to commit to you once you told him how much
you wanted children of your own. He definitely should've been
more up front about that with you. To have led you on for so long
seems like a really terrible thing to do. I'm really sorry you had
to endure that and please G-d I pray that you will never have to
endure anything like that ever again. Also, you really got me
thinking about Camus. I think I'll have to start reading him now.
Well, I should get going. Have a great night and talk soon!"

Immediately after pressing 'send,' he began to worry that he
had appended too many exclamation marks to the ends of his
sentences – it made him seem overenthusiastic, he thought. He

shook his head and grimaced; he never went about these things the right way, he muttered to himself – 'that's why you always fail with women and will fail this time and will keep failing again and again until the end of time. Forget marriage – do you even have a shred of hope of making a real connection with another human being? A connection that'll go beyond a few emails about books? An actual, personal, relational, emotional connection that'll last for more than a few weeks? It's hopeless. Forget marriage, forget trying for a long-term relationship, forget even this make-believe online dating thing – they all lead to the same place anyway: disappointment and heartbreak. Ben Azzai and Henry James had it right. Fall in love with literature, and with Torah, because unlike human beings they will never disappoint you and they will never break your heart...' And yet, without consciously admitting it to himself, he was still clinging subconsciously to the rickety hope of human love – clinging to it as if it were his only life raft in the midst of a tempest – the shaky, uncertain yet indispensable hope that one day it might just finally be his turn...

He checked his email at 10 p.m., thinking that perhaps there was a chance that Emma might have quickly responded to his brief email, but all he saw was an email from the school faculty listserv about school-day cancellation procedures in the event of a snow-day. He checked his email again at 11, 12, and once more before getting into bed at 1 a.m. Nothing. Nothing except for a notice from the school that due to the weather forecast – they were expecting a blizzard to hit New England and hit it hard – they had preemptively decided to cancel school for the following day. 'Good,' he thought, taking a deep breath and shutting down his computer. 'This will give her some more time to respond... she won't have to worry about her classes for tomorrow... she'll have the leisure to write something back to me...' As sleep overtook him, his defeatist thoughts dissolved, drowned by the dangerous dream he clung to that his turn was coming; the world had kept him locked up thus far, but soon, he fantasized, it would reward him for his good behavior and free him at last – or at least free him for a fun furlough before he was sent back to his solitary confinement for good...

When he awoke the next morning, he swiftly rubbed the sleep out of his eyes, rapidly recited his morning prayers, forced down a few spoonfuls of Rice Krispies and immediately turned on his computer. His fingers were tingling as he waited for his laptop to boot up, and his knees began to quiver as he opened up his Gmail account. But all he saw was another message from the school concerning the snow day. The meteorologists had been right; a vast swath of land from New Haven to New Hampshire had indeed been carpet-bombed with twenty-some inches of light white fluff. But Eli had not even bothered to look out the window to examine the carnage. All that mattered to him was the content, or lack thereof, in his inbox.

He slipped into a pair of red shorts, laced up a pair of black sneakers, and threw on his favorite Charles Barkley Houston Rockets jersey. Some exercise would do him good, he thought; if he couldn't go outside, a few minutes of walking, even if it was inside his building's hallways, would make him feel better. 'There's no cause for concern,' he told himself as he locked his door, readjusted his Rockets jersey, and began noiselessly pacing up and down the eerily quiet hallway. 'Nothing to worry about... she's probably just sleeping in – it's a snow-day, give her a break! And anyway, *you* had waited twenty-four hours after the video-chat date to contact *her*, so shouldn't you give her some time after your email for her to contact *you*?! Why does everything always have to happen so *fast* for you? Why do you need this instant confirmation? Have some patience! Okay, so Mar Ukva[1] only waited six hours, but for some things in life you have to wait a little longer... like here... maybe in this case you need to be more like Mar Ukva's father and wait a full twenty-four hours... yes... be patient and give her twenty-four hours to respond. And no *miktzas hayom kekulo!*[2] Give her a full twenty-four hours! A full twenty-four hours at *least*!'

And yet he *had* been patient – all he'd ever done his entire life was to be patient, biding his time, putting in his hours, waiting for his

---

1. Talmudic sage.
2. Don't try to say that 'waiting for part of the day is like waiting the entire day.'

Bashert[3] to come along. He'd been waiting for eighteen years – for eighteen years all he'd done was sit patiently in the dugout, and now that he was finally on-deck, he couldn't wait to get into the batter's box and finally have a few swings like everybody else. It was cruel, so cruel, this waiting and waiting and even once you're finally there you have to wait some more – and even if you get up to the plate you don't even know if you'll get any pitches to hit. It was totally and utterly out of your control – he'd be sitting on a fastball and she might just throw him four straight changeups and say "nice try, number 31, but you're just not my type... sorry for leading you on like this, I shouldn't have done that... that backdoor breaking ball was really nasty, I'm sorry about that... oh well, please forgive me. Take care and have a nice life... who's up next? Chaim from Passaic? Shoshana told me he can really rake. I better bring my best stuff when I face him tomorrow night. No nibbling around the edges – I'll have to really bring it..." Sure, it was completely out of his control – he wasn't the one throwing the pitches; she had to come to *him*, not he to *her* – and yet, wasn't *he* the one with the bat in his hands? Didn't he have at least *some* control over the matter, at least some ability to impose his will? He wanted to hit so madly, so inexpressibly badly, that even thinking about her toeing the rubber was enough to make him crazy – and now that it looked like she was set, locked in and winding up, he couldn't wait any longer for her to finally come home with her pitch.

At 1 p.m., with his toes twitching and fingers still tingling, he reopened his computer and logged back into his email. Still nothing. He immediately began to feel queasy. It was that awful, all-too-familiar queasiness that always afflicted him whenever a girl waited longer than seemed necessary to respond to one his messages after a date. He knew what was happening because he had lived through it – or rather "survived" through it, because each ordeal left him even more wounded – countless times over the previous ten years of his loveless life. When women were taking this long to respond to one of his simple post-date messages, it was always because they were composing something a bit more complicated than a "it was great to go out with

3. "The One."

you too! Let's do this again soon!" message. If a woman was taking this long to respond, he knew it was because she was composing her "Dear John letter" – or, as he called it, her "Dear Eli letter," because he had seen it so many times and in so many banal yet heartbreaking variations that he believed that the term should be renamed after him.

"Dear Eli, I had a nice time with you too. You're a really nice guy. But..."

"You're a nice guy *but*" – that was the line he had seen in every single one of the "Dear Eli" emails and texts he received. Every one of those messages was slightly different, but without exception, each one contained that crucial phrase – "you're a nice guy *but*." Eli was certain that whenever future English teachers would be teaching their Breakup 101 students how to write these letters the teachers would say, "you can write anything you want in these letters, but the phrase 'you're a nice guy *but*' *must* be in there somewhere – if it's not, you fail the course. This is your letter's thesis statement – the letter can contain a plethora of other information, but the statement 'you're a nice guy *but*' MUST be in there somewhere, either at the beginning or the end; otherwise your John – or, now that we've renamed it, your Eli – won't know what you're driving at."

He could already see Emma's "Dear Eli" email now, and he half-heartedly read it in his head as a painful pit formed inside his shrunken stomach:

Dear Eli,

I had a nice time with you too. You're a really nice guy, and I've really enjoyed talking with you. But I've been thinking it over, and after giving it some thought I just don't feel right about this. The talking and messaging has been nice but I just don't see it working out between us. You're clearly a very intelligent young man and I'm sure you'll do well. Your career is already off to a good start.

Take care and I wish you all the best.

– Emma

He was absolutely certain it would be appearing in his inbox in any moment – if not in those exact words, than in some similar formulation – and the letter's impending arrival was hanging over his head like a freshly sharpened pendulum. The only part about his premonition of her Dear Eli email that gave him pause was the fact that he believed that her Dear Eli email would be just as bland and boilerplate as all the others he'd ever received. Wouldn't a woman of Emma Yates' caliber write him something more original than *that*? He could imagine her artfully crafted birthday messages to him – or at least he could try to imagine them – but somehow, for some strange reason, his imagination could not stretch as far as it took to imagine an artfully written Dear Eli email from her. Maybe it was because he thought that once she would decide to break up with him, why would she put in the thought and effort it would take to write something nice and original? Artfulness and beautiful prose would be reserved for the man she would love, not for some lowlife loser like him – all he deserved was the standard Dear Eli email, so that's what he would get. Or maybe it was just because it was too painful for him to imagine Emma sending him a well-written Dear Eli email; would she really be so heartless as to send him something that looked like it was written by Flaubert in order to break up with him!? That would surely be the cruelest cut of all…

He thought about making himself a peanut butter and jelly sandwich, but his queasiness and foreboding had taken away any semblance of an appetite; his stomach and digestive system might as well have been ripped out and thrown in the dumpster, dispatched to the garbage dump to sit and rot with the pile of all the other Dear Eli emails he'd received over the past decade. When 3 p.m. arrived and she still hadn't sent him anything, he knew then that the matter was now beyond the realm of reasonable doubt – she was definitely writing her Dear Eli email. Of course she was. A beautiful, intelligent woman like Emma Yates would never settle for someone like him. Sure, these Facebook messages over the past two weeks had been fun for her – a fun, diverting intellectual fling – and the video-chat had been nice, but now that she saw he was serious about his intentions with her, she knew that the time had come to put an end to his delusions. She could have a fun time talking with someone like him online, but a *marriage* partner? For that she'd want somebody real, somebody serious, not some dilettante like him. 'She's looking for a doctor, a lawyer, an insurance executive,' Eli thought. 'A guy who can support her financially, not just intellectually. She'll always be able to get her intellectual frills elsewhere – maybe even with me, if she wants to continue this friendship – but *l'mayseh*,[4] if she's actually looking to settle down, she knows that what she'll really need is a big earner who can take care of her in all the ways that I'll never be able to…'

By Friday afternoon, as the sun began to slide behind the thick forest of red maples, black birches and eastern hemlocks, Eli had given up hope of hearing from Emma again. 'Well, it was nice while it lasted,' he said to himself, figuring that her having not written to him in over three days was a sure sign that she had decided not to pursue things with him any further. 'But, what can I do, *Hashem nasan VaShem lakach*,[5] I should really turn my attention back to other things. Like back to my *Gemara*[6]…and back to my reading… I was happy without a woman, so why should I let the thought of a woman get my hopes up? Dating has only ever caused me *tzores*,[7] and I certainly don't need any more of that. Ben Azzai and Henry David Thoreau knew what was up. They were *s'meichim b'chelkam*;[8] they didn't strive for anything more than what they had in themselves. They had nice, quiet, productive lives. They didn't need marriage; they didn't need to be "coupled up" to have good, happy, meaningful lives, so why should I? I'll be much happier continuing to live the way I've been living than actually getting seriously involved with anyone.… Still, why would she lose interest so quickly? Is she really no different than Rena? Just another white girl who comes on *b'kolos uv'rakim*[9] and then disappears without a trace?…Maybe she was attracted at

---

4. Practically.
5. "God gives and God takes away."
6. Talmud.
7. Torment.
8. Exemplars of the adage "Happiness is not getting what you want but wanting what you get."
9. Very strong.

first but then the more she thought about it the more she couldn't actually imagine being with someone like me for the long-term… maybe she can't actually imagine bringing me home to meet her father and friends…maybe she doesn't want to have children who won't look like her…maybe I just need to forget about white women… *all* women, but especially white women. They lead you on and lead you on and are so nice and polite but then when it comes time to actually pull the trigger they can't do it and they disappear…they're nothing but letdown machines and you don't need to let yourself get caught up in all this again, Eli!'

When he went to check his email one last time before the sun finally set, he saw a new unread message from Emma Yates in his inbox. His face flushed, and the plum-sized pit in his stomach expanded to the size of a small cantaloupe; with his bloodshot eyes enlarged, and while taking a few kabbalistically-inspired deep breaths, he bit his lips, prepared himself as if he were about to read his own death sentence, and read:

Hi Eli,

I'm so sorry it has taken me this long to respond. I really enjoyed talking to you the other night as well! I am working on writing my exams for my classes – my English final is this week, and my French one's the next. (Have you done yours yet? Principal Penske usually wants us to have them done by the beginning of April.) And I have been busy grading papers and planning assignments for the rest of the semester. I'm really looking forward to the Passover break. What are your plans for the vacation? Do you plan on assigning your students any work over the break? My boyfriend used to tell me not to do that because he said there's nothing students hate more than a teacher who assigns homework over vacation, so I stopped doing that a few years ago. I'm also working with Principal Penske on planning a field trip for my English Honors students to the Emily Dickinson museum up in Amherst…suffice it to say it's been a busy week. But still no excuse for not emailing you sooner.

I should be off now, and I know you need to get going soon as well – your Sabbath starts soon, right? I hope you have a good night, a "Shabbat Shalom" (see? After enough years at this high school I've learned how to say "Good Sabbath" and a few other things in Hebrew!), and a great weekend. Talk to you soon!

Stay warm,

   – Emma

He exhaled slowly. 'Well, I guess it's a good sign she wrote me such a long message,' he thought, stretching his neck and clasping his hands over his head, 'but why did she mention her boyfriend?...Why does she always talk about him? He broke up with her, what, like two years ago at this point?...Uh oh...maybe he broke up with her but in her mind she's still with him – maybe she's still not over him...maybe the fact that she mentioned him even for something that doesn't seem so consequential is a *rai'yuh*[10] that she's consciously or even subconsciously *modeh b'miktzas*[11] that she still loves him...maybe she'll move things with me up to a certain point and then when it comes time to actually commit she won't be able to do it because she's still in love with him...But *m'heichi teisi*[12] that my *havamina*[13] is a good *havamina*? How can I assume that just because she mentioned her previous boyfriend she has bad intentions when it comes to me? *B'tzedek tishpot amisecha*.[14] I can't allow the fact that she mentioned him to make me think less of her. *Ein adam meisim atzmo rasha*[15]...Or maybe I should just stop worrying so much about it...Whatever's in her head is out of my control, and *hakol bidei shamayim chutz mi'yiras shamayim*[16] so what sense is there getting so worked up about it? And anyway it was

10. Proof.
11. Partially admitting.
12. What right do I have to assume.
13. Conjecture.
14. "You shall judge your fellow righteously."
15. "A person cannot incriminate oneself."
16. "Everything is in the hands of heaven except for the fear of Heaven."

just an *agav urcha*[17] comment. It wasn't like she said "I met up with my old boyfriend last night and he reminded me not to assign my students any homework over the break," it was just some memory she has – doesn't she have a right to share a memory with me? Maybe she was just *urcha d'milsa nakat*[18] in hinting to me that it's not a good idea to assign homework over a break, and *aidi d'nakat ha*[19] it led her to remember this other related story about her boyfriend… But isn't a past boyfriend – a past *serious* boyfriend – a *davar chashuv*?[20] And don't we say that *davar chashuv eino batel*?[21] Ugh, Eli!… You're overthinking it!… learning is life but life is not learning; *efshar*[22] that not everything can be solved through *svaras*[23]… best not to worry about it too much… best to leave the past in the past – *mai d'hava hava*[24] – and just enjoy being in this relationship with her now… if what's going on between you and her is even *b'toras*[25] "relationship" yet…'

From Friday night until Sunday morning, Eli's every thought – when he wasn't intentionally directing his mind toward something else – revolved around Emma. When he was making the traditional Friday night blessings over the wine and bread, he thought about whether Emma would allow him to make those blessings out loud when they lived together – in his subconscious mind, it wasn't a question of if they would live together, but when – or whether she'd insist that he do it quietly. On Saturday morning in synagogue, during the three-hour prayer service, he thought about whether Emma would ever come to synagogue with him once they were married – 'perhaps,' he thought, while reciting the *Shema*,[26] 'since she's a curious

17. Incidental.
18. Talking about the usual way of doing things.
19. Once she started mentioning one thing.
20. An important thing.
21. Something that's important never entirely goes away.
22. It's possible that.
23. Talmudic-based logical analysis.
24. What happened, happened.
25. In the category of.
26. The Jewish declaration of faith.

person, she'd want to come at least once, or even a few times, to learn more about Judaism?' – or whether she would always stay home on Saturdays, sleeping in and reading and waiting for him to come back home, politely tolerating his religious eccentricities because she was physically attracted to him and perhaps because she even loved him. On Saturday night, while performing the ritual of *Havdalah* – while reciting blessings over a goblet of wine, a braided, multi-wicked candle, and a sterling silver spice holder filled with fragrant cloves – he thought about whether this ritual would simply be too strange for her and if she'd force him to do it privately, in another room where she wouldn't have to witness his religious mania – or perhaps she'd forbid him from doing it altogether. How much of his irrational religiosity would she actually be able to put up with? 'Best not to worry about that now,' he told himself after he inhaled the spices' tangy aroma and doused the candle in spilt wine. 'I'll find out when we're married – *b'sha'a tova*,[27] of course … but I'll found out then …'

Late on Sunday afternoon, as the dying day streaked the amethyst-colored sky with dazzling mahogany and a dark shade of gray, while Eli was halfway through typing up his lesson plan for his tenth grade Talmud class, he heard the familiar "ding" sound that signaled an incoming Facebook message. It was Yoni, with an update about Moshe Schwartz, their mutual friend from Yeshivas Chelkas Yaakov in Baltimore.

"Gut voch[28] Eli," Yoni wrote,

I hope you had a nice Shabbos![29] How are things in West Hartford? Last week I was at Moshe's *chasunah*.[30] It was *gevaldig*.[31] I always thought you were part of our *chevre*[32] so I still don't understand why you weren't invited. But they can only have so many

27. In good time.
28. Good week.
29. Sabbath.
30. Wedding.
31. Great.
32. Social circle.

guests because of all the expenses with the caterers and the band and the flowers and the photographers, you know how these things are. I couldn't stay that long at it myself because Chani actually had another *chasunah* that same night in Silver Spring that we needed to get to, so we didn't wash[33] and we left Moshe's *chasunah* early. Anyway, the bigger news is that we have a *shidduch*[34] for you! Chani met Moshe's wife's sister at the wedding. Her name is Esti Epstein. She's a speech pathologist in Queens. Lives in Kew Gardens Hills. Chani told me she's a great cook and great baker. She bakes her own challah every week. (*Agav*,[35] even though as you know I started in September at PricewaterhouseCoopers I'm still going to YCY every week for *mishmar*[36] and they asked me to give a *chaburah*[37] next month. The yeshiva's learning Avodah Zara[38] this *zman*[39] so I thought maybe since I'll be giving the *chaburah* to a group of guys who are now working that I'd give a *chaburah* on something that's more *lemayseh*.[40] So I'm thinking about doing a *chaburah* on the *g'zeiros chazal mishum chasnus*[41] that are *noheg bizman hazeh*.[42] I never learned Avodah Zarah and I'm not learning the *masekhta*[43] along with the yeshiva this *zman* so I'm really not holding,[44] but I could think of three: *bishul akum*,[45] *pas akum*[46] and *stam yeinam*.[47]

---

33. Have bread.
34. Match.
35. By the way.
36. Thursday night learning.
37. Focused study session.
38. Tractate of Talmud dealing with relations between Jews and non-Jews.
39. Semester.
40. Practical.
41. Rabbinic decrees instituted to prevent intermarriage.
42. Still in force.
43. Tractate in question.
44. My knowledge in these matters is insufficient.
45. The prohibition of eating food cooked by a non-Jew.
46. The prohibition of eating bread baked by a non-Jew.
47. The prohibition of drinking wine that was made or owned by a non-Jew.

Are there any more or is that it? You were always much more hold-ing[48] in these *inyanim*[49] than I was, I thought you'd know. Also, why is it that we're *makpid* on[50] *bishul akum* and *stam yeinam* but outside of, I don't know, like the real *yechidei segulah*,[51] people don't seem to be *makpid* on *pas akum*? *L'anius dayti*[52] people should be even more *makpid* on *pas akum* than they are on *stam yeinam*. I mean, if a non-Jewish woman in my office brought in some wine and she was saying "this wine is so good, it's the best wine, it's from France or Italy or Argentina or *ichveis*[53] and it's from this wine-maker or that wine-maker and it's the best wine and you should really try it bla bla bla," I mean, what would I care? How is any one wine different from any other? Don't they all taste the same to you? What *taka*[54] is the difference if the wine is from here or there or wherever? But if she brought in, *ichveis*,[55] a really good ice cream cake? Like how my mom makes them, you remember? With the cookie dough crust and the vanilla on the inside and the chocolate fudge on top? *Oh!* Now *that*… If she brought in something like *that*… and if I was still single? And if she looked at me a certain way, you know? Oye… For something like that, I much more understand why *chazal*[56] *asir'd*[57] *pas akum* – the whole *inyan*[58] of "*mishum b'noseihem*"[59] is *much* more *mistaber*[60] to me by[61] *pas akum* than *stam yeinam*.

48. Knowledgeable.
49. Matters.
50. Careful about.
51. Holy people.
52. IMHO.
53. Wherever.
54. Really.
55. I don't know.
56. The rabbis of the Talmud.
57. Prohibited.
58. Idea.
59. "Do not do X, Y or Z lest you come to marry their daughters."
60. Sensible, logical.
61. Regarding.

I'm not saying people should be *meikel*[62] on *stan yeinam*, all I'm saying is that *l'anius dayti* people be at *least* as *machmir on*[63] *pas akum* as they are on *stam yeinam* and *bishul akum*, no? I don't think it should just be one of these *"v'haba'al nefesh yachmir al tzmo"*[64] things, don't you agree, Eli? Or am I just really not holding in these *sugyas*[65] and totally misunderstanding *pas akum*? What do you think? Maybe you can at least help me with the *mareh mekomos*[66] for the *chaburah*?) Anyway, so to get back this *shidduch* for you, so this girl Esti – her father is a big *talmid chacham*.[67] He learned in Telz[68] for many years and now he's a *sho'el umeishiv*[69] in Lakewood. But she's not a Lakewood-type of girl. She doesn't want a guy who only learns, she wants a guy who works and learns. As long as the guy has a steady job and is *kove'a itim*[70] she'll be happy. So I told her about you and she sounded very interested. Her email is Esti12@gmail.com. You should write her soon. She's expecting your email. She's not on Facebook. She's not that type of girl. She has good *middos*.[71] She's very *makpid* on *tznius*.[72] But if you want pictures she has a dating resume that she can send. *B'hatzlacha!*[73] Let me know how it goes!

Eli cringed.

"Hey Yoni," he wrote back, shaking his head and wiggling his toes, "thanks, hope you had a nice Shabbos too. That's great about Moshe.

62. Lenient.
63. Stringent about.
64. "The spiritually sensitive person should be more strict with himself."
65. Relevant talmudic and halakhic passages.
66. Sources.
67. Torah scholar.
68. A yeshiva in Cleveland.
69. Answerer of Jewish legal questions.
70. Studies Torah regularly.
71. Values.
72. Careful about modesty.
73. Good luck.

I'm very happy to hear about his *chasunah*.[74] First of all, on *pas akum*, I think you're *mechaven* to[75] the Ramban[76] on the *sugya*[77] there on Lamed-hey[78] in Avodah Zarah. He also doesn't accept some of the *kulas*[79] on *pas akum* like *hashlachas kisim*[80] that others do, but *rov rishonim*[81] and *rov klal Yisroel*[82] don't go[83] like the Ramban. I think the Ran[84] has[85] something like this, he says by *pas akum* "*lo nispashet issuro*,"[86] but *lichora*[87] you seem to think more people *taka*[88] *should* accept the *issur*,[89] maybe you're right, I don't know. It's a good *he'ara*.[90] Maybe we should be *choshesh* for[91] the Ramban. Maybe if more *poskim*[92] tasted your mom's ice cream cake the *din*[93] would be different…Does she still make those *shtreimel*[94] cookies? The ones with the cookie dough on the outside and the chocolate fudge in the middle? Personally those were my favorite.

---

74. Marriage.
75. Thought of an idea/insight that has already been discussed by a greater authority without knowing that this authority has discussed this idea.
76. R. Moshe ben Nachman (Nachmanides), medieval Catalan Torah and Talmud scholar.
77. Passage.
78. Page 35.
79. Leniencies.
80. Having a Jew involved in the baking/cooking process.
81. Most medieval authorities.
82. Most observant Jews.
83. Follow.
84. R. Nissim of Gerona, Medieval Catalan Talmudic scholar.
85. Says.
86. The prohibition did not spread.
87. Apparently.
88. Actually.
89. Prohibition.
90. Point.
91. Be concerned for the opinion of.
92. Halakhic authorities.
93. Law.
94. Stella D'oro knockoff.

Mmmm... In all honesty I don't know if I could be *omed b'nisayon*[95] if a *nochriah*[96] came to me with some of those... The *inyan*[97] you're choosing for your *chaburah* is a pretty extensive one and too much to get into here, I'll be *me'ayen*[98] into it myself and I'll write you a separate email with some *mareh mekomos*,[99] but *al regel achas*[100] I'd suggest you check out this *sefer*[101] Chelkas Binyomin, it's a Mishna Berura[102]-type *sefer* all about *pas akum*. I've heard some very good things about it. But you should first go over the different *mahn de'amars*[103] there in the *sugya*[104] in Avodah Zarah and then you should see the Ran and the Ramban inside[105]... And *legabei*[106] your *shidduch* idea, thank you but I've been seeing someone lately and it's going really well. I'll keep Esti in mind in case anything happens."

"Ok," Yoni wrote back. "But you're not engaged yet, right? Queens is only a two-hour drive from West Hartford. It would really be worth your while to take a trip down on a Sunday and take her out. She's from a very *choshuv*[107] family. And you wouldn't have to worry about *parnossah*[108] if you marry her. Her grandfather is in real estate. Was. He owned a lot of shopping malls all across the country. He sold out at the right time and made a fortune. I really think it would be a great *shidduch*.[109] Think about it, Eli."

---

95. Withstand the temptation.
96. Non-Jewish woman.
97. Subject.
98. Look into.
99. Sources.
100. Just briefly.
101. Book.
102. Authoritative late-nineteenth-century halakhic work.
103. Opinions.
104. Passage.
105. Study the texts in the original places where they are printed.
106. Concerning.
107. Important.
108. Making a living.
109. Match.

"Sure, Yoni…will do…thanks."

"So who is this girl you're seeing now?"

Eli recoiled, sinking back in his chair. Even though there was no one else in the room, he was blushing violently.

"She's a really nice girl…a teacher."

"Sounds nice. What's her name?"

Eli took a deep breath, holding it in until his lungs hurt.

"I really don't want to say anything more right now. I'll tell you more as it *iy"H* [110] develops further."

"Alright. Sounds good, Eli. *Shkoyekh*[111] for the *Mareh Meko-mos.*[112] But don't forget to send Esti an email!"

"Sure, Yoni," he wrote, pounding the keyboard and growing pale with anger. "I gotta go. Talk soon."

"Ok, talk soon!"

Eli scowled. What he really wanted to write was: "Thanks, Yoni, but no thanks. I've been set up with dozens of these kinds of girls the past eight years and it all ends the same way. They dress up nicely and have good manners, but when I go to pick them up they always look at me funny – they exaggerate their smiles and give me that 'I wasn't expecting *this*' look and that 'I didn't realize I was being set up with a guy who looked like *that*' look. But they make nice chit-chat for the rest of the date, followed by that polite smile and that 'I had a nice time' line, followed by that polite 'Dear Eli' email and the 'you're a nice guy *but*' line. I've had it, Yoni. I've had it with these girls. They don't understand me. They never have, and they never will. And I'm finally with someone who understands me, who likes me for who I am, for *what* I am. And she's not *frum.*[113] I hate to break it to you, Yoni. She's not *frum*…heck, she's not even Jewish. I hope she'll be *misgayer*[114] before we get married. And if she doesn't, well…we'll see…but I

110. God-willing.
111. Thanks.
112. Sources.
113. Religious.
114. Convert.

can talk books with her, Yoni. I can talk about all these things I could never talk about with these other girls. And she's *into* me, Yoni. I can tell. She wants to see me again, and she wants to keep seeing me. And she's not even a 'girl.' She's a woman. A real woman. Not like all these 'girls' I keep getting set up with, these dull, unimaginative, immature girls who get all dolled up and smile so nicely but all they really care about is how much money you make, and the whole date is just *hevel*[115] and *shtus u'rus ruach*.[116] Emma's different. These other 'girls' aren't even in her class. Maybe not even in her species. Emma is incredible – indescribable, really. She's mature. Worldly. Intelligent. Understanding. I can go on and on. But the point is . . . oh, will you ever understand, Yoni? I've found a woman, Yoni. Not a 'girl' – a *woman*. I'm in love. For the first time in my life, I'm in love. Oh, and by the way, I'm done with these *shidduch*[117] dates. Send your *shidduchim* ideas to other guys. I'm outta that game – and *Baruch Hashem*[118] for that, because it was never much of a fun game to begin with."

115. Futile
116. A waste of time.
117. Set-up.
118. Thank God.

SEVEN

"How long have we been talking?" Emma asked during their second Gmail video-chat. It was a Thursday night, and Eli's throat was dry and slightly soar from all of the talking he'd had to do in class during the week, so he was glad that Emma had done most of the talking during this date. She was wearing a low-cut blue blouse, and Eli noticed that this time she had put product in hair, rouge on her cheeks, eye shadow on her eyelids, and lipstick on her lips – all of which he took as good signs. "Let's see ... wow, it's been almost two hours. Well, I'm gonna have to let you go ..."

'I'm gonna have to let you go'?! Eli blanched, repeating her ominous-sounding words in his head to himself. 'What does she mean? Is this it? Is it over? Is she ending it?'

"I still have some papers I need to grade," she continued, her cherry-colored lips spreading into a sidelong smile. "But I'd love to do this again next week. How about you?"

"Oh ... yes," he replied in a rattling voice, his surprised eyes widening. 'Absolutely ... yes.'

"Ok then. I'll see you soon. Have a good night!"

'Still,' he thought, his heart fluttering, 'how into me is she really? Why did she have to mention her old boyfriend again? When I asked her what she likes for breakfast, why did she have to say "I love eggs but I haven't had any since Todd left me ..."?

And then her "embarrassing admission" that she doesn't cook, that she "doesn't even know how to make an egg"…why couldn't she have just said *that*? She doesn't cook? So what. Plenty of people out there don't cook. I don't have a problem with that…she's too focused on her writing and teaching to bother with cooking – she could have just said that…why throw in "Todd used to do this, Todd used to do that"?…Why can't she just leave the past in the past? *Mai d'hava hava!*[1] I don't know…maybe it's not such a great sign…on the other hand, she was really enthusiastic about wanting to talk to me again… so maybe I should just enjoy that fact and not worry about what's going on in her head…'

The following morning, while eating a bowl of granola and gazing mindlessly out the window at the snow-filled sidewalks and the robust evergreens wreathed in a pearly mist, Eli involuntarily pictured Emma sitting across from him at the breakfast table. She was still in her pajamas, and she was wearing glasses because she hadn't yet put her contacts in. She was eating a small plate of scrambled eggs, and she was smiling at Eli – he didn't know why, but she was. He smiled back. They weren't talking about Keats or Camus, or about school-related matters, or even about the weather; they were not even talking at all. They were simply smiling at each other – at first coyly, then contentedly. He wasn't sure what her smile meant, but he knew what his did – it was a smile that said, "I'm so lucky to have you in my life, Emma… Before you came into my life, I was restless, a wandering soul, at home nowhere in the world. But now I finally feel at peace. Thank you for accepting me, Emma. Thank you for understanding me. Thank you for loving me. Thank you for loving every part of me – especially those parts that all the previous women in my life seemed to be scared of getting close to. Thank you for your commitment. Thank you for not running away. I know this is gonna sound ridiculous – it's not 1954 – but thank you for marrying me. Thank you for not being afraid to take me to meet your father. Thank you for not shying away from learning about what it's like to move through the world as me. Thank

1. Whatever happened already happened.

you for embracing me and everything about me in the same way that I've embraced you and everything that makes you you. Thank you for taking me on that ten-mile hike last week. Thank you for teaching me how to tell the difference between different kinds of plants and trees. Thank you for taking me to the Bronx zoo during our trip to New York last month and re-proposing to me in front of the zebras. Thank you for making sure we have a date night every week and a candle-lit dinner every month, for bringing *me* flowers every two weeks and for showing me what it's like to take a bubble-bath together surrounded by scented candles while listening to Spanish guitar music. Thank you for injecting romance into my life. And thank you for leaving your dark, painful past behind and walking with me into this bright, love-filled, wonderful future we're creating together...I'm just so filled with peace, love, contentment, and...I don't even know how to express it. If I tried, it would sound terrible – it would sound something like 'I just wanted to tell you I love you so much, you're everything to me, you're my world, my whole world,' and you would smile politely while laughing at me inside your head and thinking, 'he's so inarticulate, all he spouts are clichés about love he's picked up from books he's read, and not even *good* clichés...how did I end up with this guy and not someone a bit more sophisticated, someone on my level?, someone who wouldn't bore me with his sophomoric platitudes about love? Oh well...maybe I'll give this relationship a few more months and see where we're at then – or a few more weeks if this keeps up.' So instead of taking a risk by saying something, I'm just gonna keep my mouth shut and smile. *K'shem shekibalti s'char al had'risha kach akabel s'char al hap'risha.*[2] Because I'm really not capable of saying anything so great anyway. I'm not a poet like you; I don't know how to express myself in that super-artful way. Especially when it comes to my love for you; I can't even describe it. Even my thoughts sound like clichés to me; if I wrote them up and submitted it to you as an essay about love, you'd give me a D. The only reason you wouldn't fail me is because you're

---

2. "Just as I received reward for speaking, so too shall I receive reward for not speaking."

a nicer person than I am – *I'd* fail me. You're nicer than me, smarter than me, wiser than me, better-looking, better-dressed, more well-read, more experienced, more graceful than me – the fact that you're in my life at all is semi-miraculous. What could I possibly give you that you don't already have? So please, Emma, just accept this smile. It's all I really have to give you. Just this smile. It's all I've got…"

Later that afternoon, while cooking a filet of salmon for his Friday night Sabbath meal, Eli's mind, moving at the speed of sound, acting not according to his own conscious commands but according to the ineffable impulses of his psyche, started sketching a scene in which he and Emma were the sole actors upon the stage of his mind…

"I'm sorry, Emma," Eli said to Emma as they stood outside her book-lined apartment. "The truth is, I do want to come in – of course I want to…but…"

"But what? What is it, Eli? It's ok. You can tell me."

"Ok…well…the thing is, I'm not allowed to…I'm not allowed to be alone in a room with you until we're married…"

"But we will be married, Eli, won't we?" said Emma, wrapping her bony arms around him and looking into his lovelorn eyes reassuringly and alluringly. "Won't we?…Very soon?…So what's so wrong with getting a little head start on things now?…" With remarkable tenderness, she moved her mouth toward his, guiding his lips with hers; 'where my lips go, your lips shall go,' she said with her lips. 'Wherever my lips lick, yours shall lick; where they slither, yours shall slide. Your lips shall be mine, and mine shall be yours.…'

'What a ridiculous fantasy!' Eli thought, bursting out laughing and shaking his head as he opened the oven to check on the fish, which was starting to become white around the edges. 'I would *never* allow myself to even get *close* to being *meyached*[3] with her! That will never happen!…First she'll be *misgayer*[4] – and there's no *havamina*[5] of her *not* being *misgayer* given how much she seems to like me…and then

3. Secluded.
4. Converted.
5. Conjectural possibility.

we'll have the *chasunah*[6]... and then – and *only* then – and not before...
Everything will be *k'seder,*[7] *k'das uch'din*[8]... no reason to let yourself
even be *meharher*[9] about any other possibility...'

6. Wedding.
7. According to the prescribed order.
8. According to the stipulations of the law.
9. Think about.

EIGHT

Sunday was cool, damp, and sunless. Even though the calendar said it was the first day of spring, the blue jays and orioles that Eli remembered singing at this time of year in Maryland were still silent, the arctic wind still cut into his dry skin like a jagged shark tooth, his hands still felt rough and chapped, and the red maples and yellow birches were still as barren as they had been in late November. Normally these sorts of days would make Eli long for the warmth of Houston, but he came back from his walk feeling as if he had just taken a stroll on a Hawaiian beach. A late Friday afternoon email from Emma – "Great talking to you lastnight, Eli! Have a great weekend!" – that he had read just before sundown that day was all it had taken to render the external conditions irrelevant to him; all that mattered to him now was the glow of latent love radiating inside of him, a magical source of energy powerful enough to heat all of New England.

When he stepped back inside his apartment and checked his phone, his mood quickly soured. "Missed call: Chava Braun," read the four ominous black words inside the small white box on his iPhone's cracked screen. He flinched as if he'd been hit with a nightstick; he would have given almost anything to avoid talking to her – his savings account, his right hand, even his books; anything but Emma. But he knew he had to call her back. Yoni Braun's mother had been like a mother to him – *had* been a mother to him – during all those years in Baltimore. Every Sunday afternoon, without fail, she would bring brisket and meatballs to his yeshiva dorm room, and whenever Yoni would go home for Shabbos,[1] he would bring Eli home with him. When Eli needed a place for Passover during that first year after he had decided to cut himself off from his father, he went to the Brauns' for the Seders,[2] and kept on going to the Brauns' for every Passover since – twelve straight Passovers, by his count. Even when he moved into his storage unit-sized hole-in-a-wall of an apartment in Baltimore, Yoni's mother would still stop by regularly and make sure his refrigerator was well-stocked. But it had been almost a year since she had called him. He knew that the way things had ended between him and Rena must have been a great source of consternation for Chava; it had probably hurt her almost as much as it had hurt Eli. Chava, after all, was a semi-professional *shadchanis*[3] and practically lived for fixing people up and arranging marriages. She had been trying and failing with Eli for years, and when things went awry between Eli and Rena, Chava had taken Eli's failure with Rena as personally as if it had been she who had suggested it. But Eli's pain in losing Rena was somewhat salved by the fact that those pestering weekly check-ins from her had finally come to an end. He had appreciated her meatballs and quiches, but he would have traded them all away in a heartbeat in exchange for an end to her constant visits and incessant phone-calls, which were worse to him than dental cleanings, booster shots and post office visits combined.

"Hi, Chava," he said with a wry smile when she picked up the phone, trying to conceal his annoyance at having to talk to her again. Chava Braun was one of those titanic dynamo-women they didn't seem to make anymore, a gigantic woman – a bewigged, four-foot-eleven mammoth of a woman who somehow always managed to dominate every social interaction and reign over every conversation

---

1. The weekend.
2. The ritual feasts celebrating the beginning of the holiday of Passover.
3. Matchmaker.

as if she were Queen Elizabeth I. She was the kind of woman who wore Gucci embroidered gowns every day and garbed herself in mink furs and pearl earrings and diamond necklaces and Cartier rings and did herself up as if she were going out to a royal ball even when she was only going out to the grocery store. God bless this woman, Eli thought… God bless her… and God curse her. "Good to talk to you again. How are you?"

"*Nu*,[4] Eli, are you engaged yet?"

Chava had never been a woman for small talk. Eli simultaneously admired her and despised her for that peculiar virtue of hers, unable to make up his mind if it was a good thing to not waste time on "trivialities" and to only ever discuss "*tachlis*"[5] matters, as Chava called them. She would have made a model yeshiva *bochur*,[6] Eli used to think – she would have never *batelled*[7] and would have always been learning in the study hall; either that or she would have always been out on dates, trying with all her might to get married just as she had been trying with all her might for the past dozen years to marry off her surrogate son.

"I'm on my way to a big *chasunah*[8] now," she continued without letting Eli answer. "I don't have a lot of time to talk. My car should be here any minute. You're a good-looking boy, Eli. You should be married already. I have a *shidduch*[9] for you. Her name is Esti Epstein. She lives in Kew Gardens Hills. She's a – "

"I know, Chava," he said between tight lips, the vein in his neck starting to throb. "Yoni told me about her."

"Oh did he?… Good… You should take a drive down to Queens and take her out. She's a very nice girl. From a *choshuv*[10] family – a very

4. Well?
5. Goal-oriented.
6. Student.
7. Wasted time.
8. Wedding.
9. Match.
10. Important.

good family, Eli. You wouldn't have to worry about your *parnossah*[11] if you marry into that family, Eli. You understand?"

"Thank you, Chava…it's just – "

"Why don't you call her? I'll give you her number. She's expecting your call."

"Yoni gave me her email."

"*Nu*?! So email her!"

Eli moved the phone away from his mouth so that Chava wouldn't be able to hear his protracted sigh.

"Chava…I'm seeing someone now."

"Oh really?"

Eli wanted to reach through the phone and throttle her; the way she said "oh really?" made the bile rise from his gallbladder straight to his brain. He understood that "oh really?" perfectly well. It was an "oh really?" that said she never truly believed that a yeshiva boy who "looked like *that*" would be able to find a girl on his own; it was an "oh really?" that said that she had always believed that the only way a yeshiva *bochur* who "looked like *that*" could get married would be if he had a professional *shadchan*[12] working for him as if she were his agent, negotiating with another family and talking up his "good" qualities to such an extent that when it came time to actually meet him the girl wouldn't be taken aback by his "appearance" because she would have already heard so much about this *bochur's* virtues that perhaps, just *perhaps* she'd overlook that nonconformist "appearance" of his because of how much she respected *Shadchanis*[13] Braun's judgment. It was an "oh really?" that said that no one, not even his surrogate mother, believed in him; it was an "oh really?" that confirmed that he *was* truly alone in the world. It was an "oh really?" that drove him further into the arms of Emma – as if it were possible for his heart to embrace her even more strongly than it already had done; it was

11. Livelihood.
12. Matchmaker.
13. Matchmaker.

an "oh really?" that tore into him at his core, leaving nothing but the smoldering remains of his overheated heart.

"Nu? So what's so special about this girl?" she asked dryly, sounding as if she were a real estate agent about to lose a sale because her client had found another house all on his own that wasn't part of her listings. "She went to Harvard?"

"No, no … UCLA …" he lied, the blood inside his head pounding. "But she is very smart, yes."

"You met her in person?"

"No, just – "

"Then how?"

Why did he always feel as if he were on the witness stand when he spoke to her? Did she have no other method of communication? Was she one of these *frum*[14] housewives who had wanted to go to law school and become a lawyer but instead got married at twenty and started having children at twenty-two and never had had a career and so would act out these unfulfilled fantasies – or take out her simmering frustrations – on poor, defenseless people like him? Even when she would visit him at yeshiva it was always this way. "Eli, are you eating? Eli, what's in your refrigerator? Your refrigerator's empty. There's nothing in there. Why not? Don't you ever go out to the market? Why don't you stop learning for one hour and go to the market? Eli, are you seeing anyone? No? Why not? I have a girl for you. Her name is Shayna Moyal. She's from Far Rockaway. Very *frum*. But not too *frum*, you know? She's cooks, she bakes. She's a very good baker. What more do you need? You should see her, Eli. You should take her out. It's a good *shidduch*."[15] It never ended. And when it had finally ended after his failed relationship with Rena, it was as if a giant Juggernaut that had been weighing him down all these years, crushing his chest and smothering his mouth, had finally been lifted and he could at last breathe, truly *breathe*.

"*Nu*, Eli? How did you meet this girl?"

14. Religious.
15. Match.

"I met her...online, Chava."

"Online? What do you mean?"

"You know, these dating sites..."

"They don't have real *shadchanim*[16] working for these sites. I know these sites, Eli. Even the *frum* ones. You can't meet anybody online. It doesn't work."

"Well...I don't know, Chava.... a lot of people are doing it these days...I hear it really can work...I mean, it's working for me so far."

"You met her in person yet?"

"No, I told you. We've only been Skype-dating."

"*Skype*-dating? That doesn't work. You have to meet in person."

"Well...I'll see how it goes...if it keeps going well, I'll fly out there and meet her in person."

"*Fly? Ribbono shel olam!*[17], Eli! There are three thousand good girls right here from Baltimore to Brookline – a thousand in New York *alone* – and you want to *fly* somewhere to meet this girl? Are you out of your mind, Eli? Where is this girl?"

"Um...L.A.," he lied again, stifling a short, bitter laugh.

"Los *Angeles*?! She's a YULA girl?"

"Uh...yeah...yes..."

"You must be crazy, Eli. There are a thousand good girls two hours away from you in Brooklyn and Queens, and you want to go to Los *Angeles*?! Go to Kew Gardens Hills and see this Esti, Eli!"

"Chava, I already told you – I'm seeing someone, I can't just – "

"She's *frum*?"

".... Yes..." he said, adding silently to himself, 'she *will* be, since she's going to be marrying me...'

"In *L.A.*?...*ribbono shel olam*...what do her parents do?"

Now Eli truly wanted to throttle her. Why did it always have to come down to "what do her parents do?" and "what business is her family in?" and "how does her father make his *parnossah*?"[18] What

16. Matchmakers.
17. Good Lord.
18. Living.

about the *girl*?! Who *cares* what her father does! What about the kind of person the *girl* is and what *she* wants to do with her life!? Her father could be the King of Siam but if the girl was a complete dull bore who didn't have a thought in her head and whose only ambition in life was to mate and procreate like every other unthinking animal, Eli wouldn't care in the least about the girl Chava wanted to fix him up with – had she never understood this?!

"Well…um…" If he really had wanted to give her a heart attack and cause her to drop dead on the spot, he knew that all he had to tell her was that he was on the verge of marrying a Christian-born atheist from rural Pennsylvania whose father was a retired policeman, but he resisted the urge to tell her the truth; he was not so cold-blooded as to actually want to act out his murdering-his-surrogate-mother fantasies in real life.

"Well *what*, Eli? What do her parents do?"

"…Um…she doesn't really speak about her parents too much, so – "

"Why not?"

"Because…she's a *giyores*,"[19] he stammered, silently adding the words "soon-to-be" in front of the word "*giyores*." 'Yaakov Avinu[20] wasn't *meshaker*[21] when he told his father "*ani, Eisav bechorekha*,"'[22] Eli thought, holding his anxious arms stiffly at his sides. 'I'm not being *meshaker* either…'

"A *giyores*?! What is she, Persian?"

"Um…uh…yes…Persian…she's Persian…"

"*Ribbono shel olam*[23]…"

Eli bit his lip and bristled; it was a "*ribbono shel olam*" that said "look at you, Eli, you're already different. Why not find a nice normal Ashkenazi girl? Why make things as difficult for your children as they

19. Convert.
20. The biblical patriarch Jacob.
21. Lying.
22. "I am [Yaakov], Eisav [is] your firstborn."
23. Good Lord.

were for you? Don't you want your children to have an easier time in this community than you had?" It was a sarcastic, acerbic "*ribbono shel olam*" that Eli knew must have been the same "*ribbono shel olam*" that all those girls he'd taken out on dates in Baltimore had muttered to their roommates after the date. "So how was your date, Shoshana?" "Well, he's a really nice guy." "And?" "Well, I don't know. It was just..." "Just what?" "Well...he's...Ethiopian." "*Ethiopian?!*" "Well...I *think* he's Ethiopian..." "Ethiopian?! *Ribbono shel olam*, Shoshana...how do you keep getting set up with such strange guys? Last week it was the guy from Skokie with the funny ears, and now..."

"*Nu?!*" Chava pressed. "What makes this girl so special? She makes good brisket? Good kugel? She makes the best cholent you ever tasted?"

"No, Chava...actually, she doesn't cook."

"She doesn't *cook?!*" she yelped, sounding as if she had just been struck by a truck. "You have got to be kidding me, Eli! She doesn't *cook?! Pastnisht!*[24] What kind of good *frum* girl doesn't *cook?! Ribbono shel olam!...*Eli..." said Chava, signaling with her strident tone that she wanted to change the topic as quickly as possible. "Tzvi just got his *smicha*,"[25] she said, referring to Yoni's younger brother. "Did you know that?"

"No, I didn't know that, Chava. Mazal tov. That's wonderful."

"I was at his *chag haSmicha*[26] last week. Five hundred people, Eli. Five hundred rabbis. And all their families...They only do it once every four years and then all the rabbis that got *smicha* during those four years come and get their *klaf*[27] at the *chag haSmicha*. It's really something, Eli – what they're doing at the yeshiva here. Five hundred rabbis they've turned out in the past four years."

"I know," said Eli, knowing she was exaggerating the number by at least two hundred. "I was there for my *chag haSmicha* too once upon

---

24. Unacceptable.
25. Rabbinic ordination.
26. Ordination ceremony.
27. Ordination certificate.

a time. Yoni and I were in the same class. We walked up together to get our *klafs*, remember? And then – "

"Tzvi got a job as an assistant rabbi in Englewood, New Jersey. But I don't want him to be a rabbi, Eli. There's no money in being a rabbi. I told Yoni, 'give your brother a job at your accounting firm,' and Yoni promised to hold a spot for him. But Tzvi doesn't want it, Eli. He's crazy, Eli. He actually wants to be a rabbi. In a *shul*![28] It's madness, Eli – madness. I don't know what to do. And he's not even the main assistant rabbi – he's the second assistant…he's so smart, my Tzvi – you remember how he was, Eli. And now he's throwing his life away. He'll never get a *shidduch*.[29] No girl wants to marry a rabbi. When he was in yeshiva and getting his CPA he could've had any girl he wanted. Now no girls will go out with him. He's teaching math part-time at a yeshiva high school in Englewood, but there's no money in that either, Eli. Why don't you speak to Tzvi, Eli, and talk some sense into him? Won't you call up Tzvi and tell him to go work with his brother? He listens to you, Eli, he always did. Tell my Tzvi that a boy with a *kopf* [30] like that for numbers should get a real job. Tell him not to throw his life away."

"*Ribbono shel olam*," Eli muttered under his breath, feeling his temples exploding.

"My car is here, Eli. Do me a favor. Call Tzvi. Please."

"Ok, Chava. Enjoy the *chasunah*."[31]

"And call Esti. Forget about that Persian girl!"

"*Ribbono shel olam…*"

28. Synagogue.
29. Match.
30. Head.
31. Wedding.

NINE

Later that Sunday, as the haunting white light of the spectral crescent moon crept through his bedroom window, Eli checked his email one more time before going to sleep to see if there were any new messages from Emma; since she had sent him a few post-midnight emails, he'd gotten in the habit of checking his email when he knew he should really be reading or sleeping. There were no new messages from Emma, but Eli's face went pale and his heart began to palpitate upon seeing that his inbox displayed a new message, with the subject line left blank, from RenaBraun224@gmail.com:

Dear Eli,

I hope you've been well. I heard you're living in West Hartford now and working at NEHH. I think that's great. I'm still in Baltimore. Still working at the library. How is life in the northeast?

I wanted to say hi and belatedly apologize. I am deeply sorry for the way I behaved when we were dating and I'm even sorrier for the way I simply seemed to disappear from your life after our last date. I was going through a very chaotic time in my life, to say the least. I know that this does not excuse my conduct and my complete failure to communicate with you after what happened between us, but I did want to let you know that my head wasn't in the right place at that time.

I hope we can move on from what happened in the past and get to a better place. I have no illusions that this email can in any way rectify what I did or make up for my going MIA for a year and a half, but I just wanted to get this off my chest. You're a really good guy and deserve better than how I treated you. Please forgive me. If you ever want to meet up again, just let me know. It would be nice to see you again.

Take care,

– Rena

'Am I hallucinating?' he asked himself, suddenly feeling feverish and fatigued all at once. 'Did she really just email me? Just like that? Out of the blue? I could've sworn I'd never hear from her again…'

He rubbed his eyes, took two deep breaths, and read the email again.

'No…she really *did* email me…' He felt gimpy-armed, as if all his muscles had atrophied. 'I can't believe this. I cannot believe she really emailed me…but why? What is this all about? Is she trying to steal me away from Emma like a swallow swooping in to snatch a fly out of the mouth of a frog? But how could she have found out about our relationship? Emma's been so careful about not saying anything to anybody about us – at least I think she's been careful about it…but people have ways of finding out things these days if they really want to,' he thought, speculating nervously. '"*Ki ohf haShamayim yolikh es hakol…*"[1] So maybe she did find out. I don't know how, but maybe she did…So is that what this is about? Does she want one last chance with me? One last chance before it's too late?'

He started typing a response to her – "Dear Rena, Great to hear from you, how are you?" – but soon thought the better of it and deleted the draft. 'I need to go to sleep,' he thought, shutting down his computer and massaging his half-closed eyelids. 'I can't get involved in this now…I'm too tired…Besides, getting involved in this at all is probably a bad idea. What if I were to meet up with her again and find

---

1. "A bird in the sky will carry your words…"

out that she was interested in dating me again? How could I do that to Emma, after everything she's been through?... Yeah... best not to get involved in this at all...' He recited his bedtime prayers and closed his bleary eyes, the Connecticut quiet broken only by the tooting of an owl outside his befogged window and by the ghostly voice of a never-entirely forgotten Baltimorean inside his throbbing head...

The following day, with the scent of fresh snow hanging heavy in the air, sneaking into the classrooms like the tantalizing aroma of freshly baked chocolate chip cookies – a mere whiff of it was enough to drive Eli's students mad over the fact that all public schools in Connecticut had decided to cancel school that day while NEHH, and only NEHH, had inexplicably decided to remain open – he saw Emma twice while walking through the hallway on his way to the bathroom and received playful yet discreet smiles from her each time; he himself, though, still too nervous about what would happen to him were he to be seen smiling in that sort of way at her, kept his smiles more restrained. As soon as the school day was over, he walked back to his apartment, plodding through the cumbrous thicket of slush, snow and ice left by the previous night's late-March nor'easter, and immediately began composing a reply to Rena.

> Dear Rena,
>
> It is so nice to hear from you. Thank you so much for your message. Of course I forgive you. I really hope you're doing well. Yes, you are correct, I'm working and living in West Hartford. Other than that, not much new to report on my end. It's taken me some time to adjust to life in New England. But I don't know if I've fully gotten used to things up here. Or if I ever will.
>
> Kol tuv,[2]
> – Eli

A second after hitting "send" he shut his eyes tightly and let a loud canine howl, immediately regretting having sent the email. He thought about writing her a quick follow-up email but quickly decided against

2. All the best.

it. 'I've written her enough for now,' he thought, walking to the kitchen to make himself up a cup of decaffeinated green tea. 'I don't need to write her a whole long *arichus*.[3] Let her respond first, and then I'll write her another email…it's like what Rav Kramer always used to say about the long Tosfoses[4] – everyone always gets intimidated by the long Tosfoses but it's the shorter ones that are the hardest. The long ones are easy – Tosfos is giving you so much information to work with. But those short ones, when you're barely being given anything – you really have to work for those ones. So let her work a little, why not. Why not see if she's actually seriously interested this time, or whether as soon as things get serious she'll just back out and disappear like she did the first time…but why did I lie to her?'

He had typed "not much new to report on my end" by habit; that was what he'd been used to writing to his friends whenever they asked him what was going on in his personal life. Writing anything else seemed as farfetched as writing that he'd gone to Pluto. Still, he wondered, as he looked at his sent message again with unblinking eyes, why had he lied? Why couldn't he have simply told her that he was now dating someone? It would have been so easy: "I'm sorry, Rena," he could have written, "as much as I'd like to see you, I've started seeing someone else. But I wish you the best of luck." Did he lie to her about having "not much new to report" in his life because he was secretly hoping that he *would* see her again? Was he secretly hoping that she would ask him directly for another date? She had been very direct that day in the movie theater – maybe she would take the liberty of being that direct with him once again…

'Still,' Eli wondered, as he took a sip of his tea and gazed outside at the eerily still, soundless, cottony whiteness that lay over West Hartford like a white car cover over a convertible, protecting the delicate sports car from the elements until it was ready for summer, 'why did I lie? If Emma is everything I've ever wanted – if she really is the woman I'm preparing to devote myself to for life – then why did I so

3. Lengthy discursus.
4. Medieval commentary on the Talmud.

carelessly leave the door open for Rena to walk back in to my life?' He knew that if Emma was the true treasure that he had been waiting his entire life to find, he should have been bolting the door shut with the strongest planks and sturdiest nails he could find; instead, not only had he left the door open, but he was taking apart the panels, unscrewing the hinges and playing baseball with the knob. Before returning to his lesson-planning, he assured himself that he would rebuild the door and seal it shut; the presence of Emma in his life was more important to him than anything he could ever imagine, so why risk losing her over the infinitesimal chance that Rena actually *would* want to date him again? Eli slogged on through his lesson-planning, vowing to tell Rena the next time she emailed him that he *was* seeing someone now – and that it was going quite well – and that if he were to ever see her again, it would only be within the context of him spending a Jewish holiday with Yoni; seeing her anywhere other than the Brauns' house in Baltimore would be out of the question.

TEN

"Would you like to touch me?" she asked. Emma was lying next to him on his bed, wearing a sleeveless tight-fitting blue velvet dress; he was wearing a plain white t-shirt and a pair of red-and-white Houston Rockets shorts. He had placed two powder-blue reading pillows between them as a separation barrier, signaling to her that although he was permitting himself to lie next to her, he would still refuse to do anything further with her.

'What are you doing?!' a sharp voice in his head shouted. 'This is *asur*![1] You know you can't do this until you're married!'

'The Rambam[2] says *chuppah*[3] is *yichud*,'[4] he answered, licking his lips, upon which he could still taste a few crumbs of the chocolate chip cookies that she had brought up to his apartment when she had knocked on the door an hour earlier and had asked him if he had any tea. 'So as long as we have *yichud hara'ui lebiah*[5] this will be as good as *nisuin*.'[6]

'First of all that's only when she's *muteres*[7] to you and Emma

1. Prohibited.
2. Maimonides.
3. The marital canopy of the wedding ceremony (i.e., marriage).
4. Seclusion.
5. Seclusion that lasts for at least seven minutes (or at least five minutes – or nine; opinions vary).
6. Marriage.
7. Permitted.

is obviously not! So this *"chuppah"* you think you're doing here is a *chuppas nidah*,[8] and even though by[9] *chuppas nidah* the Rambam holds that *kiddushin*[10] is *chal*,[11] he holds that *nisuin*[12] is *not chal*! But more importantly you know we don't allow this kind of *"chuppah"* that you're trying to do here *bizman hazeh!*[13] You can't get married without a *kesubah*[14] and *bircas nisuin!'*[15]

'But – '

'And even if you *were* married you can't do this until she's *tehorah!'*[16]

'The Gemara[17] says *hu b'bigdo v'hi b'bigda*[18] with no *kiruv basar*[19] is *mutar,'*[20] he responded, dropping his arms to his sides and looking tensely at Emma.

'You know we don't *posken*[21] like that *de'ah!'*[22] the voice replied. *'V'afilu hochi,*[23] we only have that *havamina*[24] by[25] *ish v'ishto*[26] when there's *pas b'salo,*[27] not in a case of *libo gahs bah*[28] like there clearly is with you two!!'

8. A marital ceremony during which the bride is not ritually pure.
9. In a case of.
10. Betrothal.
11. Takes effect.
12. Marriage.
13. Nowadays.
14. Marriage contract.
15. The blessings of the wedding ceremony.
16. Not impure.
17. Talmud.
18. Lying on the same bed with clothes on (during a woman's period of ritual impurity).
19. Physical contact.
20. Permitted.
21. Decide the law.
22. Opinion.
23. And even so.
24. Conjecture.
25. Regarding.
26. A married couple.
27. Familiarity.
28. Pre-marital attraction.

'Yes, but – '

'And why did you allow her to come up to your apartment in the first place?!'

'She said she was cold and she wanted something hot to drink to warm up. How could I not let her?'

'She was cold?!' said the voice in a harsh snicker. 'A likely story! This is when you have to be cold with *her*! Just tell her no! It would be so easy! N-O! *"Kol mi shena'asa rach'man bim'kom ach'zari sof na'aseh ach'zari bimkom rach'man"*!'[29]

'Don't worry,' he replied nervously, watching Emma play with her hair. 'I won't do anything that I'm not allowed to do.'

'"Not allowed to do"!?' sneered the voice, spitting his words back in his face. 'You already *did* something you weren't allowed to do! You're already *over*[30] the *issur yichud*!'[31]

'Don't worry,' he replied feebly. 'I'll be careful...'

'"You'll be *careful*"?! *Ein apotropos la'arayos!*'[32]

'I put a *mechitzah*[33] up between us.'

'*Mechitzah*!? What *mechitzah*?! These pillows?! *Pillows* as a *mechitzah*!? What you need is a *metchitzah shel barzel*[34] between you and her, not a couple of goose down pillows!!'

"Would you like to touch me?" she repeated, her voice warm and inviting, her fragrance sweet, her eyes iridescent.

"...Yes..." he said, his heart banging wildly.

She reached over the row of pillows that separated them from each other and touched his left index finger with her right index finger, swirling it around the circumference of his fingernail like an illustrator tracing a circle around a penny. She then touched all the tips of his

29. "One who is merciful when he should be cruel will eventually become cruel when he needs to be merciful."
30. In violation of.
31. The prohibition of seclusion with a non-relative/non-spouse of the opposite sex.
32. "There is no such thing as too much caution in the realm of forbidden relations."
33. Partition.
34. A partition of iron.

left hand's fingers with all the tips of her right hand's lacquered, well-manicured fingers, at first tapping lightly on his fingers before coming to a slow stop and resting on them. He felt goosebumps erupting like millions of little volcanoes all across his tingling flesh. Not knowing what to do, he spun his fingers around hers in slow spiral motions just as she had done a moment before with her index finger. She clasped his hand and, as if their movements were guided by an unconscious instinct rather than by a volitional will, their fingers fully interlaced.

'What are you doing?!' shouted the voice in his head. 'The Rambam[35] holds *Lo sik'revu* [36] is a *de'oraisa!*'[37]

'The Ramban[38] says it's a *derabanan,*'[39] he replied.

'The Shulkhan Arukh[40] *poskens*[41] like the Rambam!!'

'*Ein hochi nami,*'[42] he replied to the voice, its forbidding tone echoing in his ears as Emma's cascading hair danced in his eyes. 'But Emma and I will be married.'

'But you're not allowed to marry her.'

'She will convert.'

'No she won't.'

"'*Le'asid lavo ba'im umos ha'olam umisgairim.*'"[43]

"'*Le'asid lavo,*"[44] not *bizman hazeh!*"[45]

'Except for Emma. Emma will convert.'

'No she won't. Stop deluding yourself. You know there's no chance of that happening.'

---

35. Maimonides.
36. The prohibition of touching non-family members of the opposite sex (other than one's spouse).
37. A biblical prohibition.
38. Nachmanides.
39. A rabbinic prohibition.
40. The Code of Jewish Law.
41. Holds like.
42. Yes...
43. "In the future all the nations of the world will come and convert."
44. In the future.
45. Today.

'Whatever... I don't care...'

'What?! What did you say?!'

'Go away.'

'You don't *care*?! But this is *asur*![46] What you're doing now is completely *asur*! *Asur asur asur asur*!

'Go away!'

'Asur asur asur asur!'

'Stop it!'

'This is a *de'oraisa*![47] You're about to be *over*[48] a *de'oraisa*!'

'I'll do *teshuvah*.'[49]

'"*Ha'omer echetah v'ashuv echetah v'ashuv...*"[50]

"I *know* what it says! Am I not allowed to do *one* aveirah[51] in my life?! Not even *one*?!"

'"*Ein choteh niskar!*"[52]

"Can't you just be quiet?! Please?! For once in my life, can't you just be quiet and leave me alone?! Please!...'

'But you will burn in *Gehenom*[53] for this.'

A cold knot of terror tightened around his heart. Silver streaks of lightning dashed across the sky; thunder shook the ground. He shivered, twitched involuntarily, and tried to wipe the tortured expression off of his blanched, bloodless face.

He reached for her hand again. He was surprised at how warm it was. He had always imagined that a woman's touch was supposed to feel cool and titillating, like the way he remembered Jessica's hand feeling all those years ago. He was mildly disappointed that Emma's hand felt so warm and clammy in his. It was almost like touching his own hand; he shuddered at the thought.

He tried to move his fingers around hers to see if he could create

46. Prohibited.
47. Biblical prohibition.
48. In violation of.
49. Repentance.
50. "One who says 'I will sin and repent'... "
51. Sin.
52. "A sinner is not rewarded."
53. Hell.

some sort of movement that would give him a cooler, more pleasurable sensation. He rubbed his fingers up and down hers like two sets of windshield wipers, trying to rub away the odd indifference that he was so surprised to find himself feeling. As he moved his fingers and palm over the back of her hand, she slid her hand even further forward, stroking the inside of his forearm with the back of her hand; this felt more pleasurable to him, but still not particularly stimulating.

He stroked the outside of her forearm with his palm and found it to be surprisingly hairy, like a boy's arm; his hand recoiled. He moved his hand further up her arm and caressed her upper arm, finding it rough and bumpy; he had always imagined that a woman's arm would feel soft and smooth. He made a mental note to himself that if he were to ever touch her again, he would avoid touching her arms.

"How does it feel to touch me?" she asked in a reedy, half-hoarse voice, almost whispering.

"It feels nice," he lied, looking directly into her big, green oyster-sized eyes.

"It's nice to touch you too," she said, smiling with her enormous eyes while her face remained inert, strangely expressionless.

She softly stroked the outside of his forearm and the lower end of his upper arm with the tips of her fingers, then cupped his bicep with her palm, sliding her hand over its rounded, well-defined contours as if she were smoothing a softball-sized stone.

"Would you like to kiss me?" she asked, gracefully inclining her head slightly upwards and arching her eyebrows invitingly.

'You better not.'

'I thought I already told you to go away.'

'But this is not allowed! You will – '

'That's enough out of you for tonight! Just leave me alone. Please. Just for tonight.'

'But – !'

'Ssshhhh!'

"...Yes..." he said, holding her gaze.

He instinctively drew his breath in, leaned his head to the left and bent it toward hers; she did the same. A few strands of her hair tickled his nose. He could feel her perfumed breath on the side of his neck. As soon as he touched his lips to hers, she began stroking his stiff, sloppy lips with her supple, flexible lips and plunged her tongue into his mouth.

'Why did she do that with her tongue?' he asked himself, shocked and feeling almost violated at her having unexpectedly inserted one of her appendages into one of his orifices. 'Is that how you're supposed to kiss? Like *that*? With your *tongue*?.... Does she want me to do that too?...with my tongue?...to put it in her mouth?...'

He tried sliding his tongue into her mouth, searching for her tongue with his, but he hit his upper teeth against hers instead. He pulled his tongue out of her mouth and his lips away from her face, pausing to catch his breath. When she noticed that he was ready to resume, she placed her lips back on his and once again reached into his mouth with her tongue. This time, he simply tried to mirror each movement of her mouth, matching every movement of her lips and tongue with a reciprocal movement of his, imitating her lips' pulling and sucking and her tongue's swirling and licking as if he were a six-year-old playing a game of Simons Says. This time he had a bit more success in coordinating his lips with hers but still hit her two front teeth with his teeth a few times.

He was surprised at how unexciting it felt; after all the novels he had read and all the breathless descriptions of the wonders of kissing he had imbibed, he was stupefied that it did not feel more arousing. It felt more like a strange activity that aliens from another galaxy engaged in than an act that was supposed to symbolize the height of human passion. 'What am I doing wrong?' he wondered, as he pulled his mouth away from hers. 'Isn't this supposed to feel like the most amazing thing in the world? Why don't I feel anything? What is wrong with me?'

"How does it feel to kiss me?" she asked, looking at him solicitously.

"It feels nice," he lied again, quickly becoming adept at acting despite never having taken a single theater class in his life.

"It feels nice to kiss you, too," she said affectionately, this time smiling with her lips as well.

"You realize this is the first time I've ever kissed a girl," he said, feeling the need to apologize for his ham-handed attempt.

"Yeah. It was pretty obvious."

"How did I do?"

"You did fine."

"Really?"

"Yeah."

"Oh...ok."

"Would you like to try again?"

"...Yes."

This time he felt slightly more confident kissing her, not needing to exactly imitate the movements of her lips and tongue, but he still knocked his teeth against hers once or twice. Her lips and tongue moved more aggressively around his mouth as well, as if trying to impress her attractiveness upon him by the sheer force of her mouth.

"What are you thinking?" she asked, finally relenting and releasing his mouth from the lock of her lips.

"My mind is blank," he answered, preferring to tell her nothing rather than lie to her again.

"I don't believe that," she said, stroking the back of his head with her hand. "You're a man of words. Books are your life. Your mind can't be blank."

"Well..." *What can I tell her? I can't reveal what I'm really thinking to her. That wouldn't be fair – to me or to her...* "What are *you* thinking?"

"Me? I'm thinking, 'I wonder what Eli is thinking.' That's what I'm thinking. C'mon. Tell me what you're thinking."

"Well...ok...I'm thinking...I'm thinking, 'why does this not feel like how I thought it was supposed to feel?'"

"Do you not like kissing me?"

"No – I...I mean, it's not you, it's just..."

"Just what?"

"I don't know..."

She removed her hand from the back of his head and looked at him concernedly.

"So it's not me," she said, crossing her arms. "Ok...is it that you don't like kissing women?"

He opened his mouth but no response came out.

"Maybe you like men?"

"I – no! I mean…*no*…no, it's not that – "

"It would be ok if you did. Really. It would."

"No, no, it's not that…I don't like men…it's just that…this was the first time I've ever kissed anyone, and I don't know if – I guess what I'm trying to say is, it felt strange. Not because I didn't like it. I did. Very much so. It's just that it was the first time, and I've never experienced anything remotely like this. It felt strange not because I didn't like it but because of how new it was for me. That's all."

"I understand," she said sweetly, nodding her head, but still eying him with concern. "It will feel better the next time. And even better the time after that. I promise. The more you do it, the more you'll want to do it. You'll start to really like it – I mean, *really* like it…you'll start to want to do it all the time…"

She kissed him on his left cheek and giggled like a schoolgirl.

"What?" he asked. "What's so funny?" *She's laughing at me. I know it. She's laughing at how terrible of a kisser I am; she's laughing at this pathetic, inexperienced man-boy who until the age of thirty never even kissed a girl.*

"You're just very cute," she said, smiling amusedly and tenderly stroking the back of his head again. "That's all."

She kissed him again on the lips and once again slid her tongue into his mouth, and he did the same, this time not hitting her teeth at all; their tongues twirled together like two Olympian ice skaters, and their lips looped and coiled with a surprising simultaneous symmetry that Eli found uncanny – it now suddenly felt to him as if they had been kissing each other every night for the past seven years – and, at last, arousing. She slowly pulled her lips away from his, locked eyes with him and smiled beguilingly.

"Would you like to spend the night with me?" she asked, with a charming, disarming look in her dusky eyes, the warmth of her voice melting away his inhibitions.

"Yes," he said, this time not hesitating for even a moment.

ELEVEN

On Tuesday night, instead of preparing his lesson plans for the following day's classes as he knew he should have been doing, Eli logged onto Facebook and started scrolling through Emma's pictures again. Over twenty-four hours had passed since he had emailed Rena and he hadn't heard back from her yet, but there was a new message in his inbox from Emma. "Hi Eli!," she had written; her exclamation mark next to his name alone was enough to set his mind awhirl, and he immediately started fantasizing about rendezvousing with Emma in the school janitor's closet like Mrs. Krabappel and Principal Skinner in The Simpsons, but he quickly froze the fantasy mid-scene, reminding himself that it was forbidden to entertain those kinds of thoughts for even a millisecond. He continued reading her email:

> Have you ever read Kurt Vonnegut's *Sirens of Titan*? I've never been much of a Vonnegut person, but yesterday while rearranging my bookshelves I found an old copy of it and started reading. The first line made me think of you – it was something like "everyone now knows how to find the meaning of life within himself." I'm not sure why it made me think of you, but it just did. I guess I was wondering, "What would Eli think about that? Would somebody religious – somebody whose reverence for tradition and respect for communal authority indicates that his sources of meaning are external to

himself – believe you can find meaning with*in* yourself?" Perhaps this is something we can talk about next time…

Anyway, I look forward to talking to you again on Thursday. 9 p.m. works for me again. Enjoy the rest of your night!

– Emma

He had seen her Facebook pictures five, six, maybe seven times already, so why was he looking at them again? It was as if he were a small, cold planet that was constantly compelled to remain within its sun's orbit, no matter how much it wanted to pull away from the lure of its scorching, life-giving star. He gazed at a picture of her where her upper arms did not look taut and toned but shapeless and flabby; he quickly scrolled down and found another picture where her arms looked slimmer. What was he worried about? Hadn't he by now seen her in person numerous times? Why this constant need to reappraise her? Why this constant need to continually reassure himself that he was attracted to her? Why this constant need to look at her Facebook pictures for the five-hundredth time? It was as if he continually needed to reassure himself that he found her body as appealing as he found her mind. Never before, with the exception of Rena, had he met a woman whose mind was more attractive to him than her body. If Emma aroused any degree of desire in him, it was less directed toward her hips than toward her head; his greatest, most secret desire was that he wanted – if it were somehow possible – to make love to her mind. He knew that such a notion would sound bizarre, if not downright deranged, to any sane person, but if it would have been possible to touch his brain to hers and caress its soft, tender knowledge-filled neurons and rub his enlightenment-seeking cerebellum on her scholarly cerebral cortex until their brain fluids intermingled and fertilized each other with the fruits of ecstatic intellection, he would've done it. This peculiar desire caused him so much consternation that, without realizing that he was even doing it, he constantly sought to reassure himself that it wasn't only her intellect that he found exciting. He was simply using her pictures as a kind of strange pH test, trying to ascertain whether her image was producing the proper chemical reaction in his body; he had no intention of actually doing anything about it once he found the results of the test to be successful – he merely wanted to confirm that she "worked." Why, though, was he still seeking this confirmation day after day, night after night? Wasn't one "pH test" sufficient? And weren't the "tests" that he had been conducting during their video-chats sufficiently demonstrative? '*Ribbono shel olam*,'[1] he thought, his fingers fluttering restlessly on his knees. 'I must truly be the strangest person alive. Good thing only You, Hashem, can see my thoughts, because if *chazal*[2] could see them I'd probably be *chayav makas mardus*[3] seven times over by now...'

In the sleepy silence of the mid-week night, as spring winds came swelling from the west and rain pattered against his bedroom windowpane, Eli closed his volume of Talmud and opened his computer, hoping for a new message from Rena. Upon seeing no new bolded messages from RenaBraun224@gmail, he closed his tired, irritated eyes and rubbed the back of his aching neck. 'What is going on with her *now*?' he asked himself, staring stonily at his empty inbox. 'Why would she send that email of hers and not want to follow up after *my* email? Was her email just a tease? A way to get my hopes up about her yet again?...Is this all a test? Hashem[4] wanting to find out if I can be *omed b'nisayon*?'[5] A few minutes later, as the clouds concealing the night sky began to disperse and thick, milky moonlight started spilling through Eli's bedroom window, covering his computer with a translucent, chromatic sheen, a new message appeared in his inbox:

"Hi Eli!" wrote Emma,

I hope you're having a good night. I just wanted to let you know how much I'm looking forward to our third video-chat date tomorrow night. The first couple of pages of *The Sirens of Titan* have actually been quite good... what the rest will be like I don't know, but it did kind of remind me of *The Twilight Zone*. I usually don't

---

1. Good Lord.
2. The rabbis.
3. Punished with lashes.
4. God.
5. Withstand temptation.

go for science fiction but I did like *The Twilight Zone*. Some of my only fond memories of childhood are of watching *Twilight Zone* marathons with my dad on this really old TV that we had. Most of the time I couldn't stand my father, as you know – and I still can't stand him – but this was one of the only times I can remember us actually getting along and not being at each other's throats about something... so maybe that's why I'm liking *Sirens of Titan*... nostalgia can be a pretty powerful force, I guess...

Anyways... it's almost midnight, so I should probably go to bed. Looking forward to speaking with you soon!

– Emma ;o)

After shutting down his computer, he brushed his teeth and recited his bedside prayers, his mind swirling with a strange mixture of giddiness and foreboding. He tried to read in bed, as was his custom – he had just started *The Fall* because of how much he knew Emma liked Camus – but his eyes glazed over the words, and all he could see before him were four letters: E-M-M-A... and the smiley-face icon with which she had signed her email. E-M-M-A... E-M-M-A... He closed the book and looked up at the ceiling; those four simple letters hovered before his eyes like the four letters of the ineffable name of God. "*Shivisi* E-M-M-A *l'negdi tamid*,"[6] he said to himself, his body prickling with desire. "Because she is at my right hand; I shall not be moved..." The image of the black-type letters of her name emblazoned upon the white background of his inbox hovered in the mist of his eyes like four pieces of Swiss milk chocolate lying invitingly on a white wax wrapper; he tasted the name in his mouth, letting its subtle saltiness tickle his tongue and its sinful sweetness suffuse his whole body.

The exclamation mark she had placed after his name made him so excited and filled him with so much energy that he felt that if he were to jump, his soul – if not his body – would exit the atmosphere and reach the moon. He knew how rare it was for a serious writer to use exclamation marks – Rena had once told him that exclamation marks were the "endangered species" of punctuation because writers

---

6. "I have set [E-M-M-A] always before me."

were not supposed to use more than two exclamation marks per every one hundred thousand words of prose – and so he counted the exclamation marks in Emma's emails as if they were pandas, excitedly hoping that they would procreate and reproduce themselves twofold, perhaps even fourfold, in her next email. He was particularly dizzy with delight over the smiley-face she had placed next to her name – a full, open-mouthed smile: Emma ;o)

'Oh my…' was the unfinished thought that flitted through his mind upon seeing that smiley-face for the first time. '*Three* exclamation marks, *and* a full smile…' There was something suggestive, almost sensual, about that smiley-face to him, even though – and perhaps *because* – it consisted merely of a semicolon, the lower-case letter "o," and a closing parentheses mark; if she had texted him a picture of her flashing him an actual smile it wouldn't have had the same effect upon him. The smiley-face she had emailed to him wasn't even a yellow emoji smiley-face; this smile was a smile created out of sterile letters and inert punctuation marks affixed to the name of the living, breathing, four-letter-named woman whose essence was words, sentences, letters, punctuation marks, grammar, diction, syntax…and books – and what was more stimulating to him than *that*? The mere thought of that semi-colon smile was enough to stir him out of bed and make him wish for a genie who would magically make all of the religious restrictions that were shackling him disappear so that he could go up to Emma without any fear the next day and say, "Let's drop this internet video-chatting and go out on a *real* date. I don't care if people see me with you. All I care about is you; I couldn't care less about what other people would say if they were to found out that we're together. We like each other, and that's all that matters. We should celebrate that, not be afraid of it. That's all I wanted to tell you, Emma – that I'm no longer afraid. Let's go out tonight. I'll take you to dinner. You won't have many choices of where to go if you're with me – there's only one kosher restaurant in all of Hartford – but we can do other things together besides eat…"

'Is she the one?' he found himself thinking as he struggled to fall asleep. 'Could she be…could she really be my *bashert*…?'[7] He hastily

---

7. Destined spouse.

tried to dismiss the thought from his mind – after all, as he reminded himself, the foolish notion that there was a "one" for him was only a new variation of the same reckless romanticism that had gotten him into such emotional trouble when Rena had let him down after he had gotten his hopes so dangerously up – but he couldn't help thinking that maybe, just maybe this time it would be different. "Hear O Eli," he thought he could hear a voice within him saying, "EMMA is your beloved, EMMA is the One.... Forget Rena – you have *Emma*..."

'What a ridiculous thing to think,' he said to himself, the image of the black-type letters of her name emblazoned upon the white background of his inbox still hovering in the haze of his eyes. 'You should be embarrassed that you even let such a thought cross through your mind.' But 'what *if*?' he thought. 'What if things will be different this time? Just because you've kept flipping the coin and getting tails doesn't mean the next time you're guaranteed to get tails again – maybe this is finally your time to get heads? Maybe after all this time this is *it* – you're about to finally get heads – and maybe all you need to do is muster up the courage to pick that coin up off the ground and flip it just one more time... Why not give it just one more flip? How can you be so sure it won't work out? Maybe, just maybe things *will* work out this time...' Maybe it was his *rationalism* that was reckless, he thought. Maybe it was *rationalism* that was foolish and irresponsible, because it was rationalism that would cause him to give *up* hope when perhaps the very thing he needed to do now *was* to hope, if just for a little while longer... Rationalism was telling him to cut off his budding relationship with Emma and take a drive down to Kew Gardens Hills to meet some girl named Esti – and what would be more reckless than *that*? Rationalism was telling him to go look for a 23-year-old religious Jewish girl from Queens and forget about a 33-year-old lapsed Catholic woman from Pennsylvania – but what if *rationalism* was wrong this time? What if Emma really *was* the one? Then wouldn't it be reckless to heed his *rationalism*?

He rubbed his nose, turned over in bed, and drifted off into a dreamless sleep.

TWELVE

"Well," said Emma to Eli as they entered their hotel room after the wedding, drained from dancing and exhausted from hours of small-talk but energized by the prospect of what else lay ahead of them, "I do appreciate you wearing a tux. That was really sweet of you to do that for me...I still can't believe you've never worn one until tonight...why was it you said they don't wear tuxes at *frahm* weddings?"

"*Frum.*"[1]

"What?"

"*Frum,*" he repeated, his voice hoarse and scratchy from having to shout over the absurdly loud band for four hours. "It's pronounced *frum*. Rhymes with numb."

"Oh...huh...what was I saying? It doesn't matter...well," she continued, easily sliding her feet out of her jeweled satin heels, "I guess it's time..." A sly, conspiratorial smile slowly sauntered across her rouged face, and an impish glint glittered in her reanimated eyes.

"Yeah," said Eli, feigning reluctance and modestly averting his eyes from Emma as she slipped off her wedding gown. "I guess it is..."

Eli, continuing to look away from Emma lest he catch a glimpse

---

1. Religious.

of her before she was ready for him, plopped down on the king-sized bed and began, with great difficulty, to take off his black patent leather shoes. The pair they had given him at Men's Warehouse when he had gone to rent his tuxedo had been too tight, but he had been too embarrassed to ask the slim, dark-skinned saleswoman for another pair because he hadn't wanted to come across to her as too demanding, but now he was paying for his diffidence with the very kind of awkward straining and agitated yanking that he had keenly wished to avoid in front of Emma. The most he could hope for was that she had gone into the bathroom and wasn't witnessing this pathetic spectacle. When he had at last mercifully removed the twin torture devices that had been tormenting his feet for the better part of five hours, he slowly stood up and faced the mirror directly opposite the bed in order to begin to take off his suspenders. He snatched off his watch and laid it on the dresser to the right of the mirror, next to Emma's well-worn gilt-edged copy of *Leaves of Grass*. He noticed that the tan-shaded bedside lamp had suddenly dimmed, and now cast only a faint, twilight glow upon the undone bedspread. He had only just begun to undo his clip-on bowtie when he felt two bare, slender arms smelling of rosemary-scented perfume encircle him from behind and saw two creamy white hands reach for the little black buttons of his French front shirt. Eli raised his eyes and in the reflection of the mirror saw Emma standing behind him, wearing only white panties and a Rothko-red bra, with her arms enclosed around him like a ring around a finger.

"What are you d – "

"Ssshhh...." she whispered, cocking her head to the left and bending it ever so slightly over his shoulder. She undid the buttons of his shirt one by one, letting them fall to the floor with no regard for the fact that in three days Eli was responsible for returning the entire black-and-white ensemble to Men's Warehouse completely intact, every single button included. He instinctively stooped down to collect the buttons, but Emma grabbed on to his suspenders before his hands could reach the carpet and pulled him back up.

"No," she said, beginning to unclip his suspenders. "Don't worry about that now."

She slid her hands under his shirt, running her fingers along the contours of his firm abdomen and tense chest, and began kissing the back of his neck. As his shirt and pants fell to the floor, her undone hair fell across his chest. She lifted her head again and looked at him in the mirror, and then, with her hands massaging his stiffened torso, looked back down at his chest. She curled her right leg around his right thigh, slowly sliding it up and down several times like a paintbrush on a blank canvas until she was able to ascertain that it had produced the desired effect. She moved her hands across his body, touching his tightening upper arms and kissing him on his shoulders, and then circled in front of him, wrapping her right thigh around his left leg, and began guiding him toward the bed.

'Why am I not feeling anything?' Eli fretted, his head drooping as she tugged off the bedspread and laid him down on his back as if he were a six-foot doll. 'What is going on? After all the waiting, all the yearning, all the working out just so I'd be in shape for precisely this moment…and now *this*? I cannot believe this. You have got to be kidding me…'

Emma crawled onto his lower body, her knees gracing his ankles, and bent her head downwards, caressing his convulsing feet and showering wet kisses on his quivering calves. Her perfumed breath licked at his legs, and her body heat trickled into him like decanted wine; he sipped, but didn't gulp.

'I can't understand this,' Eli said in his head, his arms hanging limply at his sides as Emma's lips began to make a slow upward progression along the longitude of his upper left leg. 'It's not like I've been waiting eighteen years for this or anything…why *now*? Why is this happening *now*? This is everything I've ever wanted, everything I've ever dreamed of…at least I *think* it's everything I ever dreamed of…unless…'

As her lips reached his lower left groin, neither his mind nor his eyes were fixed on her head; instead of thinking about how and when he was supposed to reach behind her back and unfasten her bra, he was thinking about the little black buttons of his rented tuxedo, and about how difficult it would be to find them all, scattered as they were across the thick dark-gray carpet. And he thought about how upset he would be to disappoint that saleswoman, that long-limbed, flat-chested, cocoa-skinned saleswoman – he thought about how unhappy he would be when he would go to return the tuxedo and would see the saddened look in her kindly hazel eyes when she would see that he had lost those two black buttons. And he sensed, as Emma began to do something to him that he didn't think was allowed in Jewish law, that his mind was elsewhere – in his books, in the Men's Warehouse dressing room, in next week's Vikings-Saints game – everywhere else but where it was supposed to be…

As Emma crawled further up the bed and slid her hands up along the ridges of his abdomen, her glossy, milk-white thighs resting lightly but firmly upon his, he tried to rouse himself to action, stroking her silky sun-streaked hair and setting his mouth on her licorice-colored lips. He tried to think of things he could do to her that would be as pleasurable for her as what she was doing to him, but his mind was dry, a well without water, and into the vacuum slithered serpentine statements from the Sages of the Talmud: *"Mahu liv'ol bis'chila b'Shabbos, dam mifkad pakid o chaburei michbar…Ben tesha shanim v'yom echad bi'aso biah, pachos miben shmonah ein bi'aso biah…Asurah laba'al asurah labo'el…HaKol yod'in kala lama nichn'sa lechupah ela kol hamenabel piv afilu chosmin alav g'zar din shel shivim shana l'tova hof'chin alav l'ra'a…"*

His hands were draped around Emma's waist, but his mind was wrapped around the sections of the Talmud that had once been merely academic but were now suddenly, palpably, urgently relevant to him for the first time in his life: *"Amar Rebbe Yochanan ben D'havai, chigrin mipnei mah havyan, mipnei shehofchim es shulchanam; sumin, mipnei shemistaklim b'oso makom…K'shehu mesaper megaleh tefach um'chaseh tefach v'domeh alav k'mi shek'fa'o sheid…"* The swirling sayings began to coalesce into a dense cloud in his book-cluttered consciousness, spinning like an eros-sapping cyclone and threatening to destroy any source of sensual stimulation in its defenseless path.

As his right hand softly grazed her lower back while his left hand traced the curvature of her torqueing hips, his mind finally touched upon a Talmudic teaching that he sensed was serviceable, even galvanizing: "*Amru chachamim ein halacha k'yochanan ben d'havai ela kol mah she'adam rotzeh la'asos be'ishto oseh...*" 'Okay,' he responded to the saying in his mind, his gaze orbiting the walls rather than Emma's eyes, 'but what exactly do I want to do?...And how do I do it?...And when?...Is there an order to things here?...Some kind of *seder*[2] I'm supposed to follow?...Or it's just all *b'irbuvia*?[3]...Gosh...if only the *Gemara*[4] was a little more clear in these *sugyas*[5]...maybe the Rishonim[6] go into this a bit more...Is there a *Kovetz*[7] on Nedarim?[8] *Mistama...*[9]...Gosh, what do I do...if only I had taken *chosson*[10] classes with Rav Kramer...or had learned Nedarim *be'iyun*[11]...or... or maybe I should just ask *her*?...'

She reached behind her back and undid her bra, letting it fall onto his chest, and then, with stunning dexterity, slipped her thumbs into the corners of his black boxer-briefs and slid them down his legs so that they touched his toes.

"Emma," he said, as her head was once again level with his.

"Ssshhh...." she whispered, placing her pink-painted lips on his mouth and probing for his tongue with hers.

"Wait, Emma..." He slid his head away from hers and propped himself up on the pillow.

"What's wrong, Eli?" she asked solicitously, her eyelashes fluttering and her lips protruding slightly. She lay sideways beside him, tickling his toes with hers and playfully sketching the circumference of his navel with her right index finger.

---

2. Order.
3. Anarchic.
4. Talmud.
5. Passages.
6. Medieval authorities.
7. Kovetz Mefarshim (collection of commentaries).
8. A tractate of Talmud.
9. Probably.
10. Groom.
11. In depth.

"Well, you see...I don't really know how to say this, but...it's just that...I have no idea what I'm doing..."

"What do you mean?" she asked, as a slight smile slipped across her amused face.

"I mean...that's exactly what I mean. That I have no idea what I'm doing. Literally. No idea."

An incredulous laugh escaped her mouth. "You can't be serious, Eli. You obviously have *some* idea...how can you not?" Her finger, still circling around his navel, was slowly moving ever so lower, but he was doing his best to remain undeterred.

"I mean, yeah, I have *some* idea...but it's like if you told someone to go jump into a basketball game who's never seen a basketball game in his life and knows absolutely nothing about the sport. He would instinctively figure out that the object of the game is to get the ball in the basket. That's the obvious part...but otherwise he has no idea how to pass, or dribble, or rebound, or how to do much of anything on the court...he won't know how to go to his left, how much time he's supposed to spend in the paint, how he's supposed to box-out on a rebound...he'd probably instinctively figure out how to shoot, but his form is probably atrocious. He'll have no idea about how you're supposed to bend your knees, what you're supposed to do with your elbows, how you're supposed to spin the ball on the tips of your fingers and how you're supposed to follow through after your shot...and he definitely won't know how to execute any plays. Forget telling him to make a v-cut or telling him whether to go over or under a screen, he doesn't even know what a pick-and-roll is. He doesn't even know how to run a give-and-go. He's totally clueless."

"Eli," she said, smiling weakly and shaking her head, "you know that I don't know anything about sports, so these analogies don't really help me very much...but if I understand what you're saying, you mean to tell me you don't know anything about what we're about to do?"

He sheepishly nodded his head.

"Look, Eli," she said with an exaggerated sigh, "I know that this is your first time, and you're probably very nervous, and that's okay... but even people who have never done this before at least know a few things about it ... you mean to tell me you really don't know *anything* about it?"

He nodded his head again, this time even more sheepishly.

"Are you serious? How is that even possible? How ... I mean ... you must've had sex ed at some point, right? ... Right? ... Eli?"

He shook his head.

"You've *never* had sex ed ..."

"Nope."

"I don't understand how that's possible ..."

"Emma, I've been in yeshiva all my life. In these places there *is* no sex ed."

"No? How are they allowed to not teach sex ed?"

"Because, Emma ... in these schools, in these communities, you're not supposed to do this until you're married, so from the schools' perspectives, they're like, 'why should we teach our students about any of this stuff if they're not allowed to do it anyway? Let them wait till they're about to get married. Then they can learn about it.' So that's what happens. A couple about to get married will start having these 'bride and groom classes' – the groom with his rabbi, and the bride with the rabbi's wife or another woman she trusts, and that's how they learn about it ... but for me, I'm three hundred miles away from my rabbi, and I didn't feel comfortable having these classes with him over Skype, so ..."

"Have you ever seen any pornography?"

"Why is that any of your business?" he asked, his eyes narrowing to slits.

"Because you're my husband now. I feel like I should know these things."

"Okay ..."

"Well? Have you?"

"Umm ..." He coughed, and his face turned crimson.

"It's okay, Eli," she said warmly, tenderly stroking his shoulder and grazing his thigh with hers. "If you have, you don't have to be embarrassed about it ... you can tell me. I won't judge you."

"Okay ..." He sat up with effort, upright and rigid. "Well ... yeah.

I have. Once or twice...when I was in ninth grade, but I don't really remember it. When I was on the yeshiva basketball team we had a TV in the locker room for one year. It was the only TV in the entire yeshiva. The only reason it was in the locker room was so that we could watch game film...but of course Coach Kahan never showed us any game film. He never used that TV even once. The only one to ever use it was this one kid on our team, Mordechai Menuvelstein – that was just his nickname, I can't even remember his real name now it's been so long...he was a real quiet kid, even quieter than me, but he had some interesting hobbies, apparently. After Tuesday night practices, he would wait for Coach Kahan to leave and then when the coast was clear he would put on the TV. I was kinda curious, because there were three or four other guys gathered around it, so I went over to the TV to see what they were watching...it was hard to see, because it was a small TV, and there were other guys blocking the screen, but I'm pretty sure I knew what it was...about halfway through that season the yeshiva administration found out about what was going on, and that was the end of the locker room TV."

"And you don't remember anything you saw from those films?"

"No...nothing...it was a long time ago..."

"Well," she sighed, crinkling her lips and nodding slowly, "probably better that way.... pornography is generally a terrible way to learn about these things...but I still don't understand – so even in middle school, they didn't teach you at least *some*thing? At least ways to be safe, in case kids break the rules and *do* do it? They never even taught you how to put a condom on a cucumber?"

"I don't even know what a condom looks like. I wouldn't be able to recognize one if you took one out of your pocket and shoved it in my face."

"Uh-huh...I see..." She threw a cautious glance at the window curtains, leaned back and asked him, "Do you know about the erogenous zones?"

"Like the tropics?"

"I guess not..."

She sighing, and tilted her head back. "Okay...do you know what the G-spot is?"

"You mean like on the violin?"

"Hmm...it's gonna be a long night."

"In a good way?"

"No. Not in a good way."

THIRTEEN

At one in the afternoon on a cold, cloudy Saturday, Eli returned
to his apartment after a long morning in synagogue. Still thinking about how well Thursday night's Gmail video-chat with
Emma had gone and still glowing inside like a newly formed
star fresh out of the stellar nursery, he was nearly oblivious to
the fact that the calendar now showed "April" and yet there was
still snow on the ground. 'Why should I need nice weather to
cheer me up,' he thought, slipping out of his suit and grabbing
his French edition of *The Stranger*, 'when I have Emma? Why do
I need anything else? I mean, really... *anything*...'

He lay down on his couch, exhausted from the interminable
synagogue service and post-service luncheon, and started reading.
After weeks of studying the language for forty-five minutes every
night and breaking his head over pronominal verbs and conjuga-
tions of past participles in the *passé composé*, he was finally able to
understand what he was reading, and he was looking forward to
discussing the book with Emma almost as much as he was looking
forward to impressing her with his newly acquired French. But
after twenty minutes of reading he quickly became bored with
the book. Now that Emma was in his life – or at least closer to
becoming a real presence in his life – books were starting to lose
their appeal to him. He could hardly believe this was the case, but
he was becoming aware, especially on dull days such as this one,

that with Emma now so tantalizingly close to him, everything else, even his books, seemed lackluster in comparison. When he actually tried reading the book, every other word began to look like "Emma" to him. Instead of the words of *The Stranger*, he was seeing the words of Emma's Friday afternoon email which he had read so many times that day that it had become etched in his mind like a tattoo engraved on his arm. 'I can't stand being alone anymore,' he thought, as he struggled to keep his eyes open. 'Especially on Shabbos.[1] There's nothing worse than getting back from *shul*[2] and having the whole Shabbos stretched out in front of you, the whole long afternoon, with no one to spend it with but yourself...'

The Saturday snowstorm was coating the Connecticut trees with thin layers of white powder, like vanilla frosting on chocolate cake. Plow trucks were intermittently clambering up and down the empty, slushy streets. A biting wind was driving the snowflakes that had fallen off of the tree boughs into Eli's and Emma's living room window, framing the brown-painted windowpane with a light, silvery sheen. Eli, reclining on the small three-seat sofa, was reading *Lord Jim*. The soft yellow light from the lamp next to the sofa flickered unsteadily; Emma turned it off and flipped on the apartment's recessed LED lighting.

"Emma," Eli groaned, throwing his hands halfheartedly into the air. "You know you're not supposed to do that anymore on Saturdays."

"But you'll hurt your eyes," she said, walking toward the kitchen to make tea for herself and her husband.

"You sound like a Jewish mother."

She snickered.

"At least that's what I've been told Jewish mothers sound like ..." he said under his breath, resting his book on his chest. "I never thought that even after you converted you'd still be my Shabbos goy..."

1. Saturday.
2. Synagogue.

"Your what?" she asked, turning around and looking at him cross-eyedly.

"Never mind," he muttered, picking his book back up off his chest.

"No," she snapped, flinging herself onto the cushion beside him. "What did you call me?"

"I didn't call you anything."

"Yes you did. You called me something. I want to know what you called me."

"Is this a fight? Are we fighting? We're only three months into our marriage and we're already fighting?"

"We're not *fighting*, Eli, calm down. I just want to know what you called me. You called me something in Hebrew. I want to know what it means."

"Okay, okay...it means...Sabbath queen." His thick, cracked lips coiled upwards and formed an ironic smile. "I called you my Sabbath queen."

"Oh..." she murmured, smiling and curling up beside him. She was wearing gray sweatpants and a white t-shirt and was snacking on a bowl of lightly salted snap peas. She slipped her bare feet out of her foam slippers and draped her legs across his. "So...how was the Bar Mitzvah?"

"Oh, you don't wanna know..." he began, on the verge of nodding off. "So boring. These things are excruciating. Yitzi's a great kid, but these Bar Mitzvah boys, they read so slowly, so it takes forever to get through the service. Then you gotta sit through all these speeches. You got the rabbi's speech, then the father's speech, then the synagogue president's speech, then every relative who wants to speak gets to speak. 'Yitzi, I knew your father from the time we were...' 'Yitzi, I've known your mother for decades, we go back to...' 'Yitzi, your grandfather and I learned together in Yeshiva in Brooklyn in 1940-whatever...' It never ends. And then at the end of the whole thing Harvey Greenspan collapsed, and – "

"Who's Harvey Greenspan?"

"Oh...Harvey..." His eyes were now completely closed; he sensed himself about to sink into his customary Saturday afternoon nap. "Harvey Greenspan... he's this big philanthropist who's single-handedly responsible for funding all the Jewish institutions in western New England. He practically pays my salary... I mean, not practically – he does pay it..."

"So what happened?" she asked, tickling his toes with the soles of her feet.

"The rabbi called out, 'is there a doctor in the *shul*? Please! Is there a doctor?!' And of course half the freakin' *shul* comes rushing over to him."

"Half?"

"Well, maybe I'm exaggerating... but let's just say it looked like he had the entire medical staff of the Mayo Clinic at his side in under two seconds."

"Geez... sounds like a scene out of a Woody Allen movie."

"I don't know... if it had been a Woody Allen movie Harvey would've been dead because all the people who rushed over to him would've been professors. 'But I *am* a doctor!' the guy who didn't even know how to check for his pulse would've said to the coroner. 'Would you like to see my dissertation? It was on Kierkegaard's epistemology. You'd be the second person to ever read it... well, the first – my mother put it down after the first five pages. She said she'll come back to it as soon as she retires... she's been retired for sixteen years... what's that? You mean I should've only tried to save him if I was an epi*demi*ologist, not an *epist*emologist? Now you tell me!'... It would've been a disaster..."

"Huh..."

"What? You don't find that funny?"

"I don't know... I guess I just don't really get Woody Allen's humor..."

"So what happened to Harvey? Is he alright?" she asked, sliding her right hand through his hair and enfolding her left arm around his right bicep. His eyes were still closed; '*v'hasheina meshubachas*,'[3] he said to her in his head. '*Can't you please just let me sleep? Or read?...*

---

3. "Sleep is praiseworthy."

Why do you always have to interrupt me? Can I ever get any peace around here?…Ever?…'

"Yeah, he's alright…he regained consciousness after thirty seconds or so. I was talking to Yitzi's father while the whole Mayo Clinic over there was working on him. Yitzi's father is a general practitioner. He said he had heard Harvey wheezing earlier that morning and wanted to check him out a little bit, but Harvey insisted he was fine. He's a stubborn guy. Big, tall, in great shape for an eighty-five-year-old. He walks at least three miles every day. Yitzi's father thought he could've just been hypovolemic. Either that or he could've been dehydrated…or maybe his blood sugar was really low and he just needed to eat something…I didn't quite catch everything he was saying, but basically he was saying that a guy that old can collapse for any number of reasons, so he thinks Harvey should go in for a CAT scan. Maybe he has pneumonia…who knows…meanwhile Hatzalah came and they were giving him an EKG on the spot. Right there in *shul*, in front of the Ark and everything… it was quite a scene, even without the Woody Allen part."

"What's Hot Sullah?" she asked, as her hand explored the surface of his body like a Mars rover, walking tentatively across his abdomen and probing for signs of life.

"Oh…Hatzalah…it's like a Jewish ambulance service."

"You have your own ambulances?"

"Well, not really…but sort of…"

"Do you have your own policemen too?"

"No, no," he said with an awkward giggle. "Not really…well, there *is* this group of ultra-Orthodox vigilantes in Brooklyn…but what they do is illegal."

"And your own firemen?"

He burst out laughing. Even though his eyes were closed, he could sense her smiling.

"C'mon Emma, don't be ridiculous. There'll be an all-Jewish NBA team before we ever have our own ladder company."

"So how do you like *Lord Jim*?" she asked, her hands slowly spinning around his neck and chest like two satellites orbiting the earth. "This is a hot book in graduate English departments these days."

"I don't know...I'm having trouble following it, quite frankly...I think I may need to have you explain it to me. I have no idea what's going on...Emma?...what are you doing?"

She was kissing him on his right ear, her tongue swirling like a small cyclone inside his earlobe.

"Just...you know..." she said, shyly but coyly. "Trying to see what turns you on..."

"'Turns me on'? You know what turns me on."

"What's that?"

"You."

"Me?"

"Yeah. You."

"What do you mean 'me'?"

"Just...you know...you...your.... I'm too tired to explain it, Emma...you know...just you...yourself...your presence...your essence."

"My 'essence'? That sounds a little philosophical. I thought you didn't like philosophy."

"I don't."

"So what do you mean by 'me'? What is my 'essence,' Eli Sartre?"

"C'mon, Emma..."

"You tell me what you mean by my 'essence,'" she whispered, jutting her chin forward and sticking out her lips, "and I'll tell you about *Lord Jim*. Here – I'll give you a little taste to start you off," she said, still speaking in a soft, sweet tone; he felt her eyelashes tickling his cheek. "It's really not as hard of a novel as you think. The key is in understanding how Marlow is subverting the earlier paradigm of the tale as an oral performance..."

"Huh?"

"...and how Jim dramatizes the idea of the singularity of the self."

"What? Emma, I have no idea what any of that means. You have to translate all of that for me into English."

"I'll explain the novel to you," she said, pulling up his shirt and kissing him on his abdomen, "when you explain to me how my 'essence' turns you on..."

"Emma...C'mon..."

"What?"

"Seriously? Now? Again? After last night? After everything we did last night?"

"It's 3 o'clock on a Saturday afternoon. What else are we gonna do? *Read* for the entire rest of the day?"

She placed her lips on his, and he finally opened his eyes.

"Emma..."

"Yeah?"

"It's just...I'm a little tired...I'm...I'm not in the mood...and... also...I, uh...how do I put this...I was expecting this marriage to be, you know, a little more *Middlemarch* and just *slightly* less *Lady Chatterley's Lover*...don't you want to explain *Lord Jim* to me? Can you please explain to me what in the world Conrad is doing in this book? For the life of me I can't understand it – "

"*Lady Chatterley's Lover*, huh? I'll show you *Lady Chatterley's Lover*. We haven't even skimmed the surface yet..." She started to undo the buttons of his white button-down shirt while doing something to his neck with her lips and tongue that he couldn't even attempt to describe. "*Middlemarch*?! What, you expect me to be your Casaubon? You expect me to just educate you all the time, to only talk books with you all day long and never actually do anything else with you? You made me accept all these restrictions – I can't do this and I can't do that, I can't turn on the lights on Saturday to help my husband read, I just have to sit there like an idiot and let him strain his eyes and suffer; I can't check my phone on Saturday anymore, or call my friends, or go to the mall, or listen to podcasts, or listen to music, or watch Netflix, or drive out to the Poconos, or garden, or go to one of those great used book sales in Amherst or Northampton that they always have on Saturdays; I can't go to the movies on Friday nights anymore, or to a Friday night concert, or a Saturday matinee; I can't eat out of the house – and you *know* how much I loved shrimp – and now that the only kosher restaurant around here closed all we can really do that's culinarily exciting is get some kasha from the Crown...I can't just be lazy even one night a week and not cook and order Domino's – not even *one* night a week – *every* night of *every* week I have to *go* to the grocery store, *get* more food, *cook* the food, *clean* the dishes, *rinse*, repeat…And can you please explain to me why they can't make good kosher pizza? All those pizza places we went to during our New York trip, and not a *single one* of them can make a good slice of pizza? How is that possible? It's just flour, cheese and tomato sauce, right? How difficult can be it be?! You people control the banks and the newspapers and the movie industry and send your kids to Ivy League colleges and win half the Nobel prizes every year but you can't figure out how to make a half-decent piece of pizza!?"

"*'You people?'* Emma, you *are* one of our people now."

"*And*, now that I'm keeping this Saturday-Sabbath, I can't even *write* on Saturdays anymore! That used to be my thing, Eli! Saturdays were always my best writing day! I was free from work, free from school, free from everything, and I could just sit at my desk with my notebook and look out the window and jot down whatever thoughts and images would come to me and then I'd create my poems from those notes. And now I can't even do *that*…Do you have *any* idea how much I gave up for you, Eli? *Any* idea? And now, as if all that's not enough, I give up *all* this for you, and then for a whole half of the month every month I can't even be with you?"

"Well, half the month is kind of exaggerating, it's not exactly – "

"But if *feels* like that to me, Eli. I give up *all* of this for you – so that I could be with *you!* – and even then I *still* can't even be with you?! For half the freaking month?! And then when I *can* be with you you're too tired?! Too *tired*?! Not in the *mood*?! You ask me to convert for you, you tell me that this is actually one of the few fun activities that I'm still allowed to do – but only during half of each month – you tell me that this is now that good half of the month, and then you say you're 'not in the mood'? Now, you listen to me – I want to do something fun today, and I want to do it right now. I can't write today, I have no place to go – you're not in the mood?! Well you *get* in the mood!"

"I…Emma…" He let the book slip out of his hands and let Emma slip herself onto his legs. '*Taka*[4] she's right,' he thought, as a new desire,

4. Actually.

strong and budding, sprouted inside him. 'I do have a *chiyuv onah*...[5] And it's a *b'feirush*[6] Gemara[7] – *"Kol adam she'ishto tova'to havyan lo banim she'afilu bedoro shel Moshe lo hayu k'moson..."*[8] *Lichora*[9] she's the real *tzadekes*,[10] and me, what am I? Maybe nothing more than a *hassid shoteh...*'[11]

'And besides,' he thought, as she balanced herself on his warm, unbending body, 'for the sake of *shalom bayis*[12] *Hakadosh Baruch Hu*[13] allows His own name to be erased... for the sake of my *shalom bayis* isn't it worth it to give up one Shabbos afternoon with Conrad so that I can have many more with Emma Yates?' He forced a smile, nodding blithely as she tucked her hair behind her head and lowered her lips to his mouth. '*Chalel aleiha Shabbos achas k'dei shetishmor Shabasos harbeh...*'[14]

5. An obligation to please my wife.
6. An explicit.
7. Passage from Talmud.
8. "Any man whose wife demands him will have children the likes of whom did not exist even in the generation of Moses."
9. It seems to be that...
10. Righteous person.
11. Pious fool.
12. Marital harmony.
13. God.
14. "Spend one Sabbath sub-optimally so that you may spend many more optimally."

FOURTEEN

Reading Emma's exuberant Friday afternoon email took some of the edge off of the unseasonably icy weather which had been weighing on Eli like a dozen years' worth of issues of *Brides* magazine. "Hi Eli!" she had written, sending a fathomless thrill through his body at the sight of the exclamation mark after his name,

> I hope that you've been having a wonderful day. It was so nice speaking to you again last night. By my count it was our fourth video-chat date, but it feels like our fortieth – not because our relationship feels boring to me, but because of how close to you I feel now … do you feel the same way about me?

She briefly told him about her hectic day, which involved working with an editor on last-minute changes to a poem of hers that was scheduled to appear in the Harvard Review and going back and forth to the post office because of some mix-up about packages and her mailing address, and then she had written:

> I wanted to thank you – again – for being so understanding. I was a little nervous talking to you about my past and about my feelings in that way, but you're so calm and patient and understanding and such a good listener that you put me at ease. I hope you're not scared off by me, for telling you about how I've always had these fears of disappointment and abandonment.

You asked me where those feelings come from and I didn't want to get into it too much that night, but I wanted to tell you now that I guess it comes from never feeling loved enough by my parents. Especially by my father. Never feeling close to him. Never feeling like he actually cared that much about me. I always had this feeling like he had me because having children was the thing to do and because my mom wanted a child but that he never really wanted children and was just going along with it. It's hard to explain it but it's just something I could always sense with him, this feeling that I was a burden to him. I also always had a hard time making friends and keeping friends in school. I was pretty nerdy growing up, as you know. Like a little Lisa Simpson. Whenever I actually had a friend I'd latch on to her and I'd always want to spend every night and weekend with her and I think that scared most of them away. The one really good friend I had when I was growing up was Julie, and she moved away with her parents when she was in middle school. She promised she'd write to me but after she moved I never heard from her again. I always felt so alone when I was growing up – I always had this feeling that there was no one else out there who was like me and who was interested in the things that I was into and who actually wanted to spend time with me. I didn't date in high school or college. I was attracted to different guys, for sure, but I always had this thought in the back of my mind that they'd just end up leaving me, and that kept me out of a lot of relationships. It wasn't until I met Todd that I felt safe and secure and comfortable enough with a guy to really trust him. He was really into books too, and loved hiking, and being in nature; he loved dogs too, so that was a big plus. There was something about him that I thought was different. I trusted him. And so when he broke up with me, I think you can understand how devastated I was, and how reluctant I've been since then to get into another relationship. I think you can understand now how important trust is for me in relationships. I hope my need for security and reassurance in relationships isn't scaring you away. I also hope that the fact that Todd was black isn't scaring you away either. To me it's just a coincidence. It's not something that I felt was that relevant – human beings are human beings, right? regardless of the color of their skin? – so I didn't bring it up right away. Todd was never something I wanted to discuss at all with you, actually, but it's just all come spilling out, maybe because of how good of a listener you are.

Anyway, thank you so much again for your patience, your receptive ear, and your kind heart. You're a truly special one, Eli Newman, and I'm beyond happy to have you in my life.

Have a lovely weekend!

– Emma :-)

'Did she really just write that "human beings are human beings"?' he groaned, closing his laptop and craning his neck. 'Or maybe I have the wrong *girsah*?[1] Let me reread that…No – she really *did* use that *lashon*[2]……*Ribbono shel Olam*[3]…She really *is* white. *Mamesh*[4] white…Only a white person would say something like that…only a white person would talk about this color-blindness *shtus*,[5] which is the biggest lie ever told since the South said 'what, slavery? We're fighting for states' rights…' Ha…"color-blindness" – just the latest "states' rights" nonsense that gives these wretches a cover to just keep on being racist…"Color-blindness" – would Emma say that the white guy who called me the n-word on the streets of Baltimore is "color-blind"?…Would she say that that CVS worker who'd keep an eye on me and always follow me around whenever I went into the store is "color-blind"?…Would she say that the cop who pulled me over was "color-blind?" Would she say that he thought that "all human beings are human beings"? Or was it when he called Yoni and heard his voice and then held off on putting me in handcuffs, was it then that he just maybe thought – without realizing it but I'm sure he thought it – that maybe this human being is a different kind of human being than that

1. Version of the text.
2. Language.
3. Good Lord.
4. Really.
5. Nonsense.

kind of human being?...And then there was Todd.... Todd, Todd, Todd...just a "coincidence." Sure...And I'm also supposed to believe that I'm "unique." "Special." That I'm not just a replacement for her Todd. Just another one of those "human beings" she can slot into her life to make up for the departure of the last one...So is this what she meant when she told me that I was just her "type"? Is this her "type"? These "types" of "human beings"? Did Todd leave her because he too was also getting frustrated by this color-blindness *shtus*? By this "race is irrelevant" ridiculousness?...Does she really see me for everything that I am – for everything that *I* am? Does she see me and understand me in all the ways that I am *not* Todd? *Can* she see me? Can she see everything that makes me *me*?...Including my race, and everything that that means?...Or does she prefer to be *sagi nahor*?[6]...'

He let out a heavy, anxious sigh, and propped his chin up on his hands. 'But maybe she really does like me for me...maybe she does... why can't you just accept the love of a woman when it's being given to you?' he reprimanded himself. 'Why do you have to qualify it? Ok, so maybe she has flaws, but who doesn't? Especially what white person doesn't? They didn't grow up like you. They haven't moved through life like you have. They don't know what it's like to be you. Why be so hard on them? Do you really have to be *medakdek*[7] with her *k'chut hasai'ruh*?![8] Is that fair to her? Cut her some slack...she's been through a lot...A lot of heartbreak...A lot of disappointment, rejection, abandonment...Don't be so tough on her...She likes you – maybe even loves you. Or wants to love you...Why can't you open your heart, forgive her of her flaws – *Hakadosh Baruch Hu*[9] knows you certainly have yours – and try to love her back? Why can't you love her for *her*? For everything that *she* is? Why can't you just love her *ba'asher he sham*?'[10]

6. Blind.
7. Judge her.
8. So strictly.
9. God.
10. As she is.

The following weekend, instead of focusing on the specific comments of hers which didn't sit well with him, he chose to focus instead on the two exhilarating exclamation-mark bookends in her email, her "Hi Eli!" at the beginning and her "have a lovely weekend!" at the end. The heat had been turned off in his apartment building, and he was continually rubbing his fingers and toes together to make sure he wasn't losing feeling in his extremities; he could scarcely believe it was the first week of April. Though it was as cold as a Canadian winter, inside his mind it was as steamy as a Brazilian summer. When Eli ushered in the Sabbath upon the setting of the Friday night sun, he felt so lightheaded with giddiness that it seemed to him as if the only thing keeping him from floating with Emma up to the heavens was the heavy weight of his earthly desire for her. But even more exciting for him than her email's two exclamation points was the fact that, for the first time following one of their video-chat dates, it had been she who had emailed him. Was that not a sign, he asked himself, that she desired him just as much – if not more – than he wanted her? That unimaginable thought and the boundless possibilities it brought with it tore through his mind like an uncontrollable solar flare throughout the night, inflaming his heart with passion and setting his body ablaze with unquenchable craving.

FIFTEEN

"Eli," whispered Emma as they were crawling into bed on the moon-glazed night of their first wedding anniversary. The glossy, chrome-colored light of the night fell with soft ripples on their unfolded red velvet bedspread, and the slight wrinkles in the apple and plum-patterned curtains threw subtle shadows on Emma's smooth, pastel-pink face. "I have to tell you something."

"Oh? What's that?" 'Oh no,' he thought; his stomach turned in on itself. A sinking feeling came over him. He had always known that this moment would eventually come – the moment when she'd finally have had enough of him – the moment when she'd finally tell him she needed to move on. It had been a nice run, they'd had a nice year together; they'd had a lot of fun, but it was time for her to get serious. She couldn't afford to play around for much longer. Divorces were easy to get these days. She couldn't keep up this sham of a marriage much longer; she needed something real, something substantial. She had finally met her Wallace Stevens – she had finally found her Mark Twain – and it was time to let this Eli plaything go. He knew exactly what was coming.

"I went off the pill."

"What?" He could hardly hear her above the persistent pitter-patter of the rain.

"I went off the pill," she said again, raising her voice.

"Really?" he exclaimed, flinging his head back in disbelief. "Wha... Why? Why would you do that?"

"Because, Eli..." she said, as she slipped off her red silk nightdress, draped her arms around his lower back and starting kissing his upper right collarbone, "I think it's time we had children."

"Huh?" He squinted at her as if she had just told him she had quit her job at the high school and had enrolled in a physics course at UConn so that she could pursue her long-cherished dream of becoming an astrophysicist. He held his unsteady hands together to stop them from quivering, but he was unable to prevent the rest of his body from shaking.

"Why do you seem so surprised?" she said with a delicate smile, massaging his abdomen with her left hand.

"Well...I mean..." he exhaled deeply, trying to pull himself away from the distracting movements of her dexterous hands so that he could think clearly. "It's just that...we've only been married for one year, so..."

"So? Eli. I'm 35."

"So?"

"I want children."

"Really?"

"Yes, Eli. Really."

"Oh..." He pulled himself away from her and propped himself up on the left side of the bed.

"Why does that come as such a shock to you? You knew this before we got married," she said angrily, speaking in a reedy falsetto. "You knew very well how much I wanted children."

"I don't know," he said dolefully, his baritone voice an octave lower than usual. "It's just...it's just that I never imagined that we'd actually, you know...that you'd want – "

"What?" she said, propping herself up on the right side of the bed and staring at him icily. He had never seen her look as irritated as she was looking at this moment. "You never thought that we'd actually have kids? Really? Is that what you thought? You thought that I was joking about it? That I wasn't serious about wanting to have kids? What in the world were you thinking?!"

"I don't know, Emma...maybe that – "

"Maybe what? That just because I was some literature-loving English teacher who cared deeply about books and poetry that I wouldn't want kids? That I'd just be content to teach Shelley and Keats and "Dover Beach" for the five thousandth time and write my poetry without creating anything more substantial – without creating something real?"

"Your poetry isn't real?"

"Don't be absurd, Eli. I mean something living. Something breathing."

"You don't think 'Ozymandias' is living? You don't think that 'Tintern Abbey' is breathing? You don't you think that 'Ode on a Grecian Urn' is more alive than half the dimwits walking around the mall on any given weekend?"

She drew her head back sharply, glaring at him open-mouthed and aghast as if he'd just proposed that all the brutes in the world should be exterminated.

"Don't look at me like that," he implored her, his head throbbing as if he had a migraine. "I just mean...I never thought you of all people would be the one to say that you needed children in order to be fulfilled. Especially if, you know, you have your poetry...which you do..."

"Eli...it's not about whether children are better than poetry. You can't even compare them. It's like comparing...*God*!" she exclaimed, slamming her head back against the pillow. "It's like comparing children to g@#$%n *poetry*! It's an absolutely absurd comparison! I can't believe I even have to debate this with you!"

"I should warn you – if we have children you'd have to do everything. I mean, absolutely everything. You can't leave me alone with children."

"Why not?" she asked, crossing her arms and sighing, as if to say, '*now* what?'

"Because...I'm scared."

"Scared?"

"I'm scared of children."

"You're scared of children," she said disbelievingly, rolling her eyes and shaking her head. A thin sigh escaped her lips.

"Yes...I'm scared of dogs and scared of children."

"You're scared of any creature whose poop you're responsible for disposing of?"

"No...well, yeah, there's that, and –...I'm scared of anything that I can't communicate with verbally like a normal human being."

"I know they don't talk," she said, expelling another exasperated sigh, "but babies communicate too. You just have to learn how they do so. On the surface they may be harder to understand than ordinary adults, but if you learn how to read them properly you'll see how everything they're 'saying' to you is completely understandable... much more understandable than what most adults say verbally, in fact. They're not dishonest, they don't lie, they don't cheat, they don't conceal their true feelings from you – they don't play games or practice any of the thousands of kinds of underhanded tricks adults do every moment of every day. They're never anything but completely straightforward with you. If they're telling you they're hungry, or tired, or need to go to the bathroom, you can actually believe them. It's so refreshing, don't you think?"

"I don't know," he said tonelessly, the color fading from his cracking voice. "From my experience with babies, whatever they're 'telling' you sounds exactly the same no matter what it is they want. It's all just an indecipherable babble of endless bawling for months and years until they can finally string a few words together into coherent sentences. Until then you practically need a Ph.D. in infant linguistics or some sort of Rosetta Stone for their alien language to understand a single thing they're 'saying.'"

"Oh, c'mon, Eli! Where's your spirit of adventure?! It'll be so much fun! Think of it as a challenge. It'll be like learning how to read *Ulysses*."

"I could never understand *Ulysses*."

"Fine...bad example. Think of it like...like learning how to read Faulkner."

"I never liked Faulkner either."

"Ccchhh!" she growled; it was a strange, startling sound Eli had never heard her make before. "Eli!!"

"Emma, for the life of me, I don't understand why you're so hung up on children. Jane Austen never had children...neither did Virginia Woolf.... or Walt Whitman...or T.S. Eliot...or – "

"Don't give me that, Eli – "

"Or George Eliot. Or George Washington. Or the Lubavitcher Rebbe."

"The *who*?"

"The Lubavitcher Rebbe. Probably the most influential rabbi of the twentieth century. He never had children either."

"Enough, Eli. I think you've made your poi – "

"C'mon, Emma! I'm just getting warmed up! Leonardo da Vinci! Elizabeth the First! Edgar Allan Poe! Emily Dickinson! *Doctor Seuss*!!! He was the greatest children's book author of all time and even *he* didn't have any children!"

"Eli – "

"Emily Brontë! Charlotte Brontë! Beckett! Beethoven! Nietzsche! Michelangelo! Philip Roth! Jesus Christ!"

"Hitler never had children either, Eli."

"You had to go there, didn't do? You just had to?"

"Stop this, Eli. This is absurd. This is absolutely ridiculous."

"Are we fighting? Is this our first fight?"

"Look, Eli," she groaned, her arms folded over her chest. "You're neither Christ nor the anti-Christ. Hell, for all I know you're not even the Bavitcher Rebbe."

"*Luh*-bavitcher Rebbe."

"Whatever. The point is, you're a normal person and you can – you *should* – have children like a normal person."

"Emma, it's not that. It's just – "

"And I thought you Orthodox Jews were obsessed with children. Isn't it a commandment in your religion to have children?"

"Emma – "

"*Isn't* it?"

"...Yes. Yes it is."

"And so I, the secular ex-Catholic atheist, am telling the 'commandment-keeping' Orthod3ox Jew to keep his commandments? Is that how it is?"

She scowled, staring daggers at him. The blood drained from his face. He gnawed at her words in his mouth; they tasted like poison.

"Well? Well, Mr. Commandment Keeper? Is it? Is that how it's gonna be?"

"I guess the tables have turned," said Eli sheepishly.

"I guess they have," she responded monosyllabically, giving him a steely, scornful stare.

Neither of them spoke for several more minutes; it was as if the holy hush of ancient sacrifice had suddenly interposed itself between them, and neither wanted to be the first to break the primeval taboo.

"Look, Emma," Eli finally began, hesitantly and sullenly. "What I mean to say is...first of all, I think my life is going just fine without kids. The truth is, I've been relying on an opinion in Jewish law that implies that you don't have to have actual biological children to fulfill the commandment of 'having children' – that if you teach others Torah that can be considered a fulfillment of that commandment.... and so I've, well, I made my peace a few years ago with the prospect of not having kids...and...and if we were to have kids, I just...I just worry about it, that's all...I mean, because of how things were for *me* as a kid – *still* are for me, in lots of ways...I never wanted kids of mine to experience that..."

"What do you mean?" she asked, narrowing her gaze.

"You know...growing up so different from everyone else around me...the way I was treated at school...in yeshiva...it was never anything hostile that was directed at me. I was luckier that way. But it was always there. The looks I'd get from anyone new I met...how much more careful I'd have to be than all my white yeshiva classmates anytime we went anywhere in public...how much more careful I'd have to be if there were cops around...being passed over for Baltimore Yeshiva High School teaching positions time and time again – and don't tell me I wasn't qualified for those jobs. I was more qualified than anyone in my yeshiva – you don't think I understood one-hundred-percent what they really meant when they said, 'well, Rabbi Newman, you're a fine candidate, but we just don't see you as a good fit for this school and our students' – you don't think I understood one-hundred-percent what that meant? This country is not color-blind, Emma. As much as you'd like to believe it is, it's anything but. When will you be able to open your eyes and see this, Emma?...Look...all I'm saying is, first of all, I don't think we need to have children in order to have a fulfilling life together. And secondly, if we do have children, I have to recognize – *we* have to recognize – the kind of country that we're gonna be bringing them into and the kinds of challenges they're gonna face simply because of what they'll look like...And I don't think you've ever fully recognized this. Or have *wanted* to recognize this."

"Well...I know you had a rough childhood, Eli," she said in a soft voice, gently rubbing his right arm. "Or at least a tougher one than most of your peers...but if I'm understanding you correctly, then isn't that all the more reason to want to have children with me? I mean...if you had children with me, your kids would probably be pretty white-looking...so – "

"*What?*" he hissed, his head jerking sharply and his voice turning grave.

"Isn't that what you want?"

"*WHAT?!*" He glowered at her with scorching, dragon-like eyes, threatening to incinerate her with his glare.

"You're scaring me, Eli. Don't look at me like that."

"Is that what you think?! Is that why you think I married you!? 'Cause I wanted @#$%&*g *white* kids?! @#$% that @#$%!"

Emma gasped, her rosy-cheeked face suddenly turning chalk-white. Eli leapt out of bed with a jolt and quickly slipped into a pair of trousers.

"My God, Eli...I've never heard you curse before...Eli, I – I just – I only meant that – "

"You think I married you because you think I didn't want black kids?! You're outta your @#$%&*g mind, Emma. I can't believe...I cannot believe you just said that to me."

"Eli…I'm sorry…I didn't mean to – "

"This is over," he said in a gruff voice, throwing a gray shirt over his bare body and marching out of the bedroom. "This conversation is over."

SIXTEEN

By the third week of April, Eli could finally walk outdoors without bundling himself up in ski mittens, a woolen hat, a scarf, long underwear, flannel-lined pants and a winter parka. His bones had finally stopped rattling, and he could once again hear the songbirds chiming. If this was how the weather was every year in New England, he thought, he wasn't sure how much more of it he could handle. He longed for the days of being able to play basketball outdoors in January, wearing only shorts and a Kenny Smith Houston Rockets jersey and not having to worry about slipping on a patch of black ice while walking home from school. While on his way home from work, he thought about looking for Talmud-teacher jobs in cities with warmer weather, but quickly decided against it. 'Why go anywhere else,' he said to himself, lost in thought amidst the damp odor of rain-sodden soil and the weak warmth of the late-afternoon sun, 'when Emma is here? She's all I could hope for – she's all I ever wanted. I'd be a fool to go anywhere else – worse than a fool... *Eizehu ashir – ha'sameach b'chelko*[1]... besides, in our last video-chat date, she even asked me whether I still experience any racism, so maybe she's finally starting to come around to becoming more curious about this aspect of my identity – probably a good sign...'

---

1. "Who is rich? He who is happy with his lot."

No, he had told her – he didn't really think racism was a problem for him or anyone else anymore, especially now that the country had elected a black president. 'Why did I lie to her?' he asked himself, as the tough, rocky clumps of the graveled sidewalk along Bishops Corner bit into his shoes. Black president, shlack president; having a black president didn't end racism in this country any more than *Schindler's List* winning the Oscar for Best Picture had ended antisemitism, and he knew it. He didn't need police reports and academic articles in sociology journals to tell him so – he knew it from his own experience. He didn't even need Ferguson and Freddie Gray to tell him so, though those incidents alone were evidence enough. He knew it from his own everyday life. He knew it from those ever-so-slightly-furrowed-brow looks he would get from the accountant after making an appointment to do his taxes – those ever-so-slightly-furrowed-brow looks that said, '*hmm*…you didn't *sound* black on the phone…' He knew it from those ever-so-slightly-raised-eyebrow looks he would get from the banker on the verge of denying him approval for a new credit card until Eli remembered to take off his Astros hat, revealing his black velvet yarmulke underneath – those ever-so-slightly-raised-eyebrow looks that said, '*well*, if you had *told* me you were Jewish…' He knew it from the way those Baltimore busboys at the kosher restaurants he would take his dates to would look at him after clearing his plate, with their strained, over-exaggerated smiles that said, 'how nice of that pretty social worker to take that black boy out for a good meal…' 'Oh yeah?' he would say in his head to the busboy, smiling at him contemptuously while giving him a $2 tip. 'Well, @#$% you, too.' He knew it from the way he'd be stealthily followed around drug stores by shelve-stockers as if he were a thug off of the streets – as if the color of his skin made it impossible for him to be anything other than a gangster or drug dealer. Oh how it would've blown their minds if he'd told them he was a Talmud scholar – if only he would've told them…He couldn't even go out to buy toothpaste and shampoo without being visually accosted in those and a thousand other manners and without being reminded that he was living in a country that, without telling him so, looked at him as if he was an untamed tiger who'd just escaped from the zoo. He laughed at the prospect of himself being seen as threatening to anyone – he, the least aggressive, most domesticated, most yeshiva'ized-institutionalized creature he knew? Threatening?! It was enough to make him double over with laughter were he not saddened to the core that these things kept happening no matter how many pages of Talmud he mastered and no matter how many medieval Talmudic commentaries he successfully deciphered. And these were things that happened to him in supposedly "good" states, like Maryland and Connecticut. He couldn't imagine what he would've experienced had he gone to yeshiva in Georgia or Tennessee. No...Eli Newman didn't need no New York Times news analysis to tell him that electing a black president hadn't ended racism; all he needed was the experience of living as Eli Newman.

'Why did I tell her such a blatant, bald-faced lie?' he asked himself again. 'Is it because I didn't want to scare her away? Is that why I didn't tell her about what happened that time with the cop on my way to that date with Rena? Is that why I didn't tell her about the time I got taunted by two white men when our yeshiva high school went on a field trip to Manassas National Battlefield Park in Virginia? Is that why I didn't tell her about the time in Baltimore when I was riding my bike to the bookstore and two white teenage boys behind me yelled, "hey n – ! Get off the street!"? Is that why I didn't tell her that whenever a policeman so much as even looks at me my blood pressure skyrockets? Is that why I didn't tell her about how any time I go into any store I have to remember to smile so that I don't look like Threatening Black Guy Who's Come to Rob Us? Is that why I didn't tell her about how every, single, solitary day, whether I'm at the supermarket or CVS or the bank or even the library I have to be careful to not walk too closely behind white people? Am I worried that she still might be reluctant to commit to someone whose life in the United States of America is made so much more *shver*[2] on a daily basis than hers simply because of the color of his skin? Is it because even though she's told me in so many different ways that she likes me I'm nervous that if she knows the truth about what life is really like for me she won't want to join me in living it?'

2. Challenging.

'The truth might scare her away from me,' he thought; 'better to wait until we're married to try to explain it to her...If I try to tell her too much about me too soon it could be too much for her to handle and I could lose her entirely. *Tafasta merubah lo tafasta*[3]...Better to wait until I actually know our relationship is secure...and once I know it is, once I know she really loves me for who I am and won't run away like Rena, maybe then I'll be able to burst her beloved white liberal bubble about everybody being equal in the United States of America in the twenty-first century, and her beloved blue state bubble that the country has transcended race and racism to become "color-blind"... maybe once she's living with me she'll start to understand what it's really like to be a person of color in America; maybe once she's living with me she'll actually be more curious to see what it's like to be me...' But until then, he thought, better to preserve her fantasies than to make her understand the realities – not because he didn't think she should know about them, but because he secretly believed that if she did, she might no longer be interested in sharing a life with somebody for whom that kind of treatment is a daily reality.

He wondered whether that was also why he had told her how he used to sneak out of yeshiva to see movies but hadn't told her about how he had snuck out of yeshiva to join the protests against the Baltimore police after Freddie Gray's funeral. He had had no problem telling her about the time he had put on a blue shirt to go out and see "Inside Llewyn Davis" but he couldn't bring himself to tell her about the time he had put on his burnt-orange Texas Longhorns hoodie and snuck out of yeshiva to protest in front of the Western District police station. He couldn't bring himself to tell her about how, on that warm April day, under a clear, translucent sky the color of North Carolina Tar Heel blue, with his mouth open as if to drink in the words of the empowering protest chants, he had felt something inside himself ripen; he couldn't bring himself to tell her how, upon waking up the next day, he had felt as if he had undergone some sort of intellectual puberty overnight, and that in the days following the protests he had

3. "If you have seized too much, you have not seized at all."

finally been able to understand himself, his essence, who he truly was and who he had been all along.

After getting home from work, he made himself a cup of green tea, and instead of opening up his volume of Talmud, he turned on his computer and opened up his Gmail account, curious to see if Rena had finally replied to his email. The vague stench of cholent still lingered in the apartment. '*Ucchh*…I forgot to clean the crockpot after Shabbos,[4]' he remembered, curling his lips in slight revulsion. 'But first let me just check my email…' When he still saw no new messages from RenaBraun224@gmail.com, he logged in to Facebook, curious to see if Emma had posted anything new in the past several hours. There were no new posts from Emma Yates – there still hadn't been any in over three weeks – but there was a new message from one of his yeshiva friends, Shaya Twersky:

> *Sholem Aleichem*[5] Eli! I hope all is well. Where are you holding[6] with your high schoolers in Sanhedrin?[7] Yoni and Chani ate by[8] us on Shabbos, he told me you were teaching your class the *sugya*[9] of *ben sorer umoreh*.[10] Yoni told me you're still looking for a *shidduch*. Last week Yoni gave this unbelievable *chaburah*[11] during *mishmar*[12] on *pas akum* and *bishul akum*.[13] I had been telling him, "Yoni, a lot of *balabatim*[14] will be coming to this *chaburah*, you should do something easier. Why not just say over[15] a nice *shtickl* Torah[16] on

4. Saturday.
5. Hey.
6. What part are you up to.
7. A Tractate of Talmud.
8. With.
9. Passage.
10. The rebellious son.
11. Lecture on a particular subject in a study group session.
12. Thursday night learning.
13. The laws of food cooked by non-Jews and bread baked by non-Jews.
14. Laymen.
15. Discuss.
16. Insight.

the *machlokes* Rashi-Tosfos[17] by[18] *shome'a k'oneh*[19] and *shoyn*?[20] Now that you're working why spend so much time being *me'ayen*[21] into a whole big complicated *sugya*?" But he was like, "Shaya, don't you remember rebbe's[22] schmooze[23] on *bedieved*[24] Judaism versus *lechatchilah*[25] Judaism? I don't want to be a *bedieved* Jew. I want to do things *Lechatchilah*." So he gave this whole *mechudeshdiger*[26] *chaburah* on *pas akum* and *bishul akum*. He went into *rishonim*,[27] *poskim*,[28] a *diun*[29] in *achronim*,[30] he said *lomdus*[31] on this *machlokes* Ran-Ramban[32] that I'd never heard of, he clared[33] a *chakirah*[34] on *pas akum* and *bishul akum* – he wanted to say that we're more *machmir*[35] on *bishul akum*[36] cause it's an *issur cheftza*[37] but we're more *meikel*[38] on *pas akum*[39] because it's an *issur gavra*.[40] I don't know if

---

17. Dispute between the medieval Talmud commentators Rashi and Tosfos.
18. Regarding the concept of.
19. "He who hears is like one who responds."
20. That'll be good enough.
21. Studying extensively.
22. Rabbi Kramer's.
23. Talk.
24. Sub-optimal.
25. Optimal.
26. Innovative.
27. The opinions of medieval Halakhists and Talmud scholars.
28. Rulings of modern Halakhic authorities.
29. Discussion.
30. Post-renaissance Halakhists and Talmud scholars.
31. Fancy learning.
32. Dispute between the medieval Talmud scholars Ran and Ramban.
33. Proffered.
34. Piece of Talmudic-Halakhic Analysis.
35. Strict.
36. Food cooked by non-Jews.
37. A prohibition related to the object.
38. Lenient.
39. Bread baked by non-Jews.
40. A prohibition related to the person.

it's so *muchrach*[41] but he brought[42] a lot of *rai'yuhs*[43] and at least at the time he was saying it over it sounded great. And everyone who heard it seemed to agree. You should've seen it, Eli. People were hocking him[44] after the *chaburah* like he was a Rosh Yeshiva.[45] It was unbelievable. After Maariv[46] I said to him, "Yoni, are you sure you want to spend sixty hours a week every week for the next forty years of your life going over spreadsheets and schedule C forms and w-2s and w-9s? Why not go back to yeshiva and sit and learn in *kollel elyon*[47] for a few years till you become a Ram?[48] What you did tonight was incredible." He said to me, "Shaya, this wasn't me. This was Eli. This *shiur*[49] was all Eli. He's the one who gave me the *mareh mekomos*.[50] He's the *baki*.[51] He knew where everything was. I didn't know a thing. This was all him." So we were talking after *benching*[52] and we all agreed that you need someone really special. Not just a *stam*[53] girl. Someone really special. A girl that comes from a *mishpocha*[54] that has the resources that'll allow you to learn full-time again. We all agreed that you were the shtarkest[55] guy in our *shiur*.[56] You were the biggest *masmid*,[57] the biggest *baki*,[58] the

41. Dispositive.
42. Cited.
43. Evidence.
44. Asking him questions.
45. Outstanding scholar.
46. Evening prayers.
47. Advanced yeshiva.
48. Rabbi in yeshiva.
49. Class.
50. Sources.
51. Knowledgeable one.
52. Reciting grace after meals.
53. Ordinary.
54. Family.
55. Best.
56. Class.
57. Diligent student.
58. Knowledgeable one.

biggest *lamdon*.[59] A guy like you, Eli, teaching "Talmud" in a modern
Orthodox high school?! That's *pastnisht*.[60] Especially teaching
Gemara to girls. I don't know who gave you a *heter*[61] for that but I
don't want to get into that now, the point is that what you're doing
is completely *pastnisht* for a guy like you. It's not *kavodig*[62] – the
shtarkest guy in our *shiur* stuck teaching "Talmud" in a modern
Orthodox high school somewhere out in the boonies?! No. We
won't stand for this. Eli, we all agreed that you're the one out of all
of us who has the potential to become a Yaakov of Scranton. (I mean,
a Yaakov a Scranton who didn't go off the *derech*,[63] of course...)
Okay, so you like to read *sforim chitzonim*[64] from time to time, but
who's perfect? Other than that, Eli – you're the shtarkest guy from
our *shiur*, the closest thing we have in our *chevre*[65] to a real *tzadik*.[66]
Eli, *you're* the one from our *shiur* who has the potential to become a
Rosh Yeshiva! *You're* the one, Eli, who should be sitting in *kollel elyon*
preparing to become a Ram! You should be writing *seforim*[67] and
chidushei Torah[68] and giving *shiurim*[69] and *chaburahs*, not teaching
"Talmud" at some *shvach*[70]modern place way out in G-d-knows
where! I have no idea why you chose to take such a job in the first
place but that kind of thing for a guy like you is completely *pastnisht*!,
totally not *kavodig*! Where's your *shminis shebeshminis*?![71] So after
Yoni and Chani left and Faigie and I were clearing the dishes I asked

59. Advanced learner.
60. Unacceptable.
61. Halakhic permission.
62. Befitting for you.
63. Become irreligious.
64. Non-religious books.
65. Social circle.
66. Righteous person.
67. Books on Torah and Talmud.
68. Talmud scholarship.
69. Talmud classes in yeshiva.
70. Mediocre.
71. Eighth of an eighth [of pride].

her to think of someone for you. She spent the whole day thinking, she went through her whole Bais Yaakov[72] directory to see which girls were still single and finally by[73] Shalosh Seudos[74] she came up with someone. *Agav*,[75] Faigie wanted to serve mezonos[76] rolls for Shalosh Seudos, she was like, "you don't have to wash[77] for Shalosh Seudos anyway, right?" and I was like, "no, maybe not *me'ikar hadin*,[78] but *lechatchila*[79] you should wash! With *lechem mishneh*![80] Even for Shalosh Seudos! Why do things bedieved?"[81] She was like, "but I'm a woman…" And I was like, "*Avaduh!*[82] – and women are *chayavos*[83] in the *mitzvos aseh she'hazman grama*[84] of Shabbos on the exact same level that men are!" It's *darshened* out[85] from '*zachor v'shamor*',[86] no? What are they teaching girls in Bais Yaakov these days?! How to do their veset[87] calendars and that's it?! Uchh… You know, Eli – and this is just between us – sometimes – and I know this is probably *kfirah*[88] – but sometimes I think I should've married a Stern girl. At least then she'd know something… Oye… if it wasn't for Faigie's egg noodle kugel… And besides, "*mezonos* rolls"?! What?! What is *this*?! How could they even give these things a hechsher?![89] Since when

72. Religious girls' school.
73. During.
74. The third Sabbath meal.
75. By the way.
76. Grain.
77. Have bread.
78. According to the main principle of the law.
79. If you want to do things the best possible way.
80. Two whole loaves of bread.
81. Sub-optimally.
82. Of course.
83. Obligated.
84. Time-bound positive commandments.
85. The obligation for women is derived from.
86. "Remember and observe."
87. Monthly.
88. Heresy.
89. Kosher certification.

is the OU[90] a purveyor of bedieved Judaism!? I think I might have to eat only Kof-K[91] from now on...And to want to have "mezonos rolls" for Shalosh Seudos?! That's like bedieved Judaism *squared*! *Ein bedieved Judaism gadol mizu!*[92] Ucch!...I wish you'd tell Faigie to throw out the mezonos rolls. She'd listen to you. Me, I don't know. She doesn't have the same respect for me since I took the LSATs and started at Georgetown. But you – she'd listen to you. I told her how big of a *lamdon* you are, how much of a *tzadik*[93] you are, how I never saw you *batel*[94] for even a single moment in the *Beis Medresh*[95]... You should come back to Baltimore, Eli. You should come back to yeshiva. And Faigie, *Baruch Hashem*,[96] okay so maybe she's not so great with Hilchos Shabbos[97] but she's good with shidduchim.[98] And she has someone for you. She has a *shidduch*[99] for you that'll allow you to come back to yeshiva and learn full-time like you should be doing. She says she was in seminary in Israel with this great girl who's now living in New York, in the Heights. She's 23 and works in development for American Friends of Hebrew University. She *davens*[100] at Fort Tryon. She just moved back to the states after living in Israel for 4 years. Her name is Dasi Pines. She's not on Facebook – she's not that type of girl. She's *toradig*,[101] *mamesh*[102] *toradig*. A graduate of Bais Faiga. If you want to meet her you might have to go through a *shadchanis*,[103] Chaya Mlotek – she charges 3500

90. Kosher certification agency.
91. Food bearing the kosher certification of Kof-K.
92. There's no greater example of bedieved Judaism than this.
93. Righteous person.
94. Waste time.
95. Study hall.
96. Thank God.
97. The laws of Sabbath.
98. Setting people up.
99. Match.
100. Prays.
101. Highly religious.
102. Really.
103. Matchmaker.

for a successful *shiduch* but her fee would be more than *kedai*[104] for a girl like Dasi. But I'll see if Faigie can get around that for you. (I mean, if she holds by mezonos rolls clearly she's not opposed to *ha'arama*,[105] so...) Faigie says that Dasi has excellent references. Her parents live on Bennett Ave. They know Rav[106] Leiner. Her brother's a *talmid*[107] of Rav Potek, and her younger brother's a *talmid muvhak*[108] of Rav Silverstein. Her father's a dentist, he does very well – he'll be able to support you so that you can go back and learn in *kollel*[109] and prepare to become a Ram and reach your true potential as one of the greatest *lamdonim*[110] of this *dor*[111] ... Let me know what you think!

Eli cringed.

"*Aleichem Sholom*[112] Shaya," he wrote, "thanks so much for thinking of me but I'm actually seeing someone now, and it's going quite well."

"That's wonderful you've met someone!" Shaya immediately replied. "I wish you both much *hatzlacha*![113] So happy for you! I always imagined that the girl Eli Newman would marry would be the *tzadekes hador*,[114] the Beruriah[115] of our time – can't wait to hear all about her! *Tizku lemitzvos*!"[116]

Eli winced. 'Is that really still all they care about?' Eli asked himself, closing his computer and opening his volume of Talmud. 'Fixing me

---

104. Worth it.
105. Trying to find halakhic loopholes.
106. Rabbi.
107. Student.
108. Devoted student.
109. Yeshiva.
110. Talmud scholars.
111. Generation.
112. Hey.
113. Success.
114. Most righteous woman of the generation.
115. Wife of the Mishnaic sage Rabbi Meir.
116. Good luck!

up? As if I need to be *fixed*? As if I'm a broken person and only marriage will make me whole? As if there's something deeply wrong with me just because I'm still single? I have some terrible disease that can only be cured by holy matrimony?! I'm going to *Gehenom*[117] unless I have *chuppah v'kiddushin*?[118] Is Ben Azzai in *Gehenom*?! *Nu*?! Is he?! One of the greatest Tannaim,[119] one of the *ba'alei haMesorah*[120] – and they're gonna put him *Gehenom*?!?! Because he didn't have *chuppah v'kiddushin*?!?! *Ugh*!!! … And what else do they have to tell me about this girl other than what she does and where she *davens*?![121] Don't they understand that I care almost as much about what she thinks of *Wuthering Heights* as I do about where she *davens* in Washington Heights?! *Ribbono shel Olam!!!*'[122]

He took a sip of tea and closed the volume of Talmud. 'Ugh…I can't do this now,' he said to himself, setting the large golden-brown volume aside. 'I'm not in the mood…I need something else…'

He looked out the window. A brilliant, opalescent, violet-and-vermilion dusk flared in the sky. All was quiet, save for the sound of a squirrel scurrying across the windswept street. He took a deep, kabbalistically-inspired breath, lowered his head, and opened his copy of *The Stranger*.

---

117. Hell.
118. A married life.
119. Rabbis of the Mishnah.
120. Masters of the Tradition.
121. Prays.
122. God almighty!

SEVENTEEN

"If we're going to be together," Emma said to him the next time they video-chatted – this time on Skype, because Google's video-chat service wasn't displaying Eli's face clearly enough for Emma's tastes – "we should talk about some practical things."

"Okay," said Eli, the back of his neck suddenly becoming tense. He had already been irritated that day by the sickening smell of Patchouli oil which had been wafting in to his apartment from an unknown source; he didn't know whether it was coming from the apartment below him, above him, or next-door, but, rather than knocking on the doors of all the surrounding apartments to see who the culprit was and to ask them to do something about the awful odor, he simply held his nose the entire day and prayed that the smell would eventually go away. "What would you like to talk about?"

"Well," she said, adjusting the silver magnolia-leaf pin which held together her black shawl and which made her look even more elfin, "like where we're gonna live."

"Umm...probably your place? I bet it's nicer than mine."

"You're probably right about that," she chuckled, sounding as if she was forcing a laugh. "That was easy enough...how about how many times a year we're going to go visit our dads?"

"Well...since I'm never going to go see my father, that one's easy too...and as for your father...how many times a year do you want to see him?"

"Hmmm..." She pursed her crimson-colored lips and, as she always did when thinking about something, cocked her head to the left and looked upwards. "I don't know."

"If it's more than once or twice a year, all those flights to Chicago could add up..."

"I know," she said with a subdued voice.

"Just something to keep in mind."

"Yeah...I know..."

"What else?"

"Hmm...let's see..." She ran her left hand through her hair, looked away from the screen for a moment, and then looked back at him. "What about household chores?"

"What about them?"

"Who will be doing them?"

"Umm...I suppose we could divide them up. I don't see any reason why either one of us should be doing all of them."

"Do you expect me to always put dinner on the table?"

"No..." he began, rising up in his seat. "No I don't. We can take turns doing that. I mean, sometimes you might get home later than me and I'd be the one getting dinner ready that night, and other nights I might be home later than you and you'd be handling dinner that night...I guess it would just depend..."

"And what about cleaning up?"

"I'm perfectly fine doing my dishes."

"*Your* dishes? You would do yours, but not mine? What is this, an every-man-for-himself household you want to have?"

"*No!*" he exclaimed, drawing out the word, aggravated at the way she was twisting his words by taking them literally. "I meant I'm fine doing *the* dishes."

"Then you should have said that."

"Well...." His shoulders flinched, and the corners of his mouth twitched. A sourness filled his throat. He looked at her coldly, inexpressively. A raven trilled in the distance, spoiling the delicate quiet of the calm spring evening. Black clouds bloomed in the indigo sky, like a silent poison growing in the dark. "I made a verbal mistake. Please forgive me, Ms. Yates," he said acerbically. "I apologize for not being more precise with my words."

"Apology accepted," she said dispassionately, gazing at him dimly.

This is by far the worst video-chat I've had with her since we started dating, he thought, smiling at her crookedly. *If only I could get out of this dreadful conversation…what do I need to say to her in order to be yotzeh…*[1]

"I can take out the garbage," he hastened to add, seeking to quickly re-elevate his stock in her eyes.

"That's good…"

"I can also do laundry."

"Mm-hmm…" she said, nodding her head and looking downwards as if she were evaluating a job candidate and looking to see if there was anything else on his resume she wished to ask him about. "That's good too…and who will do the ironing?"

"Ironing?"

"Yes…who among us will do the ironing?"

"I…well…" He shrugged his shoulders and absentmindedly scratched the back of his head. "I don't…"

"Don't what?"

"Don't iron."

"You don't iron?"

"No…never done it."

She looked at him as if he had just said that he believed the sun revolved around the earth.

"Then you wear wrinkled clothing?" she asked, knitting her eyebrows and staring at him uncomprehendingly.

"Well…I send my shirts and slacks to the dry cleaners."

"And what about your other clothes?"

"Umm…" *If I could only be talking to her about Dickens or Dickinson again!…or about her favorite pedagogic techniques…or even about that time her mother accidentally threw out her goldfish…anything but*

---

1. Fulfill my obligation.

this...ucch!... "To be honest...up until last year, Chava used to do my laundry, so – "

"Chava?"

"My roommate's mother."

"So she did your ironing?"

"Well...I guess she must have..."

"And since then you haven't had your clothes ironed?"

"Well..." he murmured, shrugging his shoulders again and reddening. "I guess not."

"Okay then...what about cleaning the bathroom?"

"Umm..." He slumped down in his chair. It was funny, he thought, as he tried to come up with a reasonable answer that wouldn't completely disqualify him as a marriage candidate in her eyes, that at this moment, he couldn't imagine how he had ever become attracted to her in the first place and couldn't imagine ever becoming attracted to her ever again. At this moment, any sensual excitement occurring between them ever again seemed as likely as Mongolia once again becoming a great world power. "I'm not...well...I've never done that either."

"This is something that Chava also did for you all those years in Baltimore?"

"Yes."

"So you don't know how to do it?"

"Well...I mean...I suppose I could learn...what is there, Lysol? Is that what people use?"

"And what about mopping the floors? Who will do that?"

He shrugged his shoulders instead of answering.

"Look, Eli," she said, sighing and rolling her eyes. She folded her arms and looked at him contemptuously. "I get the point...if we need to, we can get a cleaning lady. I know some other teachers who use one. We'd only have to pay, maybe, I don't know, a hundred dollars or so every two weeks...but that adds up, obviously, considering that neither of us is making a very high salary, so you might want to think about learning..."

"Alright..." he said in a toneless, deferential tone, his legs shaking as if he were riding the world's most rickety roller coaster. "Anything else?"

"Anything else? Hmm. Let's see...oh, here's an important one: when do you want to have children?"

"Children?" The word "children" fell from his lips like a wrought-iron anchor. "Well..." he stammered, looking at her as if she had just asked him if he was interested in getting a pet tiger. "I don't know... when do *you* want to have children?"

"Like, yesterday."

"Really?" he gasped, rapidly drawing his head away from the screen.

"Yeah, of course...I'm thirty-three, Eli. I can't wait forever."

"Oh...well...how about in three years?"

"*Three?*"

"Many women are giving birth later and later these days, Emma. Some even into their 40's. And very safely, too."

"But that's not what I want, Eli."

"How about two years?"

"Eli...the longer I wait, the more likelihood there will be that I could have problems conceiving...and fertility methods are very expensive. That could be financially trying on us, if we have to resort to that...not to mention emotionally trying."

"Okay...I understand...but having a child right away would be very emotionally trying on *me*. I mean, to go from being completely single my entire life to all the sudden not only married but married with children in the span of one year – I don't think I could handle all that change so soon..."

She nodded without saying anything, looking at him for a long time before speaking again. There was a trace of weary disappointment in her eyes.

"So how do you propose we put it off?" she asked, raising her eyebrows and crossing her arms in annoyed silence. Her voice sounded oddly piercing to his ears, as if she had changed the frequency to a pitch that she knew irritated him.

"What do you mean? Like, methods?"

"Yeah. What methods do you propose using?"

"C'mon, Emma," he said tiredly, feeling his face strain with frustration. "Isn't this something to discuss once we're married? I can't get into this now."

"No, Eli. This is important. What methods? I want to know. Just how do you propose delaying children?"

"*Ribbono shel Olam*..."[2] he muttered under his breath. "Well," he continued audibly, "I know that there's, um, the female method..."

"You mean birth control pills?"

"Yeah..."

"Well, I'm not comfortable taking those."

"No?"

"No. Not interested."

"Why not? Is this like some vestigial guilt from your Catholic childhood? That you would feel guilty if you were on birth control?"

"No...it's just that I'd rather not ingest substances and things like this into my body that could affect my fertility later on when I start trying to conceive."

"Uh-huh," he grumbled, leaning weakly against his desk. He squirmed; his mouth was closed, his jaw set, his eyes shut. He jutted out his chin and reopened his eyes; his voice came back to him, anxious and broken. "Well...I...umm...never heard that birth control pills could impair a woman's fertility. From everything that I know, this is a myth. I have many friends whose wives have taken them and they've all conceived and given birth just fine."

"Well, that may be fine for them," she said slowly and sternly, speaking through gritted teeth. "But I don't want to take them...I just wouldn't be comfortable if I were on those pills...it's hard enough to conceive once you're in your thirties, and then to take substances to stop me from doing so – I wouldn't want to do that..."

"What if I could show you the evidence that they're safe?"

"I'd be open to hearing it...but until I hear the evidence, I just wouldn't be comfortable taking those pills."

2. God.

"Then how else do you propose we delay children? Through the male form of contraception?"

"I heard that you're not allowed to use them."

"Who? Catholics?"

"No, Eli – Orthodox Jews. I heard *you're* not allowed to use them."

"Huh?" He scratched his stubble-covered chin and looked away from the screen, as if refusing to believe that she knew this piece of information. "Who told you this?"

"I teach in a co-ed Orthodox high school, Eli, remember? I hear things. I'm aware of what students talk about with each other. I hear some of the conversations that the rabbis here have with one another about the students and about what our students may or may not be doing with each other... I'm not completely deaf."

"What have you heard?"

"That using one is prohibited according to Jewish law. That it's the equivalent to what the biblical characters Er and Onan did."

"*Okay...*" he muttered, grimacing and smiling wanly. *Of all the things that she knows about Judaism, why did* this *have to be the one thing she knew?* "Then if you're not comfortable using female contraception, and if you don't think it's appropriate for me to use male contraception, then – "

"You can use one if you want," she interrupted annoyedly. "I have no problem with it. All these religious superstitions, as far as I'm concerned, are patently ridiculous. The Catholics' superstitions are no better or worse than the Jews'. You guys can do what you want. I'm just saying, I heard that your religion doesn't allow them. But it's fine by me. Do whatever you wanna do. As long as you don't impose your crazy medieval superstitions on me. And, like I said... I'm a rational person. I trust science. So if you can show me the evidence that the pill doesn't impair a woman's long-term fertility, I'd be open to changing my mind."

"Alright... so... where were we?... how in the world did we get here?"

"I don't know, Eli," she said in a disenchanted tone, her eyes sunken and her head slightly tilted. "I just know we have a lot of things to figure out before we get married."

Eli exhaled deeply and waited for Emma to continue, hoping – praying – that she would change the topic so that they could get back to talking about books, or about teaching, or even about their childhoods – anything but this topic would have been a welcome topic for him to discuss.

"Eli," she started, resting her left cheek in her palm and looking away from the screen. Her eyes were flat and distant, and her face was pale and twisted, as if she were concealing an unspeakable anguish. "I'm starting to get a little uncomfortable."

"Umm...why is that?"

"Because I'm feeling some hesitation on your part...it just reminds me of things, you know? Of things that I've experienced before..."

"Umm," he coughed, clearing his dry throat, "what do you mean?"

"I think you know very well what I'm talking about, Eli," she said with quiet restraint, shifting her weight on her chair and rubbing her thumbs under her eyes as if she were crying invisible tears. "I've told you about Todd...about how every time I'd try to bring up marriage, or children, or actual practical things, he'd get very hesitant and he'd change the topic...I've told you about how I should've seen it coming – I should've seen those signs, those signs that he wasn't really serious about wanting to be with me in the long-term...those signs that he was preparing to leave me...I was blind to those signs then, but now I can see them...And I don't like what I'm seeing now, Eli. I don't like what I'm feeling...I know it might be irrational, I know that I should keep being hopeful and optimistic and keep thinking about how much you've said you like me and how often you've said you like me and how often you've said you want to be with me, but – and this is really difficult for me to say but I feel like I need to say this – this conversation, and your tone, Eli – it gives me this kind of sick, anxious feeling...this feeling like that wound that I thought had healed is about to get opened again...that that trauma of being left by someone I loved is going to play itself out again...I don't want to experience that again, Eli, do you understand? I don't want to be led on again. I don't want to go through that again. I don't want to be hurt like that again. Once is enough, Eli...Eli?...Do you understand?"

'Maybe Todd was so hesitant because *you* didn't show enough signs of wanting to know what it was like to be *him*,' he wanted to say to her. 'Maybe he was so hesitant because you showed little to no curiosity of really, *actually* wanting to know what it's like to be a person of color in the United States of America. Maybe he was so hesitant because you never showed the slightest sign of wanting to see things in this country as they actually are instead of continuing to see them as you want to believe they are…And maybe I'm so hesitant because deep-down I worry that you just see me as another Todd, as just another "type" of guy that you happen to be attracted to…Maybe deep-down I'm so hesitant because I'm worried that you don't see the full me – and that you don't want to – and that you might never want to…have you thought about why *I* might be hesitant, Emma? Have you?' But instead of saying what was really on his mind, the only word that came out of his mouth was a polite, meek, half-hearted "Yes."

"Alright, Eli…it's getting late…I hope you're still enjoying talking to me despite this more intense conversation."

He didn't respond.

"Well? Are you?"

He swallowed hard, then paused to exhale.

"Yes," he said unenthusiastically, smiling weakly.

"That makes me happy…well, Eli Newman – I like saying your name – it's a fun name to say…Eli Newman…Well, Eli Newman… I won't keep you up any longer. I hope you rest well and have sweet dreams, and I look forward to talking to you again soon."

"Same to you," was all he could manage to say in response.

"I'll be thinking of you tonight."

He swallowed even harder; his breath caught in his throat. '*Thinking* of me? At *night*?…What exactly does she mean by that? Does she mean what I think she means?'

"Will you be thinking of me tonight?" she asked, smiling amiably.

'Oh God oh God oh God,' he said in his head, squirming with unforeseen delight. 'What am I supposed to say to that?! What does she *want* me to say to that?!…Is what she wants me to say the *right* thing to say?...And would it be *mutar*[3] to say that?...I don't think it would be *nivul peh*[4] to say that...at least not *nivul peh mamesh*[5]...But would it be *avak*[6] *nivul peh*?...Is there even such a thing? *Abizraihu d'nivul peh*?[7] Aye...how can it be that there's a *sefer*[8] now on every *inyan*[9] under the sun, there's even an entire *sefer* on *pas akum*[10] but there's no *sefer* yet on these *inyanim*[11] which *lichora*[12] are, at least in my case right here right now, clearly much more *noge'a lamaiseh*...'[13]

"Yes," he said, after a long pause, as his attraction to her instantaneously returned in a form that was so overwhelming that he couldn't believe he had ever not been attracted to her for even a single millisecond. "Yes I will."

It was a lie, but he had lied to her, he knew, not because he didn't want to be thinking about her at night – it was a lie because he was still withholding himself from thinking about her in that way; his desire was still not yet as strong as his discipline.

"Lilit tov," she said in a soft, throaty voice, the life returning to her eyes and the glow to her face. "Is that how you say 'goodnight' in Hebrew? Lilit tov?"

"*Laila* tov," he corrected her, her sparkling eyes intoxicating him.

"Well, then...Laila tov, Eli...and sweet dreams..."

He tasted her words in his mouth, running his tongue over them and savoring each sweet syllable as if they were chocolate-covered strawberries dipped in Tuscan truffle oil and sprinkled with edible

---

3. Permitted.
4. Inappropriate speech.
5. Outright inappropriate speech.
6. Minor-level.
7. Shades of inappropriate speech.
8. Book.
9. Subject.
10. The laws of bread baked by non-Jews.
11. Subjects.
12. Evidently.
13. Relevant.

twenty-four karat gold flakes. He closed the lid of his laptop and let out a long, deep, painful sigh, lamenting that he couldn't be with her at her side at that very instant, wishing with every fiber of his being that it could be possible for him to transport his body into her bed as easily as he could transport his words into her mind.

"Same to you, Emma...Laila tov..."

EIGHTEEN

"Eli," said Emma one night while they were reading in bed. A blood-red moon blazed in the sky – dusky, determined, obtrusive, like an unsavory relative peering through their bedroom blinds. The strange smell of Callery pear filled the air, and the sound of sleet thrashing against the window invaded their ears. "We've been married now for six years and we still have no children."

"Well," said Eli, finishing the sentence he was reading and glancing up from his copy of *Daniel Deronda* with an irritated expression on his stubble-speckled face, "what do you want me to do about it? We've tried everything – IVF, IUI, ICSI, this drug, that drug, donor eggs, going raw, going vegan, going paleo... what else is there to *do*, Emma? Who am I to give you children – *God*? I've done everything I can possibly do. And God-knows so have you. Every year around your birthday you start getting into this 'why don't we have kids yet?' mode. Well, you know what? Maybe we should just be grateful that we have each other. Not everybody can say that. There are lots of lonely people out there. But not us. We're blessed. We're blessed to have each other – what more could we want? Maybe it's a blessing in disguise that none of the treatments have worked. I mean, a child could... you know..."

"Could *what*?" she snapped, slamming her copy of *Love in the Time of Cholera* shut and throwing it at Eli's chest. "Could *spoil* things?"

"Well…"

"What exactly would it *spoil*? As if everything we have here is so great? Honestly I don't understand what's so great about this anymore. To just lie in bed talking about books every night and talking about books at the breakfast table and talking about books at dinner and while we're out walking and while we're on our way to a movie and while we're coming back from the movie and – *ughhhh*…there's gotta be something more, Eli. There's gotta be something more than just this."

"Isn't that getting a little greedy, Emma? We have everything we could ever want right here. We have great conversations, we read great books together, share great meals together, go to great concerts together…we still have a great passion for each other – how many couples can say that after almost seven years of marriage? I'd have to say we're pretty blessed, Emma. Pretty darn blessed. We've got everything we could ever – "

"*Almost* everything, Eli. *Almost*. We have *almost* everything we could ever want. You can't look me in the eyes and tell me that what we have is good enough."

"Come on, Emma," he groaned, wrenching his gaze away from her. "You've gotta stop with this…seriously…how do you like *Love in the Time of Cholera*, by the way? I always wanted to read it but somehow still haven't gotten around to it. Maybe that'll be my next book after *Daniel D* – "

"You know what I think the problem is, Eli?"

"What, Emma?" He turned to look at her and almost recoiled in fright when he saw how intently she was looking at him, glaring at him as if he were a criminal who had just been apprehended by the police for defacing a priceless artwork.

"I've been thinking about this for some time now, Eli, and I finally know what it is: it's because I haven't been a good Catholic."

Eli twisted his head to the right and squinted at her, eyeing her as if she'd just told him that she was a Martian.

"What are you talking about, Emma? All you've ever told me is that you don't believe in that stuff – that you *never* believed in it. That you would read novels in church and poetry in Sunday school and that as soon as your parents could no longer force you to go to church you never went back. Of all the ridiculous things you've ever told me, Emma, this…this is…I mean, I don't even know how you can say you're 'not a good Catholic' when it seems to me that you never even really were one in the first place."

"That's exactly the problem, Eli – I *was* a Catholic, and I'm not anymore. I haven't been one in many, many years…I left the Church during my childhood…and this is what's brought on all these problems…"

"*What* problems? Our life is fine, Emma. We have – "

"This is why we have no children, Eli. Don't you get it? Can't you see? I left the way of the truth and the life – I abandoned the Word, the Creator, the Life-giver, and so I've become incapable of creating life…*we*, are incapable of creating life…it's measure-for-measure, Eli. It's very simple."

"I…I don't understand…"

"Come back with me, Eli. Come back with me to the Church. It's where I belong…where *we* belong. It's the universal Church, Eli. It will accept you, too. You'll be much happier there. You'll finally be fulfilled – and saved…and *we'll* be fulfilled…we will have children, Eli, we *will* – but this is the only way."

"I…Emma…after all these years…I honestly cannot believe what I'm hearing. What's come over you? You don't sound like yourself… you don't sound like yourself at all…what's going on with you? Are you alright? Are you – "

"It will be very easy, Eli, don't worry. All you'll have to do is a little ceremony, nothing complicated. I had it done to me when I was a baby. Just a little water on the forehead, that's all. Your head will get a little wet…but it will feel very good, trust me. You'll feel reborn."

"Emma…" he said, shaking his head and unsuccessfully repressing a laugh. "What is this? What is going on with you tonight? HellO-oh?" he shouted, peering into her eyes and ears as if he were a detective scrutinizing a piece of evidence. "HellO-oh? Emma Yates? Has anyone seen Emma Yates? She doesn't seem to be here tonight, does anyone know where she went? I don't know who you happen to be, but whoever you are, if you see my Emma could you please tell her that I've been out all night looking for her? Please tell her to come home. I'm worried about her."

"It's a very short, quick, painless ceremony," she continued, going on as if she had not heard a word of what he had just said. "All it takes is about thirty seconds. And then you – we – will make our vows of faith and commit ourselves to the Church and to its sacraments. It's not too late, Eli. Children have been born before to women older than I. But first we have to make ourselves worthy of such a miracle. Come with me, Eli. Come with me back to the Church – the church of my childhood, and the faith of your future."

"Wha...*what*?"

"Yes, Eli. It's true.... Look into your heart...you know it's what you've always wanted...it's what you've always secretly wanted without being able to tell anyone. And now you'll be able to tell the whole world. You'll finally be able to tell everyone who you truly are..."

There was an unrecognizable tone of gravity in her voice; her gaze was impenetrable, her face impervious, her body motionless.

"Emma, I don't know what you're trying to pull here but this is truly *some* performance tonight...to carry this act out this long, without breaking character...it's very admirable. Your theater students would be proud. But it's getting a bit late, don't you think? Don't you think it's time to go to sleep?"

"This is no act, Eli. The only act is the false performance I've been giving from the time I left the Church up until this point. I've been thinking about this for months now, and I finally realized that my entire life has been a lie – a lie that has been like a shell, a husk of grain, covering up the true, faithful Catholic inside me waiting to be revealed."

"Umm...so..." he said ineptly, scratching his head and squinting again, unsure of what to say next.

"And that shell of literature, that husk of books, is covering up the true you, too, Eli. The real Eli Newman – the Christian Eli Newman – is waiting to be let out. That true you has been there underneath all along. I can see him...I can *feel* him..."

"Emma...this is...this is starting to get ridiculous...and I'm starting to get tired..."

"Will you come with me, Eli?" she asked, suddenly slipping off her nightgown and climbing on top of his prone body. "Will you come with me back to the one true faith? Will you come with me back to where you belong?...It would be easy for you, Eli – the transition would be so easy. Catholicism is not so different from Judaism. We also love ritual and ceremony and frequent communal worship. And we also have a great intellectual tradition that stretches from antiquity to modernity – Augustine, Aquinas, Pascal, Erasmus, Descartes... we revere scholarship and honor the life of the mind just as much as you do. It would be quite a rupture for you to go from Judaism to Protestantism, but not from Judaism to Catholicism. You'd feel very much at home with us. In fact, *you* of *all* people, Eli Newman, would feel *especially* at home with us. I know you, Eli Newman – you love beautiful art and sublime music, and what other faith can give you art and music as beautiful and sublime as Catholic art and music? We have Mozart, Michelangelo, Montaigne, Dante – the greatest composer, the greatest artist, the greatest essayist, and greatest poet of all time – they are all with us, and nowhere else. Look at your faith – look at it closely, Eli, and you'll see that no observant, religious Jew has ever contributed anything of significance to world culture. Look at all of your great, world-transformative figures and you'll find not one observant Jew among them: Spinoza, Freud, Einstein, Marx – all secular, non-practicing, non-religious Jews. And the same goes for the arts: Chagall, Modigliani, Mahler, Bernstein, Gershwin, Mendelssohn, Kubrick, Spielberg, Schoenberg – not a single religious Jew in that bunch. Even all your great Jewish comics – Mel Brooks, Woody Allen, Billy Crystal, Larry David, Jerry Seinfeld, Jon Stewart, Adam Sandler, Sarah Silverman, Seth Meyers – "

"You know that Seth Meyers isn't actually Jewish, right?"

"None of them are religious. Neither were Lenny Bruce, Joan Rivers or Gary Shandling. Kafka, Proust, Salinger, Malamud, Mailer, Roth, Bellow, Ozick – utterly unobservant. Billy Joel, Neil Diamond, Paul Simon, Leonard Cohen, Bob Dylan – not a kosher-eating, *shomer*

Shabbos yid among them. And do you know why, Eli? Do you know why no religious Jew has ever done anything truly artistically great? Because religious Judaism is the death of the spirit, the desiccation of the soul; any religious Jew who wants to accomplish anything truly great, any observant Jew who wants to contribute anything of lasting significance to world culture, knows that he cannot be a practicing Jew if he wants to do so. Observing this religion weighs you down, binds you to the ground, stifles your spirit – and you know this, Eli, you know this all too well. But observing *my* religion lifts you up, gives you wings, lets your spirit soar. Evelyn Waugh, Siegfried Sassoon, Gerard Manley Hopkins, Czesław Miłosz, Irène Nèmirovsky, Tennessee Williams, Johannes Vermeer, and Gustav Mahler all knew this too – and this is why they all converted to Catholicism. Caravaggio, Donatello, Leonardo, Gentileschi, Ghiberti...Mantegna, Poussin, Raphael, Titian, Velázquez, Cézanne, Dalí, Bosch, Botticelli, Bellini, Bernini – all baptized. Graham Greene, Günter Grass, Victor Hugo, J.R.R. Tolkien, Erich Maria Remarque, Walker Percy, Muriel Spark, Tobias Wolff, Anthony Burgess, Don DeLillo, Seamus Heaney, Cormac McCarthy, Kerouac, Balzac, Baudelaire, Cervantes – they're all with us too. Even Joyce could never have written *Ulysses* without having grown up with the Latin Mass. We have Chaucer and Mahler, F. Scott Fitzgerald and Flannery O'Conner – and probably even Shakespeare, too...join us, Eli, and you too can become one of them – one of *us*..."

"I...well...I don't know..."

"It will be so easy for you to convert, Eli...we won't even have to draw a drop of blood from you...it will be completely painless... and it will be so good for you...it will be a wonderful experience for you, Eli. Like a summer stroll on an English country farm...you'll finally become calm, peaceful, serene...you'll be reborn – a new man, unburdened from the traumas of your past, freed from all of your anxieties and neuroses, liberated from all your worries and fears, at last able to shed your past and to soar. *Ger shenis'gayer k'katan shenolad damei...*[1]"

---

1. "A convert is like a newborn child."

"What?! How do you know that?! Have you been reading my *seforim*?![2] This is getting too weird, Emma. You really need to stop this. Please."

"The question, Eli," she said with a solemn expression on her unblinking, unsmiling face, "that I am asking you," she continued, slipping off her white satin nightgown, twisting her taut arms around his tense torso, and sliding off his orange-striped boxer shorts, "is this: how…much…" she went further, rubbing her lithe legs against his hardened thighs and placing her full, oval lips an inch away from his twitching mouth, "do…you…love.…me…"

"I…do…I…love…you," he said breathlessly, barely able to speak, looking into her sparkling sea-green eyes and seeing his rickety reflection inside her two aquamarine orbs. "Yes, Emma…for you, Emma… I'll do it…for…you…anything for you, Emma…anything…"

"Yes, Eli," she continued, wrapping her legs around his waist and beginning to writhe up and down his supine body. "I knew…that you would…do it…for me…"

"…*Ego,*" she began, locking eyes with him.

"…Yes…" he responded, abandoning all hope of resisting.

"…*te baptizo*…"

"…yes…"

"…*in nomine Patris*…"

"…yes…"

"…*et Filii*…"

"…yes…"

"…*et Spiritus Sancti*…"

"…*yes!*"

"…*in eodem Christu Iesu Domino nostro in vitam aeternam!*"

"YES!"

He woke up panting and sweating, more terrified than he'd ever been in his entire life. He staggered to the bathroom sink, walking with leaden legs, and cleaned the pastiness off of his midriff. He peered into the mirror and two watery, bloodshot eyes stared back at him.

2. Holy books.

He wobbled to the kitchen for a drink of water. 'Not possible...' he thought, barely able to keep his balance, as he feebly lifted the glass to his mouth. 'It's not possible...no...that's absurd...totally, utterly absurd... *hevel v'shtus ruach*[3]...it was just a dream...just a dream, nothing to worry about...if I'm still bothered by it in the morning I can do *hatavas chalom*[4]...besides, the question is only whether *she* will be *misgayer,*[5] not whether *I* –.... no...what a crazy thought... never in a thousand million years.... but –...but what if....?...could it happen?...' he asked himself, as he ambled toward his bookshelf and groped for his copy of Tikkun Klali.[6] '... *Could* it??...' he repeated to himself, as he opened the well-worn pocket-sized paperback pamphlet and began reciting the first *mizmor.*[7] 'Could it really happen?...to me?...to Eli Newman?...star *talmid*[8] of Rav Simcha Kramer? *Al ta'amin b'atzmecha ad yom mos'cha*...No...no...I'm not *farfallen in ganzen*[9]...yet...am I?...It's not too late... *ad yom moso techakeh lo*[10]... I can still save myself...can't I?...?'

3. Meaningless.
4. Ritual for the Annulment of Dreams.
5. Convert.
6. A set of ten Psalms whose recital is said to effectuate atonement for certain sins.
7. Psalm.
8. Student.
9. Lost completely.
10. "Until the day of his death He waits for him."

NINETEEN

The last layers of snow that had blanketed northwestern Connecticut for nearly half a year had finally begun to melt, and the red-bellied robins and ruby-throated hummingbirds were slowly beginning to return from their southern sojourns. For the first time in what felt more like six years than six months, Eli was at last able to walk outside again without any jacket at all. He still would have preferred the seventy-seven or so degrees it likely was in Texas at the moment, but he knew that fifty-seven degrees Fahrenheit was a near-tropical temperature for New England in April, and he was grateful for the long-awaited thaw.

Even after months of communicating with Emma in some form – on Facebook and through email, via Gmail video-chat and Skype, through text messaging and even through occasional winking when they passed each other in the school hallway, and in spite of whatever concerns he may have had about her – he still could not get enough of her. The more he heard from her, the more he wanted to hear from her. Talking to her didn't satisfy his thirst; it intensified it. Hearing from her had become like a drug to him; if he did not hear from her in some form for over six hours, he started becoming light-headed and jittery and fired off text messages to her in order to get his fix. When he went twelve or more hours without hearing from her, he started becoming irritable, occasionally even sweating, growing paranoid that *now* the moment had finally come when she would send her "Dear Eli" email to him. Even after all these months, even after a folder-full of emails dotted with enough smiley-faces and exclamation points for several lifetimes, even after countless "I so enjoyed talking with you last night and look forward to talking to you again!" texts from her, and even after she sent him that birthday card on which she wrote, "I am so glad we found each other, I don't believe in destiny or fate, but I do think that, on some level, what is happening between us is meant to be" – even after all those and so many other unmistakable signs that she really did like him, he still became skittish every time more than six hours passed without him having heard from her. 'This is it,' he said to himself in late-April after he hadn't heard from her in over thirty-six hours. 'Now comes the time for the other fateful shoe to finally drop. I've had a nice run – my nicest ever, by far – but she's finally come to her senses...she's been working on a very thoughtful, carefully worded email explaining all the reasons why, after much careful consideration, she has decided that it is not a good idea for us to pursue this any further. This is how it always happens. I was stupid, so stupid and foolish, to delude myself into thinking that there was any other possible ending to this other than the one in the email she's composing to me right now...I should be mentally preparing myself, mentally preparing myself to be *mekabel*[1] these *yisurin b'ahavah*,[2] because it's gonna hurt real bad, worse than any other "Dear Eli" email I've ever received, worse than even Rena's non-responses and vanishing act... but it's the only conceivable ending. I just pray I get the email from her sooner rather than later; it would be nice if she didn't drag it out and would just put me out of my misery – and quickly. That would be the merciful thing to do. I can't take any more of this torture. It hurts so much, oh God how it hurts – why is she doing this to me? As flies to wanton boys...please, Emma – just do it quickly, that's all I ask. If it were done when 'tis done, then t'were well it were done quickly!

---

1. Accept.
2. Sufferings with love.

Z'rizin mak'dimin!![3] Just do it already, Emma! Please! Just say what I know you're gonna say: "after much thought, I really don't think it makes sense for us to be together. We're too different. I'm sorry, Eli. You're a nice guy. But this just won't work. I wish you the best." Just do it already, Emma, please. *Ha'matchil b'mitzvah omrim lo g'mor.*[4] Please, Emma…please just finish me off already…'

When he finally saw a new message from her in his inbox, he clicked on it hungrily, expecting to read the usual "Hi Eli! I hope you're having a good day, I just finished a great book that I'd love to talk to you about" email of hers that he so loved reading and which he had by now become so accustomed to receiving that he needed at least one such email from her per day to get the same thrill that he would get when he was receiving just one such email from her per week during the beginning of their relationship. He gobbled up her words with his inflamed, starving eyes, reading the email with the appetite of a prisoner on a hunger strike receiving his first taste of food in ninety-six hours, swallowing her moderately seasoned sentences whole without taking the time to savor the individual words or taste her carefully crafted clauses:

> Dear Eli,
>
> I hope you're having a good day. I apologize for not being in touch for so long. Two days ago I received word that my father has been diagnosed with lung cancer. I have gone to Chicago to be with him as he begins his treatment. I've told Principal Penske that I will not be able to fulfill my teaching duties for the remainder of this school year and I've requested that the school hire a long-term substitute to cover my classes. Because, as you know, my father has no one else, I will have to be here in Chicago for the foreseeable future. I do really hope, though, that when the school year ends, you will come and join me here. As I've told you several times, I can't describe how much I have enjoyed what has been developing between us this year. I cherish every moment that I have been

3. "The alacritous act at the earliest possible opportunity."
4. "One who starts a good deed is told to complete it."

able to spend with you. Though you may not realize this, you have changed me and my life in indescribable ways. You have a great mind, a sensitive soul, and a big warm heart. After getting to know you, Eli, I know that you're someone I can trust; I know that you understand me; I know that you won't let me down. Not now, not ever. I see us having a real future together, and once you are here, we'll be able to plan our future together – whether that means staying in Chicago, moving back to Connecticut, or going wherever else we desire to go in this great big world.

During the moments on the plane when I wasn't sleeping or reading I was thinking about how nice my time with you has been and how lovely it would be to share my life with you. I hope to see you soon in Chicago.

Yours always,

– Emma

Eli stared impassively into the corner of the room, his eyes expressionless, his mind vacant, his face pale. He reread the email – and then read it again, and again, and again, his upper lip quivering while his right hand steadied his trembling chin. 'Ribbono shel olam,'[5] he thought feverishly, enveloped in the inescapable whirlwind of his deepest anxieties and fiercest raptures. 'What now? What do I do? Ribbono shel olam what do I do?!?' A few beads of sweat formed on his creased forehead. 'I should book my flight now. Yes...that's what I should do – I should fly out there as soon as possible...She'll be so happy when she sees me after this school-year is over. Maybe during our shana rishonah[6] we'll take a trip to her hometown and I'll get to see the famous Scranton yeshiva...Where is Scranton? Is it near Pittsburgh? Would we have to fly there? Can you drive there from Chicago? Or maybe we could drive there from Hartford...all things to discuss once I'm with her in Chicago...'

He was too tired from the anticipatory excitement to book a flight,

5. Oh my God.
6. First year of marriage.

or to do much of anything else that night. He awoke in the middle of the night, anxious and sore from tossing and turning, and when he fell back asleep, he dreamt that he was back in Baltimore, at a Starbucks with Rena. He was having tea and she was drinking coffee. Her hair was tucked under a blue *tichel*,[7] and her spindly arms and legs were hidden inside a full-length white dress. "There's no sugar here for my coffee, Eli," she said softly, lifting her waifish eyes upwards and gazing at him imploringly.

"That's alright, sweetie," he said ingratiatingly, putting down his large paper cup and resting his right hand reassuringly on her left forearm. "We have some sugar back in the apartment. I can go home and get some."

"That would be great, honey. Thank you so much."

"I don't have my car here, though."

"That's okay. You can borrow mine. Here," she said sweetly, handing him the keys. "It's the navy blue Toyota right out in front."

"I know," he said, smiling affectionately. "See you soon."

On his way back from the apartment, driving briskly while humming the song "*Od Yishama*"[8] and tapping his fingers on the steering wheel, Eli merged on to the highway and suddenly noticed flashing blue lights in his rearview mirror.

"I can't believe this," Eli muttered to himself, rolling his eyes as he pulled the car over to the side of the road and rolled down his window. "You have got to be kidding me ... this cannot be happening again ..."

"License and registration, please," said the officer. Eli, not looking at the man in the blue uniform, pulled his wallet out of his pocket and began rummaging through the glove compartment.

Eli handed his license and Rena's registration papers to the officer and finally made eye contact with him. He was a stout, well-built man, with a white mustache, a sharp, chiseled chin, wire-framed glasses and close-cropped salt-and-pepper hair. A smoldering cigarette dangled from the corner of his mouth, and a copper crucifix hung from a

7. Headscarf.
8. "It Will Yet Again Be Heard."

golden chain that was wrapped tightly around his thick neck like a rope around a tree.

"Well, well, well," said the officer, smirking and nodding self-assuredly. "If it isn't my good friend Mr. Othello Shylock."

"It's good to see you again, Mr. Yates," Eli said half-heartedly, smiling feebly. "At least you finally got my name right."

"It's good to see you again too, Mr. Shylock. What's that in the plastic bag there?" asked Mr. Yates, fixing his eyes sharply on the bag of sugar that Eli had placed inside the glove compartment.

"That's sugar, sir."

"Let me see it please," said Mr. Yates in a gruff voice.

Eli handed the bag to him, flashing him a cautious smile. Mr. Yates scrutinized the contents of the bag with cold, colorless eyes; his brows knitted, and he ran his hand across his dry, leathery face.

"I'm gonna have to ask you to step out of the vehicle, Mr. Shylock."

Eli let out an angry breath and stepped out of the car. Large beads of sweat formed on his head and ran down his stubble-specked face.

"Young man, you are under arrest."

"For what?!" he snapped.

"For being in possession of illegal substances."

"What?!" he cried out sharply, as though stabbed with a dagger. "No! This is sugar! This is SUGAR!"

"I'm sorry, Mr. Shylock, but I have no choice but to arrest you," said George Yates, grabbing Eli's arms and yanking them behind his back.

"It's just freaking *sugar*!" Eli shouted, squirming out of George Yates' arms. "You can *not* arrest me for this!

"Are you resisting arrest, Othello?" said George Yates, his dark gaze boring deeper into Eli's terrified eyes. "This is a bad thing you're doing here, Othello, resisting arrest like this." He took out his baton and swung it at Eli's head; Eli blocked it with his right hand. A dull pain coursed through his arm. "A real bad thing. This is gonna get you in some deep trouble."

Mr. Yates swung it again, and Eli blocked it with his left hand. Mr. Yates tried to knee him in the stomach; Eli blocked his leg with his fists.

Mr. Yates lunged at him, and Eli pushed him away, knocking him into the car and causing him to tumble on to the white-lined asphalt.

"Oww!" shrieked George Yates, clutching his hip and slowly rising from the ground. "Now you've really done it, Othello...committing an act of violence against a sworn officer of the law..." He fumbled for his pistol and drew it out of his holster. "Violence against an officer of the law of the United States of America," repeated George Yates, clutching the Glock 22 and leveling it at Eli's head.

Eli heard the gun click. His heart began pounding violently. He dashed behind the car, gulping great mouthfuls of air; a shot went off, shattering the passenger's side window.

"Come out come out wherever you are, Mr. Shylock!" yelled George Yates gleefully, hobbling over to the other side of the car.

Eli dove into the car, his face frozen with fear; two more shots went off, shattering the windshield and the driver's side window.

"You can't hide from me forever, Othello Shylock! Your time has come!"

As he heard George Yates reloading his gun, he glanced at the backseat and noticed an AR-15 rifle, an AK-47, a Sig Sauer pistol and a pump-action shotgun. Eli grabbed the shotgun, jumped out of the car and aimed the gun at George Yates' chest.

"@#$% *yeah* my time has come!" shouted Eli, his eyes blazing and his nostrils flaring. "*OUR* time as come! We've had enough of this! *Enough!*"

"Now you be a good boy and put down that gun there, Othello," said George Yates in a deadly serious tone, aiming his pistol at Eli's head. "You put down that gun right now or there sure gonna be some consequences you ain't gonna like, Mr. Shylock!"

"I am *not* putting down this gun until you put down *your* gun!"

"Put down that gun right now, Mr. Shylock!" repeated George Yates, his voice cracking, still aiming his pistol at Eli's head.

"No! I will *not* put down this gun until you put down *your* gun! We've had enough of this! *ENOUGH!* We were told that racism was over! We were told that antisemitism was over! You promised us that blacks and Jews would be equal citizens in this country! That we would have peace! That we wouldn't be terrorized and enslaved and slaughtered on the streets anymore! We were told this! Over and over and over again! And for a time we were even gullible enough to believe you! But you're *still* terrorizing us! You're *still* persecuting us! You're *still* scrawling swastikas on subway cars and you're *still* burning crosses in front of our homes! You're *still* slaughtering us on the streets and in our churches and in our synagogues! After all these hundreds of years and after all this 'progress' you're *still* treating black and Jewish blood like it's less red than yours! You're *still* treating us as if we don't have the same eyes that you have, the same hands that you have, the same lungs and kidneys and emotions and sensations that you white Christians have! Why can't you see that?! Why can't you take those bloody white robes off your heads and open your @#$%*@# eyes and *see* that?! And meanwhile you *continue* to call us the worst names you can think of and you *continue* to blame *us* for all of *your* problems and you continue to put *us* down as a way to raise your sorry racist @#$%# *up*! All throughout history all you people have done is persecute us and enslave us and gas us and massacre us *and what has changed?!* NOTHING!!! Not even *here*! Not even in the United @#$%*@# States of @#$%*@# America, *no-thing has changed!!!* Charlottesville, Charleston, Ferguson, Freddie Gray, Pittsburgh, Poway – *what* has *changed*!?! You abuse us and harass us and terrorize us and massacre us – *you*, the very people that were supposed to *protect* us from all that, are *slaughtering* us! And now you're coming into our churches and synagogues and massacring us even *there*! That ends NOW! It ends RIGHT HERE!, RIGHT NOW!!!"

"You put down that gun right now young man," said George Yates, his forehead glistening with sweat, still aiming his pistol at Eli's head.

"No! *You* put down *your* gun!" Eli cried, his voice rising and his grip around the trigger tightening. "You put down *all* of your guns! We've @#$%*@# had it with you people gunning us down in the streets *and we're not gonna @#$%*@# take it anymore!*"

"I bet you don't even know how to use that thing, you dirty black Jewboy scum-of-the-earth kike ni – "

"Oh yeah? @#$% you, you @#$%*$@#$%@#$ white supremacist neo-Nazi @#$%@#*#!"

Eli fired two shots into George Yates' heart and placed a third bullet right between his eyes. George Yates fell to the ground with a sickening thud; Eli pumped the gun again and fired another round into chest.

As he pumped the gun yet again, the dream melted away and Eli woke up with a start, bathed in cold sweat and breathing harder than he ever had in his life.

'*Ribbono shel olam*,'[9] he gasped, clasping his heaving chest. '*Ribbono shel olam*...*Baruch Hashem*[10] it was a just a dream," he thought with relief, his teeth still chattering. "*Baruch Hashem*...Definitely just a dream – I would never use *nivvul peh*[11] in real life...*chas v'shalom*[12]... never in a thousand million years...*Ribbono shel olam*, what a terrible dream...Maybe I'll message Yoni and Shaya to see if they're free today...Can you do *hatavas chalom*[13] over Skype?...'

---

9. Good Lord.
10. Thank God.
11. Obscenities.
12. God forbid.
13. Ritual for the annulment of dreams.

TWENTY

The next day, as he was teaching the passage from the Talmud about 'those who do not have a share in the world to come' to his ninth grade class, the impending decision he knew he would soon have to make began to weigh upon him like a down comforter – warmly and comfortably at first, but the more he struggled to think underneath its dense weight, the heavier and more oppressive it began to feel.

He put off purchasing a plane ticket for another week. He lumbered through the next few days as if his shoes were filled with iron, and he ate and drank as if he were on death row; some days he had the appetite of a lion after three days of fasting, and on other days he could hardly force down a single pea. When he lay down in bed at night, he once again felt like a skittish child, fearful of falling asleep lest some monster in the closet or demon under the bed attack him once he was defenseless. When he sat in faculty meetings and listened to Principal Penske list the dates by when each teacher would have to have the following year's course-plans ready, his toes twitched more than usual, and he couldn't stop his knees from continuously clapping against each other. Whenever his mind had a free moment – and even during moments when it wasn't truly free, as when students or other teachers were speaking to him – his mind drifted directly to the thought of Emma eagerly awaiting him in Chicago; when students asked him questions in class, he had to ask them to repeat their questions a second time, and sometimes even a third time, apologizing to them for not catching their question the first time.

When he finally booked his ticket and printed out his boarding pass, he felt as if a boulder from his chest had been lifted; he hadn't been able to take deep breaths for nearly five days. He was able to smile once again when students and other teachers greeted him in the morning, and he found himself humming the song "*Vayivaser Yaakov Levado*"[1] as he strode about the New England Hebrew High School hallways; he hadn't walked with this much confidence since he had won a *bekius*[2] prize in his third year at Yeshivas Chelkas Yaakov in Baltimore and was awarded with a brand-new Ritva[3] on Kesubos.[4] He once again was able to eat to the point of satisfaction, no longer feeling that every meal was his last, and slept as soundly as if he had just been bequeathed an inheritance from a rich relative that would allow him to never worry about the price of gasoline or avocados ever again.

When the school year ended and the time came for him to leave Hartford, he had all of his belongings shipped ahead of him and ordered a taxi to take him and his one navy blue carry-on bag to Bradley International Airport. As he made his way through the small airport, passed through the security clearance – never had he more eagerly removed his belt and shoes in his life – and found his gate, whenever he passed by a window and caught his reflection in the glass, he was surprised to see himself still smiling; it was as if, at the moment when he had booked his ticket, Velázquez himself had painted a gleaming safflower-oil smile on the canvas of his countenance, and all he had to do in order to reap the rewards of owning a priceless masterpiece was to take care to not wipe it away.

When he arrived in Houston four hours later, he calmly and contentedly collected his carry-on bag from the overheard compartment,

---

1. "And Jacob Was Alone."
2. Knowledge in Mishnah and Talmud.
3. Medieval Talmudic commentary.
4. A tractate of Talmud.

quietly humming "*Vayivaser Yaakov Levado*" as he exited the plane and strolled through the airport. He immediately boarded a bus bound for Austin, intent on checking out the city's popular new downtown bookstore that Emma had told him about in April. She had said that even though it had only been open for two years, it had already established a reputation as one of the best independent bookstores in the United States; she was eager to visit the store herself, she had told him, but she preferred to wait so that she could visit it with him.

During the three-hour bus ride, he held his paperback copies of *Invisible Cities* and *Mishnayos Kiddushin*[5] in his hands without opening them, and instead gazed meditatively at the silent power of the familiar scenery that he had not seen in eighteen years – the gleaming glass skyscrapers of his native city, shining like the sunlit sea; the short, thin, tattered trees hugging the low-hanging heaven; the wide-open ocher-colored plains and prairie grasslands to the west of Houston, the rolling hills and large silver boulders of central Texas, the natural springs and the cedar tree groves underneath the crystalline sky. Upon arriving in Austin, he took a city bus to the University of Texas campus, got off across from the Blanton Museum of Art, and started walking west, luxuriating in the warm, relaxed, spring-scented air, which was bursting with bluebonnets, red yucca and purple penstemons. When he arrived at the sunbaked intersection of MLK Boulevard and Trinity Street, he saw a small shop with the purple-painted letters "JESS'S BOOKS" stenciled upon a wide white awning. Breathing deeply, he stepped into the cozy store, treading lightly on its carpeted floors and moving leisurely past several inviting easy chairs. As he gazed up at the store's timbered ceilings and beheld the shop's thousands of carefully arranged multicolored volumes, he felt as if he had just entered a secret treasure trove to which only he held the key. And then, as he lowered his head and set his eyes back upon the books, he saw her. She was shelving books in the fiction section, carefully inserting volumes by Alighieri, Austen, and Allende into a nearly full row, with her nimble, dew-scented hands – hands which for eighteen years he had never

5. Mishnah of Tractate Kiddushin.

stopped dreaming of holding once again. She looked up from the shelf, and the glance she cast around the store suddenly fell upon him.

"Eli!" exclaimed Jessica, raising a hand to her gaping mouth and letting the books in her arms fall to the floor. "Oh my God... it's really you..." She exhaled, and a golden glint surfaced in her clear blue eyes. "It's been so long, Eli, so long... but I always believed you'd eventually come back home..."

He met her eyes and smiled, remembering her cool touch and warm breath on his cheeks all those years ago. She reached for his hand.

"No," he pronounced, withdrawing it. "Not yet..."

A look of concern clouded over her good-humored face.

"I want to do things the right way this time," he said, speaking with a calm, clear voice. "I've made some mistakes this year... some very bad mistakes... It's a long story... I'll explain. I'll tell you everything..."

She nodded contentedly, the glow returning to her face and the smile to her lips, and listened attentively.

"It all began in Baltimore, when I was returning home one night after yet another terrible date..."